There's one gang you don't piss off at Prescott High, not unless you want them to destroy you.

H.A.V.O.C.

My enemies turned friends turned lovers.

BOOKS BY
C . M . S T U N I C H

ROMANCE NOVELS

HARD ROCK ROOTS SERIES
Real Ugly
Get Bent
Tough Luck
Bad Day
Born Wrong
Hard Rock Roots Box Set (1-5)
Dead Serious
Doll Face
Heart Broke
Get Hitched
Screw Up

TASTING NEVER SERIES
Tasting Never
Finding Never
Keeping Never
Tasting, Finding, Keeping
Never Can Tell
Never Let Go
Never Did Say
Never Could Stop

ROCK-HARD BEAUTIFUL
Groupie
Roadie
Moxie

TRIPLE M SERIES
Losing Me, Finding You
Loving Me, Trusting You
Needing Me, Wanting You
Craving Me, Desiring You

A DUET
Paint Me Beautiful
Color Me Pretty

THE BAD NANNY TRILOGY
Bad Nanny
Good Boyfriend

FIVE FORGOTTEN SOULS
Beautiful Survivors

DEATH BY DAYBREAK MC
I Was Born Ruined
I Am Dressed in Sin

STAND-ALONES & BOX SETS
Devils' Day Party
Baby Girl
All for 1
Blizzards and Bastards
Fuck Valentine's Day
Broken Pasts
Crushing Summer
Becoming Us Again
Taboo Unchained
Taming Her Boss
Kicked
Football Dick
Stepbrother Inked
Alpha Wolves Motorcycle Club:The Complete Collection
Glacier

HERS TO KEEP TRILOGY
Biker Rockstar Billionaire CEO Alpha

RIICH BOYS OF BURBERRY PREP
Filthy Rich Boys
Bad, Bad BlueBloods
The Envy of Idols
In the Arms of the Elite

ADAMSON ALL-BOYA ACADEMY
The Secret Girl
The Ruthless Boys
The Forever Crew

THE HAVOC BOYS
Havoc at Prescott High
Chaos at Prescott High
Mayhem at Prescott High

BOOKS BY

C . M . STUNICH

FANTASY NOVELS

THE SEVEN MATES OF ZARA WOLF
Pack Ebon Red
Pack Violet Shadow
Pack Obsidian Gold
Pack Ivory Emerald
Pack Amber Ash
Pack Azure Frost
Pack Crimson Dusk

ACADEMY OF SPIRITS AND SHADOWS
Spirited
Haunted
Shadowed

TEN CATS PARANORMAL SOCIETY
Possessed

TRUST NO EVIL
See No Devils
Hear No Demons
Speak No Curses

THE SEVEN WICKED SERIES
Seven Wicked Creatures
Six Wicked Beasts
Five Wicked Monsters
Four Wicked Fiends

THE WICKED WIZARDS OF OZ
Very Bad Wizards

HOWLING HOLIDAYS
Werewolf Kisses

CAMERON DARK NOVELS
Stiltz

OTHER FANTASY NOVELS
Gray and Graves
Indigo & Iris
She Lies Twisted
Hell Inc.
DeadBorn
Chryer's Crest

SIRENS OF A SINFUL SEA TRILOGY
Under the Wild Waves

CO-WRITTEN
(With Tate James)

HIJINKS HAREM
Elements of Mischief
Elements of Ruin
Elements of Desire

THE WILD HUNT MOTORCYCLE CLUB
Dark Glitter
Cruel Glamour

FOXFIRE BURNING
The Nine
Tail Game

OTHER
And Today I Die

UNDERCOVER SINNERS
Altered By Fire
Altered By Lead
Altered by Pain

CH A

AOS

ABBOTT HIGH

THE HAVOC BOYS #2

*this book is dedicated to my most insidious
character inspiration.*

*just because all is quiet on the Western front doesn't mean
I've forgotten you, sweetie.*

AUTHOR'S
NOTE

*** *Possible Spoilers* ***

Chaos at Prescott High is a reverse harem, high school, enemies-to-lovers/love hate/bully romance. What does that mean exactly? It means our female main character, Bernadette Blackbird, will end up with at least three love interests by the end of the series. It also means that for a portion of this book, the love interests are total assholes; there are also flashbacks of past incidents involving bullying. This book in no way condones bullying, nor does it romanticize it. If the love interests in this story want to win the main character over, they'll have to earn it.

Might be hard though, considering the Havoc Boys are dicks.

If you've read my other three high school romance series—*Rich Boys of Burberry Prep, Devils' Day Party,* or *Adamson All-Boys Academy*—then just know this one is a bit more intense, and character growth/redemption are needed more than ever. Stick with us. It's fairly similar to *I Was Born Ruined* (the first book in my *Death by Daybreak Motorcycle Club* series).

Any kissing/sexual scenes featuring Bernie are consensual. This book might be about high school students, but it is not what I would consider young adult. The characters are brutal, the emotions real, the f-word in prolific use. There's the aftermath of a suicide, mentions of past abuse, sexual situations, and other adult scenarios.

None of the main characters is under the age of seventeen. This series will have a happy ending in the final book.

Love, C.M. Stunich

CHAPTER
ONE

Two months earlier ...

Victor Channing

*"We can't do this to her," Aaron says, looking me dead in the
face. I try to keep the ugly smile off my lips. He doesn't stand
up to me often; he must really love Bernadette.*

I almost scoff but manage to keep the emotion to myself.

Of course *he loves Bernadette.*

We all do.

But none of them more than me.

*"Do this to her?" Oscar echoes, looking askance at Aaron.
He's sitting in the front row of the school theater, iPad in hand,
as shrewd and calculating as always. More often than not, I let
him come up with Havoc's price. He understands numbers and
risk in ways I never will. I'd trust him with my life.*

1

Just … not today.

Things are going to be a little different today.

"*You know what I mean,*" Aaron says, pushing up off the prop he's leaning against to come stand near the edge of the stage. I look up at him, but even though he's a good six feet above me, I'm not intimidated. I'm not intimidated by anything anymore. Shit, I haven't felt real fear since I was five years old. "*We owe Bern in a way we don't owe anyone else.*"

"*Let's just give her something easy, smack her ass a bit, and send her on her way,*" Hael says, taking a black leather devil mask from Callum's fingers and slipping it over his face. "*Shit, I'd pay to kick Principal Vaughn's ass for her.*"

I slide my fingers into the pockets of my jeans and lean back against the stage, pretending to contemplate their words. I'll admit, when Bernadette stormed up to me in the hall on the first day of school, opening up those poison-painted lips to call Havoc, I was surprised. Then pleased. Then desperately, unbelievably sad.

Because if she's calling Havoc, then it means she has nothing to lose. It means the butterfly I tried to set free no longer has wings. I can keep her, but she'll never fly again. Instead, if she wants to rule in this world, she's going to have to do it crawling on her belly like a snake.

A gruff laugh escapes me as I light up a cigarette and take a long drag, the cherry crackling in the quiet theater.

I know all about snakes. I'm one myself, a venomous motherfucker who knows where and when to strike to inflict the most damage. That's what I specialize in now, inflicting damage, dispensing nightmares.

Victor, *you lonely, desperate asshole, I think, as Oscar makes a sound of disgust.*

"She came to us," *he says, but I know he's just like the rest of them. He doesn't want her around, not the way I do. Nobody wants her around the way I do.* "We have to at least give her a presentable price or our reputation is shattered."

"Hasn't she paid more than her fair share for our bullshit?" *Cal asks, his broken voice like a shattered star. There used to be light there, but now ... ain't nothing but a black hole. I frown and lift my head up. Aaron is still staring at me, always fucking staring at me. He blames me for taking his girl away. If you ask me, he should've fought harder if he wanted her so bad.* "Ask her to kick Kali Rose-Kennedy's ass for us." *He flashes a dark grin before slipping a monster mask over his face. Not much difference between the mask and the man, not for any of us.*

We are all monsters.

And you're about to make Bernadette one, too, aren't you, Victor?

"We need to make use of her," *Oscar muses, like he's actually considering that bullshit price.* "But I'd prefer it if she were as far away from us as possible. Let's have her move, say, fifty thousand in product. As pretty as she is, it shouldn't be hard to do by the end of the year."

This time, when I laugh, the sound is loud and raucous, echoing around the dark space of the Prescott High School theater. Really? My beautiful Bernadette's time wasted selling weed? Not while I'm still breathing; my girl has potential.

"No, I don't think so," *I say, studying my cigarette. I can feel Aaron's eyes narrow on me, even before I turn around. He knows how selfish I am, how much I want the girl that was supposed to be his. "If Bernadette wants Havoc's help, she'll have to become one of us."*

"What?!" Aaron roars as I turn my head slowly to look at him, a wicked smile blooming across my face. He looks at me like he wants to kill me. Maybe he does, I don't know, but this is Havoc. Blood in, blood out. Who knows what might happen?

"I want Bernadette Blackbird to be ..." I almost say my girl, but I don't. That's not a fair price for anyone. Everything we do, it has to be for Havoc, for the benefit of Havoc. "Our girl. A Havoc girl." I stab my cigarette out in the built-in ashtray on one of the theater chairs. That's how old this place is; the chairs haven't been replaced since the early nineties. "I want her to be one of us."

"You've lost your fucking mind," Aaron snarls at me, visibly shaken. He runs his fingers through his chestnut hair and looks down at me with violence brimming in his gaze. "You can't wish that on her." He slaps the back of one hand into the palm of the other for emphasis. "You can't want that for her."

I just shake my head, turning and putting my palms on the edge of the stage. Without much effort, I haul my body up and over the side, rising to my feet in front of the kid I used to protect on the playground. He's come a long way since then, but he'll always be little Aaron fucking Fadler to me.

"But I can. And I do." I smile. It's a patronizing smile, I'll admit, but I can't help it. When it comes to Bernadette Blackbird, I've never been very rational. Once, in the tenth grade, when I was pretending to hate her, and lying with every breath I took, Sheldon Ernst murmured something about how

sweet her cunt must taste.

I beat him until he couldn't stand.

Because I'm jealous.

And I'm in love.

I've always been in love with that girl.

Now, without any guilt or regret, she can be mine.

I intend to see that through.

"Don't do this, Victor," Aaron pleads, gritting his teeth, his hands curling into fists at his sides. I just keep smiling at him. If he wants Bernadette, he's going to have to fight harder than that. In a surprising move, he falls to his knees and puts his hands together in a prayerlike position. The move pleases me far more than it should. I must be wicked. "Please. Don't bring her into this mess. Our lives will never be normal, and that's all she's ever wanted."

I stare down at him. Maybe he thinks I'm being cold or apathetic; I'm anything but. On the inside, that careful numbness I've tended and stoked for years is starting to disintegrate. I feel alive in a way I haven't since I locked that girl in my closet.

Does she know I used to press my palms against the outside of that door, put my ear to the wood and close my eyes, just to hear the sound of her? When she cried, I broke. When she screamed, I shattered.

"You don't really want to rope Bernadette into all of this?" Callum asks, but I don't turn around to look at him. Instead, I keep my focus on Aaron. Despite his outward appearance, he's the one I need to watch, the one I need to worry about.

Bernadette loved him, probably still loves him. This'll

destroy them both, I bet.

"Come on, boss, that's taking it a little far, don't you think?" Hael adds, but I don't look at him either. He always acts on impulse, and even if he can be brutal in a fight, he's too soft on women. Bernadette, in particular.

I crouch down in front of Aaron, putting us on eye level with one another.

"I think that Bernadette has had her chance." Aaron's mouth opens and closes in response to my statement, but he doesn't actually say anything. Maybe it's my eyes? Sometimes when I look in the mirror, I have no goddamn clue who the man is that's looking back at me. My brown eyes seem black, like a reflection of my heart. "We did our best, but you know what they say: if you love something, let it go, and if it comes back, it's yours forever."

"That's such bullshit," Aaron grinds out, on the verge of angry tears. He wants to kick my ass right now, more than anything. Last night, when I was gripping my cock in my hand and dreaming of Bernadette's narrowed green eyes and pursed lips, I wanted to kick my own ass.

She's going to bleed for this; she's going to hurt.

Ultimately, though, she'll be right where she belongs.

"I strongly advise against this," Oscar says, now standing at the bottom of the stage, inked fingers tight around the edges of the iPad, like if he squeezes it hard enough, that'll erase all the feelings he keeps trapped inside. "The last thing we need in Havoc is a slice of trouble with tits."

I rest my elbows on my knees as Aaron drops his hands to his lap. He's shaking all over, murder in his eyes. He'll never forgive me for this, but who cares? He hasn't forgiven me for asking him to give up Bernadette in tenth grade. What's so different now? He'll never truly have her again, not to himself.

"We will have Bernadette," I say, and I only use the word we *because these boys are my family. My gang, if you will. We were here first, but our prologue was Bernadette. Apparently, she's desperate enough to become our epilogue, too. Just ... hopefully not our epitaph.* "I will have Bernadette," I *emphasize, staring into Aaron's eyes.*

On the outside, I'm as calm as I always am. On the inside, I motherfucking *burn.*

Bernadette, Bernadette, Bernadette.

Her name repeats in my head like it's on a loop, and my cock stiffens inside my jeans. I squeeze my hands into fists, and Aaron notices.

"You've never been able to accept that she really did love me," he growls, and my smile turns into a maniacal smirk. I'm probably showing far too much teeth.

"I'm a jealous, selfish man, Aaron Fadler. And you no longer have the protection of the innocent. Your hands are just as covered in blood; your soul is just as dark." I shrug my shoulders and rise to my feet before turning to Oscar. "Write it down." I nod my chin at the screen of his iPad, but he doesn't move to obey, not right away.

I'm vaguely aware of them arguing around me for a while longer, but I'm not listening.

Instead, I'm trapped in a nightmare I've entertained for years, one where Bernadette is looking at me like she hates me.

Like she did when she passed me in the hall today.

Like she did on the first day of school.

Like she did when I held her prisoner in my closet.

Some men dream when they sleep. Some of us live in nightmares, whether we're asleep or not.

And if I can't get Bernadette to see who I really am, then I'm afraid I'll never wake up.

It strikes me suddenly, what I've just said, and a laugh spills from my throat.

"Boss?" Hael asks, watching me skeptically. I shake my head at him and rub my chin in thought.

"The discussion is over," I say, letting my voice drop to a dangerous low, caught somewhere between a purr and a growl. Like I said, I haven't felt fear—true fear—since I was five. I'm sure as shit feeling it now. "Bernadette is mine, or no deal."

I hop off the stage and slap my palm on Oscar's iPad.

"Write it down—now. I'm off to find our new girl." I lift my hand up and keep going, shoving open the doors to the theater and storming down the hall. Students scatter in my wake, as they should.

When I first started this gang, others tried to copy me. Hell, they still do—just look at Mitch Charter. They can pretend to be inspired by me all they want, but they're nothing. Poor imitations at best, plagiarists at worst. I'm content to watch them scrabble like rats for my crumbs.

Because I'm Victor Channing. This is Havoc. We're OG, and everyone else can get fucked.

And Bernadette Blackbird … she's going to be my goddamn wife if it kills me.

Which, thinking about it now, it just might.

Halloween night, Now ...

Bernadette Blackbird

There are two sides to every story, but usually, only one of them is true.

According to my stepfather, my sister Penelope was a sad, lonely, little girl who was desperate for attention. It's why she made up those lies; it's why she killed herself.

Looking into his dark gaze, I can tell we both know better.

"Take a seat," Neil Pence repeats, dressed in his uniform and smiling like only he can, like a gator who's just scented his next meal at the edge of the swamp. His brown hair is disheveled, his stubble thick around those fat, worm-like lips of his. I've never wanted to see someone dead the way I do him. "That blood real?"

He knows it is. The question mark at the end of that sentence is just for fun. See, my stepfather doesn't have hobbies like a normal person. He thrives on pain, discomfort, and repartee edged in violence. *Asshole.*

"Costume blood," I say, worrying about Callum, about all the boys really. Wondering if Danny Ensbrook really would've shot me in the face if given the chance. Aaron is stone-still behind me, so I reach back and grab his hand. It kills me a little bit, to touch him like that, but there are bigger things at play here than our bullshit feelings for each other. "What are you doing in Aaron's house?"

I don't acknowledge my ex-bestie Kali Rose-Kennedy or our disgraced Principal Vaughn; they're not worth my time.

Mostly, I'm concerned with making sure Aaron doesn't start anything violent just yet.

Or … maybe I'm the one most likely to start something violent? If I find out that the Thing laid a single finger on my sister, God help him. I'm more than happy to go down and take Neil Pence with me, engulfed in flames and enjoying the burn.

Anything to see him suffer.

Principal Vaughn watches us warily, and I can tell Havoc has done it: he's really and truly afraid of them … of us?

Us.

Havoc Girl.

Kali smirks at me, and I come to the understanding that if she weren't pregnant, I might just leap across this table and hit her as hard as I could in the tit. Maybe I still will? Her flat-ass boobs aren't currently enveloping a fetus, now are they?

The worst part about the whole situation though, is the way Neil looks at me. He stares at me like he always does, like I'm a horse that needs breaking. He undresses me with his eyes, too. He does that to every girl—even his flesh and blood daughter. My mouth fills with bile, and the step-thing grins like a crocodile. He's loving every minute of this interaction.

"Where the fuck are our girls?" Aaron asks, still bleeding, still with a goddamn bullet in his arm. He resists when I pull him down toward the sofa, but he hasn't got a lot of strength left and finally gives in. *This couch is gonna end up drenched in blood* ... Aaron and I, we're covered in it. The smell is actually starting to make me dizzy.

"Your girls?" the Thing asks, lifting one scarred eyebrow. Want to know how that happened? Our neighbor's super sweet golden retriever broke out of the fence one day, charged Neil, and attacked his face. Clearly, he knew something about Neil that nobody else but me seems to notice.

He's a bigger monster than all five Havoc Boys combined.

"You heard me, you pedophile piece of shit," Aaron grinds out, his hands shaking but his gold-green gaze steady and fierce. I have no doubt that he'd bleed himself out going after Neil if he had to. He'd do anything for his girls, even bully me. But would I want a man that *wouldn't* do those things for the children he loves like his own?

No. No, I would not.

I squeeze Aaron's hand a little harder. Sometimes, it feels almost impossible to see past one's own hurt, like looking directly into the sun. The brilliance of it is blinding. But if we close our eyes, we can feel the warmth of those rays on our skin.

"Our. Girls." Aaron lifts his chin up and flashes the nastiest smirk I've ever seen on his face. It's a mask, I see that now, but we're both players in a much bigger game. What choice does he have? His father is dead; his mother is gone. This is all he's got left, the grinning maw of a master thespian. "Because you lost that right when you raped Penelope Blackbird. Matter of fact, you lost the right to *life*."

"I told you this was a bad idea," Vaughn simpers, and I flick my green gaze his direction, making him flinch. "They probably killed somebody tonight. That blood ... that's not costume blood at all, is it?"

"Keep talking and maybe you'll get to see the difference for yourself?" I say, my voice a cold deadpan that doesn't quite match the frantic beating of my heart.

"Oh, Penelope," Neil says as Kali bristles and glances his way with narrowed eyes. "She certainly was a pathetic little fuck-up, wasn't she?" The step-thing turns toward Kali, like he's about to explain a sad truth. "Brought her into the station drunk on more than one occasion. She was a fucking delinquent, but nothing like this bitch." Neil gestures my way. "This bitch has gotten herself tangled up in a gang."

"I'm going to kill you one day," I tell him, shaking with rage, the words from Penelope's journal echoing inside my head. *He said he'd kill my sisters if I told, that he'd kill my mom. He says he's killed before and gotten away with it. That look in his eyes when he said it ... there's no doubt in my mind that he was telling the truth.* "And I'm going to cry tears of joy."

"Are you threatening a cop?" Neil asks, cocking his head to the side. His eyes shimmer with loathing and licentious greed, a want so strong it makes my head spin. Underneath that average Joe persona he has going on, his need to break and consume innocence shines brightest. If you know to look, it's impossible to miss it. "You know how serious of an offense that is?"

"You better have a fucking warrant, considering you're sitting in my house," Aaron says, his hand clenching hard to mine. "Now, where the fuck are our girls?"

"Sound asleep in their beds," Neil says in that infuriatingly calm voice of his. The way he says the word *beds,* however, frightens me to my very core. I don't *think* he would commit his dark deeds with Vaughn and Kali as witnesses, but you never know. Fear flutters in my chest like a bird with broken wings. "Such sweet, beautiful little babies. Angels, really. I sent that babysitter home a few minutes ago, gorgeous young thing."

I'm surprised Havoc's safety net didn't alert the boys to what was going on, but then … maybe they did, and we were just too busy to see the messages?

"If you touched them," I begin, because at this point, all gloves are off. I'm sitting here covered in both my ex's blood, and the blood of a boy who tried to kill me tonight. A boy who's now dead. All Neil has to do is call us in, that's it. The question is: why hasn't he?

"Listen, Bernadette," Neil interrupts, smirking as he leans forward, a shimmer in his eyes that says he has me right where he wants me. "If you don't want your little gang to go to jail, you'll shut the fuck up and say *yes, sir* to every word that comes out of my mouth."

My entire body goes ice-cold, to the point that I just don't *smell* blood, I'm *choking* on it.

"Talk to my girl like that again, and I'll break your face," Aaron says, and my gaze snaps his direction. My girl? He's like an echo of Vic right now. I don't … hate that though.

"Listen, you little prick, you've got no fucking choice."

"Watch me," Aaron says, standing up so fast that he ends up stumbling and slamming into the coffee table. He's dizzy from blood loss; I'm seriously worried about him. I stand up, too, grabbing onto his shoulder as he braces both palms on the table, panting for breath. I need to get some fluids in him, and fast.

"Forgive me if I'm not running in fear," Neil says as that little rat Kali giggles next to him.

"Tough guy," she says, playing off her perceived seat of power next to Neil. But she has no idea what Havoc has in store for her. Hell, neither do I. All I know is that if the boys were willing to castrate Donald, Kali is going to suffer just as much.

What was it that Callum said? *Her face isn't pregnant.*

Principal Vaughn doesn't look quite so smug, eyes darting from the front door to the back, like he expects trouble. No, no, like he expects *Havoc.*

"Sit down," Neil repeats, eyes hardening as he looks at me. "And say *yes, sir.*"

"Bernadette," Aaron says, panting as he looks over at me. "Don't do it. We have Neil by the balls; he can't touch us."

"How?" I ask as Vaughn makes a small sound of protest, wringing his hands as he paces in front of the fireplace. Aaron just glances my way, meeting my eyes, and shaking his head slightly. Fuck. Whatever it is they've got on Neil, I'm not going to like it.

"You said you'd bring them to heel," Kali demands, standing up from the couch and turning on Neil with a pouty expression on her pretty little face. *Is it Neil's baby that she's carrying?* "Well, I'm still waiting."

Neil rises to his feet at the same time I notice movement in the shadows near the staircase and in the small hall by the master bedroom.

"Last chance, Bernadette," the Thing says, putting his hand on the radio at his hip. "Say it, or I call you and your friend

Aaron here in." He pulls the radio out and pauses as a clicking sound comes from behind his head; it's the distinct sound of a gun's hammer being pulled back.

"Don't make your final mistake here, Neil. I'd hate to have to scrub your brains off the walls of Aaron's living room."

Vic's voice is ice-cold, his full mouth twisted in a dark frown. His purple-black hair is slicked back from his face, still wet from a shower, his makeup wiped clean, clothes fresh and blood-free. As soon as I see him, a dark thrill travels through me, one that tastes like sweet, heavy poison.

"And if you think I'm bluffing, go ahead and test me."

The fury that lights my stepfather's face scares the crap out of me. He has friends; he has connections.

And he came here for a reason.

"I knew I shouldn't have followed you here," Vaughn murmurs, still wringing his hands.

"Excellent observation," Oscar says, suddenly standing behind the principal. A chill traces over my skin. *How the fuck did he get in here without me noticing?* His gray eyes are focused on the back of Vaughn's head, his revolver held rock steady in a single hand. He pulls the hammer back and keeps smiling.

Hael swaggers in from the kitchen (I figure he, at least, must've used the exterior door that leads into the laundry room), while Callum slides open the patio door. He has the bat in his hand still and while he's cleaned up, the weapon's still stained red.

The energy in that room suffocates me, climbing down my throat like smoke. I find it suddenly hard to breathe.

"Don't worry, Bernie. Neil's just a dickless, neutered dog," Vic reassures me, stone-cold, immovable. But he strikes that chord deep within me, shaking away the ice crystals that cling to my soul. He eats away the numb and leaves me bleeding. Who can staunch that bleeding? Me? Am I supposed to bandage my own emotional wounds? "His hands are tied; we have dirt on him."

"And why don't you tell my lovely stepdaughter what, exactly, that is?" Neil asks, turning around to face Victor, not at all concerned about the gun in his face. The way that man smiles, it cuts to the marrow in my bones and rots me from the inside out. Right here, this is the type of person who only gets pleasure from watching others suffer. "You can't though, can you? Because you're afraid to."

The thing about Neil though, is that he's underestimated Victor Channing.

"We have a video of him," Vic says, nodding his chin in Neil's direction. "With your sister Penelope."

On the outside, I do nothing. I'm still standing there, trying to help Aaron keep his feet, blood smearing across my hands. On the inside, I'm shattering into a mosaic of hurt and pain and *rage.* It's leaded glass, that mosaic, and my anger is the iron that holds all the pretty pieces together. One day, I'm going to pick up one of those pieces and I'm going to stab Neil Pence through the empty cavity where his heart should be.

"Neil, what the hell is going on?" Kali asks, crossing an arm over her still-flat stomach and looking between Victor and the Thing with a particularly vacuous facial expression. Nobody ever said the lying little twit had any working brain cells.

Principal Vaughn looks like he might shit his pants. "You said we were going to come over here and put a stop to all this."

"A stop to what?" Oscar asks innocently, pushing his glasses up his nose with an inked middle finger while at the same time keeping his revolver trained on Scott. "A raucous Halloween night? I see Kali came in costume. It's quite popular for girls to dress up like whores on All Hallows' Eve, isn't it?"

"Fuck you, Montauk," she snarls, smoothing her hands down her pale pink skirt. Despite Oscar's quip, she didn't dress up, she didn't come to Stacey's party. She abandoned Mitch's pathetic clown crew, but why? What is she doing here? What is Vaughn doing here? And why are three of the seven people on my list standing in this room?

"You have one minute to fuck off out of here before we make all three of you disappear—permanently." Victor steps back and drops the gun to his side. His eyes are like two dark pools, ready to swallow me up and drown me. But his attention keeps flicking to Aaron. He's worried, and so am I. My ex-boyfriend doesn't look so hot right about now. "I'm going to count down from sixty."

"You don't want to know why I'm here?" Neil teases, eyes narrowing as his thin lips curl into a smirk. "What Scott's doing here? He came to me, you know, after you trashed his cabin and made him do all those nasty things on the Internet."

"Sixty." Vic nods, and both Callum and Hael step forward to flank him. Nobody's smiling tonight. Nobody's reveling in this moment, not like they did before when we went after Don. "Fifty-nine. Fifty-eight."

"Let's just go, please," Vaughn says, shaking, his gaze

latching on me like I'm the sole party responsible for this mess. "This was a bad idea in the first place. You didn't tell me they had a video."

"Fifty-seven." Vic barely looks like he's breathing, he's standing so damn still. Callum's hood is pulled up over his blond hair, his face bathed in shadows. He probably needs me as much as Aaron does right now, just in a different way. *Did you hear yourself, Bernadette? He needs you? Havoc doesn't fucking need you. And you don't owe them your emotional energy or support.*

And yet here I am, wanting to give it.

My hand curls around Aaron's arm as he pants beside me, fighting to maintain at least some semblance of power and control.

"We're at a crossroads here. You move on me, I bury you," Neil growls out, never taking his eyes off of Vic. "And leave Kali out of it."

"What about me?" Principal Vaughn bursts out, putting one hand on the mantle to steady himself. "You said you'd help me out of this mess! I helped you when you asked for it."

"That confession of yours is gone," Neil says, sniffling and backing up a few feet. My blood chills because I know my stepfather; he's only telling us what he wants us to hear. *See how powerful I am? See what I can do? Don't you ever forget that I have fingers in many pies.* Kali clings to his arm and then turns a poisonous glare on me, dropping her poor-me act for once. There's no audience around to lap it up, so she doesn't bother. "That's all I've got. Scott, you're on your own now."

Neil turns and takes off for the front door with Kali in tow.

Principal Vaughn scrambles after him, and the boys let them go. I realize then that maybe we're stretched too thin. I did this. I called Havoc, and I started this mess.

I grit my teeth.

The shittiest part about all of this? I actually feel *bad* about it, like I'm inconveniencing the Havoc Boys. They ruined my life sophomore year. Does it matter what their twisted reasons were, what price Kali paid? They did it, and I suffered, and now here I am praying to what little good is left in the universe that Aaron Fadler doesn't fucking die on me.

"They've all gotten into the cruiser; it's pulling out of the driveway," Oscar says, looking out from between the sheer curtains that line the front window. "Off they go down the street."

"Fuck," Aaron says, and then he falls. Hard. So hard that I can't keep him up even though I try. Hael is there in a split-second, grabbing onto his friend's arm and helping me push him back onto the couch. I climb onto the cushion next to him and start to undo his sweater, helping Hael remove his clothes so we can assess the damage.

"He's still bleeding," I murmur as the other boys move in around us. "The bullet's still in his arm." My fingers just lightly skim the bruise on his chest, but it's nowhere near as important as the wound in his left bicep. Or the dead kid we left at the Halloween party. *Damn you, Danny Ensbrook, you piece of shit.* He just had to do it, huh? Aim that gun at me ... "He needs a hospital."

"Mm," Vic says, rubbing at his chin, a sign that he's deep in thought. "Hospitals are full of mandated reporters. A minor with a gunshot wound is bad news for us. It brings inquiries and questions and police reports."

My head snaps around to level a glare on Havoc's boss; I must look pretty scary, too, because he raises his eyebrows at me in mock surprise.

"We're not letting him die," I say as Aaron groans, his head leaned back on the cushion, eyes closed. I'm not fully certain that he's still conscious.

"No, of course not," Vic scoffs, like I've lost my damn mind. "Let's get him in the van and take him to Whitney's house."

"Nurse Yes-Scott?!" I choke out, but it's the obvious choice. She'll have heard from Vaughn by now about what happened. She'll know her ass is on the line. What choice will she have but to help us? Besides, she was hired at Prescott for a reason. Most schools don't need trauma nurses with gunshot wound experience. In the southside, it's practically a requirement. "Fuck. Fine. Let's get him outside."

I stand up, still shaking with the rush of adrenaline, still covered in blood.

"Oscar, you stay with the girls," Vic commands, and I just know I'm not going anywhere either until I know they're alright. I pull away from Aaron and walk backwards for a moment, bumping into Victor. He puts his hands on my shoulders and leans down to put his mouth near my ear. "Don't worry about Aaron: I won't let anything happen to him." His lips press against the side of my neck, branding me in a way I can never wash off. "I'll even stitch him up before we leave to stem the flow; take a quick shower and get that blood off of you."

Even though it probably shouldn't, his voice comforts me, and I nod, heading up the stairs and cracking the door to the girls' room. All three of them are fast asleep, like maybe they never knew Neil was here in the first place. I stand there for several minutes, watching Heather's chest rise and fall with steady breaths, and then I slip back out and duck into the bathroom.

Blood is not the easiest substance to wash off. It's sticky and viscous, and it clings to the skin like paint. By the time I get out of the shower, my skin is pink and irritated, and the spot where Billie stabbed me is throbbing and oozing fresh crimson, soaking the black t-shirt I stole from Aaron's dresser. At least you can't see the stain, and right now, that's good enough for me.

"You're hurt," Oscar says when I step out of the bathroom. He's standing in front of me, shirtless and wearing a pair of plaid pajama pants. His tattooed chest and belly are on full display, and if circumstances were different, I'd very much appreciate the view. My breath catches as he reaches out and presses his thumb against the spot on my right sleeve, making me hiss between gritted teeth as he pulls his finger back, stained with blood. "Let's take care of that, shall we?"

"No time. I'll worry about it when I get back." I move to shove past him when he reaches out and snatches my upper arm in tight fingers, making me cry out. More blood oozes out and dribbles down my arm. With his other hand, Oscar traces the wound on my face, the one I'm too afraid to look at because I know it's going to scar.

"It'll only take a minute," he says, pushing me back into the bathroom and forcing me onto the closed lid of the toilet. I'm getting mad déjà vu here from when Victor stitched up my arm, looking up at Oscar's gray eyes through the thick lenses of his glasses. I sneer at him as he pulls a first aid kit out from under the sink, but I don't have the energy to protest. Oscar turns back to me and shoves my shirtsleeve up, making me gasp. He's not at all gentle as he goes about inspecting the wound. "You really could use a hospital visit as well. Have that bitch nurse take a look at this while you're over there."

"Aaron is the one who needs help. Slap a bandage on it and let me get out of here." This bone-weary fatigue washes over me, and my lids close of their own accord. My entire body hurts from the fight, and I'm bruised all over. Strong fingers touch the underside of my jaw, lifting my face up. I open my eyes to find Oscar staring down at me.

"Chin up, Bernadette. There is no rest for the wicked." He releases me and tackles both wounds with an antiseptic wipe as Hael pops in the door, worrying at his lower lip. Some of the black hair dye still stains his red faux hawk as he reaches up and runs tattooed fingers through it.

"Aaron's all loaded up in the van," Hael says, studying me, his honey-brown eyes dark. He hesitates for a second before adding, "and he's asking for you." My heart twists into a knot as I watch Oscar take some antiseptic gel and squeeze it onto a cotton round. He swipes it over my face and arm then applies some bandages.

"I'll add *tetanus shot* to our list of things to do," Oscar murmurs, releasing me and stepping back to lean against the opposite wall. He crosses lean, muscular arms over his chest as I notice that his nipples are pierced with little swords. *Interesting.*

I stand up, yanking my shirtsleeve down, and exit the bathroom, following Hael downstairs and outside, into the crisp, fall air. Jack o' lanterns flicker in the yard across the street, but the magic of Halloween is dead to me right now.

Victor drives us for once while I sit next to Aaron in the middle row. He's groaning, mumbling things under his breath, but at least when I grab his hand, he squeezes back.

"Bernie," he whispers, his head leaned back on the seat. I frown, scooting closer to him and then glancing back to check on Callum in the last row, leaned over with his hood covering his freshly washed hair.

"You okay?" I ask him, and he lifts his head up just enough to look at me, a frown darkening those perfect pink lips. He's still holding the bat, like he can't bear to let it go.

"I'm okay," he replies, but I'm not sure that's true. He killed somebody tonight. For me. He's bound to be a little fucked-up. Callum smiles, like he can sense the direction of my thoughts. "Just to be clear: I'm not upset that Danny Ensbrook is dead. I'm upset that I did it with too many witnesses, and that I put as all at risk. I'd kill the world to save you, Bernadette."

My cheeks flush, and I look down, running my tongue over my lower lip.

"I appreciate it," I say, and even though our situation tonight is beyond fucked, I can't help but like what he's just said to me. Like I said, I've grown up in the dark, so I appreciate the shadows. His darkness is beautiful to me, like a night sky bereft of stars. The sun is just too bright, and it burns. I belong here, in eternal midnight.

Cal reaches up and takes my other hand, giving it a squeeze as we snake through town toward Nurse Whitney's house. He doesn't let go until we pull up outside a modest two-bedroom with fresh paint and a Lexus in the driveway, a vehicle that's certainly way above the paygrade for a school nurse of any kind, most especially one from Prescott High.

Vic and Hael climb out, leaving me in the car with Aaron and Cal, and knock on the front door. Slowly, hesitantly, the door opens, and I can see a crack of light from inside. Nurse Yes-Scott was smart enough to leave the chain-lock in place, but surely, she must know that that won't stop the Havoc Boys. If they want into her house, they'll get in.

Speak of the devil and he shall appear ...

Hael shoves his boot into the open door to keep Whitney from closing it. In the same breath, he hefts up a pair of bolt cutters that he's holding by his side and snaps the lock in its sharp jaws. He shoves the door open and steps inside while Victor comes back to help us with Aaron. I'm fully prepared to get under one of Aaron's arms and brace him until we get in the front door, but Vic just grabs his friend under the legs and around the waist and hoists him up into his arms.

My brows go up as I watch Vic carry him toward the front door and up the few steps that lead to the porch. Aaron Fadler is no lightweight; he's built and muscular, but Vic carries him like he weighs little to nothing at all, setting him gently down on Nurse Yes-Scott's pretty yellow couch. *Well, that's ruined.* I sneer at her as she stands nearby, wringing her hands.

"He really should be at a hospital right now …" she says, sweat beading on her forehead. She's dressed in a loose white t-shirt and lace-trimmed black silk shorts, clearly ready for bed. Her blond hair is piled in a messy bun on her head, her brown eyes flicking from Callum and his bloodied baseball bat to the boy moaning on her ruined sofa.

"Not happening," Vic says, standing up and turning to face her. "Do what you can do here and give me an assessment of where he's at."

Nurse Yes-Scott swallows hard and then moves into a small bathroom off the main living area, grabbing some supplies, and coming to sit on the coffee table in front of Aaron. He's shirtless now, so I can see his bruise, the wound in his arm, and the fresh, shiny blood that won't stop coming.

"I can clean this up, but he really needs a blood transfusion."

"Aaron's O-positive," Vic says, his voice like ice. "Where can we get some?"

"Get some?" Whitney asks, turning to look at him like he's lost his mind. "What do you mean?"

"I mean, where can we fucking get some?" Victor repeats, and Nurse Whitney goes completely pale. She knows what she's done, what we did to Scott Vaughn, and she better believe we'll burn this place to the ground if she doesn't cooperate. My hands curl into fists at my sides as I stare at her, wishing I'd added her to the list, too. We haven't had much in the way of personal interaction, but she's a big part of Vaughn's operation, tricking the poor girls of Prescott High into making her money off their own backs. "Can we rob an ambulance or something?"

"A-ambulances don't carry blood," she whispers, biting her lower lip as she turns back to Aaron. "He needs a hospital—"

"The hospital then," Victor says, not skipping a beat. "What all do we need?"

"You can't be serious?" Whitney chokes as Vic passes over his phone, his expression a dark slice of hell.

"Make me a list. *Now.* I really hate repeating myself."

Nurse Whitney grabs Vic's phone and quickly types up a list of supplies before passing it back to him.

"Let's hit Joseph General," Victor says, glancing over at Hael. "Security is much lighter, and the place gets tons of trauma patients; it's a madhouse over there, so they don't notice shit. Let's grab some cash before we go. Might be easier to bribe somebody than it would be to just pinch it."

"Got it," Hael says, nodding as I gape at the two of them.

"You can't be serious?" I ask, looking between the boys. I'm torn between being worried and being pissed off. Glancing back at Aaron, I see his pallid expression and my heart seizes in my chest. *He can't die on me, not when things are so … confusing between us.* Putting my hands over my face, I drag them down and then give Victor a look that could kill.

He smiles at me, but it isn't a nice smile.

It's a smile nightmares are made of, and I hate how much I love that.

At this point, I'm fairly certain we're soul mates. We must be, with how fucked-up we are. Put us together, and the fucked-up factor amplifies by about a hundred times. I put a finger up, pointing directly at Vic. He's the leader: Aaron is his responsibility.

"Fine," I start, poking him in the chest. "You let him die, and I'll cut your fucking balls off." Nurse Whitney makes a small squeaking sound behind me, but I ignore her. She reaped the fruits of others' suffering, of their labor, their sacrifice. She recruited girls for Principal Vaughn's bullshit and reveled in that glory. I *really* should've added her to my list; Oscar was right.

Vic snorts and grabs my hand, bringing my finger to his lips and sucking it between them in the lewdest possible way. Hael shakes his head and puts his hands on his hips, clearly annoyed with Vic and me and our weird shit.

"If he dies, I'll sharpen the knife," Victor says, dropping my hand, but I snatch his wrist before he can turn away, raising his dark brows my direction. "Yes, darling?"

"Don't pull that darling shit on me," I growl, yanking him close. He comes to me, but not because I actually have the strength to move him, but because we're drawn together. Because we're beautiful poison together. Perfect toxicity. "You and Hael come back to me. If either of you gets arrested …"

"Yes, balls, knife, no Havoc babies." Vic grabs me by the back of the hair with a punishing grip and crushes his lips to mine, taking down my walls with that lush mouth of his. "Don't worry: I'm not going to the hospital." He lifts his head up and gestures in Hael's direction. "He is. I'm going to find out why none of our crew told us a goddamn pig was at the house." Vic scowls as he pulls away, nodding at Callum as he passes.

My eyes meet Cal's blue ones, and I lick my lower lip.

Aaron's body is broken; I'm worried about Callum's soul.

"This is so crazy," Whitney murmurs from behind me. I turn

my head slowly as Vic and Hael slip out the door, just two shadows in the night. Whatever she sees on my face must scare the shit out of her because she stands up, leaving a pale-faced and groaning Aaron alone on the sofa.

"What can we do to help him while we wait?" I ask, my voice a cold thread of steel. "Because if he dies here tonight, so do you." Whitney's face pales and she takes another step back, looking at me like she's considering calling the cops and risking sending us all to jail, just to save her own ass. What she doesn't know or maybe just hasn't figured out, is that Callum isn't going to let her get anywhere near a phone, a door, or a window. She's stuck here, for better or worse.

"We need to elevate his legs and keep him warm," she says, swallowing hard, stray strands of hair coming loose from her bun and sticking to her sweaty forehead. She's got full-on hooker makeup on her face, probably from some long-ago Halloween party. My throat tightens up as I think about the altercation in the fun house, of Danny aiming the gun at me, of Callum lifting the baseball bat.

Fuck.

"He could go into shock …" Whitney continues, giving Callum a wary look.

But she needn't worry about him.

If something happens to Aaron, I'll become her worst nightmare.

"Fine. Get a warm rag, some blankets, pillows. Get him orange juice or something." I bark out the orders, even though I have no clue what I'm doing. But somebody has to do something, so it may as well be me. *Take him to a hospital,*

Bernadette. The rational part of my mind is screaming at me, but the other part, the darker part, is fully immersed in the world of Havoc.

No cops, no hospitals.

Aaron could lose his sisters. He could go to jail. We all could.

We deal with this our way.

"Did she stutter?" Callum asks, leaning casually against the wall, hands in the front pocket of his hoodie. His voice is pleasant enough, his expression serene, almost too calm, as he turns blue eyes over to Whitney, spurring her into action.

I give Cal a look of thanks as I sit down on the edge of the sofa, sweeping Aaron's auburn hair back from his forehead. My throat feels tight, like there's a sob stuck in there somewhere that I'm just too stubborn—or perhaps just too broken—to let out.

"He isn't going to die," Callum tells me, like he somehow knows this for certain. I look down at Aaron for several quiet moments, trying to commit his face to memory, the smooth line of his jaw, the tiny scar on his right earlobe. But then I realize I'm doing it and *why* I'm doing it, and I get furious all over again.

"You can't know that," I growl, turning back to Callum and finding his eyes not on Aaron, but on me. We stare at each other for a long time before he finally speaks in that beautifully dark voice of his, like his vocal cords are shaped from the shadows of Halloween night.

"He won't go, not when there's so much uncertainty between the two of you. He's never stopped loving you, and he's never had the chance to truly prove how sorry he is for the things that happened." Cal pauses as Whitney comes back into the room, carrying a glass pitcher of orange juice and several glasses. He takes one from her and then looks her dead in the face. "Sit down at the kitchen table, and don't try anything I might not like." He taps the end of the bloodied baseball bat with the toe of his boot and her face pales even further, a feat I hadn't considered possible.

Callum brings me some juice, letting his fingers linger against mine for longer than is really necessary. Neither of us misses how much they shake, but we both know that emotional wounds can be dealt with later. Physical ones have an expiration date.

I try my best to get Aaron to sip some juice, but he isn't moving. Fuck, he's barely *breathing*. After a while, I give up and drink it myself. The sugar rush goes straight to my head, giving my adrenaline-addled body the boost it needs. I set the glass down on the pristine surface of the coffee table, hoping it leaves a ring and ruins the furniture.

"Happy Halloween," I whisper to Aaron, leaning down to press my lips to the clammy skin of his forehead.

I'm going to give Vic and Hael two hours, no more.

And then, even if it costs me everything, I'm taking Aaron to a fucking hospital.

If he dies, something inside of me will die with him, and there isn't that much left of me to give. I'm a tree with barren branches, one lone blossom clinging to a wooden wasteland. I will not let this part of my childhood go, no matter what the cost.

CHAPTER
TWO

Pretty sure the Havoc boys like to torture me. Must help them get off or something. It's quite literally two hours and three minutes into this nightmare before we hear back from Hael and Vic. There's a loud knock at the front door of Nurse Yes-Scott's house, a sound like a cop's knock, the pounding of a frantic fist.

Callum checks the peephole, and then wrenches it open, revealing a blood-spattered Hael Harbin.

"What in the actual fuck?!" I shout, standing up as Hael steps inside, clutching a plastic grocery bag by his side. His face and chest are drenched in crimson, and he scowls as he swipes a hand over his full lips, smearing blood across his too-handsome features. His honey-brown eyes look wicked, surrounded by all of that crimson. I'm surprised by how scared I am for him. *Little bit more than just a sidepiece, eh, Bernie?* That's when I know for certain that I'm well and truly screwed. Havoc has its claws in me, and it's never letting go. I force my next words out through clenched teeth. "Are you okay?"

I pray to every dark god I don't believe in that it's not his blood. How messed up is that? I *want* to hear that he slit some asshole's throat, that Hael isn't hurt in any way, shape, or form.

"I broke one of these fucking things," he says, handing me the bag. When I glance down to see what's inside, I find several sealed bags of blood and some clear bags of saline, among other things. My stomach turns as I lift my head to look at him. "Ran into trouble on my way back. Mitch is on the warpath tonight; our boys are even starting to refer to his goons as the Charter Crew." He shakes his head and drags his arm over his mouth again, flicking the blood onto Whitney's perfect white walls as I pass the bag to her.

She looks into it, face paling, before lifting her brown eyes up to Hael's bloodied face.

"How did you get this?" she whispers, but Hael just laughs. He's not going to answer her. She should know better than to speak to us like we're anything but her captors.

"Never you mind that, sugar tits," he says, lighting up a cigarette with shaking hands. Hael might look like a cocky asshole right now, but he's as afraid for Aaron as I am. I flick my attention back to him as Nurse Yes-Scott starts to set up a blood transfusion, right there in her Pottery Barn-inspired living room. Fitting, I think, since everything in here was paid for with blood money. "Use some of your wasted medical knowledge on fixing up our friend."

"I'm not a surgeon," Whitney begins, but the look she gets from Hael clearly relays the fact that we give zero fucks. "But I'll … I'll try."

"Try really fucking hard," Hael warns as Callum closes the door behind him, and Hael strips off his shirt, using it to scrub the blood from his skin. If this were any other moment, I'd most definitely appreciate his crimson-covered chest. "Vic'll be back soon. Doubtful you want to hear what he'll say if you screw this up."

Whitney purses her fuchsia-painted lips, giving Hael a side-eye as he smokes a cigarette in her living room, but she gets to work, inserting an IV into Aaron's arm. The bullet is still inside of him; what if it's lodged next to an artery or something? What if Whitney's right, and we really do need a surgeon to get it out?

Minute by minute, Bernadette. Take it minute by minute.

Hael takes a seat on the coffee table while I stand near the foot of the couch, watching as Whitney does her thing, removing Victor's careful stitches and digging into the wound with what I can only hope are a clean pair of household tweezers. *This is so wrong, so wrong on so many levels.* I turn away, but only for a minute. I can't let that bitch work on my ex without at least keeping an eye on him.

Even though it turns my stomach to see Aaron opened back up, I glance over and watch Whitney remove the small piece of metal from his bicep. With a frown on her face, she drops it into my empty orange juice cup.

"He could very well have internal damage in his arm that we don't know about," she murmurs, but she keeps working until the wound is closed and bandaged.

While we wait, we watch Aaron go through two pints of blood. He eats up everything Hael brought and looks like he could use a little more.

I feel like I'm imagining it, but his face seems a little less pale, his cheeks a bit pinker. I touch my fingers to the wound on my own arm, but I don't want Whitney distracted with my injuries when she needs to be keeping an eye on Aaron. *My face is going to scar,* I think, but I push the thought back. It isn't important, not right now anyway.

Although when I next have a dark moment alone with Billie Charter, I'm going to kill her.

Make no mistake about that.

After a while, I end up curled on the couch beside Aaron, my head resting against his chest, just so I can make sure his heart is still beating, that he's still breathing. *That he's still around for me to hate.* Part of me wonders what I'd do if I lost him now, how I'd react. For someone I supposedly despise, I sure have a lot of feelings on the matter.

When Vic appears several hours later, he pauses in the living room and gives his friend an assessing look.

"What are his chances?" he demands, and it's quite clear that he's addressing Nurse Yes-Scott and not us.

"He seems stable enough," she says, checking Aaron's blood pressure for the umpteenth time. "He's going to need time to heal, and he'll scar, but—"

"I don't give a shit about scarring. Will he live?" Vic demands, lighting up a cigarette of his own and making Whitney frown dramatically.

"He'll live. As far as gunshot wounds go, it isn't overly serious. Likely, his poor condition is a result of pushing too hard and refusing to seek medical treatment right away. But I really should insist that you have him see a doctor—"

"I don't give a fuck what you insist," Vic says, moving over to stand beside her. The look on her face is priceless. Two parts fear and one part, sickening, disgusting lust. Guess she likes 'em young, same as Principal Vaughn. They deserve to share a coffin together, preferably sometime soon. If only the devil worked on karma. Too bad nothing about life is fair. "Hael, Cal, load Aaron up and let's go."

"What am I supposed to do about all of this blood?" Whitney whines as Hael and Cal gingerly lift their friend between them, carrying him to the door. I move ahead of them, opening it wide, and pausing just briefly before following them out, so I can hear Victor's answer.

"You're going to clean it up," he says, crouching low next to Nurse Yes-Scott and putting his lips near her ear. "And then you're going to erase this night from your memory. If you choose to do anything outside of that plan, I'll send the most depraved men I know to pay you a little visit." Vic stands up, staring down at Whitney's wide eyes and quivering form with zero empathy. Her face is paler than Aaron's was when we first got here. "Oh, and if you see Vaughn around, you tell him to fuck off. If I find out you're entertaining him …" Victor just shakes his head, but he doesn't need to say anything else. It's quite clear from Whitney's expression that his message was heard loud and clear.

Turning away, I head down the steps and open the sliding door to the minivan.

The sky is beginning to warm with color from the rising sun, a cheeky blush that annoys the shit out of me. How dare the day be threatening to start when the night seems so endless and bleak? That endlessness, it suits the situation. A gentle pink blush does not.

"Hey." Vic grabs my chin, but I tear my face away from him, turning away to stare down the street, at a perfect row of suburban houses lined up like toys, dollhouses for people crafted of plastic dreams. I don't belong anywhere near here, not by a long shot. Aaron's dream of seeing me reach for the stars, like some sort of bullshit poster on the wall of an elementary school classroom, it was never going to happen for me. Even if I didn't have Heather to worry about. Even if I didn't drink darkness and sip pain. "He'll be okay, Bernie."

"Yeah, but that doesn't mean we didn't kill a kid tonight," I say, turning back to look at Vic. He just stands there, a mountain of muscle and immorality, and smiles tightly at me.

"What happens on All Hallows' Eve, stays on All Hallows' Eve. Don't bring it up again." He starts to move past me, but then grabs my face and presses a scalding kiss to my lips that has me thinking all sorts of depraved thoughts that don't belong in the middle of a crisis, thoughts that pertain to naked flesh and hungry mouths and roving hands. "That's not a request."

Vic lets go of me and slips into the driver's side of the van. I hesitate only briefly before climbing in to join him.

I don't remember falling asleep, but I'm just grateful that I wake up with zero nightmares. All I can figure is that I was just too fucking tired to have them. When I crack my lids, I find Aaron staring back at me, sitting propped up in the king bed in his parents' old bedroom. Vic is on my other side, his breathing deep enough that I can tell he's still asleep.

"You're awake," Aaron says softly, and I cock a brow, pushing myself up into a sitting position.

"Shouldn't I be the one saying that?" I reply, pushing white-blonde hair over my shoulder. The pink at the ends is starting to fade; time to re-dye it. I wonder if I should choose another color? But no, Penelope's favorite color was pink. I wet my lips and scoot a bit closer to Aaron, until our shoulders are so close that one deep breath would press our bare skin together. "How are you feeling?"

Aaron scoffs a laugh and shakes his head, cringing a bit as he reaches up a hand to press against the bandage on his left shoulder.

"Like I got run over by a fucking truck," he says, cocking a smile that reminds me of the ones we used to share on bright, sunshine-y days, back when life didn't feel quite so … desperate. That's the only way I can think to describe the way I feel right now, *desperate*.

The Thing was here last night. Kali was here. Principal Vaughn was here.

Callum killed Danny Ensbrook.

Shit.

You're not in this alone, I remind myself, looking up and catching Aaron's green-gold gaze. *Havoc Girl. Not Havoc's girl. We might be in hell, but we're burning together.*

"I thought you might die last night," I whisper, without even meaning to. Emotion catches in my throat, surprising me. With Vic on one side, and Aaron on the other … the numbness inside of me feels like it's been shattered, like I'm being cut apart with every thought, every feeling. I'm bleeding profusely, and I don't know how to stop it. Unlike with Aaron's wound, there are no transfusions for the emotionally repressed, no IV doses of happiness or clarity or mental wellness.

"Yeah?" Aaron asks, shirtless and covered in tattoos, beautiful and broken. I want to reach out and touch him, but I don't dare. There might only be inches between us physically, but emotionally, there are miles. "And how did you feel about that?"

I snort and shake my head.

"Don't ask stupid questions, Aaron Fadler. They don't suit you." We both pause as a soft, little knock sounds at the door.

"Bernie?" Heather calls out. "We're hungry, and there's cereal but no milk."

Aaron and I exchange a look, and he grins.

My heart stutters in my chest and I know I'm balancing on a dangerous precipice here, one where I forgive Aaron for the things he did to me, where I find myself slipping into a routine as warm and familiar as any I've ever had in my life. Aaron and I were good together, but we were kids. Maybe we're still kids, but things are different now. I'm not sure how safe or smart it is to let my heart believe we can ever recapture the past.

"I wouldn't mind something to eat, if you're up for having food delivered." He glances down at his phone, twisting his mouth to the side in a sardonic smile. "It's nearly five o'clock anyway, so pizza seems appropriate."

"Five o'clock?" I choke out, pushing up to my feet and heading for the door. I'm no longer wearing my bloodstained clothes from last night, just an old t-shirt I stole from Aaron's dresser. The smell of it—like sandalwood and rose, like Aaron himself—lulled me to sleep last night. Underneath, I'm not wearing shit, but luckily the shirt is long enough to cover me. We're all about casual here, in fucking Havoc House. "Hey," I say as I open the door to find my sister, along with Aaron's sister Kara and cousin Ashley. "Sorry we slept so late. We … had a long night." I clench my jaw against the stark reality of that statement.

It's Friday today, a school day, but only technically speaking. Prescott High would've been a ghost town. Nobody in the southside goes to class the day after Halloween, regardless of what day of the week it is. I do feel kind of shitty about not taking the girls though.

"We don't care," Heather says, peering past me to see both Aaron and Vic in the bed. How weird is that, that we all slept in there together? A tingle passes through me, and I have to wrap my arms around myself to keep it contained. It feels like a sparkle, and I don't like sparkles. They're nothing but bullshit covered in glitter. "We played video games with Hael and ate chips and Twinkies. Ashley puked on Hael's jeans." She points back at Kara's younger cousin, and the little girl hides behind Kara like she has something to be ashamed of.

I just roll my eyes and run my fingers through my hair.

"Anyone would throw up after a night of candy and a day of junk food." I glance back at Aaron, sitting in bed with a bandage on his arm, his muscles those of a man, his boy's body shed along with his old life. What was I thinking? He hasn't been a kid for a long time, and neither have I. "I'll cook something. I just need someone to take me to the store."

"You'll make tacos?" Heather asks, clasping her hands together in a prayer position. The golden highlights in her light brown hair remind me of Penelope. So much so that I find that I suddenly can't breathe. *Shit, fuck, bitch.* This is all Vic's fault. And Aaron's, how dare he almost die on me. That's so not freaking fair for him to do that, to trick me into thinking I might lose him so that my walls could come tumbling down. And Callum? He just risked life in prison to save me.

Screw these Havoc Boys, and everything they stand for.

If I were smart, I'd just take Heather and run.

Instead, my blood is thick with vengeance, and the more the boys push, the more of my emotional walls they knock down, the harder I want to fight. The more I hurt. For myself, for Penelope. Like a caged cat, my claws are out.

"Oscar can take you in the van," Vic murmurs, surprising me. I glance back, but his crow-black eyes are still closed. I'd have known if they were open and boring into me; I'd have felt them.

"Fan-flipping-tastic," I growl, stepping out of the room and closing the door behind me. As soon as I do, I feel a brief moment of respite. Victor is a lot; Aaron and I have baggage. I just need a minute.

"Shall I make a list?" Oscar asks, looking up from his iPad to stare at me through perfectly clean lenses. I've never seen them with a smudge or a speck; they're almost *too* clean. He's practically inhuman. "I don't like to dawdle in supermarkets, especially when we're in the middle of a turf war."

"I'm not exactly the list-making type," I quip back, giving him a look. He stares right back at me, cutting through me with a slate-gray stare, and then lets his attention dip to my thighs. The shirt is just barely long enough to cover my crotch, leaving little to the imagination.

"Well, then, I suppose *I'll* make the list while you find something appropriate to wear."

"How's this for appropriate?" I snap back, lifting the front of the shirt and flashing him tits and bush, all in one go. The girls have wandered out the back door to the yard, so they don't see it happen, but Oscar most certainly does. An unreadable expression crosses his face before he goes right back to making a list on his iPad, seemingly unaffected by my naked body. *Psycho.* I drop the shirt back into place and grab the booty shorts I wore beneath my cheerleading skirt last night. I yank them on, twist my hair up into a messy bun, and use the hair-tie on my wrist to keep it in place. "Let's go." Slipping my feet into my combat boots (the tennis-shoes are covered in blood and should probably be burned), I head for the front door, exhaling sharply as soon as I step out into the wet, cold November morning.

November.

Just last night, there was a harvest moon, a Halloween party … and a murder.

Speaking of, as I close the door behind me and rest my back against it, gathering a bit of peace for myself, I see Callum on the edge of the sidewalk, the hood of his navy-blue sweatshirt over his head, the sleeves torn at the shoulders, his muscular arms and scars on vivid display.

"Hey," I start, moving across the wet grass to stand beside him. The cold dew seeps through the laces on my boots, chilling me to the bone, but I ignore it, crossing my arms over my chest to ward off the frigid air. My breath escapes in tiny, white clouds as I pause next to Callum, our shoulders pressed as close as I was with Aaron just a few minutes prior.

But between Callum and me, there's a hell of a lot less baggage.

I scoot a bit closer, so that we're touching.

"Good morning," he says, giving me one of those cryptic smiles of his. The look in his blue eyes is telling, a somber sort of acceptance. *"Sometimes pain is pretty, to the people who have too much of it."* Callum Park has already accepted that his life will never be what he wanted, that he will never achieve his dreams. He's come to the realization that some of us just exist in nightmares. "Taking off so soon?"

A shudder comes over me at the thought of returning to my mother's house, of sleeping under the same roof as the Thing. I'm not sure that I can do it, muster up that level of courage just about now.

"Not really. More like, I can't feed the girls junk food for dinner, not after a day of eating chips and cake." My mouth twitches into a bit of a smile as I remember playing with Penelope, running around the house dressed in Mom's fancy dresses and laughing, stuffing our faces with snacks. When Pamela came home and saw what we were doing, she cracked Pen across the cheek so hard that her face swelled up for almost two weeks. Mom told the school she'd been stung by a bee, that she was allergic. "We're going to the store for supplies."

My smile disappears as quick as it came.

"Well," Cal starts, giving that husky laugh of his as he pulls out a pack of cigarettes from his hoodie pocket. "If you need something to do today, stop by the studio." He lights up, the orange glow from the lighter pushing away the shadows in his face, warming up the darkness inside his hoodie. Beneath all the scars and the bullshit, Callum looks tired and stretched thin.

Nothing I'd ever thought I'd see from a Havoc Boy.

"Yeah?" I quip as the front door opens and we both glance back to see Oscar stepping outside, the gray glare of the sky cutting the lenses of his glasses in half. I can't see his eyes, and I don't like that. There's no telling what he might do if he isn't watched. And if he thinks I've forgotten what he said to me last night—*You know I can't stand you; go bother somebody else*—then he's got another thing coming.

"I'm teaching a beginners' class, for adults," Cal finishes, reaching up to push blond hair away from his forehead. He gives me a tight smile and a wink before taking off down the sidewalk, hauling his black duffel bag up his shoulder.

I wait until he disappears around the corner before I turn and head up the driveway, pausing as I see Oscar inside of Hael's Camaro instead of the minivan.

"Pretty sure Vic didn't stutter when he said *the van*," I murmur, sick and tired of Oscar's crap. This morning, I am precisely out of fucks to give. I climb in as Oscar tilts the edge of his sharp mouth up into a smile, turning the key and warming the engine up to a gentle purr. When I'm sitting in here, I feel like I can figure out where Hael's coming from. I know who he is. Saucy little playboy with a heart of gold, a love for cars and kids, and ... an ex who could be dangerous to us in so many ways.

I slide my hands over my face again as Oscar reverses down the driveway, pausing at the next stop sign to select a song from his phone. *Homicide* by Logic and Eminem starts to play, and I frown hard.

Maybe I only *think* I know Hael Harbin? Shit, maybe I don't know any of them?

I haven't forgotten what I overheard at the party.

The boys castrated Donald. They carved the word *Rapist* into his forehead.

What the actual fuck are they going to do to the Thing?

I also haven't forgotten what I heard *after* the party.

"We have a video, of him with your sister."

But I need time to process that, along with everything else. Some part of me wonders if I'm suffering from some sort of emotional shock.

"I want to talk about the next name on my list," I start, and Oscar laughs. It isn't a pretty sound. No, actually, it sends chills down my spine. I flick my gaze his direction, trying to align the boy who made a paper princess dress for me in elementary school to the whip-smart gangbanger sitting beside me. There's no correlating the two.

"Of course you do, Bernadette. We can't let such an important matter slip through the cracks. Perhaps we should talk about you flashing me first?"

"Oh, you're still on that?" I quip, feeling this warm, gooey sense of smug satisfaction steal through me. "And here I thought only the idea of Vic's bare cock could get you going."

"If it's between him, and that terror you call a cunt, then I'll choose him every time," Oscar agrees, maliciously smirking at me. He's acting like he doesn't care, but it's quite clear that he's got my naked body on the brain. "Do you need me to set you up with a waxing appointment this weekend? Bushes like that haven't been in since the seventies."

"Don't start with me this morning," I warn, giving him a sideways look and wishing like hell I'd brought a hoodie with me. It is cold as *fuck* this morning. Leaning forward, I turn the heater on and sit back as warm air drifts over my chilled skin. "I put my hands around your throat once; don't make me do it again."

"You think you're tough, don't you, Bernadette?" he asks me, his voice deceptively mild. If he thinks I don't notice the way his fingers curl around the steering wheel, then he's grossly underestimated me.

"No, I don't *think* anything. I've proven it. I want to go after my social worker, Coraleigh Vincent." Oscar's eyes widen slightly at the name, like he expected me to mention the Thing or Kali. But even I understand they're a bit more complicated than some of the other names on my list. As far as Principal Vaughn … I have no idea *what* to think.

"I know all about Ms. Vincent," Oscar says, his smile growing in depravity. It's practically obscene now, almost wantonly uncivilized. "She's been promoted, you know, since you last saw her."

My jaw clenches as I think of Coraleigh Vincent and her plastered faux smile, her murmured words of comfort, her promises.

"Don't worry, Bernadette. Everything will be different here; you can start a new life."

She delivered me into the hands of a monster, my foster 'brother', Eric Kushner.

A social worker who takes money to deliver pretty girls to ugly monsters.

She handpicks 'em, girls who seem like victims, who don't have any extended family that might care what happens to them, girls who are pretty.

I've always hated being pretty.

I wish the scars I had on my soul showed on my face. Touching gentle fingers to the bandage on my cheek, I wonder if I'm not already on my way to getting that shit granted.

"Promoted, huh?" I ask, thinking about how a woman paid to rescue children from bad circumstances cares more about money than actually helping people. Hell, she went out of her way to make sure I was hurt.

"Come sit next to me, Bernie. I'm your new brother, after all."

Memories swirl like a dark storm inside my head, pushing against the emotional levees I've built over the years. My protective layer of numbness is falling apart; these next names on the list are going to hurt.

1. the stepdad
2. the best friend
3. the social worker
4. the ex-boyfriend
5. the principal
6. the foster brother
7. the mom

One down, just six more to go … which, unfortunately, is one *more* than I thought we had to deal with last night.

"She's now the director of DHS's new child welfare program."

I throw my head back with maniacal laughter at Oscar's words. The thought of Coraleigh being in charge of protecting children … that's priceless.

Life isn't fair.

But if I have to sacrifice my life to make sure the people who hurt me suffer, then so be it.

Even if it means siccing villains on villains, I'll do it.

Even if it means becoming one.

"She lives in a big, fancy house in Oak Park with her husband Marcus," Oscar continues, his voice as smooth and even as a snake's scales. I don't liken his relative calm to tameness because, like a viper, he could strike at any moment and I wouldn't see it coming. "They have a Ferrari now, and a vacation home in Newport."

I punch the dashboard and then immediately regret it, clutching my fist against my chest as my ears ring and my heartbeat thunders like a herd of horses.

Oscar smiles.

"You're not nearly as put together as you'd have the world believe," he tells me, as if he knows the dark, twisted depths of my soul better than I do. What he doesn't know is that I once heard him crying in the boys' bathroom when we were eight. One of the boys in the class had pulled his glasses off and crushed them, and Oscar couldn't see anything. The boy and his friends took his backpack, ate his lunch.

Eight years later, I saw him curb stomp that kid's head outside of Prescott High.

I lick my lower lip to wet it and shake my head.

"He who is without sin should throw the first stone, Oscar…" I warn, and he laughs again. Maybe he finds it funny, me using a religious story to chastise him. We both know we're headed straight for hell.

"Your stepfather's becoming a problem," Oscar admits as we pull into the parking lot of the grocery store. Across the street is the pharmacy where Hael took me to get a morning-after pill. "Seeing him at Aaron's house last night was a concern, to be sure."

"Isn't that why Havoc has people?" I ask dryly, glancing over and finding Oscar's trenchant expression resting on me. He pushes his glasses up with an inked middle finger, flashing the 'V' of his H.A.V.O.C. tattoo. *Jesus, what have I gotten myself into?* "To warn us about that shit? How did the Thing get into the house? And with Kali and Scott on top of it?"

"That's what Victor was dealing with last night," Oscar says as he pushes open the driver's side door open. "Several of our guys were left bleeding and broken by Mitch's crew; the rest are now bleeding and broken because Vic cannot stand failure of any kind." He slips out and closes his door behind him, leaving me to catch up.

I take my sweet time, refusing to be intimidated by Oscar Montauk.

Once I get inside, I find him sitting at the café near the front door, sipping a coffee and fucking around on his iPad.

What a drama queen, I think, setting my jaw as I pause beside the table. Oscar gestures at the empty seat across from him with an elegant hand, wrapped entirely in ink. Out of all the boys, he's the most covered in tattoos. He must've really worked his ass off to get so many at such a young age. Not for the first time, I wonder about Oscar's family—or if he even has any. Sometimes, it's a blessing to be alone.

"Take a seat."

There's a second coffee sitting there, waiting for me. I slump down into the plastic chair, listening to the incessant beeping of products being scanned at the registers. People wheel carts past as I sit there in a sea of normalcy, more aware than ever before that I will not be living a life like any of them. My biggest worry will never be about what's going to happen for dinner. Instead, I'll always wonder if calling out *Havoc* was the biggest mistake I ever made.

My fingernails tap against the surface of the table before I finally reach for the coffee. Oscar ignores me like he always does, zoned in on the screen of his tablet. He's basically glued to that thing. I figure it holds all of Havoc's secrets. One of these days, I'm going to get a hold of that thing and unearth every dark story it holds.

After a moment, I pull my phone out and turn it on, nausea taking over my belly as I wait to see the impact of last night's charades on the Prescott High gossip circle. There are photos of the Halloween party on every student's social media accounts, hundreds of them, videos, too. But ... nothing about clowns and boys with skeleton makeup on their faces.

Nothing about murder.

I do, however, have several texts from Kali Rose-Kennedy herself.

Hah.

Kali Rose.

Liar. Thief. Coward.

And the Havoc Boys and I ... we were going to kill her. I just didn't know that yet.

Where the hell is Danny, you psycho?

That text is followed by a dozen others, accusing me and the boys of kidnapping Danny, threats to call the cops. No matter how well the boys buried Danny, this problem isn't going away. No, it's only going to get worse.

I exhale sharply, a fear taking over me that I've never felt before.

For some stupid, silly reason I was certain that I had nothing to lose, that I'd fallen as hard and as far and as fast as was possible, that I was truly at rock-bottom. But I was wrong. We always have more to lose than we think we do, don't we?

"Kali's been texting me," I say, pushing my phone across the table to Oscar. He looks up briefly, his gray eyes catching mine. He doesn't want me here; he doesn't want me to be a part of Havoc. And every time something happens between me and

Victor, I get the sense that I'm making him like me less and less. Why, I have no idea. The way he looked that day he caught me with the paperwork I'd stolen from Vice Principal Keating's office, it was as if he were desperate for me to fail. Like he'd take any reason he was given to get me kicked out of Havoc. "My inclination is to tell her to fuck off, then block her."

Oscar reads the messages carefully, looking for meaning beneath the lines. And then he passes the phone back to me.

"Do what you'd normally do," he tells me, sipping his coffee, and then spinning his iPad around so I can see the screen. There's an entire thread on Mitch's Facebook page about Danny; nobody's seen him since last night. Nobody knows.

At least, not yet they don't.

"Have you guys ever ..." I pause, looking up from the screen to see Oscar's stoic face. He's beyond handsome, like some billionaire born in the wrong part of town, so cultured and elegant, so beautiful with those high cheekbones and that full lower lip. The tattoos on his neck and his hands almost add to the illusion, providing a sort of contrast to his unearthly beauty. "Well, ever done anything like that before." *Has Havoc ever murdered someone before, that's my question and he damn well knows it.*

Oscar just smirks at me, his devil-may-care attitude pissing me the hell off.

"Unlike Vic, you don't have a stranglehold on my heart, Bernadette. I'm not about to give you all my naughty, little secrets." He stands up, taking his coffee and his iPad with him. "Let's shop. Our budget is three hundred dollars; we need food for the week as well, not just today." He opens a list on his iPad, and I see that it's like, some sort of master list of basic shopping needs.

"God, you guys are weird," I murmur, taking a cart as we pass by and pushing it down the aisle. "Gang members don't generally shop for food together, you know that right?"

"Whoever said we were a gang?" Oscar asks, pausing in the middle of the aisle and giving me a look that says I've disgusted him. Seriously, I can't win with this guy. Fluorescent lights beat down on my head, the rolling of cart wheels and the whining of small children near the checkout making me feel trapped. Itchy. Desperate to escape. "We're a family, Bernadette. I'd have thought you figured that out already?"

Oscar takes the cart, heading down the aisle in black jeans and a white t-shirt, one of the most casual outfits I've ever seen him wear. I let him go, grabbing a small red basket instead and loading it up with the ingredients I need for tonight's dinner. Once I'm finished, I wait near the self-checkout, sipping my coffee and waiting for Oscar.

As far as mornings go, this one is terribly boring.

But I have a feeling this is just the calm before the storm.

You don't murder a teenage boy and just walk away from the ramifications.

Oscar rejoins me a while later, but we don't talk to each other.

Once we've paid for the food and loaded it up, I climb back into Hael's car and sit in silence while Oscar starts some orchestral piece that gives me the chills. Checking the title of the song on his phone, I see that it's *Heaven, We're Already*

Here by The Maine, only … a music-only version of the original. The sound of it gives me the chills.

"Do you have the video?" I ask as we make the turn into Aaron's quiet, little suburban neighborhood. I don't have to specify; Oscar knows what I'm talking about. The video with … Penelope. And the Thing.

They have a video; they have proof. All this time, they've held the one thing I needed in their clutches. Havoc's reaching claws have no qualms about drawing blood from the innocent.

They're using Penelope's pain to keep the police at bay.

They're using mine.

Oscar says nothing, pulling into the driveway and then handing me his iPad.

I wait until he's climbed out before I press play on the video he's pulled up.

My mind goes blank, and everything that makes me, me … it all just disappears.

The world is evil; I've always known the world is evil.

But this, it's even worse than I ever could've imagined.

My hands shake and fat tears roll down my face as I watch what I already knew to be true take place on a shiny glass screen sitting in my lap. My sister's most unbearable pain, and there it is, etched into technology forever.

I make myself watch the whole thing; if Penelope suffered then I can at least watch. I can watch. I can fucking watch.

Throwing the passenger side door open, I fall to my knees with the iPad clutched against my chest. Pushing up to my feet, I start running. I have no idea where I'm going, but I can't stay here. *Heather will be safe with Havoc.*

Despite everything else I know about them, I believe that part to be true.

So I run and I don't stop, holding the iPad like I'm holding Penelope's heart in my hand.

"Bernadette!" It's Oscar's voice, calling out to me.

But he doesn't stop me, and I don't slow down, pushing myself so hard that I trip and fall more than once, bruising my bare knees on the concrete, turning them bloody.

Numb, numb, numb.

All I want to be is numb.

Numb, like when I was locked in the closet. Numb, like when my foster brother smoothed his hands over my budding breasts. Numb. Forever numb.

How could they? All this time, they had this video. All this time.

The Thing knew—he *knew*—that this would freak me out, that it would make me question everything I thought I knew about the Havoc Boys. And he was right. I hate that more than anything, that he knew exactly how to get under my skin and destroy me.

There's video proof of Neil Pence raping my older sister.

And I hold it in my hands.

But if I turn it in, he goes to prison … and so do the boys.

At first, I don't realize where I'm going, not until I find myself outside the door to the *Southside Dreams Dance Company.*

I push my way in, my face wet with tears, my legs wet with blood, and I find my way down the hall to Studio C.

"Get the fuck out," I snarl as soon as I step inside, still

clutching the iPad, my skin soaked in fresh sweat, my heart in pieces. Callum pauses at the front of the room, turning to look at me with eyes the color of melancholy. That's what they are; they're not even blue, not really. Blue doesn't look like that, like a pool of a thousand tears, like crushed dreams and fragmented realities.

"Excuse me?" one of the girls at the front asks, and I flick my green eyes over to hers. If I were certain I could stop myself just short of murdering her, I'd storm over there and tear her pale pink leotard from her anorexic body.

"*Out,*" I repeat, and then I throw the iPad as hard as I can against one of the walls, shattering both the screen and the mirror. It comes down in silvery shards, sparkling as it falls, like my pain's an art project, on display for everyone in that room to see.

"Everyone out," Callum confirms, turning fully around, his sleeveless navy hoodie unzipped over his black tank top and leggings. "You'll all get a full refund for today, and a free class. Go." He waits as his students file out, moving past me to lock the door and draw the shades behind them.

"How could you?" I ask as he turns back to look at me, fully aware that I'm crying again. Silent tears, though. My pain is always silent. If I let it go, the monster inside of me will start screaming, and she won't stop until I'm deaf, until the world falls quiet around me and leaves room for only the worst thoughts. "All this time …" I start, a harsh laugh slipping past my lips. I should've painted them with that teal-gray color I like, the one that reminds me of zombies and graveyards. *Pretty Little Dead Girl* is the name of the shade. It seems appropriate in this moment. "How did you get it?" The words come out like a bite, a verbal punch to the gut. And then, the worst part of it: "and if you saw it, why didn't you stop it?"

Callum moves back to the front of the room, pushing play on his stereo and starting up *Sex Metal Barbie* by In This Moment; I recognize the haunting darkness of it right away. When he turns around to look at me again, he offers up a hand.

My footsteps are loud as I move across the well-worn floors of the studio, placing my hand in his and then kicking off my boots.

Cal pulls me close and then uses the force of his body to guide us into the center of the room again, spinning me and then letting me fall into his arms. Our gazes meet, and hatred ripples through me in a brilliant and violent wave.

After all the things they did to me, I *still* liked them all. I still wanted to be a part of their group, more than anything.

And now this?

I feel like a reaper's come and stolen my soul away, leaving me truly empty in a way that I never was before. No, instead, I was only trapped. Now, how am I supposed to survive this emotional blow? Because after everything, despite everything, I still had the Havoc Boys. I still had them. Even if this is a life lived in darkness, it's at least a life.

Now I have nothing.

Now I *am* nothing.

Callum guides me around in a circle, my hand in his, our bodies circling each other as the soles of his slippers whisper across the floor. When he drags me in close, slamming us together front to front, the music grinds on, desperate and low and angry.

I fucking lose it.

My fists pound against Cal's chest before he grabs my wrists, the strength in his grip surprising as he tries to hold me back. Meanwhile, Maria Brink continues to let the husky purr of her words weave through the still air in the studio, creating magic where there was none.

Today though, right now, it most definitely feels like black magic.

"Think about it, Bernadette," Cal whispers, his voice just barely audible over the music. His eyes look down into mine, asking me to understand. He doesn't beg, doesn't plead, just asks. And all with a look. Tearing my arms from Callum's, I put my face in my hands as the song ends and a new one from the same artist—*Big Bad Wolf*—starts up. "If we'd seen it while it was happening, we would've done something about it."

"Really?" I ask, dropping my hands down and turning to look at him. I'm not sure I've ever identified with a song more than I do right this second. *"Even in these chains, you can't stop me."* "Because I don't know that. You guys are more than aware of all the seedy shit that goes on in this town. You knew about Principal Vaughn, but you didn't do fuck-all until I asked you to." I storm back over to Callum, fully aware that I'm taking every bit of rage I'm feeling toward Havoc as a whole out on him. Maybe I feel safe to do that, like I'll somehow get a better reaction from him than any of the others. If so, it's a false sense of security. "You *know* about Nurse Yes-Scott, and yet you do nothing about her either. So don't lie to me and say you'd have stopped it. If it didn't interfere with Havoc's plans, then maybe."

Those full pink lips of his twist up into a smile, the darkness in that expression at odds with the rest of his appearance. Callum looks like a fairy-tale prince, ready to ride in on a white horse and save the day. In all reality, he's the villain, the one you're supposed to hate, but can't because he's too damn pretty. That's how he gets you in the end, like a poisonous butterfly, too beautiful for the crow to resist.

"What I mean to say, Bernie, is that we weren't there when it happened; we didn't film it."

I turn in a small circle, pacing in place, trying to keep my hands to myself. My go-to reaction to everything is violence. Despite my anger right now, I don't actually want to hurt Callum. To be quite honest, I'm not sure that I *could* hurt Cal, even if I wanted to.

He might be able to beat me.

Maybe.

"Even if you didn't film it," I bite out, pausing and curling my hands into fists at my sides, "you knew about it. All this time, you've held Neil Pence's smoking gun in your hands, and you *chose* not to pull the trigger." Callum watches me carefully, his blond hair bright beneath the track lighting above our heads, the muscular curves of his biceps dotted with sweat.

He's staring at me like he … feels *sorry* for me.

That look makes me want to kill him.

"What do you want me to say, Bernadette?" he asks me, cocking his head slightly to one side, as cute as a puppy gazing at his master. Only, this boy is no puppy. He's cute, sure, but underneath all of that pretty, there's a whole hoard of ugly. "I killed a man to protect you last night. Do you think I would lie to you now?"

I grit my teeth.

I'm obstinate, but even I can't deny that.

"Why?" I ask, putting my hands together in a prayer position and gesturing at him with them. "Just tell me *why*."

Callum pauses for a moment, pulling in a deep breath, and then holding out both hands for me.

It doesn't take a genius to know he wants me to dance with him again. Why, I'm not sure, because I'm a shitty dancer. Maybe because it's the only way he knows how to express himself?

Even though it fucking *kills* me, I put my hands in his and let him pull me close. The track switches to *Rise Above It* by I Prevail and Justin Stone. The song starts slow, so Callum and I do, too.

He pulls me close, plastering us front to front, his movements forcing my own. He turns me into a decent dancer by simply using his form to dictate what I do with mine.

Doesn't make me any less pissed.

My very cells vibrate with rage, and I know he can feel it. I *know* he can.

His hands, my hips, it's impossible to tell where Cal's body ends and mine begins. He walks me backward, until we're in the center of the room, using his foot to sweep one of mine out from underneath me. I dip back, and he catches me like it's nothing, lifting me up and then hauling me into his arms. We turn in a slow circle before Callum sets me down again.

His fingers trail down the side of my face as our mouths

come close enough to kiss, but then the drop in the song comes, and Cal pulls back from me, encouraging me to spin in place. He lifts me up by the hips and my legs go around him, the music fading to a slower beat. My fingers dig into his blond hair as he turns us in another circle, my gaze tilted down toward his.

I don't quite expect him to push me against the mirror, to let my body slide down the front of his until we're face-to-face. Cal leans in and captures my mouth with his, leaving me with the taste of regret and pain on my lips.

It's a kiss for the ages, a defining moment in the storybook of my life. Callum's kiss forces his spirit into me, brushing his very essence up against mine. I can see now why he didn't kiss me before. It's too personal for him, too deep.

Yet … he's giving it to me now.

I gasp as we separate, like I'm coming up for air. Like I just found myself sweetly drowning and didn't care if I died or not. Now that, that is one dangerous motherfucking kiss.

"Whatever is best for Havoc, Bernadette, that's what we do." His mouth is pressed up tight against mine, but I can barely think beyond my anger. Even if my body is flushing hot, and all I want right now is to fuck Callum against the wall of his dance studio.

"Yeah, well, screw you." I shove him back, letting my feet fall to the floor, but he doesn't let me go, grabbing my wrists and slamming them into the mirror behind my head. "I bet there isn't a single one of you who would've told me about that video." I sneer at him and then, when I try to pry out of his grip and he doesn't let me go, I spit at his feet. "I had to hear about it from the Thing. Do you know what that was like? It was like being taunted by the devil himself. He took pleasure in telling me. *You* gave him that pleasure by keeping this from me."

"Bernadette," Callum growls, surprising me as he grabs me by my hair, keeping the fingers of his right hand around my wrist. "I spilled blood for you last night, and I'd do it all again in a heartbeat. I'm not sure what it is you're looking for, an escape route, or a reason to run, but you won't find it here."

"Let me go," I grind out, but Cal ignores me, leaning in to put his lips near mine. My heart is pounding like crazy, but I'm not sure what to do. I want to leave here, but then where will I go? *Liar. You don't want to leave at all, do you?*

And that's the worst part of it all: I don't.

I want to stay with the Havoc boys; I want to *be* a Havoc Girl.

I always have, since I was eight years old. They might not've called themselves Havoc back then, but they were still my boys.

When Cal turns and presses his mouth against mine, I see stars. The fingers of my right hand dig into his shirt and my body arches, like we're dancing all over again. His arm, the one with the ballerina tattoo, wraps around my waist as he releases my other wrist. When he picks me up and slams me into the mirror again, I gasp against his lips, my legs curving around him, ankles locking.

Callum is soaked in sweat, his cheeks pink from whatever workout he must've gotten in before I got here. I wonder if I'm too much for him to hold up, with his injuries and all, but he doesn't act like I weigh anything at all. His fingers slide from my hair to cup the side of my face, thumb dipping between my lips. This time, when he leans in toward me, he kisses the side of my neck instead of my mouth.

The sensation burns like fire through my veins, traveling to my fingers, my toes, making my cunt pulse and throb as he grinds his erection against my pelvis. It's impossible to miss, behind those sweatpants of his. Callum waits for the beat of the song to pick up and then starts to move in rhythm to the music, stirring up this delicious friction between my thighs.

That's when the power cuts again and the studio goes dark.

"Fuck." It's the only word he manages to get out before the rain starts to come down, battering the old skylight. The song ends and suddenly, it's just way too fucking quiet in that studio. Part of me wonders if some of those pinging sounds I hear are Callum's dreams, shattering to glass on the tin roof above our heads. "It's always bad timing with us, isn't it?" he asks, but I'm not entirely sure what he means, other than that I was just here, with the rain coming down in sheets.

Cal releases me, and I shove him back. He stumbles a bit, but only because he's letting me push him around.

His blue eyes watch me as I head for the door, shoving it open with both palms. I've left little spatters of blood in my wake, and my bare feet smear them as I continue down the hallway, not caring that I've left my shoes behind.

Regardless of where and how they got it, the Havoc Boys had that video.

They didn't tell me about it.

Worse, they let the Thing taint Aaron's house, ruin an already shitty Halloween, mock me.

They let him get a leg up, and I'm not sure if I can ever forgive them for that.

I'm soaking wet and my feet are killing me by the time I get back to Aaron's place, but I ran out of fucks to give a long time ago.

A rough hand grabs my wrist as I pass by an overgrown yard, and my fight-or-fight-harder instinct kicks in. I throw a hard punch with my left hand, but my attacker intercepts it, keeping me from killing him long enough for me to realize through my adrenaline-soaked haze that the person I'm fighting with is Victor Channing.

"Oh, great," I snap, tearing my arm away from him and wishing it didn't feel like my skin was branded by his touch. "The absolute *last* person I want to see right now." I look up into his ebon eyes and feel my rage begin to crack and burn around the edges of my vision. Vic is the leader. He's the one who's supposed to be in charge. Ultimately, this decision fell to him and he fucked it all up.

"How could you run off like that?" he asks, his voice dark and low and dangerous, his hair wet and hanging in his beautiful face. He's frowning at me, nostrils flared as he takes me in like a runaway kid who needs to be kept in line. So much for being a Havoc Girl, right? If I were, they'd have told me. *"You're a Havoc Girl now, and we don't keep secrets from each other."* What a crock. "We're in the middle of a *war*, Bernadette. Do you understand that? You could've been killed." He pauses for a brief moment before flicking those dark eyes away from mine. "Or worse." Vic spits into the wet grass, and then pulls a pack of cigarettes from his back pocket.

I say nothing.

I'm afraid to say something, the way I feel right now. Likely, it'd be something I'd very much regret.

Victor tries and fails to light a cigarette, the rain soaking his clothes and plastering them to his muscular body. My eyes find their way down to his chest, despite my reservations, despite my hatred. Part of me is an animal, and she still very much wants her alpha male. I grit my teeth against the impulse.

"You *lied* to me," I say, the words coming out in a hiss. With everything that happened last night, I think I was in some sort of shock. Right now, the world seems crystal clear. "After all that bullshit about *the one currency you can carry is truth.*" I imitate Vic's voice, and he smirks at me, as if he has any right to look at me like that.

"Nobody lied to you, Bernadette. We have a lot of information; we're disseminating it on a need-to-know basis." He reaches out to grab me again, but I take a step back, putting some much-needed space between us. Vic lets out a long sigh, and I swear, if I couldn't hear Heather laughing through an open window, I might have attacked him. "There are no secrets in Havoc; there are no lies."

"Where did you get the video then?" I snap, taking note of Oscar as he moves halfway across the front yard, pausing with one arm over his chest, the elbow of the other resting in his palm. He cradles his chin in his hand and watches me, but I ignore him, too. If he wants his shattered iPad back, he can get it from Callum.

Vic sighs again and stares at the tip of his soggy cigarette. He holds it between two fingers and studies it carefully, like it holds all the answers he could ever need.

"Oscar," he says, like that's explanation enough. The rain stops and Vic gets out another cigarette, offering it up to me, but I'm not taking his metaphorical fucking olive branch. "For Christ's sake, Bernadette, have you not noticed he's got some skills with computer shit? He got them off of your stepfather's laptop."

"Why did you have Neil's laptop?" I whisper, burning up on the inside. My eyes are narrowed on Vic, homed in on him like weapons. He's just lucky that looks can't actually kill.

"Because we were in your house," Vic growls out, stepping close to me again. This time, when I take another step back, I can see in his face that he knows he fucked up. And it's terrifying to him. Absolutely terrifying.

We're toxic, Vic and me.

We'd be better off apart.

The thought kills me.

"We were in your house, to drag you out of bed, to send you scurrying through the woods like a little mouse." There's bite to his words, a rancid sort of anger that I can't abide by. I slap him hard across the face, but he does nothing to stop it.

"All this time, you had that video …" I start, disbelief making me feel insane. When did I start thinking of these guys as allies? They've only ever been the enemy of my enemies. That's it. What the actual fuck is wrong with me?

Callum killed Danny to protect you, Bernadette. That must count for something. It has to.

"What would seeing it have changed?" Vic retorts, smoking his cigarette. He doesn't lift a hand to his cheek, even as it turns

65

a warm pink color. "You knew what Neil was doing; you read Penelope's journal. The only thing that video did was upset you," Vic snarls, sneering as he turns his attention on Oscar.

The two of them maintain a long, terrifying sort of stare, one that says they're long overdue to vent some frustration at each other. I'd love to be a fly on the wall when that happens.

"Seeing it …" I start, images flashing in my mind that make me feel dizzy. Images that I never wanted to see, that I now can never *un*see. My attention slides back to Oscar, and I can't decide if I want to kill him *more* or less than Vic. Either way, they're both dead to me. "Seeing it doesn't matter. But you could've put him away with that video, saved me and Heather both. All these years, I've been fighting, and you could've ended it at any time."

"Every action has consequences, Bernadette. Everything. If we'd turned that video in, Neil would've buried it. His brother, that fancy ass DA, he would've buried it. Or what about his father? He's a circuit court judge. Even if—and that's a big *if*—someone took it seriously, what sort of time would he be looking at? I hate to tell you this, Bernie, but our world is fucked. It's fucked up and broken and ugly as hell." Victor steps toward me again, but this time, I don't pull away. How can I? He has me in orbit, and I despise him for that, too. "People don't care about girls who get raped."

My throat starts to close up, and white splotches flicker across my vision. I am *this* close to passing out. Screw the tacos, I guess. No way in hell I'm cooking tonight.

"People don't, but *we* do," Vic corrects, his words commanding me to look his way. But I won't. If I can at least withhold this one thing from him, then maybe I'll feel better. "And we're going to get Neil, but these things take time. If we turn the video in, eyes will turn his way. We need as many of them to look away as we can, before we act. Do you believe me when I tell you that we'll get him?"

"Hey, I called out Havoc. Make a deal, pay a price." I start to move away, and Vic comes after me. The look I throw him must change his mind about grabbing me. "Do not touch me, Victor Channing." Hurt flashes across his face, rapidly replaced with a scowl and a snarl that I just don't have the time for today. "And don't talk to me for the rest of the night."

I storm across the street, across the front lawn and past Oscar, and into the house.

Aaron is sitting on the couch when I come in. He glances back at me, his gaze snagging on mine and holding me captive.

"I'm sorry about the video, Bernadette," he says, closing his eyes briefly. When he opens them back up, he looks about as devastated as I feel. "You shouldn't have had to see that."

I just stare at him, sitting there with a bandage on his shoulder, and I think about the way he tried to defend me last night. Not just against Mitch and his crew, but against the Thing. Even when he was suffering from severe blood loss, even when he might've died.

I say nothing, turning away and finding myself face-to-face with Hael.

He seems to understand that I'm not ready to talk, stepping aside and holding out a hand to usher me past, like a proper gentleman.

I head up the steps, check in on the girls, and then lock

myself in Aaron's room for the rest of the night.

None of the Havoc Boys bother me.

Good for them.

Because I'm not ready to talk, not even fucking close.

CHAPTER
THREE

Two years earlier ...

*By the time I get home from school, I'm exhausted, mentally
and physically. Emotionally. Spiritually. The Havoc Boys own
Prescott High and right now, they own me, too. I can't take one
step, can't speak one single word, without them breathing down
my neck.*

*Today, they took my lunch away and made me run laps
around the track until I collapsed in the hot heat of the
afternoon, waking up in the nurse's office.*

*"Hello, Bernadette," Nurse Whitney said, smiling at me like
she had a secret she just couldn't wait to tell. "Are you feeling
better?" I sat up, shrugging and then reaching a hand up to
press against my throbbing head. "Once you've got yourself
together, Principal Vaughn wants to speak to you in his office."*

I shudder as I close the front door behind me, closing my

eyes against the memory. I'd thought at first that the principal might want to talk to me about Havoc. Oh, how wrong I was about that. Touching my hand to my thigh, I can still feel the slimy trail of Vaughn's fingers as he caressed my bare leg.

"Fucking pervert," I murmur, pushing up off the door. "Penelope!" I call out, noticing her backpack on the floor near the front door. I can't think about Havoc, or creepy Principal Vaughn, not here. Because this place is as much of a battleground as school—if not more so. "Pen!" I call again, popping into the kitchen for a glass of water. I'm starving, but there's no food here, and I'm not likely to get any tonight.

Sometimes, the Thing will take us all out for a surprise dinner, but it's rare, and I've noticed that Penelope always looks so empty on those nights. Besides, just sitting at a table with that monster is torture. Frankly, I'd rather starve.

When I don't hear anything from my sister, I head upstairs.

Pen's door is locked when I try the handle, but I figure she's just listening to music and head into the room I share with Heather. Sitting down on the edge of my bed, I clutch the glass of water in my hands and play a game I'm well-familiar with, one where I try to see if I can cry without making a sound, and if I can keep my tears from filling the glass.

I'll always regret that, sitting there and crying while Pen was dying.

The logical part of me knows that she was dead long before that, because she never went to school that day. I was just too busy running from Havoc to notice.

After a while, I set the water glass aside and use one of the bobby pins from my hair to pick Pen's lock. It shouldn't be so easy, like it isn't fair she doesn't have any privacy. I've seen her get in throw down brawls with our mom over having a deadbolt, but poor Pen's never had her wish granted.

The knob gives a satisfying click, and I push the door in.

Pen is sleeping on the bed, wrapped up in her blankets, like it's not the middle of the day with bright sunshine streaming in through the window. Her room smells strange, not like it usually does, like bleach and the sweet lilac scent of our laundry detergent. She cleans it constantly, scrubs every surface, washes her sheets three times a week.

I've always thought it a strange tic, for someone who keeps such a messy backpack and locker.

I wrinkle my nose, ignoring the sounds of children playing in the backyard of our neighbor's duplex. Despite the smell, I don't rush to Penelope's side. Maybe something in me knew that that day, everything would change for me.

Because I wasn't born Bernadette the bitch, the badass, the leather-wearing cynic with a fondness for sarcasm and a mean right hook. I used to cry over little things. Big things, too, obviously, but little things constantly. The world held promise before that day, like I could find a future waiting in the stars for me, no matter how distant or dim it might seem.

I sit down at Penelope's desk. She's left her phone plugged in, and when I touch it, I find that it's unlocked. Definitely unusual for her. She craves privacy, wherever she can get it. There's a note there, open and written with a discarded stylus.

"I'm so sorry, Bernadette. Out of everyone, you and Heather are the ones I owe the world to. But I can't take it anymore. When I try to run, he chases. When I tell the truth,

she calls me a liar. I can only take so many dark showers, stay awake so many nights. No matter what they say to you, always remember that I loved you both."

I lift my head up from the phone screen to stare at the blanket mound on the bed.

Slowly, carefully, I set Pen's phone aside and stand up.

This isn't what you think it is, Bernie, *I tell myself, my hands shaking as I stand there in a pink plaid skirt and a white cardigan, twisting my fingers together and doing my best to keep breathing. My head feels disconnected, and my heart thunders like a mad thing.*

"Penelope?" I ask, but there's no answer.

Closing my eyes, I try to listen for the sound of her breathing, but the fucking kids outside are too loud. Storming over to the window, I lean out and shout down at them to shut the hell up before I slam it closed. Spinning around, I close my eyes and perch my ass on the windowsill.

For several more minutes, I just sit there. Because the longer I do, the longer I can pretend that everything is okay. Like, if I don't check her, then I can't find anything wrong, and if I can't find anything wrong, then she'll be alright.

Finally, I open my eyes and look down to see her face, still and waxy and perfect. Trapped forever in a single state, draped in youthful skin and silken hair.

I choke on my own saliva as I fall to my knees in front of her.

I don't have to touch my sister to know that she's dead.

"Hey, Penny?" I whisper, calling her by a name that I haven't used since Dad died. "Where did you go?" Reaching

out, I pull the blankets back and find her clutching one of her stuffed animals, dressed in her favorite pj's. There's a bottle of Pamela's pills on the nightstand, but I hardly register that. I just remember sitting there and watching her chest, waiting for that rhythmic rise and fall, that predictable constant.

It never comes.

After a while, I climb into bed beside her, looking into her face, committing it to memory.

I don't remember crying, but when I finally get up the courage to grab Pen's phone and dial 911, I look back to see the sheets soaked where I rested my head.

"My big sister was murdered," is what I tell the operator on the end of the line.

Despite their findings to the contrary, I know better.

Penelope might've taken those pills, but she didn't want to die.

Someone drove her to it, and I know exactly who that person was.

I still do.

And I'm willing to sell my soul to the devil to watch him suffer. That's how important his pain is to me; I need to see him bleed.

Two and a half years later, I find my chance in Havoc.

The next morning, I wake up on Aaron's bed, wrapped in his scent, decimated by memories. My eyes find this spot on the door where we accidentally dented it with my head. Yep, my fucking head. Aaron and I tumbled against the door in a frenzy, hands tearing at each other's clothes, adrenaline pumping through our bodies.

Youthful rage and desire, all mixed into one. I stand up and put my fingers against the dent before opening the door, fully expecting to find Vic looming over me, staring down at me with those crow-black eyes of his. Instead, I find an empty hall, the distant giggles of the girls drifting to me from a cracked door at the other end.

Relief surges through me and I slump against the wall with my right shoulder, closing my eyes and listening to the sounds of play, sounds that I left behind a long, long time ago. It feels like it's been centuries since I was a child.

The Thing stole that from me, my innocence and my childhood.

My sister.

Gritting my teeth, I open my eyes and then push up off the wall, moving down the hallway to open Kara's door. The three girls are sitting around an iPad, watching a TikTok video about eye shadow. They look up guiltily as I pause in the door, leaning against the jamb.

I feel exhausted, emotionally and physically.

Between the Halloween party, the Thing's visit, and Aaron's near death ... I'm dead on my feet. Add in the video and I'm about half-ready to crack, steal one of Oscar's guns, and go take care of my stepdad myself.

"We were just looking," Heather says, pausing the video, like wanting to learn how to put sparkly eye shadow on is the devil's work. It's Mom's fault that she feels like this. Pamela has never kept her jealousy or distaste hidden from us, calling me and Pen whores and sluts for dressing up and wearing makeup. She's scared Heather out of having any interest in fashion or makeup or fitness. Or at least, I thought she had.

"If you guys can stay up here for a little while, and keep the door closed, I'll take you to get some makeup later. If you're *really* good," I tease, crouching down next to them and pressing play on the video, "then I'll show you how to put it on, Bernadette style."

I reach out and cup the side of Heather's head, giving her a kiss on the forehead, even as she wrinkles her nose at me and sticks out her tongue. I'm glad she thinks something as simple as a kiss from her big sister is icky; that's how I used to feel. It means she believes I'll be here forever.

I intend to be, even if it means putting my faith back in Havoc.

When I made the decision to call out that word, to bring their dark wrath down on me, I knew what I was getting into, knew I was climbing into bed with demons so they might fight my devils. Lesser of two evils, that's all they've ever been. Somehow, I let myself be tricked into believing that my childhood fantasies about the boys might actually come to fruition. I lost my mind in a pretty black wedding gown, tattooed hands, and sultry smiles.

"We'll stay upstairs," Heather agrees, eyes sparkling at the idea of some colorful new eye shadow. She won't pick pink like Pen, that's for sure. More than likely, she'll choose something I'd like. Purple. Teal. *Black.*

"Good girls," I say, giving Kara a kiss, too. Ashley is still a little shy when I'm around, clutching a stuffed narwhal and leaning away from me, so I don't bother her. Nobody should have affection forced on them, not even children. Even when it seems innocent—*go sit on your new daddy's lap, Bernadette*—it might not be.

With a groan, I shove to my feet, feeling like an old lady as my joints protest. All that running I did yesterday has shown me exactly how out of shape I really am. Add in the bruised knees from my many falls, and I'm practically limping.

I head down the stairs, fully expecting a confrontation with the guys. Instead, I find Aaron, slumped over on the couch, shirtless and bandaged and sleeping. I pad over to stand in front of him, watching his eyelids flicker as he dreams, wondering if they're more nightmares than anything else. He doesn't stir, not even when I reach out and brush some auburn hair back from his sweaty forehead.

"You still love him."

I turn my head to find Vic, leaning against the arch that leads into the kitchen, his inked-up arms crossed over his equally inked-up chest. My breath comes out in a rush as my body comes to life, my heartbeat racing, my skin flushing with heat. Nobody ever said we were lacking chemistry. It's trust, apparently, that's missing here.

And when I was *just* starting to believe their bullshit, too.

"You're a Havoc Girl now, and we don't keep secrets from each other."

"You must've gotten a good laugh out of all this," I say, stepping back from Aaron and turning to face the leader of the

Havoc Boys dead-on. Vic stares back at me, his arms a mosaic of color, his face a study in masculine architecture. Whatever dark god created him, they should be proud. He oozes sexuality and confidence, danger, violence. He's the perfect alpha male, the perfect leader.

He's also a liar.

"A good laugh?" Vic asks, cocking a dark brow. "Out of what? You seeing your sister raped on film? No. I never wanted that."

"If you didn't want that, you should've told me sooner. You should've let *me* make that choice," I growl, pointing to my chest as I grit my teeth and feel my lust quickly being replaced with anger. "After all your bullshit, all your reassurances, you and the others, you're *exactly* what I thought you would be."

"And that is?" Vic asks, uncrossing his arms and moving toward me. He keeps a healthy distance between us—smart move on his part—but it still feels too close. He's always too close to me, always digging beneath my skin and into my soul with those depthless eyes of his. Unending. Infinite. Eternal. Victor Channing will outlast an apocalypse, I'm sure of it.

"Monsters," I clarify, exhaling sharply and then moving past him to get into the kitchen. I forgot to eat yesterday and I'm starving. When I open the fridge, I find leftovers from a taco dinner: cooked ground beef in a Tupperware container, chopped green onions and shredded cheese, all of it wrapped up and carefully put away. Havoc is far more domestic than they first appear, and you know what? That makes them even scarier. There's nothing they can't do, no chasm they can't cross.

"Hael cooked for the girls last night," Vic explains, without my even having to ask. "He's surprisingly good at it." He lets out a low chuckle and shakes his head, stepping back into the archway and blocking me into the kitchen. I'd say I didn't think he meant to do that, that he's just big and muscular and the space is small, but I don't believe that for a second.

Nothing Vic ever does is by accident.

"Must be all those morning-after breakfasts he cooks for his one-night stands," I quip, despite the fact that tacos aren't exactly a breakfast food. When I suck in a deep breath, I can smell the weed curing in the bathroom around the corner, just past the laundry room. There are joints all over this house; I just need to find some, light up, and try to calm my head.

"Bernadette, I need you to listen to me," Vic says, but I ignore him, getting out the leftovers, and opening a fresh pack of flour tortillas. I turn the gas stove on and then throw a tortilla directly onto the burner. It cooks fast that way, and there's no oil involved. Win-win. Victor watches me as I pretend he doesn't exist. Pretend being the key word. I could never truly forget about Vic, no matter how hard I tried. Shit, I'm wearing the guy's family heirloom on my finger. "We never meant to keep that video from you. I'd always intended on showing you, but it got lost in the hustle and bustle of everything else. There's so much, Bernadette. So damn much. We're taking this one step at a time."

"Why does it seem like everyone else in Havoc wanted me gone?" I ask, lifting my eyes up to look at Vic. He repositions himself on the opposite side of the peninsula, putting his palms atop the counter and leaning in to look at me. "But not you. According to every other asshole in Havoc, my being here was your idea."

"Let's talk about the video," Vic says, redirecting the conversation and making me grit my teeth. "You're upset, understandably so. What you saw, no person should ever have to witness. But we didn't intentionally hide that from you, and we never lied."

"You had the video for years and did nothing with it," I repeat, feeling my eyes begin to sting, my lips quiver. I don't want to cry. I cried enough yesterday. But somehow, with my sister dead and gone, lost in the claws of a monster that makes Havoc look like good guys by comparison, it doesn't seem like I can truly cry *enough*. It'll never be enough, not when it comes to Pen. She was my older sister, my best friend, the only family I had that truly cared about me.

And now she's gone.

And I've sold my soul to see justice. My body. My heart. My dignity.

"I explained that to you yesterday," Vic says softly. "And we *did* do something with it; Neil has known all along that we have that video. We leveraged it against him so that he'd keep his fucking hands off of you. We didn't know Pen was going to die the next day. Nobody could've known that." There's something about the tenderness in his voice that really gets me, cuts right through the flesh and bone of my body and delves into my soul. I'm bleeding again, just splashing crimson everywhere, and I don't know what to do about it.

That's what sets me off, how gentle and vulnerable he sounds.

No.

I'm not letting him or any of the others pull the wool over my eyes again.

I throw the tortilla on a plate and then lift my eyes up to meet Vic's.

"You're right," I tell him, and he cocks a brow, seemingly pleased with himself. But if he thought things would be that easy, then he doesn't know Bernadette Blackbird for shit. "I do love him."

"What?" Vic barks on the end of a harsh laugh. He's forgotten about his statement from just a few minutes ago.

"Aaron," I repeat, putting another tortilla on the burner and shrugging my shoulders like it doesn't matter. But it does. It matters in innumerable ways, too many to count or quantify. It matters because that statement isn't just a way to make Vic hurt; it's an admission to myself. Seeing Aaron covered in blood, his face ashen, his lips pale, that was a wakeup call for me.

Nothing lasts forever.

And a lie you tell yourself can be just as damaging as one you tell to somebody else.

I love Aaron Fadler, and I've never stopped loving him.

That doesn't mean I forgive him or that I want to get back together, but it's something.

"I love Aaron," I repeat again, loving the way Vic's jaw clenches, the muscle in his neck ticking as his pulse picks up, fueled by jealous rage. I love it, too. And I'm not ashamed of that. I want him to hurt the way I'm hurting right now. See, told you we were both toxic.

"Why are you telling me this?" he asks me, his voice just this side of a snarl. If I weren't certain he was in love with me, too, I'd be scared right now. I mean, if I had anything left to fear, that is.

"Because I want you to get out," I tell him, flipping over the next tortilla and starting another. "I want you to leave so I can spend time with Aaron *without* you." *I'm being a petty bitch right now.* I know I am, and I don't care. Why should I? The boys have wounded me in an irreparable way, shattered my fragile trust, twisted my reality.

"Is that so?" Vic growls, coming around the counter. My breath catches as he gets too close to me, pressing his body against my back, putting his big hands on my hips. I hate how much I love it, how much I crave him. "You want me to leave so you can fuck his crippled ass on the sofa?"

He thinks he's being cute here.

I'm most definitely not.

"That was the plan," I lie. I'm not up to having sex with anyone right now. Aaron might not be the leader of this sordid club of assholes, but he knew about the video, too. They all did. "So take your hard-on away from my back and fuck all the way off with it."

Vic's hands tighten on my hips, and I have to close my eyes to keep from reacting to that. If he gets even the slightest inkling of how much I want him, he'll push me, and I won't be able to say no.

A low, sinful laugh escapes Vic's lips, ruffling the hair on the back of my neck.

"You test my patience, Bernadette."

"The feeling's mutual," I quip back, putting the last tortilla on the plate. I'm trapped here, penned in by his arms, desperate

81

to escape but also … desperate to stay. I close my eyes on the realization. *You're in love with Victor, Bernadette. You have been for years. No matter how nasty he is, how cruel, how inhuman … it doesn't matter.*

Love knows no boundaries.

"You could've had a much different life than this," Vic whispers, bending low and putting his head up against the side of my face. He rubs against me, teasing my smooth cheek with his stubbled one. It should be sweet, the way he's nuzzling me, but instead, all I can think of is a lion, maned and wild, rubbing up against his female.

It's a possessive move, a dominant one.

He wants to own me. Little does he know that a lioness can *never* be bought or sold.

I glance over, putting our faces precariously close together.

"They all wanted that for you," Victor says quietly, dark eyes simmering. "An escape. A different life. A chance to be something better than a gangbanger."

"They all …" I repeat slowly, thinking of the other Havoc Boys.

"Except for me. Some men sleep and dream. Some men have nightmares. You're a nightmare, Bernadette, a beautiful nightmare." Vic grabs my arm and leans in even closer, sending my pulse racing. "We're both nightmares; we belong together."

He kisses me, but it isn't a nice kiss. It's a move meant to seal this deal, mark me, stamp me with his name. I tear away from him and he pauses briefly to turn off the burner, glancing over at me as my heart races and I struggle to find my breath.

"That's what happened, Bernadette. We met up to discuss

your price. They fought against me. They demanded we give you some bullshit, made-up price, some nonsense." He laughs again, and the sound is that of a villain, staking his claim on the princess' heart. Just like Callum. None of these boys are princes, not even Aaron. "We could've … no, no …" He rubs at his chin for a moment, the *HAVOC* tattoo on his knuckles making me shiver. No part of me believes I'm exempt from having that mark needled into my skin. "We *would've* done all the things you asked of us, and then set you free."

"What the fuck, Vic?" I ask, backing up until my body is pressed against the fridge. I'm not afraid of him, far from it. I'm fighting the desire to throw myself at him, to tear his shirt off, to open his pants and free his cock. He can't know that I feel that way, not a chance in hell.

"But not me," he repeats again, stopping to look me dead in the face. There's no sign of humor anywhere in his expression; this is not a joke. "I wanted you here. My love is selfish, Bernadette."

"Love?" I ask, but Victor just smiles at me. You can only deny reality for so long without it coming back to bite you in the ass.

"*I* am selfish," he says, exhaling and then moving forward. He pauses just two feet in front of me. "I could've let you go, but I wanted you here instead, wrapped up in Havoc. Wrapped up in *me*." He turns and takes off toward the front door. I try to tell my feet to stay where they are, but I end up scrambling around the corner as he grabs the door handle and then pauses to glance over his shoulder. "So go ahead. Fuck Aaron if you want. I'm sure he'd be better for you than I am." Victor opens the door and then pauses again, like he's just thought of something. "Better, maybe, but not like me. Nobody will love you the way I do, Bernadette Blackbird."

Victor leaves out the front door, slamming it behind him.

I wait about three heartbeats before I turn and throw a punch at the wall. It cracks the drywall and leaves my knuckles a bleeding mess, but I don't care. It's better than what I really want to do right now: murder Victor fucking Channing.

"Did you mean what you said?" Aaron asks softly, surprising the hell out of me. Cradling my bloody hand to my chest, I turn around to look at him. He's sitting up now, his right shoulder still swaddled in a white bandage, his green-gold eyes hooded and dark with emotion. "That you love me?"

"Love isn't everything, Aaron," I quip back, feeling wounded. *They all wanted that for you.* How dare he. How fucking dare he?! Victor pulled me into this mess because he wanted me? How messed-up is that?

I can't decide if I want to kill him or fuck him right now. Best we just stay away from each other.

"It isn't nothing either," he replies, exhaling sharply. His eyes drift to my hand, still cradled to my chest, still bleeding. "Are you okay?"

"I just punched a hole in your wall," I respond dryly, sick at the idea of going back to school on Monday. Of seeing Kyler and Timmy, of knowing their brother is dead because of us. Because of Havoc. "What do you think?"

"I think," Aaron starts, groaning as he moves to stand up. He barely makes it to his feet before he stumbles, going down to one knee beside the coffee table. If I still had a heart to break, the sight would shatter it. "We really need to talk."

"No shit," I murmur, moving over to him and helping him back onto the couch. He slumps into the cushion with a groan, letting his head fall back into the pillows. His eyes are closed, but his teeth are clenched. It's pretty obvious he doesn't like feeling so helpless, but he just needs to give his body time. He'll be back to being an asshole before the week is out. "You need to sit down. I'll … bring you tacos." I start to turn away, but he curls his fingers around mine and squeezes them tight.

He may as well have wrapped that inked grip around my heart.

"Bernie," he pleads, and the depth of emotion in his voice makes my heart stutter. I close my eyes against a surge of my own feelings; I'm just not ready to face them all yet. "Please, sit down."

"The tortillas will get cold," I argue, even though my hunger pangs have disappeared completely. How can I eat after what Victor just told me? He made me sign my life away in blood, but … he also just told me the other boys didn't want that for me. I'm so confused. What does Oscar care about me? Likely, he just wanted me gone, but Aaron … I look back at him, and our gazes lock. "I can't go to my grandmother's house, not now, not ever," I tell him for the second time, just to make sure he's really getting it. I got no response last time, none at all. "You understand that, don't you?"

"I do," Aaron chokes out, closing his eyes. He lets go of me, but I don't leave. I can't imagine being anywhere but here right now. This is where I'm meant to stand. "I know that, but I worry about you."

"Really?" I ask, cocking a brow in a way that makes me think of Vic. I scowl, but Aaron's eyes are still closed, so at least he can't see me. "Could've fooled me. How do you show that worry, Aaron? By watching as your friends drag me off, by letting them lock me in a closet?"

"Bernadette," he starts, dropping his chin to his chest. He drags both tattooed hands over his face. "There was no winning for me, you know that, right?" He drops his hands to his lap and looks back up at me, anger darkening his face. "I had two choices: lose my sisters and be a piece of shit not worthy of you … or I had to give you up so you could have a better life."

A sick sad feeling shoots through me, taking over my body, infecting my bloodstream. I don't want to feel this way right now, drowning in empathy. I'm pissed. I have a *right* to be pissed.

"That's what I thought I was doing," Aaron continues, leaning back and putting his left arm on the edge of the couch. The way he tilts his head and frowns at me, he's got the cocky asshole thing down pat. From here, it looks an awful lot like a defense mechanism. "I thought I was setting you free, Bernie. You don't need to be stuck in Springfield with a bunch of kids and a whole lot of baggage."

"It's a little late for that now, isn't it?" I snap back, turning fully around to face him. "So maybe you stop with the bullshit and man up. I'm not going anywhere now; my fate is sealed in blood."

"It doesn't have to be," Aaron says, breathing hard, like maybe this is too much exertion for him. My eyes slide down his chest and stomach, admiring the deep grooves of his muscles. He's bulked up a lot. When we were in freshman year, he was just a skinny little thing. Skinny little thing with a big cock, but still. I frown. "We can talk to Vic; we can talk to Oscar. After graduation, you can walk away from all of this."

I just stare at him.

"You castrated a boy because I asked you to. Callum killed a boy because he had to. All of that blood, it's on my hands, Aaron. There's nowhere else for me, so stop looking for a distant locale to drop me in, some fairy-tale of a life you wished I lived. Vic is right: I'm a nightmare. I exist in the night; my only light is the moon and the stars."

"Stop that shit," he snaps at me, acting like he's going to get up again. I move forward and push him back with a hand on his chest, shoving him back into the cushions. And then, for some reason entirely unknown to me, I straddle him, pinning his body to the couch with my own.

He looks at me like I've just gut punched him.

"You don't have to take what Vic says at face value," Aaron pleads. Unlike Vic and Oscar, he's not above it. Underneath the pleading though, his hatred for Vic is just barely concealed. "You're not like this, Bernadette. You're not one of us."

"Stop acting like I'm the girl you gave up years ago," I growl back, curling my hands over his shoulders. I dig my nails into his skin, refusing to stop, even when he cringes. Underneath the heel of my left hand, there's a healing wound, but I don't care. My own shoulder twinges in pain. The bandage hidden beneath my borrowed tee is likely wet with blood, but I don't feel like leaving to change it right about now. "You're not the same boy either, and I will *never, ever* be the sweet little thing you abandoned when I needed you most."

"Don't talk like that," Aaron snarls back at me, hissing in pain when I grind the heel of my hand against his shoulder. "I believe in you, Bernadette, even if you don't believe in yourself."

I throw my head back with a laugh, wondering if I really am a perfect slice of sin, Vic's wicked other half. We could do horrible things together. Fuck, we could topple cities. We could rule the world. Or the underworld, at the very least. Despite his tough, new exterior, Aaron is still trying to be the good guy. It's a tired shtick.

I drop my head back down, so I can look at him. And then I roll my hips.

Aaron groans as the baggy t-shirt rides up and my panties slide against the bulge in his sweats. He's hard for me, despite our arguments, despite his pain. I push against the bullet wound in his shoulder even harder, staining the bandage red with blood, and he sucks in a sharp breath between his teeth.

"Aaron," I begin, rocking against him again, knowing that Vic won't have gone far. Likely, he's right outside the front door. Shit, maybe he's watching me again? One can only hope. He deserves to see this, deserves to see me and Aaron wrapped up in each other. "If you don't start treating me like a member of Havoc, instead of your childhood sweetheart, we're going to have problems."

"How do you want me to treat you then?" he barks back at me, gritting his teeth. I'm pissing him off. Good. That's how I want him. I don't want him gazing at me like I'm the love of his life, like he needs to set me free, send me off to Nantucket to lounge on the beach and sip cherry cola as I make eyes at the town cutie. That's not my life. That's not what I'm destined to do.

Fate has never been kind to me, so I decline to be kind to fate. I'm going to twist my entire destiny and put it on a course that I've chartered—even if that course sends me straight into the pits of Hades.

"Treat me like the newest member of your little gang. Treat me like an initiate, but keep in mind that one day I'll be queen." Aaron's eyes narrow, his mouth tightening into a thin line. He doesn't like the implications—that by marrying Vic, I'll be his queen—but he doesn't challenge them. Not yet. That's what I want. I hadn't realized it until now, but that's what I *need*. I want Aaron to stand up for me, to fight for us, for what we could have been.

Whether he likes it or not, I'm a part of Havoc. Blood in, blood out, right? And I don't know how long this particular arrangement—that is, me being the only woman in the group—is going to last, but for now, I'm going to take advantage of it.

These boys are mine, even if they've managed to royally piss me off. I'm going to use them the same way they're using me.

"You want me to treat you like shit, huh?" Aaron quips back, scowling at me. I'd say it doesn't fit his face, but I have to face reality the same way he does: Aaron is not the boy I grew up with. I am not that girl. We have to accept who we are together, or else we're never going to get along. That, and I have to know all his secrets, all of Havoc's secrets. I need to know if they've castrated someone and carved *Rapist* into their forehead. I need to know if they have a video of my sister and the Thing. I need to know what Kali truly paid them and why they did what they did to me. "Because I can do that."

"How many girls have you been with since me?" I ask, rocking my hips again, feeling his muscles tighten underneath me. Carefully, I peel the bandage from his shoulder, staring at Nurse Yes-Scott's tiny, little stitches, watching the blood ooze out from between them. He's going to have a nasty scar there, no doubt about that. Aaron doesn't say anything for several minutes, so I push my panties against his crotch again. They're soaked straight through. I wonder if he can feel that when he reaches down and grabs my ass in two tattooed hands.

"Are you hoping for a specific answer?" he asks, looking me in the face, his eyes the color of the fall leaves outside, this glorious mix of green and gold and brown. Nuanced, just like he is. "Because you're not going to like it."

I go still, pausing the movement of my hips, waiting for an answer to a simple question.

"Will I be jealous?" I ask carefully, feeling that hungry monster inside of me, green with envy and eating up self-confidence that I know I have. I've got plenty to burn, so it doesn't shake me too much, but I need to hear this answer. I need him to tell me he slept with a hundred girls, but that all of them had my face, that he used them because he couldn't have me. That's what I want to hear. Instead, he surprises the shit out of me.

"I haven't slept with anyone since," he tells me, and he sounds almost … shamed by it. "I gave up the only girl I ever loved; I hurt her. I don't deserve to be happy, and I most definitely don't need to fuck somebody I don't like. That I'll never love."

I stay stone-still, unsure about what to think. He said I wasn't going to like his answer: he was right. He isn't supposed to be able to surprise me, to convince me that he's got a spark of the old Aaron deep inside somewhere. That isn't fair, not when I've just finally embraced the dark side.

"You're lying," I snap back at him, moving to stand up, to storm out, to get the fuck out of this house and away from these boys. I don't know what to think when I'm around them, how to act. But Aaron doesn't let me go; his hands tighten on my ass, bruising me, holding me in place. In retaliation, I stick my thumb into his wound, and he grits his teeth so hard I'm afraid he's going to break one off.

"Why the *fuck* would I lie about that?" he snarls back at me, using his hands to guide my hips, so that our pelvises grind together. It's been years since I last slept with Aaron, since right before we broke up. *Well, except for that one time ...* I don't let myself go back to that memory, focusing instead on the ardent intensity of the moment.

"Because you thought I'd enjoy such shallow sentimentality?" I quip back, cocking a brow and then reaching down to curl my fingers beneath the bottom of the t-shirt. With an indolent sensuality, I strip it off and toss it aside, leaving my breasts bare and right at the level of Aaron's face. He exhales, and his warm breath feathers across my nipples, hardening them to fine, pink points.

"It isn't sentimentality, Bern. It's just how I fucking feel." Aaron gathers me close, wrapping tattooed arms around me.

They feel like home, those arms, but like I've walked into an entirely new renovation. I'm liking it, I'm just not used to it, not yet.

My head falls back as I groan, tangling my fingers in Aaron's auburn hair as he swirls his hot tongue around my nipple. His arms hold me tight, almost possessively. No, not almost. Definitely possessive.

Well, if Aaron wants to take me away from Vic, he's going to have to stand up for himself. He's going to have to *fight*.

I'm not expecting him to bite my nipple, and I cry out, clamping my hands over my mouth and closing my eyes as I remember the girls are upstairs. I told them to stay put, but … Shit. The fact that we could get caught should make me stop. But I can't. Guess I'm just that weak.

My hips seem to be moving of their own accord, stroking Aaron's bulge against the torrid heat between my thighs. It's not enough though, not even close. Just a fucking tease.

Aaron lifts his head up, running his tongue across his lower lip. The sight of that just undoes me. I drop my head to his, thrusting my tongue between his lips as his arms tighten around me. Our hips start to move faster, his pelvis coming up off the couch to grind against me. Our mouths feast on each other, like two hungry beasts in desperate need of a mate. I can taste Aaron on my lips, like sweet cherries and heartache, that's what he tastes like, what he's always tasted like.

Someone like Vic is easy, because you always know what to expect, where you stand.

Someone like Aaron is dangerous. He's unpredictable, his morals mean too much to him, and he has the potential to crawl inside your soul and ruin you, wreck you from the inside. I let him in once; I let him have all of me.

And he threw it away.

For Havoc.

For motherfucking *Havoc.*

"Havoc," I murmur, and Aaron groans against my mouth as we kiss. "I'm calling Havoc."

He grabs a handful of my panties and then simply tears them off, rending the fabric and chucking them to the floor. His right hand finds its way between my legs, stroking my wet folds and making my hips buck with pleasure. When he slides two fingers into me, I work my pelvis even harder, grinding into him and fucking his hand like it's his dick.

The movement of my body is working Aaron down there anyway, my ass rubbing up against him as he flicks his thumb across the swollen nub of my clit. His mouth envelops my right nipple again, scalding me, chasing the pert pink point with his tongue. My breath is coming in shallow pants as I hold his head against my chest, his tongue greedily lapping at my flesh.

"So good," I murmur without even meaning to, my mind flickering back to a moment I'm not particularly proud of. It's a moment I try to pretend doesn't exist, that I've attempted to wipe from the narrative of my life. But it's there, and I can't forget it. Neither of us can, I bet.

"Shit, Bern," Aaron growls back, curving his inked fingers against the back of my neck and giving me goose bumps. He pulls my face back toward him, kissing me again and then pressing our foreheads together. Our breath mingles as my eyes close and I'm reminded of that time in tenth grade when, in the midst of all Havoc's bullying, Aaron and I fucked each other.

It was hot and desperate and sweaty, much like it is now.

It was also a mistake. I'm not sure yet if this is or not.

My hips move faster, increasing the frequency of our shared breaths, our mouths nipping at one another as we push closer and closer to the edge. I'm not expecting to have an orgasm, but it hits me anyway as I open my eyes and find his, watching me, always watching me.

The front door flies open and slams into the wall, but that doesn't stop me. When I look up and see Vic scowling at me, I shove my hand into Aaron's sweats and slick my thumb across the salty wet pre-cum at the head of his cock. He's close, fingers digging into my upper arms as I give him a few hard, punishing pumps of my fist. Like a good boy, Aaron comes right in my hand, filling my palm with his seed.

Oscar and Callum appear behind Vic, stepping in from outside.

The former doesn't appear to have any reaction whatsoever, but the latter … Cal smiles at me in a way that sends heat shooting through my belly, like he's remembering what happened between us yesterday. As for my part in the matter, I just sit back and look them over as Aaron pants beneath me. He doesn't even flinch when I wipe my hand on his sweats.

"Mitch is out for blood," Vic snarls, looking at me like he's torn between kicking Aaron's ass or fucking mine. "We have a problem." His head snaps up and his eyes narrow, causing me to turn and look. I don't expect to find Hael, leaning in the doorway to the kitchen, watching me with an inscrutable gaze. He grins, like he always does, but there's something missing, some key ingredient to his usual cocksureness. "The hell are you doing anyway?"

"Maybe you're not the only one who likes to watch?" Hael quips back, and I swear to god, you could hear a pin drop in that room.

"For the love of the devil's cock," Oscar murmurs, which is actually a pretty fucking unique expletive. "I knew this would happen." He moves over to my discarded shirt and picks it up off the floor, thrusting it out to me with a curled lip, like even the thought of touching something that was on my body disgusts him. Pig. I take the shirt, but I just use it to clean the rest of the cum from my fingers, staring Oscar's gray eyes down like I've got nothing to lose.

No, wait, not *like* I've got nothing to lose. I'm already there.

"You see a pair of tits and forget what's going on here?" Oscar snaps again, drawing Vic's sharp gaze. "The Charter Crew is at your house, Hael."

"Fucking what?!" Hael snaps, breaking out of his strange reverie. He tears his eyes from me and then rakes his tatted fingers through his hair. "You got the boys on it?"

"They're on it, but we need to go," Vic says, that booming voice of his cutting through the bullshit in the room. That's not a request; it's an order. I chuck the cum-covered t-shirt at Oscar's face, but unfortunately, he's a dexterous motherfucker and manages to catch it. Once he does, he drops it like it's hot and then scowls at me.

At least that's something, right? An actual expression of emotion.

"Bernadette, stay here with Aaron and Callum." Vic moves

to turn away, but I'm already standing up and facing him down, naked in a sea of tattooed demons. There are five very dangerous, very pretty men in this room with me. But the way they all look at me? I've never felt more powerful.

"You messed up by failing to show me that video; I'm coming." Vic works his jaw for a moment, but then just shakes his head at me.

"You're going to be the goddamn death of me, Bernadette. Get dressed. You have two minutes, and if your ass isn't sitting bitch-seat, you're not going."

I flip his back off as he storms outside, leaving me to stalk past Hael and up the stairs to grab my clothes. After I get dressed, I head out the front door and down the driveway, passing by Oscar as I go. He watches me, turning those gray eyes of his down to mine when I pause beside him. On impulse, I lean in toward him and lift up on my tiptoes, careful not to touch him.

It's clear he doesn't like to be touched.

"Don't pretend you didn't get off on seeing me with Aaron," I whisper with my lips hovering near his ear. He scowls at me, but I've very clearly found a weakness in him that can be exploited: he doesn't notice me slip his revolver out of Hael's open trunk. It's in a black leather gun case that I very quietly slip beneath my own leather jacket.

"Get away from me, Miss Blackbird," Oscar purrs, in the most vitriolic way possible. But fuck him, mission accomplished. He clearly has no idea how much I mess him up. He must really freaking hate me.

Doesn't matter, I got what I wanted, smiling as I move

around him toward Vic's bike.

I feel almost maniacally excited at the prospect of violence. After all, if I'm shedding blood, I don't have to give a second thought to what happened with Aaron. Or why Hael Harbin, of all people, was watching.

CHAPTER

FOUR

The Charter Crew—Mitch's insane motherfucking clown posse
—are waiting outside this small white cottage in a shady part of
town. Well, I think the cottage used to be white. The exterior
walls are in desperate need of replacing; the bottom row of
siding is covered in moss and clearly succumbing to the
elements. Oddly enough, there are flowers planted in neat rows
on either side of the walkway, some fall-blooming yellow thing
that I'm pretty sure is an Oregon Grape.

Vic pulls right up into the middle of all that shit on his
Harley, knocking the kickstand into place with his foot and then
lighting up a cigarette, all before ever turning off the engine.
Hael is right behind us, driving his Camaro right up and over the
curb to park in the lawn. There are tire tracks there in the grass,
making it fairly obvious that this is where he always parks.

He steps out of the driver's side, looking like a devil with that red hair of his, his beautiful mouth turned down in a frown. Oscar isn't far behind him, hands crossed pleasantly over the end of one of the baseball bats from Halloween night, still studded with nails but blessedly free of bloodstains. Chills chase up my spine as I think of Danny, lying dead on the bloodied floor. Where did they take him? Where did they bury him? And how did they get back so quickly? Supposedly, there are no secrets in Havoc, but is that really something I *want* to know?

"Where the fuck is my brother?!" Kyler snarls, getting right up in Vic's face.

For his part, Victor doesn't react, continuing to smoke his cigarette as my eyes pan past Kyler to find Billie and Kali. The former has red-rimmed eyes like she's been up all night, but the latter … she just smirks at me when she sees me, sending my pulse racing. How *dare* she flaunt herself in front of me like that. How goddamn dare she. I wonder, not for the first time, if the baby she's carrying is my stepdad's.

Kali keeps smiling at me, but it isn't a nice smile. As they say, every rose has its thorns. But I'll be damned if I let Kali Rose make me bleed. One day, the world is going to realize that she's a lowlife, scummy, thieving bitch.

"What are you doing here?" Vic asks calmly, smoking his cigarette like he has all the time in the world. The wind catches the gray ash from the end, sending it spiraling down the quiet street. It smells like bum piss and neglect over here in the Four Corners neighborhood. On my right, there's a row of shitty, rundown houses from the 1940s. On the other side, the railroad tracks. Other than South Prescott, this is considered one of the worst neighborhoods in Lane County.

That, and it's Hael's home.

The look on his face as he leans back against the Camaro, muscled arms crossed over a red wifebeater, is pure murder. It's one thing to start a gang war in Prescott, it's a whole other thing to bring that shit to his fucking house.

"We're making a stand," Mitch says calmly, reaching out to put a hand on Kyler's shoulder. He pulls his friend away, leaving Kyler to pace and run his fingers through his dirty blond hair. "Tell us what you did with Danny."

Vic laughs, the sound like rusty nails and forgotten dreams. Mitch grits his teeth, brown eyes narrowing on Havoc's leader. Mitch gestures with his chin, and then glances up in the direction of the chain-link fence that cuts across Hael's driveway. Just a few seconds later, several thugs in clown masks appear, dragging a redheaded woman between them.

She's wearing an apron, her face covered in bruises. One pink heel is still clinging to her foot, the other is missing.

"What the actual fuck?!" Hael roars, and then everything just happens in a blur.

Dozens of boys appear from the bushes, wearing skeleton masks—just like they did on Halloween night. Guns are drawn, and in less than a minute, Vic, Mitch, and I are in the middle of a stand-off.

"Let her go," Hael growls out, losing every ounce of his usual cool. There's a deep-seated fear behind his eyes, a long-held terror finally realized. Mitch's cronies toss the comatose woman down on the gravel driveway and leave her in a heap.

It doesn't take a genius to put the pieces together: that's gotta be Hael's mom.

"Ballsy," Victor says, still smoking, acting like he doesn't give a fuck about any of this. I can read the bullshit in his tense shoulders, but the show he's putting on must be good enough for Mitch because fear flickers in his gaze for the briefest of seconds before he banishes it.

Vic swings a leg over the motorcycle and stands up, leaving me straddling the back. Without being asked, I get off, too, and head straight toward Hael's mother.

"Tell your bitch to back off," Mitch snarls as one of the clown-masked assholes turns his weapon on me. I ignore him, kneeling down next to the woman and swiping some of her red hair back from her face.

"If you call my girl a bitch one more time, I *will* kill you, and I won't care who sees me do it." Victor's gaze follows me for a moment before he turns back to Mitch. "You think you can waltz into my brother's home and assault his mother and there won't be consequences? I sure hope you know what you're up to, Mitch."

Mitch laughs, but the sound is strained. He's playing the nonchalant act, too, but he's not nearly as good at it as Vic is. In fact, that's Mitch in a nutshell, isn't it? A less good Vic. A watered-down Vic. A charlatan. A fucking copycat. Call him an inspiration, if you will, but Havoc was here first. *We* were here first.

Do it first or do it best, but when somebody does it first *and* best, well, you're fucked.

Good choice for the Charter Crew, to choose those clown masks, because that's all they are. Imitations. Shadows.

Havoc, they're OG.

And I'm one of them.

"You think we knocked this bitch out?" Mitch asks incredulously, pointing over at Hael's mother. "We *found* her like this." A smirk lights his lips as I glance back to watch the interaction between him and Vic, sitting down to pull Hael's mother into my lap. "Looks like her ol' man was knocking her around a bit."

"Fuck," Hael growls, the pain in his voice like broken glass. It cuts me to hear it, deeper than I ever could've expected. Even after seeing the video, even after knowing they kept it from me. *Shit, Bernadette, you're getting soft.* Only … I don't feel soft. Instead, I feel the opposite, like something inside of me is solidifying, turning my heart to stone.

I turn my eyes back to Mitch and frown.

The Charter Crew, what a joke.

In this world of sinners and saints, there is only one authority.

Havoc.

"What goes on with our families is none of your business," Vic says as Mitch circles him. Victor doesn't even bother to follow him with his eyes, so unconcerned by his rival that he'll show his back to him. Pretty gutsy, if you ask me.

The woman in my lap stirs, murmuring in French as she struggles to sit up. I try to soothe her, smoothing back her hair with my fingers, but she shoves me away, pushing herself into a sitting position, red hair disheveled, pretty face mottled with bruises. She looks around the mess we've made of her neighborhood before her eyes settle on Hael.

"*Qu'est ce qu'il se passe?*" she whispers, brown eyes widening. One of her hands comes up to tangle around a cross hanging at her throat. "*Ils ont fini par venir pour moi c'est ça?*" I have no idea what she's saying. There aren't exactly a lot of foreign language classes at Prescott High. We have an English as a Second Language class for Spanish-speakers, but that's about as close as we get to culture in South Prescott.

"*Calme toi Maman. Ça va bien se passer,*" Hael pleads, taking a step closer to her, and even though the situation *sucks,* and I'm royally pissed at the Havoc Boys, I have to admit that it's hot when he speaks French like that. When one of Mitch's guys pulls back the hammer on his revolver, Hael stops in his tracks, scowling and cursing under his breath. "*Nique ta mère, Mitch,*" he murmurs, but nobody but Hael knows what that means so the insult is lost in translation. "Let her go back in the house, and we'll deal with this like real men."

"Real men?" Mitch asks as Kali watches me with dark eyes from across the street. I can only pray her ass gets hit by an oncoming train. If only the universe were so kind. "Real men don't play games in the dark. *Where. Is. Danny?* Either you take us to him now or else this shit gets real."

"Wrong," Vic snaps, flicking his cigarette aside and pointing at Mitch with a tattooed finger. He looks like a dark god right now, commanding an army of undead delinquents. It shouldn't make him more attractive to me, but it does. I both crave his commands and despise them, all at the same time. "Real men, as you've so eloquently put it, are as at home in the dark as they are in the daylight. If we want to play games with poor little Danny, who's to stop us? Besides, there's nothing for us to take you to. We fucked around with him and he ran off into the woods. Not our fault if he fell into a cougar's jaws."

"Goddamn it, Victor," Mitch snarls, but before he can get another word out, Hael's mother starts screaming.

"They're coming for me!" she screams in a strange accent, digging her fingers into her hair, eyes darting wildly around the neighborhood. "They're already here; I can smell them. I can smell them. *Je les sens.*"

"*Arrête ça, Maman,*" Hael pleads, his teeth gritted, shame coloring his face. This isn't something he ever wanted anyone else to see, let alone Mitch and his crew. Things start making sense: the way Hael acts when his mother is mentioned, the way he avoids her calls, the pair of them homeless and sleeping in the shelter with me and Pen and Pamela.

Clearly, Hael's mom has some serious mental health issues.

She tries to tear away from me, and several guns swing our direction. I stand up after her, trying to keep her still and quiet, but she's fighting me, clawing at my skin with long nails, weeping and shaking and murmuring in French.

"Get that crazy cunt to calm her tits down or—" Mitch starts, but I'm just done listening to men squabble. This woman needs help. Now.

"Or you'll show us all what a real man can do?" I interrupt, reaching beneath my leather jacket and removing the revolver I pinched from Oscar. As soon as he sees me going for it, his gray eyes widen behind his glasses. He didn't expect this shit, now did he?

Glad to know I can pull one off on these boys.

I level the weapon on what's left of Mitch's El Camino. It's *fucked* from when Hael ran the SUV into it, and I feel my lips split into a grin as I fire a round into the rear windshield, shattering what's left of it.

"What the fuck?!" Mitch howls, but there are too many witnesses here for anyone to actually put a bullet in another person. This is all for show, all an act. Well, I'm tired of playing my part. I want a new role. I fire off another round into one of the rear tires as chaos erupts around me.

This dark, horrible part of me cackles as fists fly and the boys spill blood, and I'm tempted to point this gun at Kali and cross her name off my own list. But I don't. I know better. Besides, Hael's mother is in full hysterics now, sobbing and clinging to me like I'm her only way out.

"They're after me," she whispers in that unusual accent of hers. "And they'll get you, too, *cher*," she sobs as I tuck the gun back beneath my jacket, catching her before she falls to her knees. While the world around me falls to violence and turmoil, I take Hael's mother by the hands and lead her up the front steps and into the house, closing the door behind us.

Nobody notices us leaving, so I take advantage of the moment and get her situated on the couch as she cries. The house smells like bleach, but underneath it, there's the acrid stink of piss and cigarettes. This woman, in her pink apron, she clearly cleans it, but there's somebody else here who messes it up, and I'd bet the very few pennies I have to my name that it isn't Hael.

"*Cher*, listen," she says, taking my hands in hers as my eyes flick to the front door, wondering when or if someone might come storming in here with a gun in their hands. Or if the cops will show up. Unfortunately, the Four Corners neighborhood is technically unincorporated Springfield, meaning the city police won't show up here for shit; this is county territory, so we'd have to wait for the sheriff. Likely, none of the neighbors will bother. The people who live here are well-aware of the costs of getting involved in a gang war. "They're coming for me."

"Who?" I ask, even though I know I probably shouldn't engage this woman without Hael around. She squeezes my hands, digging her nails into my skin. The move triggers something inside of me and I tear away, stumbling back several steps as old memories come flooding into my brain, a broken dam that rages and destroys as it overflows its banks.

"Bernadette," Mom snaps, turning around to look at me, digging her red nails into my arm hard enough to draw blood. Her face is a mask of rage; I can't bear to look at it. Instead, I focus on the crescent marks in my skin, unsure of where my blood ends and her red nails begin. "This man is going to be your new daddy. You will show him respect, or I'll beat it into you."

The front door flies open, the knob smashing into the wall, and Hael storms in, sweaty and shaking as he kneels down in front of his mother.

"*Maman,* listen to me," he says as she fights against him, trying to tear her hands from his.

"They're coming, *mon fils,*" she murmurs, eyes flicking to the doorway as Vic walks in, scowling and speckled with blood. He gives me a look that says he isn't happy with my escalation of the situation, but fuck him. I'm not happy about the video; we all have to learn to live with disappointment. "They're out to get me."

"What on earth is she muttering about now?" Oscar asks, flicking an imaginary piece of dust from the arm of his dark suit as he joins us, closing the door behind him.

"Show some goddamn compassion, would ya?" Hael snaps back at him, moving to sit on the sofa beside his mother and smoothing back her hair. He murmurs quietly to her in French until she stops fidgeting, her honey-brown eyes remarkably similar to her son's. She darts her gaze between us, finally landing her attention on me.

"Who is this?" she asks in a heavily accented voice, gesturing at me. "I'll make cookies. You want some? Of course you do," she mutters this last part, like she really doesn't care what Hael's going to say; she's making those goddamn cookies.

"We don't need any cookies, *Maman*," Hael groans, closing his eyes in a way that reveals how tired he truly is. And I don't mean physically, I mean in his fucking soul. It's a weightiness, a heaviness, that sort of melancholic fatigue. It eats at you like moths at a sweater, leaving little holes, weakening the knit. You can still put it on, but it'll never keep you warm, not ever again. Eventually, the whole thing just unravels.

"All little boys like cookies," his mother says, pushing away from him and standing up with a smile, like she didn't just see two dozen teenagers brandish illegal weapons at each other in her front yard. Hael scowls as his mother totters off, pausing to pat me on the cheek. "You Hael's girlfriend?" she asks, but before I can think up an appropriate answer, she's talking again. "You like chocolate chip? Nobody don't like chocolate chip."

His mother disappears into the kitchen area, leaving the four of us in a bubble of awkward-as-fuck. I raise an eyebrow as Hael swallows and swipes a hand down his face.

"Interesting accent she has," I remark, and he shakes his head with a sigh.

"She's from Louisiana," he tells me, shrugging his big shoulders. "My *maman* is Cajun."

Ahh, so that explains both the French *and* the unusual accent.

"And as far as who's actually coming for her ..." I start.

"My mom's sick, okay?" Hael snaps, a bit of that darkness I remember seeing in him during sophomore year coming to the surface to play. Doesn't offend me, but at least he has the common decency to look chagrined. "Sorry, Blackbird. I just ... I don't want to talk about it, okay?" He gives me a look that says this is as deep as he goes, this thing with his mom. I'm not going to get to see this part of Hael, not yet. Maybe not ever. All of his playfulness, his flirting, his smirks and his sultry chuckles, all defense mechanisms to keep the world from seeing this part of him.

"Marie suffers from various mental illnesses," Oscar explains in a deadpan, causing Hael to grit his teeth and clench his fists in a way that reminds me of Vic. For his part, Havoc's leader says nothing, staring at me from dark eyes in such a manner that tells me I better get the hell out of Dodge or pay the consequences. "I maintain that while *some* are a matter of imbalanced brain chemistry, most are Martin's doing."

Martin, who the fuck is Martin?

"Enough," Hael growls out, the word the final nail in the coffin of this conversation. "Mitch and his crew just rolled up into my neighborhood and dragged my mother to the lawn. What else would they have done if we hadn't shown up?"

"Moot point, we did show up," Vic says as Marie begins to hum in the kitchen. "This was all just a farce to get us out here, to spew some bullshit about Danny."

"Yeah, well, it hit a little too close to home for me," Hael snaps back, taking off down the hallway. I hesitate only briefly before taking off after him. Vic grabs my wrist before I can go, squeezing just a little too hard. When I look back at him, I can't decide if the expression on his face is one of disappointment … or jealousy. Probably a mixture of both.

"Listen, princess," he starts, but I just laugh. Princess? Nobody's ever called me princess before. Besides, what little girl would want to be a princess when they could be a queen? "You could've messed things up bad today. I thought you'd learned your lesson when you stabbed Kali. I don't mind if you want to knock some heads together, just ask me first."

"You're just lucky I didn't shoot Kali today," I retort back, twisting my arm from his grip and ignoring Oscar as he watches me from behind the lenses of his glasses. "Don't lecture me about my mistakes when you could raze an entire city with the heat of your own. Don't talk to me again unless you're going to apologize."

Victor scowls at me as I take off down the hall, finding Hael sitting on the edge of his bed.

One look at his bedroom tells me everything I need to know about this family: the Harbins have no money, but someone clearly cares about Hael. The bed is made and dressed in clean blankets and sheets; the windows are free of streaks and dead bugs. There's even a threadbare rug, freshly vacuumed and laid out at the foot of the bed.

I hesitate in the doorway, my fingers lingering on the jamb as I watch him. It's weird, to see Hael Harbin in his bedroom, surrounded by his things. He's always seemed so impossible, a character of his own making, larger than life, a walking-talking slice of sex and violence.

In here … he almost looks his age.

Almost.

"You okay?" I ask, which is a stupid question. Such an empty question. None of us is okay. Not a single one. If we were, we wouldn't be a part of Havoc. If we were, we wouldn't have killed a kid in a funhouse at a Halloween party. No, we're far from okay. We're antonyms of okay.

Hael lifts his face up, honey-brown eyes dark, shoulders slumped. He forces a smile, but that just makes me frown harder. I don't want to see him smiling his way through this shit. I want to see something that's fucking real.

I step into the room and close the door behind me, leaning my ass up against it and wondering what, exactly, Mitch and his crew planned to get out of coming here. Thought they'd shake our tree up and Danny's ass would fall out like a rotten apple, maybe.

"I'm okay," Hael says finally, and I laugh, the sound as bitter as cheap gin. Hael cocks a brow at me as I push up off of the door, taking note of the extra locks on the inside. My eyes flick from the deadbolt to Hael's face.

"No, you're not. Why lie to me? I thought there weren't any secrets in Havoc?" This last part comes out a tad salty, but I can't help it. I'm not over the video thing, not over being lied to, even if it was by omission. Hael is just as guilty as Callum, as Oscar, as Aaron … maybe not quite as guilty as Victor. As the leader, he gets the most blame. It's a double-edged sword, isn't it? Being in charge.

"I'm sorry about the video, Bernadette," Hael says, looking away from me, toward a shelf stuffed with comic books. There must be thousands of slim volumes stuffed into the cheap, little Wal-Mart bookcases. I move over to stand next to them, pulling one out and examining the cover. It's a superhero story, but not one that I recognize. Flipping through it, I see there's a pretty clear-cut beginning, middle, and end. Good guy meets bad guy, shit happens, good guy triumphs. Switching it out for another volume, I find different characters but the same story. Over and over and over again. "When we first found it, we thought about turning it in, but then we thought about it. For a long, long fucking time. You know how the world really works."

Hael stands up from the bed, moving over to hover behind me. I can smell him, that pungent mix of sweet coconut oil and dirty grease from spending so much time beneath the hood. I inhale, just to bring it all in, but I keep it quiet. No need to let Hael know that I enjoy his personal scent so damn much.

"It's not like it is in the comics, you know?" he says, his breath feathering against my hair. Hael reaches around me to grab one of the volumes from the shelf. He flips through it as I stay where I am, acutely aware of his proximity to my back, acutely aware of the distance between our bodies. "Life isn't fair. It doesn't have story arcs with satisfying conclusions. Shit, it doesn't make narrative sense at all, does it?"

"Have you ever noticed that the good guys in these books are too concerned with their own morality to make hard choices?" I ask, staring at the conclusion of the story in my hand. The hero has locked the bad guy up, but on the very last page, he escapes, leaving room for a sequel. The thing is, how many people are going to die before the villain is caught again? How many have to suffer? It would be better if he were dead.

But people who kill other people are murderers, right? Villains. Only a villain can truly stop another villain. There is no room in this world for heroes; they only get in the way.

"A lot of shit has happened in my life," Hael says, moving away from me and pausing to look at a poster of a girl in a bikini, straddling the hood of a Ferrari. He smirks at it and shakes his head, turning away from the wall to look at me. "I always wanted to be the good guy, you know. But, uh …" Hael pauses to laugh, the sound as dark as the black paint on my nails. "If you want justice, you have to seek vengeance." He shrugs his big shoulders, looking me dead in the face. "You understand that, right? That's why you're here."

"I'm not afraid to sully myself to make things right," I admit, flashes of that awful video playing in the back of my skull. I can never unsee it. I can never shake those horrible images. Bile rises in my throat, but I swallow it back. The Thing will get what's coming to him. No matter Havoc's other faults, that I don't doubt. "But I have to ask …" Hael reaches down and tucks a strand of white-blonde hair behind my ear, his fingers lingering at the pink-tipped ends. "Is it true that Vic is the only one who wanted me in Havoc?"

Hael hesitates, like he's debating the merits of answering

me, when the door opens. Of course it's Vic, and he doesn't bother to knock. He looks around the room like he's familiar with it but hasn't been here in a long time. Memories flash across his face, a flicker of nostalgia that makes me hate him just a little bit less than I love him.

Ugh.

Fuck.

Of course I love Victor Channing. I always have. From that first moment on the playground, he took my heart in his hands when he shoved that brat down the slide for me. *Victor Channing punched me in the face between first and second period for saying Bernadette Blackbird was hot.* I can't forget that even when they were kicking the shit out of me during sophomore year, they were still on my side.

Which means that whatever price Kali paid must've been good.

"We should go," Vic says, his voice a thread of ice and steel. He gives Hael a look. "He just pulled into the driveway."

"He?" I ask as Hael grits his teeth, exhaling and nodding sharply.

"My dad," he says, giving me a look that communicates volumes without a single word. "We don't exactly get along."

"Is it true that he cut you up with a hunting knife?" I ask, pointing at the scar on Hael's arm, the one that goes from fingertip to shoulder. That's the rumor at Prescott High, that his father did that to him. But then, rumors at Prescott High are a lesson in the game of telephone; they grow leaps and bounds with each fantastical retelling.

Hael licks his lips and gives a curt nod.

"Yeah, something like that …" he starts as an unfamiliar male voice sounds from down the hall. Oscar's smooth, cool reply comes in response, and a shiver traces down my spine. "Tell ya more later, Blackbird, I promise." He gives my shoulder a squeeze as he moves past, and Vic and I exchange a look.

"You're not going to like Hael's dad," he tells me, and I cock a brow, so done with his bullshit I could scream. We're going to have to have it out soon, Vic and me.

"Why's that?" I quip back, popping my hip out and putting my hand on it.

"Because he murdered a pregnant prostitute," Vic replies with a sardonic smile. He moves past me and down the hall, leaving me to gape behind him. A million questions slither through my mind, but I'm not about to miss out on this interaction. I move down the hall as quick as I can, expecting to find a man like my stepfather, a wolf in wolf's clothing. The Thing never tries to hide what a monster he is. He feels protected, by his badge and his brother's law degree and his father's gavel.

Instead, I find a slender man in a baseball cap, smiling as he pulls the hat from his head and holds it against his chest.

"Long time, no see, son," he says as Hael stares at him from across the width of the small living room. The sweet smell of creamed butter and sugar wafts out from the direction of the kitchen. It's at odds with the tension in the room, reminding me that not everything is as it seems. The air smells sweet, the sound of Hael's mother's humming is comforting, but the look in Hael's eyes promises there's much more to this happy, little story than he's letting on.

"I mean, that's what happens when you go to prison," Hael retorts, shrugging again, like this is no big deal. He plasters one of those cocksure smiles on his face, putting a bit of swagger back in his step.

"I've been out for damn near a month, and yet, you haven't bothered to see me," the man—his name was Martin, wasn't it? —smiles as he glances from his son to Vic, then over to Oscar and me. "Do you want to introduce your new friend?" Martin continues to smile at me, like we're old buddies. "I remember the others. Victor and Oscar, right?"

"Guess the meth hasn't rotted your brain the way it did your judgement, huh?" Hael asks, throwing out a laugh. He gestures back at me. "This is Bernadette. We met a long time ago, right after you went to prison for the first time, and Mom and I were homeless. Spent the night in the same homeless shelter."

Something strange and dark flashes across Martin's face, and I can see that the smile on his lips isn't the whole story. There are monsters buried underneath all that nice.

"Let's go," Hael says, but then his mother comes out of the kitchen in her apron, wielding a wooden spoon covered in cookie dough.

"*Ne me laisse pas fiston,*" she pleads, her voice cracking a bit, like she can't bear to see her son go. I have no idea what she's saying, but it's pretty clear she wants Hael to stay here. He sighs heavily and nods, murmuring something to her in French that makes her smile.

"I gotta take Oscar back, and I'll come home," he promises, giving Martin a look. "Wouldn't want to leave you home alone with him very long anyway." Hael takes off for the front door, letting it slam into the wall on his way out.

"Lovely to meet you, Bernadette," Martin says, nodding as we pass by. He seems nice enough on the surface, but we all know that what lies beneath could be a vastly different story.

CHAPTER
FIVE

Sitting on the back of that bike, my arms wrapped around Vic, I'm forced to confront everything I'm feeling. How can I sit here and smell him, that musky mix of leather and bergamot that makes my heart flutter and melts the ice around my heart, and not evaluate everything that's going on inside of me?

Maybe, if I were to dig a little deeper, I'd realize that the reason I'm so upset with Havoc is because I *wanted* to trust them. I wanted to believe that I really was a Havoc Girl, that I was a part of the gang. But finding out they kept something so big from me, it seems impossible.

"Are you planning on going home tonight?" Victor asks me after we park on the curb in front of Aaron's house and he kicks off the bike's engine with his boot. He doesn't move, so neither do I, waiting with my arms wrapped around him as dusk settles over the quiet neighborhood. A child's laughter drifts back to us from down the street, a potent reminder that even if it feels like everything is going to shit in my own life, other people are still living theirs.

It doesn't seem fair, somehow. But, like Hael just said, life definitely isn't fucking fair. If it were, Penelope would still be alive, and my stepfather would be rotting six feet under.

"I kind of have to, unless you're willing to move on the Thing tonight. If I don't bring Heather back soon, Pamela will call the cops on me again." Vic nods, but I'm guessing his lack of a response is all the answer I need. They're not going to move on Neil, not tonight. Technically, I could probably stay here until tomorrow; it's only Saturday.

But if Neil came to find me and the boys, that means he senses a threat. Monsters always know to look for other monsters in the dark. Maybe if I come home a day early, Pamela will chill, and she won't poke the bear before we're ready? *Or maybe you just need space to think because the guys pissed you the hell off?*

"I'll have Hael give you a ride on his way back home," he says, and then he starts to stand up. Instead of releasing my arms, I squeeze him a bit tighter and he pauses. I close my eyes against the cool, night breeze, the scent of the white roses in the yard carrying over to me.

"Whatever reason you had for keeping that video from me, it wasn't good enough. It wasn't your choice to decide what to do with it. It was mine."

Vic stays quiet for several seconds, and I wonder if he's going to bring up the thing with Aaron today. Between all the bullshit at the Harbin house, I'd almost forgotten about that. Almost, but then there's a sore spot inside of my heart where

Aaron sits, and it's quite obviously bleeding. I take one of my hands away from Vic's waist and press it against my chest.

"That's where you're wrong, Bernadette. I'm the boss here, no matter how you feel about it."

A scowl forms on my lips, and I swing my leg over the side of the bike. Victor grabs my wrist, but I shake him off, spinning to face him with a sneer.

"You might be the boss, but you told me there were no lies in Havoc, no secrets. Tell me then, what did Kali give you guys that was so goddamn special that I deserved to suffer for it?"

"It wasn't just about the price she paid, Bernie," Vic tells me, turning slowly to look at me as he pulls out another cigarette. Smoking seems to be a nervous tic of his. I must be making him nervous a lot as of late. "It was about you. You were attached to Aaron; you were too attached to us. We needed to show you this wasn't a life you wanted to live."

I just stare back at him. On the outside, I'm stoic as fuck. On the inside, I feel like I've just been hit with a tidal wave, like cold, frothing waters are raging around me, like my legs could be knocked out from under me at any moment.

"You said you wanted me here, even though nobody else did," I repeat, trying to understand the inner mechanics of this group. For some stupid reason, I thought I'd pegged their motivations. Silly me. I don't understand Havoc at all.

"After I saw what you'd become, I knew," Vic says, lighting up and watching the stars flicker to life in the black velvet sky. "I knew we belonged together. Before that, you were too sweet, too soft. This life would've eaten you alive." He glances my way. "I was willing to let you go. Not anymore. I'm going to marry you, Bernadette."

My heart stutters in my chest, but I refuse to let Vic get to me, not right now.

Somebody has to stand up to him. It might as well be me.

I cross my arms over my chest, the pulse in my head throbbing as I try to rationalize what he's just said to me. *"It was about you."* They tortured me, not for Kali, but to get *rid* of me? I can't decide if that makes the pain I suffered worse … or better?

Goddamn, I must be irreparably broken.

"*If* you can get Pamela to agree to sign off on it," I quip back, running my tongue across my lower lip and tasting the waxy texture of my lipstick. "If, after everything I've learned in the last few days, *I* agree to it." Vic turns to look at me, anger building in his dark gaze. I stare right back at him, and I refuse to flinch. "And if that's the case, then remember, there won't just be a king in Havoc; there'll be a queen." I turn away before he can respond, shaking as I head across the grass toward the front door.

It's unlocked, so I let myself in, ignoring Aaron's stare as I pass by.

"Welcome back, Bernadette," he says, but I don't look at him. Instead, I gather Heather from upstairs, promise the girls I'll make good on my promise about the makeup, and head outside to the Camaro.

I need some time away from the boys to think.

Even if it means going home to my worst nightmare.

To fight him, I'll have to become one myself, but I'm not afraid, not anymore.

Pamela is waiting for us when we get home, sitting on the living room sofa with a fan of stolen credit cards on the coffee table in front of her, her laptop open beside them. I see an order confirmation from Nordstrom on the screen, thanking her for her fifteen-hundred-dollar purchase. Guess at least one of those stolen Visas had some room on it.

"If you're going to steal credit cards and commit felony fraud, why not get your daughter some new shoes?" I quip as Heather heads up the stairs to her room. The Thing isn't home just yet, but he will be soon. I'm curious to see what his next move will be, now that he knows I'm plotting against him. I'm going to have to be extremely careful for the next few weeks, watch my every move. If I hit him, he'll send me to juvie faster than you can say *sociopathic pedophile pig.*

"I taught you manners, Bernadette," Pamela says, lifting her martini to her lips. She rarely drinks, but when she does, her fights with Neil get even worse. They deserve each other. "Don't you talk to me that way."

"What way?" I ask, coming around the table with my ratty backpack slung over my shoulder. "Like I think you could do better? That you *should* do better? Why is it okay for you to waltz around in stolen pearls, but you can't at least pinch Heather some new shoes?"

Pamela waves her hand absently in my direction, her attention focused on the screen of her brand-new iPhone instead of on my face.

"If it's that important to you, take a card and order some shoes. I don't care." She gestures at the credit cards on the table, but I know that if she's being that generous, it means they're all used up. I've never once had Pamela gift me with anything, not even a piece of something she's stolen. After a moment, she finally looks up at my face. It's clear from her expression that Neil hasn't told her shit—not even that he's possibly gotten an underage teen pregnant. "What? You think you can stay out all the time, ignore my calls, and I'll start showering you with gifts when you deign to return home?"

I just stand there for a moment, staring at her. Her nails are long and red, the pearls around her neck real, her hair coiffed and freshly dyed from a recent salon visit. Pamela's clothes are designer, the gin in her martini top-shelf. She even sits on a beautiful silk couch, but it all looks so strange, paired with the dirty off-white walls of the duplex, the water-stained ceiling, and the open kitchen with its '70s cabinets. We live in a shithole while Pamela drapes herself in luxury. She's the epitome of selfish.

"You know why I don't come home, right?" I ask, and Pamela laughs, casting her green-eyed gaze my direction. I hate that I have her eyes, that I have her lips, her curves. I hate everything that ties us together. She can't make me forget that once, when I broke a plate on accident, she forced me to sit outside in the cold in nothing but my underwear while I watched her and the Thing eat a hot meal inside with Penelope and Heather.

Pen tried to sneak me some chicken later, but the Thing

caught her, grabbing her by the arm and dragging her away before she could unlock the sliding glass door. I always wondered what happened after that, but she never told me.

Now I know.

I recognized her outfit in that video as the one she had on that night. Everything about that dinner is engraved inside my skull, carved into my bone, a storybook in ivory without a happy ending.

The sound of the police cruiser pulling into the driveway is unmistakable, but instead of running to my room like I usually do, I stay right where I am, facing off against Pam.

"Why don't you tell me?" Pamela quips right back, raising a micro-bladed eyebrow in my direction. "Because you've been whoring yourself out to those thugs?"

A laugh slips past my red-painted lips as the door swings in and there he is, the monster himself. He smiles at me, clearly remembering our interaction on Halloween night, how I was covered in blood, how Aaron could barely stand, how Vic put a gun to his head.

My mind reels at the sight of him, my psyche cracking and splintering into ragged pieces. For a moment there, I can't see straight. Fuck, I can't see anything at all except that video, of Neil licking his fat lower lip, of him thrusting into my struggling sister.

Nausea roils in my stomach, and I bend over, vomiting right on his shoes. Pamela recoils with a gasp, clamping a hand over her mouth and spilling her martini all over the couch with a curse.

"What the fuck?" Neil snarls, stumbling back as I stand up

straight, running my arm across my lips. Our eyes meet, and I hope he can see in them just how much I hate him. If I have to drag him to hell myself, I'll do it, and I'll enjoy the eternal torment, just so long as I know he's suffering, too. "The hell is wrong with you?"

"You," I say, feeling like my spine is made of steel, my heart forged in iron, my willpower wooden and immovable. I wasn't able to be there for Penelope when she was alive, but I'll be damned if I don't avenge her now. *Kill him, kill him, kill him,* my psyche whispers, but as pissed as I am with Havoc right now, I trust in their plan.

Neil Pence will pay; it's just a matter of time.

He sneers at me, kicking his foot and spattering the wall with vomit.

"Clean this shit up," he barks at me, but I just smile back at him. The video of him and Pen is playing across my vision, my worst nightmare on repeat. I can't erase that trauma, but I sure as shit can hone it into a sharp edge and spill blood with it. I feel twitchy right now, and if Heather weren't here and counting on me, I'd probably just head outside and start running. I don't think I'd stop until I collapsed.

"I have no intention of doing any such thing," I tell him, completely unafraid. *Havoc Girl, Havoc Girl, Havoc Girl.* The words echo around in my skull, helping to banish the sounds from that awful, awful video. "I'm sure you're tired from all of that protecting and serving you've done today, but you have two hands. Clean it up yourself."

Neil clenches his teeth, still dressed in his uniform and sneering like the wicked, evil thing he is. His expression reminds me of a spider's web, of the dried insect carcasses caught in the silk, spinning beneath the pointed legs of a venomous arachnid. He loves to see his victims squirm, so I refuse to give him the pleasure.

"You're gettin' a mouth on you, girl," he says, moving closer in an attempt to intimidate me. "Almost as bad as Penelope was before she died." He smiles now, and my vision goes red. It takes everything I have inside of me to hold back. I'm better than that, better than him. Whatever small amount of satisfaction I'd get from hitting him right now, it'll be a drop of water in the ocean compared to Havoc's plans. "Must be because of that gang you're running with. It's time we had a talk about those hoodlums."

I look back at Pamela.

"Better to whore myself out to 'those thugs'," I make quotes with my fingers, "than let your husband fuck me into an early grave."

The room goes silent, and then Neil is coming at me, getting up in my face as Pamela sloshes what's left of her martini all over the coffee table as she slams it down on the glass surface.

"You want to say that again?" Neil threatens, the toes of his shoes just an inch from my own. "Considering all the things I know."

"What about the things *I* know?" I retort, my heartbeat thundering as I smell his sour breath, and the reek of old sweat from his uniform. Unfortunately, Neil Pence isn't a particularly unattractive man, but over the years, he's gotten uglier and uglier to me, to the point where I'm not even sure what he really looks like, without that filter over his better-than-average features. He sickens me, he smells to me, and I don't know if it's all in my head or not. The mind can play strange tricks, can't it?

"You think you can shake me with that shit?" Neil asks, reaching out to touch my hair. I slap his hand away as Pamela scrambles up from the couch, shoving between us to take her husband's side. Like always.

"Keep your hands off of my man," she snaps, looking at me like I'm the greatest mistake she ever made.

Frankly, I think she might be right about that.

I'm going to make it my mission to become her worst nightmare.

"Just a bunch of brats playing a game with rules they don't understand," Neil tells me as I move past them and head up the stairs. "Keep pushing, little girl, and you'll find yourself in that metaphorical grave."

"Likely," I start, pausing at the top of the stairs and leaning over the railing. "It's going to end up the other way." The video flickers in my mind again, and I brush it away as Pamela starts to scream at me. *I'll see him fucking buried for what he did,* I think as I push open the door to my room and slam it closed behind me.

I've trained Heather well, so she's already situated on the bed with her headphones in, using my phone to watch YouTube.

Good girl.

I flick the locks on the door, grab Pen's journal, and sit in the bathtub with all my clothes on to read it. Fortunately, Heather can't hear me when I start to cry.

CHAPTER
SIX

Prescott High, November fourth. Total shitshow.

As soon as I get there and see Principal Vaughn standing in the front hallway, I almost lose my shit.

"What the fuck is he doing here?" I whisper as Aaron pauses beside me, his body cloaked in a baggy hoodie to hide his injury, his green-gold gaze locked on the principal. "He's not supposed to be here, Aaron."

"No shit," Aaron murmurs, glancing down at me. I look back at him, and this moment passes between us, one where I remember his hot cum in my palm, and he's probably thinking about my tit in his mouth. Doesn't matter. I can't focus on personal stuff, not right now. I'm too angry with Havoc as a whole to think past business. Having to ride with Aaron all the way to school this morning was agony though. I'm just not built to deal with feelings.

"Well, this is unexpected," Oscar quips, moving up to stand beside me. He taps his fingers on the screen of a brand-new iPad, glancing my way and noticing the direction of my stare. He smiles, a slow, awful smile, the smile of a devil. I ignore him, turning back to look at Principal Vaughn instead. If he's here, it's because the Thing encouraged him to be. I could see it written all over my stepdad's face this morning: he thinks this is *fun*. That, and he intends to win. "I don't like surprises."

"And I don't like people on my list popping back up in unexpected places," I growl back at him, shaking with anger. This isn't fair. I called Havoc. This is my time. *Mine*. Sophomore year was stolen from me; I deserve senior year to go right.

"This oversight will be corrected, I assure you," Oscar purrs, but I just scowl at him, moving down the hall and toward my first period English class with Mr. Darkwood. It's the only class of the day I share with Kali, so this should be fun.

After that nightmare yesterday, I can only imagine how full of herself she's going to be. I'm not in the mood to deal with it today either. If she tries me, she's going to see what happens when I clap back.

Slumping into my seat, I drop my ratty backpack to the floor, leaning back in my seat and finding the back of Kali's head. Her green-streaked dark hair cascades over her shoulders in a glossy, raven wave. The sight reminds me of a sleepover we had, years ago, when we took turns braiding each other's hair. Hers was blond back then, too, but she didn't like the brassy shade of it. We stole some money from her mother's purse, bought some shitty black dye from the grocery store, and it's been dark ever since.

My lips purse tight.

She let jealousy rule over our relationship, tear us apart, break us. She could've had me forever, and I would've been her ride or die bitch.

I tap my black-painted nails on the surface of my desk, twisted up from my interaction with the Thing, from the altercation with the Charter Crew—as they're now also calling themselves.

A gang war, on top of everything else. Fantastic. And now Principal Vaughn is back? I feel like things are spinning out of control. My trust with the Havoc Boys is broken; my hatred toward Aaron is draining from me like the color out of the fall leaves. My whole world is topsy-turvy.

The only way to deal with it all is to take control, wrap my fist around the heart of the situation and squeeze until it stops beating.

As if she can sense the direction of my thoughts, Kali turns around to look at me, purple-painted lips curving up into a smirk. There's something nefarious about her expression, something twisted, like the branches of the tree outside the classroom window. Almost wicked.

Is she pregnant with the Thing's baby? That's the question here. She's dating Mitch, but fucking Neil? And she was seeing someone at Oak Valley Prep on the side? I smell a plot.

"Better get used to seeing me in front, bitch," Kali says, and instead of reacting in the moment, I internalize my rage, smiling at her in a way that I hope brings nightmares. My hands twitch with a surge of rage, but I still them in my lap. "Oh, and I like the new look." Kali runs her finger from the edge of her eye to the corner of her lip, mimicking Billie's knife wound before she throws her head back with a plastic-sounding laugh.

I stay completely still, mind spinning with tainted thoughts. There are several places in Prescott High that the students call 'dark zones', spots in the hall or in empty classrooms where you're unlikely to run into the campus cops or security guards.

Kali passes one on her way to second period.

Sucks to be her. I'm going to make certain of that.

It occurs to me then that she's jealous of me for a reason, because Kali Rose will never be able to reach my level. She will never be able to do the things I do. It's why she stole from me. It's why she plays the victim, why she lies. It's why she sent Havoc after me.

Mr. Darkwood comes into the classroom, and Kali turns away, pretending like she gives a crap about schoolwork. We both know she's never planned on using education to escape South Prescott. Instead, she uses her body and her bullshit as weapons. I mean, I've seen her writing during peer reviews. Sorry, but Kali can't write for shit.

Seeing her walking around like this though, a free woman, girlfriend to the new leader of the Charter Crew, it infuriates me. I'm paying Havoc's price to see her downfall and yet, here she stands, more confident than ever.

My boys better have a good plan in place.

If they don't, I'll take things into my own hands. I'm done with being the victim here.

During class, I start a new poem, one that I don't turn in at the end of the period, electing to take a zero on the assignment so I can slam the paper down on Kali's desk.

He who dares not grasp the thorn
Should never crave the rose.
Anne Brontë was overlooked in her time.
I've stolen her words.
You will not steal mine.
I'm not afraid of thorns; I will pluck the petals from your rose.
Even if I have to pay the price in blood.

To be fair, it's a shitty poem. But it does the trick. Kali looks up at me, confusion written across her painfully average features.

"What the fuck is this?" she asks, but I ignore her, heading out into the hallway and hiding myself behind a bank of lockers, one foot propped on the wall behind me. I'm aware that I'm not functioning as I should, that something in my brain is broken, that maybe I'm still in shock over what happened on Halloween.

But I don't care.

I'm standing up for myself. Against Kali. Against the Havoc Boys. Against the *world*.

Unaware that she's being stalked, Kali saunters down the hall like she's queen, greeting Billie briefly and talking long enough that the other students clear out before she heads for the east hall. For the dark zone.

I slip out from behind the lockers as soon as Billie's disappeared into the bathroom. I walk quickly but quietly, my boots gliding across the scratched and stained tiles that have lined these halls since my grandparents went to this stupid school.

C.M. STUNICH

As soon as I turn the corner and spot Kali, I start to run.

She turns around to look, tucking some hair behind her ear in the process.

"The hell?" That's all she manages to get out before my fingers are digging into the back of her head, nails gouging her scalp as she gasps and reaches up to pry my hand away. "I'm pregnant," she gushes suddenly, a truly cowardly move meant to save her own skin. Guarantee you the second I let go, she'd attack me instead.

"Oh, I already know that," I purr, channeling Vic, channeling Oscar, channeling the pure emotional malevolence that is Havoc. Leaning in, I put my lips against Kali's cheek, kissing her and staining her skin with my bloodred lipstick. "But as a friend once said, your face isn't pregnant."

I shove Kali forward and slam her face into the front of one of the lockers. She chokes on blood as hot red liquid streams from her nose and over her lips. I know she's working to become a model. This incident might not change her life, but she won't be pretty for a while, that's for sure.

"You can thank Billie for this," I hiss at her as my own face throbs. I cleaned it again last night, reapplied some butterfly bandages. The whole time, all I could think about were Oscar's long, tattooed fingers caressing my cheek and arm. "Consider it an eye for an eye."

Kali struggles, but my grip on her is too good. I shove her into the locker a second time, and she tries to scream. Too bad for her, I know exactly how to hold a bitch's head back so that it's hard to make a sound. With her neck curved the way it is, the best she can do is gasp and whimper.

My mind flickers back to Halloween night, to Kali sitting all cuddled up next to the Thing.

She could be a victim of his, too. I know that, and yet … nobody made her call Havoc.

She did that all on her own.

"You fucking whore," she gasps out, but then I shove her forward again. Too hard maybe. Her knees buckle and she flags to the floor. There's blood everywhere, but my vision is colored red, too, so it's hard for me to tell.

Danny Ensbrook lying on the floor in a puddle of blood. Penelope screaming beneath the Thing. Kali laughing as she slipped into my stolen homecoming dress.

I think if gentle hands hadn't grabbed me from behind, I might've killed her then.

"That's enough, Bernadette," a dark voice whispers in my ear, and then I'm overwhelmed with the smell of Callum's aftershave. It's a hard scent to describe, like private exchanges behind closed doors and pillow talk on a rainy morning.

I gasp like I'm coming to, releasing Kali's hair as he hauls me backward, enveloping me in those strong arms of his.

"I've got you, Bernie," Cal whispers, squeezing me tight, his head bent over mine, the hood of his sweatshirt hiding us from the world. "I've got you." He holds me tighter than I'd ever imagine to be comfortable, but there's something soothing about it. I feel my rage melting away, logic trickling back into my clouded vision.

Kali is on the ground, covered in blood and groaning.

Callum leaves her there, taking me by the hand and pulling me down the hall to the boys' bathroom. He sits me down on the closed lid of the toilet and gathers up a wad of paper towels, letting the water in the old sinks run hot before he gets them damp.

"I can't believe I just did that," I say, my voice colored with dark wonder. Cal crouches in front of me, smiling tightly as he reaches out and takes my hand in his, carefully brushing aside Kali's blood spatters.

"I can," he says, voice gravelly and broken, but beautiful anyway, like a shattered tombstone on a sunny day. It's a little sad, but the sun is warm, and the view is right. "Because I've been there. Remember how I told you that I almost killed the boys that did this to me?" He points to the scars on his neck. "You're drowning in your own pain, Bernadette." Callum swipes the wet paper towels across my face, and they come away red with blood. I must've gotten Kali even worse than I thought. "You need to learn to swim before you try to push someone else's head under."

I scowl at him, turning my head to look at the graffiti scratched across the walls of the bathroom stall. There are things written there that I'd never dare repeat. Boys are fucking gross sometimes. I wonder how many times my name has been scribbled across these walls? Looking now, I see nothing, and I just know deep down that Havoc had something to do with that.

"What happened to the boys that gave you your scars?" I ask mildly, because while Callum said Vic saved him, taught him how to seek revenge the right way ... what is the right way? Castrating someone and carving the word *Rapist* into their face?

"They'll never walk again," Cal says, nodding his chin

briefly before standing up. "They took my dreams away from me, so I took theirs, too." He smiles again, and the sight of it gives me the chills.

"About the other day …" I start, because we can't just forget that we almost had sex at the studio. I *certainly* can't forget that out of all the boys, I chose to run to him. What the fuck does that even mean?

"It either means nothing," Cal starts, shaking his head slightly. He reaches up to push his hood back, revealing that pretty blond hair of his. "Or it means everything. We don't have to talk about it. Just decide what it is that you want."

Callum turns away, flushes the paper towels down the toilet in the next stall over—likely to hide the evidence—and then disappears out the door.

I stay in the boys' bathroom, crouched on the seat of the toilet in a locked stall, until lunch rolls around.

Nobody bothers me, and that's just the way I like it.

There's not a goddamn student at Prescott High who isn't aware of our little war with the Charter Crew. I can feel their eyes following me as I walk down the halls, and it would be impossible to miss all of the money changing hands as students place their bets.

I just hope everyone who bets against us knows they're placing their eggs in the wrong basket.

"This is not the senior year I signed up for," Hael says,

leaning back on the front steps as Callum sips a Pepsi, his hood flipped up over his blond hair again. The conversation stops as soon as I come out the door, taking a seat next to Oscar because, let's be honest, knowing that he hates me means we have the easiest relationship out of everyone here. We know what we want—and don't want—from one another.

He stares at me like I'm some sort of diseased slag, and I curl my lip his direction.

"This isn't the senior year I was expecting either," I quip, giving Vic a sideways look. He laughs at me, making me bristle. How fucking *dare* he. After what he said to me the other night, I oughta dump his entire soda on his head and then curb stomp his balls. "My question is: what are we going to do about it? Vaughn is here, like nothing happened. That's as much a slap to our authority as Mitch and his buddies."

I glance briefly at Callum, but he isn't looking at me, and it's quite clear from Victor's lack of violent rage that he doesn't know about Kali yet. Surprisingly enough, she hasn't narked on me either. Likely, she won't. It'd put her new crew at too much risk. The shitty part for me is, I *will* have to tell Vic at some point.

Just … maybe not right this second.

"So it's *our* authority, now is it?" Vic asks, and Aaron throws him a goddamn death glare.

"Lay off of her," he growls, and the tension—and the testosterone—ramps up to dangerous levels. I probably shouldn't have gone after Aaron the way I did. It's turned an already messy situation into a filthy one. "Bernadette deserves better than that, after the way we've treated her."

"After the way we've treated her?" Oscar echoes, the lenses of his glasses flashing as he lifts his gaze up from the surface of his iPad. Apparently, nobody's going to mention the one that I threw against the wall. "How, exactly, are we treating her, Aaron?"

"You know what I mean," Aaron says, not looking at me. He's just staring across the street at the row of modest suburban houses. You can tell by the aged siding and the sagging roofs that even the homeowners who do care about their homes are limited by funds. Makes me think of the assholes in the Oak Park neighborhood with their luxury cars and soaring mansions, and I scowl. "The video. The thing with Kali. Everything."

Aaron turns to look at me, his green-gold gaze cutting right through me as he furrows his brow. Are we going to talk about what happened on the couch? Are we going to talk about the fact that I said I still loved him? Looking at him right now, my heart breaks all over again, and I feel a lump forming in my throat. The day he broke up with me, I thought I would die. I truly and utterly believed that my broken heart would kill me. Somehow, I managed to patch it together and keep going, but the patchwork quilt of my soul is not the same as it was then. Aaron isn't the same either, not even remotely. I'm not even sure if it's *possible* for us to bridge the gap between us.

"I don't see the problem; you were shown the video. Is your problem then that you just weren't shown it sooner?" Oscar asks, his voice a derisive slight that I do my best to ignore. Kneeing him in the balls and wrapping my hands around his throat at Vic's house is one thing, but I can't do it here, especially not with things the way they are.

I lean back on the steps, basking in the sun like a snake. I don't belong in the daylight, but every now and again I need to absorb a little light to keep me warm.

"You know," I start, tilting my head to one side as I watch students shrink and cower past us. They might bet against us, but they know better than to show open defiance. Unless they're willing to join the Charter Crew and fight the war, they're nothing but peons. "Once Victor and I are married—"

"Oh, so you *have* decided to grace me with your hand in marriage then? After the other night, I wasn't sure you were still interested." Vic's dark voice reeks of butthurt, but you know, it's not my fault if he feels emotionally raped by my words. I offered him an olive branch, and he essentially spit in my face.

I ignore him.

"Once we're married," I start again, raising my voice and turning my attention on Oscar. "You aren't going to speak to me like that anymore."

"How so?" Oscar asks, carefully setting the iPad aside and leveling his gray gaze on me. He obviously isn't afraid of me. Either he can learn to respect me, or I'll show him the true meaning of fear. "You think marrying Victor gives you some sort of status upgrade? Don't fool yourself."

I laugh, letting my head fall back, sunshine caressing my throat. I've bared it to this group of dangerous assholes, like a wolf who isn't afraid to let her inferiors sniff her neck. I'm not afraid. Let them try to bite me and see what happens.

"Marrying Victor *does* give me a status upgrade," I say, turning to look at the man in question. It's impossible not to look at Aaron, too, seeing as he's sitting on Vic's other side, looking at me in just such a way that I wonder if today he might actually speak up, fight for me the way I've been craving since moment one. But, I guess not today, Satan. "Doesn't it, Vic?" I ask, quirking a brow. He shifts uncomfortably on the step for a moment, turning his obsidian gaze to the street and narrowing his eyes.

I have his balls in a vise, and he doesn't even know it.

Actually, the only reason that *I* know that is because he has my heart in one. I want to please him so badly and yet, I hate myself for it. I'm sure Victor feels the same way about me. That, at least, levels the playing field.

"You might be king of Havoc, but if you think I'm going to marry you and keep this crappy omega status you've granted me, you have another thing coming."

Hael grins and offers me up a high five. I hesitate for a second, but decide to slap my palm against his in solidarity. He ends up yanking me down the steps and into his lap instead, putting his lips up against my ear.

"If Vic doesn't want you to be his queen, I might have an opening you could fill?" Hael pauses for a second, frowning, and then flashes a shit-eating smile that makes my stomach flip. "Actually, it's the other way around, isn't it? You're the one with an opening that needs filling."

"Knock that shit off," Vic snaps, watching us together. His dark eyes take me and Hael in with no small amount of jealousy. While it's obvious that Victor doesn't like what happened between me and Aaron yesterday either, it's clear that finding Hael watching us pissed him off even more. *And yet another thing I have to tell him: me and Cal at the studio.* Fantastic. I'm sure that'll go over about as well as a hurricane in Florida. "I'm not having this conversation here. We can talk about it later." Victor lights up a cigarette, saluting one of the on-campus police officers who turns a blind eye to his disobedience, leaving me with a sick feeling in the pit of my stomach. How many cops does Havoc own? More or less than Neil?

I turn in Hael's lap, straddling him and weaving my hands together behind his neck, his red hair tickling my fingers. It's bloodred, so clearly a dye job, but after seeing his mother, it's likely that he really is a ginger underneath.

His honey-brown eyes look down into mine, sharp fragments of pain hidden behind those vibrant irises. He's still shaken from the incident on Saturday, and obviously there's still something going on between him and his father. All the smiles, the braying laughter, the flirting, it's a front for an entire firestorm of pain.

"I won't let Oscar treat me like shit," I tell Hael, stroking an ebony fingernail down the side of his smooth face. He never lets his stubble get the better of him, not like Vic or Aaron. Told ya, he's the southside version of the popular boy—vibrant, charismatic, gregarious. If only he lived a different life, Hael could be something special. "But if Vic won't stand up for me, will you?" I ask, glancing over at Aaron.

Callum watches us from the shadows of his hood, sipping on his Pepsi. It's not uncharacteristic for him to be so quiet, but after what happened at the Halloween party, I'm seriously worried. I'll admit, I'm struggling with all of the revelations.

The video.

The information about my Havoc price.

The fact that Vic told me they tortured me to put distance between us.

All of that.

Hael is just so … plucky, sometimes it's hard to remember that he's just as culpable as the rest of them. I mean, he is the H in Havoc, isn't he?

"You want me to whip Oscar's ass for your honor?" Hael asks, still grinning maniacally. "I mean, I'm not opposed to it. He's skinny as fuck; I outweigh him by like seventy pounds."

"Bernadette …" Victor warns, leaning over and putting his elbows on his knees. The look he throws me is cold hell.

I ignore him, putting my forehead up against Hael's. He exhales and wraps his strong arms around my waist, smelling like coconut oil and old cars.

"Fucking grease monkey," I murmur, and then I kiss him.

It's pure fire, that kiss. We could light up the night with it.

Hael's tongue slips between my lips as his hands slide down my sides to cup my ass through my leather pants.

"Jesus Christ," Vic growls, throwing his soda can on the ground. It explodes in a rush of foam as he reaches down and grabs my chin. Hael's jaw clenches tight and his hands squeeze even tighter on my ass. "When we get married, Bernadette Savannah Blackbird, you will be mine. And I'll treat you as such. Oscar will mind his tongue. And next time he tries to do something stupid—like show you a fucking video of your sister being raped—it won't be Hael that puts him in line, it'll be me."

"You can't be serious?" Oscar asks, scowling as he puts his iPad aside. "You're on a very short leash, Victor. Can't you see it? This girl is going to ruin us." Oscar gestures at me with one of his tattooed hands. His easy calm is slipping as I smirk at him, watching the repercussions of that expression ripple through his body. "She's already creating cracks between you and Hael, you and Aaron."

"Don't use me as an argument against Bernadette," Aaron says, turning away and subconsciously reaching across his chest to touch his shoulder. He grimaces slightly and grits his teeth, fingers curling in his sweatshirt. I'm surprised he even showed up to school today, everything considered. I would've preferred it if he'd stayed home to rest, but I guess that's not how Havoc functions.

"Think what you want," Victor says, scanning the street like a predator on the hunt. He doesn't look at me again, but that's okay. I've won a battle today. Maybe not a war, but definitely a skirmish. "When Bernadette is my wife, you'll treat her like it."

"How, might I ask, is that?" Oscar grinds out as Callum pushes his hood back, blond hair catching the sunlight. "I seem to have missed the memo. I wasn't aware you two were soul mates; I was under the impression this was a marriage of convenience."

"What did you mean by 'you'll be mine', exactly?" Callum asks, smiling slightly. "Just clarifying."

"All of your questions are self-explanatory," Vic says, flicking his cigarette onto the cement and turning to head back inside. "We're having a group meeting on Friday. We'll hash whatever out then. For now, keep on your toes. Mitch isn't as stupid as he looks."

Victor heads for the double doors that lead into Prescott High, shoving through them with both palms.

"Fuck, he's an asshole," Hael says, closing his eyes for a brief moment. I notice, though, that he doesn't let go of me. I'm not really sure what Hael and I are to each other right now, but … we must be something, right?

"You see that, Oscar?" I say, looking past Hael's shoulder to the gray-eyed prick behind him. "You keep berating me for giving into Vic. Little did you know it was the other way around."

Oscar's face tightens as he shoves to his feet, snatching up his iPad in the process.

"I say this with the utmost respect, Bernadette," he purrs, leaning down to look at me, almost close enough to kiss. "Fuck you."

I find myself laughing as Oscar takes off after Vic, leaving me alone with Hael, Aaron, and Callum.

"Hey, Bern, can we talk?" Aaron asks as Hael studies me, still sitting in his lap, his arms still wrapped around me. He said he would stand up to Oscar for me, but what about Vic? Can Hael stand up to him for me? Can Aaron? I'd love to see either or both of them try.

"Like Vic said, meeting on Friday. We can talk then." I push up off of Hael's lap. I might be the *least* mad at him, but I'm still pissed. I feel like I'm playing an entirely new game here, and I don't like it. At least with the old game, I knew the rules. Now, I'm starting from scratch.

Havoc kept secrets from me.

They're just as bad as I always thought they were, and I won't make the mistake of underestimating them again.

CHAPTER
SEVEN

After school, I head down the front steps to find Hael waiting beside his cherry-red Camaro. Our plan this week is to lie low, but that doesn't mean I don't need a ride home.

"Hey Blackbird," he calls out, smoking a cigarette, leaning casually back against the car like everything is fine and dandy. One might think he didn't have a crazy mother, or a father recently released from prison. We all have our masks, and Hael Harbin wears his well. "Have I told you how beautiful you look today?" He takes in my leather pants and halter top with stark appreciation.

With the sun on my back, and Hael's smile warming up the rest of me, I almost feel for the briefest of moments like this might be at least an okay afternoon. *Neither Pamela nor the Thing should be home today, so maybe I'll invite him up?* Hael and I haven't talked about what happened after Victor kicked him out of the room, but maybe we need to?

I should've expected trouble.

And I mean, I did, but from Kali and the Charter Crew, not from some cunt with a Starbucks cup in her hand. I'd have preferred to be knifed, to be honest.

"Havoc," a voice calls out, and a white streak of rage flashes across my vision. It's mixed with a healthy dose of fear as I turn my head to the right and find Hael's ex, Brittany Burr, standing on the sidewalk in front of Prescott High. She goes to Fuller High; there is absolutely no reason she should be on this side of town. You know, except to fuck up my entire life.

"Excuse me?" I say, and if I were Brittany, I'd probably run. Can she hear the murder in my words? If not, she clearly has no sense of self-preservation. The bourgeois cheerleader cunt stares right back at me with weepy brown eyes. She's looking at me, and not at Hael, but if she's just called out Havoc then there's a reason for it.

Somehow, it never really occurred to me that someone else might call Havoc. I mean, logically, I always knew it was a possibility, but I guess I was showing my naivety by believing it wouldn't happen. Even weirder than hearing Havoc called out, is knowing that I'm as beholden to that word as any of the boys. As a member of Havoc, it's also *my* duty to carry out requests—and to determine price.

How the tables have turned.

I narrow my eyes on Brittany's pregnant ass, wondering if there's something in the goddamn water here in Springfield for so many girls to be pregnant. Brittany, Kali … hopefully not me. I bite my lower lip and wonder if I shouldn't take a pregnancy test. I haven't been careful enough, and as much as I believe in a woman's right to choose, I'd rather not have to deal with any of that. Doctors, nurses, questions, medical procedures. It's an invasion of another sort, and I'm not interested in subjecting myself to scrutiny of any kind.

For right now though, I'm not thinking about birth control. Nah, instead it's violence that's in the forefront of my mind. But I already beat up a pregnant chick today. Restraint is key.

"What did you just say?" Hael asks, his face going ashen as Brittany makes her way over to us, dressed in an oversized cable-knit sweater and leggings with UGGS. She's got her basic bitch uniform down pat, pumpkin spice latte included. I can see the letters *PSL* scrawled on the side of the cup.

"Havoc," Brittany says again, lifting her chin in defiance. "I'm calling Havoc."

"You don't even go to Prescott," Hael chokes out, but he knows as well as I do that that was never part of the bargain. Call out the word, state your needs, pay the price. That's it. "Holy motherfucker son of a bitch," he groans, letting his head fall back and sliding both hands over his face.

"I need you, Hael," Brittany says, leveling a death glare on me, like it's my fault she got pregnant with some random guy's kid. Looking at her, I can see that we've devolved into something primal here. She wants this man standing between us, but even though I'm loath to admit it, the thought of her taking him from me fills me with a white-hot fury. "This baby needs you." She puts her hand over her belly, finally turning her attention away from me and over to her ex. "That's why I'm calling Havoc. I want you to be in my life, in this baby's life. I want you to be a father."

Hael drops his hands at his sides and gives her a long, suffering look. His expression is strained, almost dejected. He wants this about as much as I do.

"That's what you called Havoc for?" he asks, studying her in a way that says he looks back on their relationship with about as much fondness as I look back on Donald. What a mistake he was, a nightmare of national proportions. Clearly, anyone can see what a divisive little psycho he is. "To ask me to be a father?" Hael laughs, the sound dry and disconnected. "You understand that's a lifelong commitment. You'll never be able to pay our price."

"Look, I'm going to be honest with you, okay," Brittany says, casting me a look that says I'm not welcome to be a part of this conversation. "But I want to talk alone. Can we take a drive maybe?" She takes another step forward, reaching out to put her hand on Hael's muscular arm. I step between them, cutting her off from touching him and staking my claim in a man that I'm still royally pissed off at. But I can't help it. This is getting primal: two bitches fighting over a bastard. And I'm not about to lose. If Brittany wants to see claws, I'll show her mine. Guarantee mine are sharper, longer, and tipped in venom.

"You're not taking a drive alone with my man," I say, and there it is, just sitting out there for the entire world to hear. I don't give a shit if I sound ratchet as hell either. It is what it is. I might've been born into wealth, but I grew up in poverty. South Prescott is in my blood, and I'm a stronger person for it. What does bourgeois Brittany and her upper middle-class bullshit have on me? I'll tell you what: fucking *nothing*. "And he isn't carrying your baby."

"You'd know that how?" Brittany asks, clutching her drink close to her chest. "He fucked me enough times that it's a possibility." Without thinking, I step forward and hit the bottom of her cup, upending the coffee all over her pale red sweater. She gasps and steps back, shaking out the fabric to keep it away from her skin.

"I know that he always used a condom with you. I know that I don't like you. And I know that Hael belongs to me now. That's what matters."

"Holy shit," Hael whistles from behind me, but he doesn't step in or stop me from doing my thing. He doesn't contradict me either, despite the fact that we've never once had a conversation about our relationship or lack thereof.

Something happened to me on Halloween night though. I can't quite put my finger on it, but I feel like I'm being pulled apart by the wicked fingers of the universe, and only I can figure out how to put myself back together.

"Bernadette," Oscar says, appearing at my side like a summoned ghost. He freaks me the fuck out, this motherfucker. Like, how does he materialize out of nowhere like that? I haven't gotten the chance to ask him. "You know we treat potential clients with respect," he says, giving me a look before glancing back at a fuming Brittany. "I hear you've called Havoc. What is it that you want?"

"I want Hael to step up and be a father to his goddamn kid," Brittany snaps back, tearing her sweater over her head and leaving only her tank top. She's so skinny that even though she isn't far along, her baby bump is showing. The sight of it makes me feel nauseous. Some distant part of me recognizes that I'm being a bad feminist. I should support Brittany honestly. In all reality, it probably is Hael's kid. But I don't like that. It doesn't work into my goddamn narrative, and you know what? Senior year is *my* year, and I don't want to share.

"If it even is my kid," Hael growls back at her. He snakes an arm around my waist and pulls me back against him, claiming me. I love it, and I revel in the look on Brittany's face, even though I know I rightfully shouldn't. Even though I sort of hate Havoc right now.

"Let her finish," Oscar purrs, turning to look at us, taking note of Hael's arm around my waist, and then turning back to Brittany. "Go on."

Brittany swallows hard, tossing espresso dark hair over her shoulder.

"I want Hael to take responsibility for the baby, to be a father, to come with me to my appointments." She swallows hard and looks away, like we're about to get to the core of what she really wants here. "And I want him to come with me to tell my dad."

"Fuck no," Hael snaps back, his arm tightening around me. "Are you kidding? Do you want to see me dead or behind bars? Your father will fucking kill me."

"No," Brittany cries out, her voice this reedy plead that makes my teeth hurt. She takes another step forward, but I press my body back into Hael's. I licked him; he's mine now. "I won't let him hurt you, but it has to happen. We *have* to tell him."

"*We* don't have to do shit," Hael snaps, but Oscar gives him another long, studying look and he snaps his teeth together.

"What else?" Oscar asks, turning back to look at Brittany.

"Because once we calculate a price, there's no going back."

Brittany nods and swallows.

"I need you guys to deal with … another guy I'm having problems with." She exhales and pulls her balled-up sweater against her chest. "That, and I want to get back together," she adds, and I feel myself go hot and then cold on the inside. "That is, if the baby is his."

"If?" Hael repeats, and I swear, I can feel his heart beating against my back. My fingers trace across his tattooed arms, teasing the hair there with my nails. He shudders behind me, but I can't tell if that's because he likes me touching him or because he's completely freaked out by Brittany's presence.

"Another condition I have is that I want time to talk to Hael alone." Brittany narrows her eyes on me. "And if the baby is his, then I want us back together, and I want her"—Brittany points a French manicured nail tip at me—"to keep her slutty hands off of him."

A laugh bubbles up from out of nowhere, and it takes every ounce of self-control I have not to throw myself at that girl, to hit her somewhere that isn't her belly and listen to her howl in pain.

"That won't be possible," Oscar amends, before I get a chance to second-guess my own self-control. "Bernadette is a member of Havoc; Hael is a member of Havoc. These things are signed and sealed in blood; they cannot be undone."

"You're a member of Havoc, and you don't fuck him," Brittany blurts at Oscar, throwing her arm out for emphasis as she clutches her ruined sweater even closer. Oscar gives her a long, studying sort of look.

"No, I don't, but I could if I wanted to. Havoc is family, and you are not family and will never be. So. I will look into your request and get back to you with a price, but what Bernadette and Hael do in the bedroom is not and will never be your business." Oscar turns away from her and moves over to the Camaro, pausing to glance over his shoulder at Brittany. "Meet us at the drive-in after school tomorrow, and we'll give you our price."

"On your side of the tracks?" Brittany manages to choke out, but there's no need for any of us to answer her in that regard. We all know that the answer to that question is yes.

Hael opens the passenger side door for me, and I climb in, deciding that for today, at least, I'll accept his gentlemanly advances. Brittany gawks at us as Oscar and Hael move around to climb in on the driver's side, but she knows better than to say anything. Most students at this school would rather commit hara-kiri than call on Havoc; she has to know she's walking on thin ice.

"About all that shit you said about me being yours," Hael starts, but I ignore him, leaning forward to push play on the stereo and starting up *Lion* by Hollywood Undead.

"Don't push it," I tell him, melting back into the seat and closing my eyes.

I'm exhausted, but I could sleep for a thousand years and find no rest in it. No, I won't truly rest until every name on my list is crossed off in bloodred lipstick and buried.

"Her entire request is bullshit," I grind out, sitting on top of one of the old picnic tables as I watch Fuller High kids pull into the drive-in across the railroad tracks. It's been a while since we visited the old grease pit, but I have to say, it feels good, sitting here surrounded by other rejects from Prescott High, like I'm exactly where I should be.

"That doesn't matter," Vic says absently, leaning back on the table in a black wifebeater, his hair greased back like he thinks he's John Travolta or something. I'll never admit how handsome he looks like that; I'd rather die. "You know as well as anyone else that when someone calls Havoc, they set the terms, we set the price."

Hael is sitting quietly across from us, head buried in his hands. His bloodred hair catches the light as he goes through what looks like a mourning process, like he's saying goodbye to life as he knows it. I'd ask how things could possibly get any worse than they are, but then, I know that rock-bottom is just an illusion. Fate is a cunt, and she will drill down into that stone beneath your feet and send you straight to hell first chance she gets.

What's worse than having a mentally ill mom, a murderer for a father, and a gang war on your hands?

That's right, adding a squalling infant birthed by a woman you hate.

"I've calculated the cost of her request already," Oscar remarks, consulting his iPad like he always does. Wouldn't surprise me if he lubed up and fucked it, too. "A lifetime commitment from Hael would require a life in return; that's not something she's going to be willing to pay."

A shiver chases over my skin as I bite into my burger, slowly licking the sauce off of my bottom lip as Aaron watches me. He does the same with his burger, and I almost smile. I mean, I would if Oscar hadn't just suggested that the price for Hael's fatherhood is murder.

"But?" Vic asks, closing his eyes against the sunshine, like he's in a world far, far away from here. Flicking my attention to Callum, I see him unloading his extra-large fry order onto a tray and dousing it in ketchup. He pauses just after he does that, staring down at the viscous red liquid like perhaps his mind is somewhere else, too. Maybe at the party, with Danny's blood staining the floor.

He notices me looking and hooks a cruel smile, flipping his hood up and hiding the golden shimmer of his blond hair. When he puts a long fry between his lips, it's not a particularly innocent move.

"It either means nothing or it means everything. We don't have to talk about it. Just decide what it is that you want."

I flick my attention back to Oscar.

"You assume there's a *but* involved," Oscar says, smiling in a way that reminds me of cold graves and mausoleums with weeping angels. That thought soon devolves into one of us fucking in a graveyard, and I grit my teeth, wondering where the hell that came from. Another bite of my burger banishes the day-mare into oblivion.

"There's always a conjunction with you, Oscar," Vic murmurs as I pick up my chocolate shake and take a sip.

"Well, in this case, you're right," Oscar says, and I have to wonder if this isn't how the discussion of my price went down.

"Tell her we want to own her—body, mind, and soul. She'll never accept." I frown as I think about what Aaron and Vic told me, about how every letter of Havoc *but* the V wanted me gone, shipped off to Nantucket to work part-time at the ice cream parlor. My lip curls. "There is a but. We add in a condition that she have the fetus DNA tested at the earliest available opportunity. According to my research, Brittany should be about seventeen weeks along. That means conception would likely be on or around August twenty-ninth."

Oscar pauses to look up from the iPad as all eyes turn to Hael. He's still slumped over, leaving his triple-meat burger and cheese fries cooling on the table. Nobody talks, but voices drift across the railroad tracks from the Fuller High hangout. We cut class early to have time to talk this out; guess we aren't the only ones who skipped out on sixth period today.

I watch them, in their pre-ripped department store jeans and Lululemon leggings, and wonder what life is like when you're just … normal. And no, it's not just a setting on a dryer. It's a reality. Either you blend in, or you stick out. And we, we most certainly stick out, like broken graves in a green lawn.

Hael finally lifts his head up as I glance back at him, his jaw tight, his eyes flinty.

"August twenty-ninth?" he asks, like that's not a date he wants to hear. "Fuck my life."

"You screw her on the twenty-ninth or what?" Vic snaps, lifting his own head back up and leaning forward to put his elbows on his knees. The way he looks at Hael, well, I don't envy the guy. "Speak up. I'm not exactly thrilled with you. On top of everything else, we now have to deal with this shit. The load's getting a little heavy, Hael."

"Don't you think I fucking know that?" he snaps back, his skin ashen as he rubs at his face again. His stubble is just starting to come through, and it's a much redder color than I expected. Just yesterday, I was admiring how clean-shaven he was. Just one day of thinking about Brittany, and he's stopped that routine entirely. "If you're starting to wonder if I might be getting psyched about this whole 'raising a baby with Brittany thing', then you clearly don't know me for shit." He pauses, working his jaw as his eyes flick back in the direction of the Fuller High kids. "Late August, Brittany stole the keys to her dad's lake house. We spent a weekend up there. I don't know if it was the twenty-ninth or not. Thing is, she didn't cheat on me until *after* we got back from that trip. So far as I know anyway."

Oscar checks something on his iPad and makes a hiss of disapproval.

"You were at the lake house on the twenty-ninth, most definitely," Oscar agrees, frowning as Vic sighs and grabs his cherry soda, flipping the plastic top off and using a flask of whiskey from his pocket to spike it.

"Alright, fine, you fucked her on the twenty-ninth or thereabouts. Keep going, Oscar. I haven't heard the tail end of this *but* just yet." Vic swigs his whiskey-laced soda, and then offers the cup up to me. I just glare back at him until he scowls and takes it away again. We are not friends, not today. I'm still pissed, and we have yet to actually talk about my feelings in detail.

"Did you use a condom?" Aaron asks, which, apparently, is

the wrong thing to say to Hael right now. He stands up and grabs his own milkshake, throwing it as hard as he can against the side of an old train car. It sits in the grass nearby, all its wheels missing save for one that's being eaten by rust. The side is covered in graffiti and now, strawberry milkshake.

It doesn't need explaining that the graffiti tagged on that car says *HAVOC.*

"Of course I used a condom!" Hael roars, and I'm surprised to see so much emotion from him. Gone is the cocky swagger, and the cocksure smirk. He looks like any other member of Havoc now, just a tortured, tattooed asshole with a chip on his shoulder. "Keep going, let's just roll through the possibilities." He snaps his fingers to get Oscar to keep going.

Oscar sits there with the iPad on his lap and gives Hael such a withering look that he finally sits down again, lifting a hand in an indication that Oscar should continue.

"We give her what she wants on the stipulation that she takes a DNA test at the earliest opportunity, and we require her honesty beforehand, to see if there's any other possible father."

"There's no way," Hael says, but almost like he's pleading, wishing he could change the past with a snap of his fingers. "It was just us at the lake house, and we were there for an entire weekend."

"Four days to be exact," Oscar corrects, and I wonder, if he's keeping such good track of everything, is he monitoring my fucking menstrual cycles, too? Dick. "But Brittany is— excuse the language—a whore. Likely, there are other candidates for her child's father."

"So we give her what she wants on a trial basis, and we

schedule a DNA test?" Vic asks, like he's mulling this over. "If the baby is Hael's?"

Hael makes a noise of protest but doesn't say anything.

"We tell her to kill Kali," Callum says, speaking up for the first time. He's eating his fries one by one, carefully pushing the length of each one between his full lips. His voice is as deep and dark as usual, like black velvet and forgotten promises. "Pretty little white girl like her, she'd get away with it. Then we'd have Kali off our backs, but a smaller body count to our own names."

"What is your body count by the way?" I ask, leaning back against the table and propping my elbow on the surface. "Because I'd love to know. You're all acting like …" I trail off for a moment and shrug again. "Like the other night wasn't the first time."

"It wasn't," Vic says, and my stomach drops. He turns back to Oscar. "Keep going. I'm not happy with any of this; it feels like we're getting screwed either way."

"If the baby is his, then we have her kill Kali. If it's not, Hael walks free and clear, but"—Oscar holds up a finger and smirks like the sociopath he so very clearly is—"she also has to sic her father and his task force of pigs on the Charter Crew."

Goose bumps rise on my arms, and I find myself grinning, even though I simultaneously want to punch Oscar in the nuts.

"Either way, it's a win," Oscar explains, folding the cover on his iPad and setting it aside. He isn't eating anything—in fact, I've never actually seen him eat before, not once—but he does have a cup of crushed ice next to him. Casually, he picks it up and places a single cube on his tongue, crushing it with his teeth as I stare at him. "I like the odds on this one, to be honest with you. Besides, it isn't like Hael would abandon his child anyway, so we may as well get something out of it."

"Although if it is his kid, we'll need to figure out a way to get rid of Brittany," Victor muses, just casually pondering the fate of some random teen like he wouldn't lose a minute of sleep over separating a mother from her child.

I always knew they were monsters, nice to see that I wasn't just running from shadows.

Everyone falls quiet for a moment, me sucking on my milkshake, Vic downing his booze-laden cola. Callum eats his French fries in silence while Hael sulks and Oscar crunches ice. Brittany arrives just fifteen minutes later, right on time.

Today, she's wearing a pretty yellow dress with an empire waist. It hides her growing baby bump admirably well.

"Hael," she says, looking right at him and refusing to acknowledge the rest of us.

"Sit and let's talk, Brittany," Vic says, and I get chills all over as I remember him saying the same thing to me as he kicked out a chair from under the library table. *Alright, Bernie, sit and talk.* "Let's discuss price."

"This better be something fair," Brittany whines, moving over to sit next to Hael. He scowls, but doesn't move, clearly resigned to his fate. Our eyes meet across the narrow space, and I feel a tug inside of me. It's one-part jealousy and two-parts regret. If we'd been able to reconcile our differences just a little bit sooner, then he wouldn't have slept with Brittany, and maybe she wouldn't be pregnant.

"Are you questioning us?" Vic asks, looking at her in just

such a way that most people would probably piss themselves. Giving credit where credit's due, Brittany just shifts slightly and looks away, refusing to make eye contact with anyone—even me. "Here's the deal: you're asking a lot. You're asking for a man's lifetime commitment."

"But it's his kid!" Brittany blurts, whirling around to look at Vic and then cowering back slightly. "If he didn't want to make a lifetime commitment, he shouldn't have slept with me."

Hael just folds his arms over his chest and refuses to look in her direction, leaving the interaction up to Vic and Oscar. Aaron and Callum are quiet, too, and I can't decide if that's just because they don't like Brittany or if there's something more to it. Aaron is still hurting from his GSW, I know that, and Callum … he's probably hurting on the inside, even if he won't admit it.

"We want you to get a DNA test as soon as possible," Victor says, nodding his head in Oscar's direction.

"I can get you in for an appointment at the Northwest Pregnancy Project in late November." He looks up from his screen to find Brittany staring at him. She has goose bumps all over her arms as she swings her attention over to me. I'm honestly surprised—but pleased—to see her shudder in horror. A grin spreads across my lips as I lean back, resting my elbows on the surface of the table. The pink demon tattoo on my chest catches the sunlight, and Brittany fixes her gaze on it. Probably safer to look at my tits than my face. If I were her, I'd avoid pissing me off if at all possible.

Bernadette Blackbird has a very short temper.

"So for the next few weeks," Vic says, lifting two fingers, "you'll have Hael as a partner, regardless. He will speak to your father with you; we will kick the shit out of whoever it is you want beaten up. You can even go on a fucking date together tonight." Vic ignores me as I narrow my eyes, turning my glare onto him. Some part of me recognizes that he's doing this shit on purpose.

He's jealous of Hael, no doubt about it. My eyes end up sliding over to Aaron's, and something unspoken passes between us. We need time to talk, just me and him, whether Vic likes it or not.

"Okay …" Brittany starts, putting her hand on her belly. "So then what's my price?"

"If the baby is Hael's, we're going to give you one of two options," Victor says with a smile. "One, you take on a very special mission and you get to keep Hael for yourself. For now though, we'll keep that mission a secret. If the time comes, and the DNA test agrees with your assessment, we'll re-evaluate things. You can take that deal, or you can choose option two." Vic's smile turns into a feral grin. "That is, you let Hael go and never speak to him again. In that case, you can either keep the baby for yourself or give it to us to raise."

"Are you fucking kidding me?!" Brittany chokes out, brown eyes going wide. "I'm not giving you my baby; I'd rather die."

"That's your choice to make," Vic says smoothly, and I can't decide if he's telling her that it's her choice to keep the baby or not … or if it's her choice to die. Knowing him, it could very well be either. He stands up, cracking his knuckles and shrugging his shoulders. "If the baby is not his, then you're going to fuck all the way off. Regardless of parentage," Vic takes a step forward and crouches down in front of Brittany, reaching out to lift her chin up. The way he does it, there's a sense of menace in the air. "You're also going to get your dad to sic his dogs on a target of our choosing."

"I can't control what my father does and doesn't do," Brittany snaps back, and Vic grabs her chin harder, yanking her face down toward his.

"Well, you better figure out a way to turn his head and *quick*. We wouldn't send him on a wild-goose chase: there's another gang we want him to deal with, that's it. Just redirect his attention away from Havoc and over to the Charter Crew."

"I don't know anything about the Charter Crew," Brittany simpers, but I notice she doesn't try to pull her face away from Vic again. Good girl. I just sit there, content to watch things play out. My gaze drifts back to Hael's after a minute though, searching for some sign that he feels this strain between us. My heart aches when I think of him leaving in the Camaro with Brittany.

He was always meant to be mine.

I turn away to look back at Brittany and Vic.

"Of course you don't," he purrs, reaching out to push some hair back from her face. She cringes and squeezes her eyes closed, all of that bitchy bravado she had yesterday fading away to nothing. Underneath it all, Brittany Burr is just a terrified preppy Fuller High brat. "And you won't learn anything about them until it's necessary. Let's just set this agreement up and then see how the DNA tests goes, shall we?"

"What if I can't get my father to agree?" she asks finally, as soon as Vic lets go of her face. I notice he's left red marks where his fingertips pressed into her skin. He stands up, looking down at her with an expression that reminds me that, no matter what sort of chemistry we have between us, I really don't know him for shit. I don't, I think, know what he's truly capable of. For some reason, the boys chose to go easy on me during sophomore year. If they'd wanted to, they could've destroyed me.

But not anymore.

I'm not the same person now as I was then.

I get up and move over to stand next to Vic, putting my hands on my hips and hoping I cut a pretty figure in my leather pants and jacket.

"You don't want to know what'll happen to you if you renege on this deal," I tell Brittany, loving how meek she is. Does that make me a bad person, that I enjoy power? That I enjoy finally being on the other end of the bullying? I think that maybe it does, but I can't help myself. The old Bernadette, the one who believed in daisies and dreams, she was shattered to pieces by the hammer of reality. There is no getting her back, no going back to who I used to be. As Alice once said, *there's no use going back to yesterday; I was a different person then.* "If you don't think you can pay up, then don't take the deal. Fuck off and raise your bastard kid by yourself."

"I'll do it!" Brittany snaps, shoving up to her feet. She glares at me, nostrils flaring, and then turns away again, like she can't bear to hold my attention for any longer than that. "What do I have to do?"

"Take Hael and go, tell him what you promised to tell him —who the other possible father is. And also who you'd like us to take care of. Don't let us see you before then. If you need to talk to Hael, text him but don't expect him to be a slave to your whims." Vic hooks his thumbs in the waistband of his jeans and looks Brittany over carefully. "For the next two weeks, he'll behave as a respectful boyfriend should, but not like a trained dog, do you understand and accept?"

"I accept," Brittany agrees, sealing her fate in blood.

"Jesus Christ," Hael murmurs, swiping his hand over his mouth as he grimaces. There's zero hesitation on Brittany's end as she grabs his arm and encourages him to find his feet.

"We have a prior engagement for Friday night, so don't expect cuddles and kisses all night long," Vic tells Brittany with a sharp laugh. *God, he's an asshole.* I stare at him and he stares right back in challenge.

"Fine," she snaps, clearly over her groveling for the time being. She proceeds to drag her ex toward his car.

On their way past, I grab Hael, my fingers burning as they curl around his wrist.

"Don't forget about me when you're on your little date," I say, hating the way the jealousy pulls me apart on the inside, like my bones are separating from the muscle, making my entire body ache.

"How could anyone ever forget you, Blackbird?" Hael says, the edge of his mouth curving up into a slight smirk. He flicks his honey-brown eyes my way as I release his wrist, and then turns abruptly in my direction. I don't expect him to touch me, or put up much of a fight, considering that Brittany's standing right there, and we just made a goddamn Havoc deal for him to be her boyfriend.

But, apparently, unlike Aaron, Hael is willing to test the

limits.

He puts his hands on my hips and leans in close, letting his lips brush against my ear.

"I feel like we owe each other a good, long fuck. What do you think, Blackbird?"

"I think if you screw Brittany—or hell, kiss her—even once during these two weeks, I'll castrate you the way you did Donald Asher." Hael lets out a howling laugh, and then reaches up to cup the side of my face. His thumb plays across my lower lip before he leans in and takes my mouth with his, searing me with an intensity that I didn't expect. Everything between me and Hael thus far has been … I don't want to say casual, but it hasn't been serious. This kiss is different. It's dead serious, a promise made with lips and teeth and tongue.

"This is bullshit," Brittany whines, standing off to Hael's right. "What sort of boyfriend act is this? Is this what I'm really paying for?"

A caustic laugh slips past my lips as I pull away from Hael and move over to stand in front of her, grinning like a goddamn maniac.

"Oscar already explained this to you: we are Havoc. You are not. You can't police what I do with my own family—no bargain can ever infringe on that."

"Blood in," Victor says, lighting up a cigarette. "Blood out."

Hael winks at me as he steps back, leading Brittany to the Camaro, and taking off with a squeal of tires and a cloud of dust.

I pretend like that doesn't bother me, but it does.

"Didn't realize you two were so close," Vic murmurs as he

pauses behind me.

Slowly, I turn over my shoulder to give him a sharp look.

"Then you weren't paying attention," I quip back. He scowls at me, but that's about it. Maybe he knows what a thin line he's walking?

I might be a part of Havoc, but if he wants me to be *his* girl, then he better shape the fuck up.

"Oh, and I have a few things I need to tell you," I start as Cal looks up, studying us with bright blue eyes. Victor just cocks a brow, and I feel this near-orgasmic satisfaction at the idea that I'm about to piss him off. "First, Callum and I almost had sex on Saturday, at the dance studio." Victor's eyes go wide, and he turns in a very slow, very scary sort of way to stare at his friend. Before Vic even gets the chance to respond, I forge on. "Second, I smashed Kali's face into a locker until she was bloody and unconscious. We might have some extra problems with the Charter Crew this week."

Victor's cold, dark gaze swings back to me, but for several minutes, he says nothing, just stares down at me with an inscrutable demeanor.

"You've managed to surprise me, Bernadette. And I'm not one who's easily surprised." Vic turns and heads over to his bike, climbing on and taking off in a cloud of dust, leaving me behind.

"He'll get over it," Callum says, but I notice that Vic isn't the only one who's irritated with him. Aaron looks pissed, too.

"I knew this was a bad idea," Oscar murmurs, but I can't decide if he's talking about Brittany … or me.

No, he's definitely talking about me.

Seeing how easily I can fracture these boys from within, I'm not sure that he's entirely wrong about that.

CHAPTER
EIGHT

The rest of the week goes by fairly quickly, but that doesn't mean it's peaceable or pleasant. I've got Principal Vaughn breathing down my neck, the Thing on the offensive, and a whole basket of trouble to unravel with the boys.

Also, Kali doesn't come back to school after our incident on Monday. Not once. That doesn't bode well for me. She's like a black widow, crouching in her web, waiting for the right time to strike.

By Friday afternoon, I'm actually looking *forward* to our usual weekend sleepover.

After class lets out, I meet Aaron out front for a ride. Now that Hael's on Brittany duty—fucking *Brittany*—I've been getting rides home with my ex. We've barely spoken to each other since I ground myself into an orgasm on his lap, but it's not the sex that makes things awkward—okay, maybe a little—but mostly, it's the feelings.

All the fucking feelings.

"You don't have to stay at Pamela's anymore if you don't want to," Aaron tells me, driving the minivan like a grandma through the school zone. I appreciate it, dare I say *find it cute*, when he does that next to an elementary school or something, but let's be honest: the world would probably be better off if he ran down a few Prescott High kids on the way.

"I know," I say, because the implication was always there. If I want to stay at Aaron's house with Heather, I can. Knowing I have a safe space to retreat to makes the stress-filled nights at home much more bearable. "But at least for now, Pamela still owns my ass. Heather's, too. I can't poke the bear until I'm ready to weather the bite."

Aaron doesn't say anything, keeping his green-gold gaze focused out the front window.

I shift in my seat, fully aware that we've got a ton of unspoken bullshit brewing between us.

"About the other day," I start, but he just shakes his head.

"We don't have to talk about that," he says, but how can we not? How can we keep going if he's going to play hot and cold faucet on me? Sometimes scalding, sometimes freezing. I can't deal with that crap.

"Yes, we fucking do," I snap, leaning back and putting my boot up on the dash. I don't look at Aaron, focusing instead on the white and black stripes of my shoelaces. "You told me you hadn't had a girl since me."

He clenches his teeth, like this is a sore subject for him. Can't say I blame him. It makes him sound … vulnerable. Desperate, even. Half of me is a little freaked out that he's managed to abstain from sex for so long while the rest of me is terrifyingly excited. Aaron is still mine. He's always been mine. If I wanted him, I could have him, couldn't I?

"I slept with two guys between you and Vic," I tell him, thinking about those one-night encounters. They were fine, adequate. I mean, I managed to get myself off, but I wouldn't write home about them. "One guy was a Fuller High basketball player. The other was an Oak Valley Prep student—not Donald though."

Aaron raises a brow at me, turning slightly to give me a questioning look.

"Really?" he asks, like he's having a hard time imagining it. I shrug my shoulders.

"The first guy's name … I can't remember to be honest with you. The second one, pretty sure his name was David, but I could be wrong." I muse over that for a moment, trying to get back into the headspace I was in when I slept with two strangers. Life has given me plenty of reasons to self-medicate, to turn to drugs, or alcohol, or even sex to numb the pain, but that's never been my forte. I don't internalize my pain, not anymore. No, the reason I hired Havoc was to *externalize* it. I don't want to punish myself over the bad things that've happened in my life. Instead, I want to punish the world.

"Why them?" he asks, and I just shrug, my leather jacket creaking. It's pink and cracked in places, but it's been through a lot, seen so much, and yet it still shines. I look fucking fly in it, I won't lie. Besides, it reminds me of Penelope.

"Because they were hot and available," I respond honestly. "I didn't sleep with them to forget you or anything else honestly. I'm a woman with needs, and that's it." I pause, thinking about it for a minute. "But they only satisfied me physically, that's it."

"You mean, not emotionally like Vic or Hael?" Aaron asks, his voice acidic. I chuckle, but I still won't look at him. Trapped in this car with Aaron, with all our baggage spilled around us in a gigantic mess, I feel like that girl who shook as she stripped her clothes off for the first time, who was afraid to take the plunge into sex, but who did it anyway because she was so in love. Aaron never pushed me, but I wanted to be as close to him as I possibly could. I got there, and then I was punished for it. When he pushed me aside, it hurt twice as bad as it could've if we'd never slept together.

"I wouldn't call Hael an emotional outlet," I say with a smile. Then again, knowing he's out with Brittany right now fills me with an impossible fury. But I've got enough going on that I don't need to dig into that. "Vic ..." What the hell do I say about Vic? Even I don't fully understand what he means to me, what he *does* to me. "Dude, you need to tell me what the hell is going on between you and Vic. I can taste your loathing like ash on my tongue." I make a clicking noise and a dramatic exploding gesture with my fingers.

"It's complicated," Aaron says, getting in line with all the soccer moms and stay-at-home dads to pick up his sisters. He even does it the right way while several parents struggle with the parking arrangement and end up driving the wrong way around the traffic circle, fucking up the flow of parent pickup time. Aaron kills the engine and sits back to wait for his sister and cousin. "I owe Victor everything, but at the same time, he *took* everything I had. So, I guess we're just even and floating in limbo."

"By take everything …" I start as Aaron turns away, staring out the window at passing traffic. It gets crazy over here at this time of day. By evening, it's one of the quietest, most pleasant streets in town. If I had the choice, I would send Heather to this school, instead of the one on the opposite end of town.

"I mean you," Aaron says, turning back to me with a deep frown etched onto his face. "He took you from me, in exchange for helping me with my sisters, that's what." I just stare at Aaron, willing him to keep going, to shatter a mystery I've pondered over for years. "I called Havoc before there even *was* a Havoc," he tells me, his tone acerbic and biting. "Part of my price for joining them was to give you up."

"See, that's the part I don't understand," I snap, sitting up, already shaking with the rush of emotion. I need to approach this conversation in a different way than I have before, because that's never gotten me anywhere. But I need to understand this. If I don't, I'm afraid I'll always be stuck in this rut, running over the same problems again and again. To truly and utterly become a part of Havoc, I need Aaron to be honest with me. "Why would they care if you were dating me or not?"

Aaron turns to look at me, narrowing his eyes like he thinks I'm playing dumb here or something.

"Are you kidding me?" he asks, his voice dry and bitter. "Vic is goddamn obsessed with you." I shiver and lick my lips, but I don't say anything. I can't let Aaron know that I *like* hearing that, that I want Victor Channing to be as obsessed with me as I am with him. "He's been obsessed with you for years.

Even in elementary school …" Aaron starts, trailing off.

"Even in elementary school, what?" I ask, but then Kara's tearing the back door open and scrambling into the van.

"Bernadette!" she says, reaching around the seat to hug me. I grin as I turn around, and she settles into her own seat, reaching out to take Ashley's backpack so her cousin can get in, too. "Are we going shopping for makeup? You said we could get makeup."

"I don't see why not?" I start, looking back at Aaron. He smiles at me, as if he didn't almost just admit something happened in elementary school, of all places. "Let's grab Heather, and we can go to the drugstore or something."

"Your wish is my command," Aaron says, but with a surprising lack of sarcasm. He starts the van and we head over to grab Heather. I feel like a shitty sister-mom, pulling her out of the afterschool program so often, but it's whatever works, right? Whatever it takes to keep her happy and away from her father's idle hands.

We go to the same drugstore where Hael and I got the morning-after pill, and I help the girls choose their makeup carefully. Aaron stands back at first, but Kara and Ashley are far more skilled at engaging him than I am.

He ends up posing with his hands out so they can use the tester makeup on his skin, deciding what they think will look best on their own eyelids. Aaron's gaze lifts up to find mine, and we both smile. It's a surreal moment, like something out of a fairy-tale that can never last. If Aaron hadn't joined Havoc, if we lived in a different world …

"This one," Kara declares, the last one to make her

selection. She's picked out a sparkly pink shadow that I know Penelope would've loved. My own sister can't abide by pink in any way, shape, or form, and has chosen a neon green that makes my teeth hurt. But that's okay, we'll figure out a way to blend it, so it doesn't look garish.

"What happened to your face again?" Heather asks as I grab some concealer and foundation for the angry pink gash on my cheek. I glance down at her and then lift my eyes up to find Aaron's. He's pursing his lips, a fire burning in his gaze that makes me awfully glad that I'm not Billie Charter.

"I got hurt at the Halloween party, I told you that," I say, refusing to lie, but unable to tell my little sister the truth. She narrows her eyes on me, and we both know she's smart enough to figure out that I'm not telling her the most important part of the story. I've been beyond careful to keep the stab wound on my arm hidden from her, too, but I know she doesn't miss the bloodstained bandages in the trash can in our bathroom. "Why don't you each pick out a piece of candy, too?" I suggest mildly, and it only takes the three girls a split-second to race toward the front counter together.

"Candy, huh?" Aaron asks, following me as I switch aisles and pause in front of the pregnancy tests. I don't even care that he's watching as I grab a few boxes. "Shit, Bern," he murmurs as I tuck them under my arm, grabbing some tampons and a box of disposal menstrual cups in case I get my period. "Do you think you might be pregnant?"

"I have no idea," I snap back at him, even though he's honestly being pretty damn nice right now. "I hope not." Closing my eyes, I take a calming breath and then glance over my shoulder at Aaron. He looks as ridiculous as Hael did in here, tattoos bathed in fluorescent light and silhouetted by sterile white walls. "If I were, would you hate me for it?"

He cocks his head at me, like he can't even fathom where I'm coming from right now.

"Are you fucking with me, Bernie? I could never hate you."

I look down at the items in my arms, and I feel so goddamn stupid all of a sudden. Victor is going to be the death of me. I'm going to end up pregnant and ruling the underworld of this stupid city. My breath escapes in a strong exhale, and I just feel so heavy all of a sudden.

"I'm not stupid; I understand how birth control works," I say, more to myself than to Aaron really. He reaches out with an inked hand and takes the boxes from my overburdened arms. The brush of his fingertips across my skin leaves me breathless as I lift my gaze again.

"You're not stupid at all," Aaron says with a bit of a scowl, his attention fixing on the kids for a minute, calculating their distance from us, determining their relative safety. It's what he lives for, after all, to protect his girls. "It's Vic. He's too intense for his own good. Havoc might be an acronym of our names, but it's his brainchild." Aaron turns back to me, expression softening as he taps his fingers against the side of one of the boxes. "Don't let him get to you, Bern. If you want to be with him, fine, but don't let him rule you."

There's no time for me to respond to that. Heather comes slinking around the corner, like she thought she might be able to eavesdrop on us for a minute. Too bad for her that I'm a master at that game.

"Ready to go?" I ask, ignoring her inquisitive stare as she tries to puzzle out what I'm holding in my hands. Luckily for me, Aaron has the pregnancy tests, so she doesn't see shit.

"Yeah, I guess," she says, getting pouty on me. She doesn't like how much time I'm spending with the boys. She hasn't said anything, but I can see it in her eyes. The thing is, she doesn't understand the half of it. I'm not just hanging out with friends here; I'm seeking justice for Pen. For her.

For myself.

We head to the front and Aaron pays in cash, taking the paper bag in his right arm as I lead the way to the door.

I'm not two steps into the parking lot before I realize something's wrong. The air smells strange, like gasoline and burnt rubber.

"What the hell is—" I start as Aaron reaches out and grabs me by my upper arm, yanking me back and out of the way of a speeding car. Several boys in clown masks lean out the window, chucking Molotov cocktails at the rear windshield of Aaron's van. They smash right through it, turning the vehicle into a blazing inferno within seconds. The fire sweeps over it like a gluttonous demon, gobbling it up with orange tongues and oppressive heat.

"Say hi to Vic for us!" one of the boys shouts as they speed off in fits of laughter.

Meanwhile, the girls scream, the van burns, and people come pouring out of the store to watch.

Guess that's it, isn't it?

This war is officially fucking *on*.

"Hell is empty, and all the devils are here," Oscar murmurs, frowning as Aaron paces ruts in the freshly mowed grass of his backyard. That's the first thing he did when we finished with the police and got Vic and Hael to pick us up, mowed his damn lawn. He did it shirtless, too, with a lit joint hanging out of his mouth.

Despite the shitty turn our Friday afternoon has taken, I won't lie about my panties being soaked from the sight. Sitting in a plastic chair with my knees to my chest, I wrap my arms around my legs and give Oscar a strange look.

Apparently, I'm not the only one here who thinks that was a weird thing to say.

"Dude, what the fuck are you talking about?" Hael asks, shaking his head and shoving his sunglasses up and into his red hair. He had to cut his date with Brittany short, and, since he only has four passenger seats in his car—I rode with Vic on the Harley—he had to drop the bitch off *here* before he could come to the police station for the girls and Aaron.

Brittany's inside now, sitting on the couch and scowling as she browses TikTok videos on her phone.

"It's a Shakespeare quote," Oscar replies smoothly, clearly annoyed at us for having to explain his intellectual prowess. "Which you'd know if you actually managed to pass your classes. It was a reference, to explain our current situation. Victor?"

Vic is watching Aaron carefully, like he expects him to fly

off the handle at any moment and go batshit. He rubs at his chin, proving that he's already deep in thought.

"Our plans for this weekend don't change," he says, and Aaron turns on him, the joint toppling from his parted lips.

"The fuck?" he asks as Callum kicks a leg up onto the plastic table between us and lights up another joint. He offers it up to Aaron, but he's not paying attention to anyone but Vic.

"We need to be proactive, not reactive," Vic says, which is probably true. My attention shifts to Aaron. Every fiber of his being screams violence. It's written in the tenseness of his muscles, the tightness of his jaw, the clench of his teeth. "Next weekend, we will deliver a package to the Ensbrook place. I have something nice in mind."

"They could've hurt the kids," Aaron snarls, shaking as he bends down to grab his discarded shirt. He drags it over his sweaty face, leaving bits of grass on his skin. I imagine if I were to get close to him, he'd smell like fresh grass and new sweat. My body tingles and I shift uncomfortably in my chair. "They could've killed them. Shit, they almost ran Bernadette over."

Vic glances briefly in my direction, but quickly turns his focus back to Aaron.

"And they'll pay handsomely for that—in time. If we start reacting to every little thing the Charter Crew does, that means they own us. Unfortunately for them, that's not the case. We are the masters of this city, Aaron."

Aaron just scowls, spitting at Vic's booted feet as he storms past and into the house. He heads straight for the staircase, pounding his way up. Even over the distant buzz of the neighbor's lawnmowers, I can hear his door slam upstairs.

He's in his room which, oddly enough, has sort of become my room when I'm here. Not sure what to make of that, but I like sleeping wrapped in his sandalwood and rose scent too much to bring it up lest I get banished to the room with the bunkbeds. Come to think of it though, after my marriage to Vic, I'll probably be sleeping in the downstairs bedroom with him.

"We'll need to procure Aaron a new vehicle," Oscar says absently, one, long finger sliding across the screen of his iPad. "I'll schedule it for next week, when we deal with Bernadette."

"Deal with me how?" I ask, but Callum's smiling, so it can't be all that bad. He lifts his hand up and flashes me his knuckles with the word *HAVOC* scrawled across them. He wiggles his fingers at me, and my own hand throbs in response. I cradle it to my chest, desperate to hide the sudden beating of my heart. Somehow, the idea of getting that tattoo makes this all seem more real, like … once I take that step, I can never go back.

"I'll take the girls to school for now," Hael muses, his face falling. "But they'll have to deal with Brittany's bitching on the way. Speaking of, what do you want me to do with her?"

"I already explained we had plans for tonight," Vic says, turning back to his best friend. "I don't give a shit if her date was cut short; shit happens. Take her home."

Hael works his jaw for a moment before turning and heading back into the house. It only takes about five seconds before the screaming starts.

"God help me, but I hate that woman with a passion," Oscar says, setting his tablet aside and steeling his inked fingers beneath his chin. He looks ridiculous, sitting out here in the sunshine in a suit and tie. He also looks dangerous as fuck. "We should kill her after the baby is born."

I choke on my own spit, but Vic just rolls his eyes, making me question whether that statement was serious or not. He did flat-out admit to me the other day that Danny wasn't their first body in the ground. How many others are there? I wonder if I should even ask.

"Finish that joint, and then get up. You and I have errands to run," Vic says, nodding his chin in Cal's direction. I wonder if the two of them have talked about what happened between me and Callum at the studio, or about what I did to Kali. I'm not about to ask because that'll give Vic exactly what he wants: confirmation that I can't get him out of my head, no matter how hard I try.

Cal salutes Vic with the joint and then takes a long drag, passing it over to me as he sits up. Our fingers brush, but I keep my body's reaction as hidden as I possibly can. But to deny there's chemistry there? I once read a book, some time loop story called *Devils' Day Party*, where the main character said, *"Lying to other people is insane; lying to yourself is suicidal."*

Pretty sure she was right about that. Oh, and her name was Karma. Talk about hitting readers over the head with metaphors, am I right?

"Bernie," Vic says, crouching down in front of me. This zing passes between us, making my breath catch in my throat. *Fuck you, Victor Channing,* I think, but I can't make my lips say the words aloud. "You and Oscar are going to run an errand of your own." He reaches out to take my hand, pressing something into my palm. I'm overwhelmed with the feeling of burning, certain that every place his fingers touched must be blistered beyond recognition. When I look down though, everything is as it should be, but for a single key. "Don't say I never did anything nice for you, princess." He leans forward, cupping the back of my head and pressing a scalding kiss to my lips before he stands back up.

"You and I have an errand to run?" I ask, looking askance at Oscar and doing my best not to curl my lip. Callum rises from his chair, leaning down to whisper against my ear before he goes.

"Good luck," he says with a small chuckle, disappearing into the house with Vic.

"And then there were two," I say, saluting Oscar with the joint the way Cal did to Vic. He stares at me with a wrinkled nose and a deep frown, like one might stare at a pile of dog shit. "What is this key for?"

"Well," he says, reclining back in the chair and letting his long body stretch out like a cat's. That's what it is, what he reminds me of. A fucking housecat, one who's well-fed but kills for fun, one with sharp claws and glistening canines. The thing is, for his threats to be effective, I'd have to be a mouse. Maybe, once upon a time, when the Havoc Boys chased me through the woods, I was one. Not anymore. "Despite the fact that you've barged into a smoothly running operation and thrown it entirely off its rails, Victor wants to continue with your list. I suggested we step back from it and deal with more pertinent matters, but apparently your cunt is made of glitter and rainbows."

I smirk at him, taking another drag on the joint.

"Curious about it?" I quip, raising an eyebrow, but Oscar just smiles at me like a shark who's scented blood.

"Not particularly. I'd rather eat razor blades. What are you doing here anyway, Bernadette?"

"Seeking vengeance, finding justice," I reply with a smooth smile, wondering how I'd have felt if Havoc really had come back at me with some bullshit price. They can't have known how deeply the thorn of want had embedded itself in my heart, how desperately I wanted to be one of them.

On the inside, underneath all of my ramblings about revenge for Pen and safety for Heather, am I just as selfish as the rest of the world?

"Boring," Oscar replies, standing up from the chair and loosening his tie. "And here I was actually starting to wonder if you were more interesting than that." He pauses next to me, leans down, and captures the joint between two inked fingers. "Now, let's go find your foster brother, shall we?" He flicks the joint into the ashtray and then disappears inside, leaving me to stare down at the smoking ruins with wide eyes.

My foster brother, Eric Kushner. Name number six on my list.

Well, fuck.

CHAPTER
NINE

Eric Kushner lives in a builder's grade McMansion on a quiet street. His is, surprisingly, the prettiest house on the cul-de-sac. It's a three-story white colonial with a red door and spiral-cut boxwoods that frame the large porch. He's even added to the charming ambiance of his all-American house by putting a bulb with a flickering flame in his outdoor light, making it look like a gas lantern.

When I first saw it, at age eleven, I was impressed.

It looked like such a nice place. When I walked in and smelled the lemon and sugar scent from the freshly baked cookies, I thought it smelled like a nice place, too. My foster father, a man named Todd Kushner, seemed like a nice guy, too. He was relatively young, only sixteen years older than his eldest son, and an investment banker to boot.

The Kushner Family was my first experience with the foster care system, and it was everything I'd dreamed it would be. I'd fantasized about what life would be like when I escaped my mother, when I finally had a real home with people who loved me, who wouldn't hit me, who'd buy me pretty dresses and fancy toys.

For about two weeks, the Kushners were everything I'd dreamed they could be. At first, I was disappointed that there was no mother figure here for me and Pen and Heather. But Eric and Todd, they were as nice as could be.

Until … they weren't.

Bile rises in my throat as I stand on the sidewalk, looking up at the five-thousand square foot house with a sense of dread. I barely escaped this place; Heather barely escaped this place. I don't think about Penelope, not right now.

"What are we doing here?" I ask as Oscar strides up the front walk like he owns the place. He gestures for me to follow him, pausing on the front porch and waiting for me to join him. It doesn't take a genius to figure out that the key in my hand goes to this house. Swallowing past the memories, I reach out and unlock it. When I hesitate, Oscar opens the door for me and gestures with his hand to indicate I should follow him in.

I glance toward my right, finding a blond woman standing on her front lawn, one hand over her eyes as she shields them from the sun, watching me. Her kids tumble around her feet, one on a plastic tricycle, the other waving around a hose. If I stand here for too long, she'll call security on us.

I smile, resist the urge to flip her off, and then stroll casually after Oscar, like I belong here. After all, I used to be a part of this family, too. From my mother's clawed grip to the Kushners' depravity to the insanity that is Havoc, it's no wonder why Vic referred to me as a beautiful nightmare. I've never been allowed to dream, after all.

Oscar closes and locks the door behind me. Not that it matters, considering we parked right in the driveway on Victor's Harley. It's so fucking flashy, impossible to miss. I had no idea Oscar knew how to drive a bike, but I guess he's just full of surprises, isn't he?

"Someone in the neighborhood is going to tell the Kushners we were here," I say, trying to resist the shiver of revulsion that comes over me as I stand in that palace of lies, as I think about Eric, pulling me onto his lap, his breath hot and stale against my ear. I was okay sitting there, at first, not like I was with the Thing. I wasn't afraid to sit with Eric; I was excited. He might've been a decade older than me, but he was my new brother, right?

"Does that feel good, Bernadette?" He'd asked, sliding his hand up my leg. I can't forget that moment, no matter how hard I try. I was wearing tights under my new dress, all gussied-up for a school play that both Eric and Todd had attended, sitting in the front row and filming me with their phones, beaming as proudly as the other parents in the audience. That's the part I can't forget, the way Eric smiled at me when I was performing, how happy I was. That, and the skim of his palm along my tights. *"Would you like it if I touched you just a little bit higher?"*

My hands curl into fists as Oscar takes in the place's mettle, making notes on his iPad. I'm just assuming he has all his work tied to the cloud. We haven't talked about the iPad I threw into the mirror, or the fact that I'm certain he still has access to that horrible video. How many times has he watched it? I decide I don't want to know the answer to that question.

"I'm counting on the neighborhood telling them," Oscar says, smiling sharply. His glasses flash as he turns to look at me. "What are they going to say? Two kids on a motorcycle walked into the house and then left, but yet nothing was disturbed?" He pauses for a moment, like he's thinking. "Well, I suppose you could steal a few small things, just for fun."

I narrow my eyes as Oscar continues down the hall, toward the gym and the bathroom that functions as a changing room for the outdoor pool. My nostrils flare. Pen and I had so much fun swimming out there. It didn't occur to me that Eric was filming us in our bathing suits for any reason other than posterity's sake.

Hah.

And at age eleven, I'd thought I was hardened to the world, that my experience with my father's suicide, and my mother's abuse, the Thing's rage ... I thought those things had taught me to see evil. How wrong I was.

I wait for Oscar, standing in the open kitchen/living room area with the faint smell of Eric's stupid *Straight to Heaven* cologne wafting in the air around us. The smell of it—like dark rum and patchouli—makes me sick, churning old memories that are better left buried.

When Oscar comes back and heads for the stairs, he pauses with one, elegant, inked hand waiting on the banister. As he glances down at me, I can see the challenge burning in his eyes.

"Coming with?" he quips, and then he continues on up the stairs, like he truly doesn't expect me to follow, like he thinks

I'll chicken out. Guess he doesn't know me as well as he thinks he does.

With a long exhale, I start up the stairs, pausing on the landing, my eyes focused on the door to the room that used to be mine.

One night, after weeks of discomfort, where Eric touched and cuddled me in ways just this side of inappropriate, he came into my room at night. He laid down beside me and pulled my nightgown over my shoulder, pressing his lips to my skin. I woke up right away, my body freezing up as his hand slipped down between my legs.

He still has a scar, you know, from where I hit him with the vintage toy firetruck that was decorating the nightstand beside my bed. Eric almost lost an eye. Every day since I've wished that I'd robbed him of his sight the way he'd robbed so many girls of their sense of safety.

Pursing my lips in determination, I follow after Oscar, taking the curving staircase one step at a time, the sound echoing in the vast palace that is the Kushner's home. My palm skims up the banister, caressing the metal railing as I remember running down these stairs in my nightgown, Eric's blood on my hands.

I ran down the street, and I didn't stop running until my feet were bleeding and my entire body ached. The next morning, I called my social worker—Coraleigh Vincent—from the phone at the antique store. She came alright, but when she got there, she wasn't on my side. Not even close.

I pause on the top landing, looking down the hallway at the rows of doors on either side. Oscar takes a separate key from the pocket of his slacks and unlocks one, like he's been here plenty of times before.

"Where did you get that key?" I ask, hanging back, hating the dark wave of suspicion that's washing over me. I should trust Havoc, trust their twisted view of the world. I paid them, fair and square. I'm one of them.

"Off a hook in the kitchen," Oscar says smoothly, pushing the door open and stepping inside. It takes me a minute to follow after him, wrapped up in old memories and pain. Penelope suffered here, too. Not quite as badly as she did with the Thing, but only because we weren't here long enough for her to be raped. Just molested. Just. I hate that I can even use that word in reference to my sister's sexual abuse.

After a moment, I gather my courage and move down the hall, entering an innocuous looking bedroom that's quite clearly decked out in Pottery Barn and high thread count sheets. Money. That's what it's decorated in: cold, hard cash.

Oscar starts looking through drawers right away, meticulously examining every inch but without disturbing anything. It's impressive, I'll admit.

"What are we looking for here? Evidence?" I ask dryly, raising an eyebrow. All Oscar does is laugh.

"What do you think this is?" he asks, his smooth voice a balm to the rage burning within me. Oscar is so goddamn calm, so cool-headed, so well-collected. "*Dexter?* We don't need any evidence. You said you wanted Eric Kushner dealt with, so he'll be dealt with." Oscar pauses to smile, reaching out a finger to touch a framed photo of Eric, all dressed up in his hunting gear and hauling a rifle, his dog by his side.

"Not the dog," I tell him, my voice threaded through with a deadly ribbon. Oscar glances my way, but just barely. "I hope you can see how serious I am about that."

"Don't worry, darling," Oscar oozes, infuriating me even further. "We're not such monsters that we need you to tell us the basic rules of morality. No kids, no dogs. Don't worry: there are other ways to make pigs squeal." Oscar picks up a photo of Eric and his father next, examining it carefully before turning it over. He removes the velvet backing and extracts the photo, folding it and sliding it into the front pocket of his suit. "How about the old man? Any qualms about taking him out with the trash?"

I think about Eric's father, Todd, smiling as he handed me a pink bikini and then sat down by the poolside to watch me swim, eyes hungry, tongue running across his lower lip.

"I don't care what happens to him," I say, shaking my head. "He never touched me, but he might as well have. He knows his son's proclivities and has no qualms about paying for them."

Oscar smirks at me, turning and heading purposely in the direction of a decorative bookshelf. Its shelves are covered with pieces of African art, a giraffe carved from wood here, a metal elephant there. Eric thinks of himself as a white savior, heading to other countries to 'save' people who don't need saving. Knowing what I know about him now, I'm guessing he does a hell of a lot more than just virtue signaling.

"What are you doing?" I ask as Oscar digs his inked fingers beneath the edges of the bookcase, swinging it open toward us and revealing a hidden room. My mouth drops open, but Oscar just smiles at me.

"Have you ever seen a bookcase with hinges?" he asks, cocking a brow before continuing inside. As soon as I get close to the opening, I know there are going to be things in there I don't like.

"It's a pleasure dungeon," he adds, and I just shake my head.

"No," I growl back, feeling my skin crawl. "This is a torture chamber."

Oscar doesn't say anything, moving into the room to look at the devices and their leather straps, their handcuffs, their ball gags. It's basically a BDSM paradise, but one where the participants have no say.

I vomit. For the second time in a week.

I don't mean to, it just happens.

Oscar doesn't look very sympathetic about it, wrinkling his nose slightly in disgust as I turn away from the smell.

"Don't clean that up; leave it for Eric to wonder about," he tells me, moving further into the room and letting his long fingers play across a Saint Andrew's Cross, a sex bench, a wall covered in handcuffs. There are cameras everywhere, but none of them seem to be on; their wicked eyes are dark and shrouded. *Eric doesn't just rape girls in here; he films it.*

I gag again, but nothing comes up, so I spit on Eric's bedspread and swipe my arm across my lips. The further Vic digs his claws into me, the more my numbness, my shield against the world, gives way. And the further I get into my list, the more wicked my reality becomes. It's no surprise that I've been vomiting lately. Over the Thing's video. Over Eric's torture chamber. My body is full of wickedness and hate, and it's only natural that I should purge.

Without a second thought, I move into the room and shove the cross over. It crashes into the floor, denting the shiny, dark wood planks and splintering in several places. Oscar raises a brow and turns back to look at me, crossing his arms over his chest. Panting, I start in on the bench, pushing it on its side and then yanking open a black cabinet on the wall. Inside, there are whips, chains, belts, dildos, all manner of filth and fury. I grab a *knife* that's stained with blood and try not to think about the things it's been used for—or the way it might've been used on me, if given the chance.

Tears are streaming down my face as I plunge the knife into the cushioned surface of the upturned bench, rending the leather to shreds, turning the room white with fluff. I don't stop there, emptying the cabinet and throwing everything on the floor. I'm not even thinking at that point; I'm reacting.

Oscar says nothing, does nothing, just simply stands there studying me as I bare myself to him in a way I never meant to. He's seeing the raw, unedited side of me and I find the reality of that terrifying. I'm pretty sure Vic sent us here together to, like, make us bond or some stupid shit. He's worried that we hate each other; I'm worried that he's right.

"Are you quite finished?" Oscar asks, lifting a delicate brow after I slump to my knees in the center of the ruined room. I can barely see the destruction in front of me. Instead, all I can see are memories, memories of Pen's face after she stepped out of Eric's room one night. Memories of her sad smile as she ushered me back to bed.

It was my fault that we came here, a place arguably worse than home.

I had no idea how bad Eric Kushner was, no fucking idea.

"I want to kill him," I say, looking up at Oscar. He doesn't seem surprised. Instead, he unzips his pants and my eyes go wide. If he seriously thinks something sexual is happening between us in this disgusting hellhole of a room, I may very well take the knife that's still clutched in my hands and cut his dick off.

So ... the reason nothing sexual could happen between you is because of the setting, Bernie? And not because he hates you, and you hate him?

Hate sex is pretty amazing though, right?

Instead of propositioning me, Oscar turns and pisses all over the wall. You wouldn't think someone could look arrogant or sexy taking a piss, but somehow, in his suit and tattoos, he does. His obvious disrespect and hatred for Eric doesn't hurt either.

My eyes find his fingers, holding his cock, and it's impossible to miss the tattoos on it.

An inked cock. A *pierced* cock.

Huh.

When he's finished, Oscar fixes his pants, and then retreats to the attached restroom to wash his hands.

"Let's burn it down," I say, after shoving to my feet and stumbling over to the doorway. At this point, I'd gladly do just that—with both Eric and his father inside—and then fuck Oscar in the ashes. It takes me a minute to realize the significance of that thought. Not the burning Eric and his dad alive part, but the fucking Oscar part.

"In good time, Bernadette," he tells me, lathering his hands up with careful efficiency and then drying them on a nearby hand towel. "In good time."

Oscar turns back toward me, studying me like he's never seen me before, and then proceeds to breeze past me and down the hall. I wander after him, lost in a daze. As I walk, I break things. A vase, a framed picture, a stabbed oil painting. I don't steal anything though. I want Eric to know that the motive here wasn't theft. Besides, I don't want anything from this place. Every item in here is tainted goods.

We hit up every room, and as we go, Oscar collects a few things here and there.

Once we're done, we head right back out the front door, and I watch as Oscar locks the house up tight. Instead of getting on the bike however, he opens one of the saddlebags and pulls out two cans of red spray paint. Across the street, one of the neighbors is mowing their lawn and watching us curiously.

"Leave a message," Oscar tells me, nodding his head and shaking up the cans in his hands before passing one over to me. I take it from him, studying the color printed on the label. *Violently Red.* Appropriate. "Something that'll make him think twice about reporting the break-in."

It only takes me a second to figure it out.

I take the top off the can and hand it over to Oscar, stepping up to the pristine white of the garage door and starting on the first word. He waits patiently behind me, watching as I leave my dark mark in the heart of suburbia.

"Hey!" the neighbor calls, moving across the street, his overalls covered in grass. "What the hell are you kids doing? Knock that off." Oscar reaches into his jacket and pulls out his revolver, drawing the hammer back before pointing it at the man. He glances lazily in his direction.

"Be quiet and bear witness," he tells him as the man's eyes go wide. I finish off the first can and trade Oscar for the full one. When I'm finished, I step back to examine my handiwork. "Read it aloud for us," Oscar muses, tilting his head to one side.

"I …" the man starts, his voice quivering. As soon as we're done here, he's going to call the cops, most definitely. Guess that puts a bit of a wrench into our plans. I decide I don't give a shit. "I … I fuck …" the man continues, choking on the awful words.

"I'm getting impatient," Oscar purrs, pushing the gun against the side of the man's head. "Say it."

"Kids," the man chokes out, falling to his knees in the grass. Oscar puts the gun away and nods briskly.

"Before you call the police, think about me coming back to your house and burning it to the ground with you inside of it. Otherwise, we have no qualms with you, just your pedophile neighbor. Something to think about." Oscar chucks the empty spray cans into the saddlebag, closes it, and pulls the key from his pocket.

We climb onto the bike together and take off.

Oscar offers me the first small kindness he's ever granted by pretending he doesn't see me cry.

CHAPTER

TEN

"How did it go today?" Vic asks, standing outside the front door to Aaron's place, his big arms crossed over his broad chest. His ebon eyes track my every movement, taking me in, absorbing me. We just stare at each other, and it becomes obvious that fighting this attraction between us isn't going to work. I can't just stand here and pretend like I don't want to forgive him for the things he's done.

"Why did you send us together?" I ask him as Oscar pauses beside me. He smells like cinnamon, something I never expected from him. That's a warm, homey sort of smell, and Oscar Montauk is anything *but* warm and homey. "You know how we feel about each other."

Victor just stares down at me, chewing on a piece of gum, and looking at me like he'd very much like to throw me against the wall and ravage me. I almost wish he would. I just … it's only been a week since the Halloween party. One week since I saw the video. Since Vic told me he was the only one who wanted me to be a part of Havoc. One fucking week since he told me that the Kali thing was more for my 'benefit' than hers.

"We're family, Bernadette," Vic says, looking up and away, and appearing far more regal than he has any right to. "The two of you are going to have to deal with your shit sometime, don't you think?" He pauses for a moment and then looks back at me.

It's impossible to miss the double meaning in his words.

"Why did Aaron dump me?" I ask him, tilting my head to one side. Maybe today isn't the best day to broach this subject, especially considering I've already picked a metaphorical scab and find myself bleeding a red as violent as the color of that spray paint. "When he joined Havoc, I mean. Why dump me? Clearly, you guys are okay with dating. Hael dated Brittany. So what the hell is up with that?"

Vic exhales and leans his head back against the side of the house as Oscar stands silently just behind and to the right of me.

"Not everything is my fault, you know?" Victor starts, closing his eyes.

"Yes, it is," I retort, crossing my arms under my breasts and wishing Oscar wasn't standing so close or listening so intently. "You're the boss, Vic. All the positives and negatives of that apply to you. So it is your fault. Aaron joined Havoc; I lost him." My nostrils flare as I stare at Vic, waiting for an explanation that I know is only going to make my shitty day worse, rather than better. "Why? Why couldn't you just let him have me."

"Everything comes at a price, even joining Havoc." Vic turns back to me and opens his eyes. "You know that, Bernadette."

"So, Aaron's price was to dump me?" I ask, my hands curving into fists. The front door opens and there he is, the man in question, watching me from gold-green eyes.

"Bern," he starts, resting a hand against the doorjamb. "Let's go for a walk, okay?"

"Victor isn't getting out of this!" I shout, losing my shit for a second. The last few months have given me a lot to take in. I act so badass on the outside, but buried deep down, there's a broken little girl crying her shattered heart out. That doesn't make me weak, though. No, instead it makes me stronger. I have to remember that. If you're just steel through and through, you'll sink. "He gets final say in the price. You didn't want Aaron to have me if you couldn't, is that it?"

"Bernadette," Aaron repeats, reaching out to take my arm. His fingers burn where he touches me, but I don't pull away. Instead, I turn to look at him, wondering how many more secrets I can take before I start to lose it. "Let me get my shoes on and we'll walk and talk, okay?"

I tear my arm away from him and turn toward the quiet street instead, moving through the grass to put some space between myself and Vic.

"For what it's worth, this particular incident wasn't just Victor's fault," Oscar says, and I glance back to see that Vic's already gone. Oscar stares back at me from behind the lenses of his glasses, as unreadable as always. "Some boys just don't know how to share their toys," he murmurs, moving into the house before I can respond.

What the actual fuck is that supposed to mean?

I stare after him for a moment, until Aaron steps outside in brown work boots with no laces, his jeans low-slung. He's in the process of pulling a clean, white t-shirt over his head. My eyes watch as the tight fabric clings to the hard planes of his chest, his erect nipples impossible to miss. He tugs the shirt into place, noticing me watching him, and flashes a small smile. It's a sad smile, though. It'd have to be, to pass between me and him with any sort of genuine feeling.

We've been through a lot, Aaron Fadler and me.

"I brought my wallet," he says as he comes up beside me, tucking a brown leather square into his back pocket. "We can stop and grab a milkshake or something."

I snort.

"You're still trying too hard to be the good guy," I tell him with a small shake of my head. "We aren't in junior high anymore. We're not going to stop and get a shake at the fucking soda fountain."

"Why not?" Aaron asks, pausing beside me. "What's wrong with that?"

"That's just not who we are anymore," I say, remembering a time when we were both relatively … normal. I look away, the wind catching strands of pink-tinged blond hair and swirling it around my face.

"See, that's where you're wrong, Bernie," Aaron says quietly. I turn to find him staring at me with an intensity I wasn't sure he was capable of. On the inside, I'm still waiting for him to stand up to Vic for me, to fight for us. On the outside, I give him nothing, despite the desperate pleading in his stare. "We might live in the dark, but that doesn't mean we're not allowed to enjoy the moonlight."

With another scoff, I turn away and start down the sidewalk. With his long legs, it doesn't take Aaron long to catch up to me.

"That's something the girls have taught me," he says, tucking inked fingers into the front pockets of his jeans. He almost looks his seventeen years when he does that, hunching over slightly. Most days, I'd peg him in his mid-twenties. Guess that's what hardship and violence will do to a person. We age faster than most. "You have to find happiness wherever you can, whenever you can, because you never know when you might be sailing into a storm."

I walk faster, acting like I'm annoyed at him and his stupid metaphors. Little does he know, I like metaphors. The world is too complicated sometimes. It's much more palatable if you break it down into pretty words and flowery phrases.

"Bernadette," Aaron repeats, reaching out to grab my arm. I try to tear away from him, but he doesn't let me go, yanking me close so that we're chest to chest. I look up into his face and something dark clogs my throat. *You're not allowed to look at me like that,* I think, heart thundering. *You're not allowed to look at me like I matter, not after what you did.* "Being a part of Havoc has to mean something." He pauses, but he never takes his eyes off of mine. "There *has* to be a sacrifice of some kind, or it's just a meaningless oath."

"Yeah?" I quip, trying to swallow past the darkness clogging my mouth. It's thick and cloying, and it tastes like ash on my tongue. *Maybe this is what Aaron meant when he said that to me?* Because it feels like my mouth is coated in charcoal. "What was my sacrifice then?"

Aaron's face softens, and he reaches up an inked hand to cup my cheek.

"You always wanted a normal life; now you'll never have one," he says quietly, almost reassuringly, like he expects this revelation to rock me. "That's all you ever wanted, Bernadette." I shove his hand away, but Aaron just puts it on the curve of my waist instead. "And all I ever wanted was you."

"Whose idea was it?" I ask, shaking all over. I have that urge to start running again. If I wasn't worried about the Charter Crew picking me up off the side of the road, I might do just that. "For you to give me up."

"All of them," Aaron says, sighing and finally dropping his hands to his sides. I hate to admit how empty and lonely I feel without him touching me. "You've seen how it works, when we come up with a price."

"You could've said no," I snap back, all of that old hurt and anger rushing to the surface. No matter how many times I try to pretend like it doesn't affect me anymore, it's a lie. I'm not sure I'll ever truly heal from that pain. "You could've walked away."

Aaron turns his head and puts a tattooed hand over his mouth, closing his eyes.

But just as I've told him before that I could never go to Nantucket, he could never pass up on Havoc's protection for his sister and cousin. We're both just repeating the dreams we had for each other, dreams that are too far from reality to ever come true.

"They're your friends," I choke out, on the verge of tears

again. For two years, I didn't cry. I missed Pen with every breath I took, with every step, every heartbeat, but I didn't cry. I can't seem to stop doing just that now. Like I said, it must be a purge of some sort, a chance for my rattled spirit to expel all of that darkness out through my mouth. "They could've helped you without bringing you into the gang."

"We're not a gang, Bernie, we're a family," Aaron says as he drops his hand to his side. There's a tattoo on his right bicep that I've seen before, but that I've refused to acknowledge. It's my name, written in cursive across a red heart for all the world to see. I haven't let myself really *look* at it until now. Because it means too much. Because me being in Havoc means that Aaron and I … don't have to be apart anymore.

Havoc is a family.

I'm a part of that family.

Aaron is a part of that family.

"These things are signed and sealed in blood; they cannot be undone." That's what Oscar said, isn't it? Aaron and I are inextricably tied now. Forever and always.

"Why couldn't they help you without giving me up?" I ask, and this time, I just acknowledge the fact that I'm crying again. *I must be about to start my period,* I think, but that's such a stupid copout and I know it. "They knew how happy we were together; they could see it. Vic was jealous." This last part comes out as sharp as a whiplash. Aaron looks back at me and nods.

"He was. He's always loved you, Bernadette. I'm sure you've noticed that?" I say nothing, because it's true. I've noticed. There's proof of it enough on that paper. *Victor*

Channing punched me in the face between first and second period for saying Bernadette Blackbird was hot. "Sometimes I hate him so much it hurts. Sometimes, I even want to kill him for what he made me do." Aaron leans back against the trunk of a tree edging the neighbor's yard. I wonder how long it'll take them to come outside and yell at us? "But then I remember that he let us have each other, once upon a time. Freshman year was ours. I didn't know my dad was going to die, and my mom was going to leave. I thought we had forever, Bernie, that we could be normal *together.*"

Aaron shrugs his big shoulders and sighs again, kicking one boot up to rest the sole against the tree trunk. He doesn't look at me as he continues.

"If I was stronger, we could've been. But I wasn't. And neither were you." He turns back to me, but I can't deny it. That memory of his father's funeral plays fresh in my mind. I can hear my own thoughts echoing back at me. *I don't know how to help. That happens sometimes, when one broken person tries to lean on another. We're too rickety to keep the other standing.* "So I let you go. It killed a part of me I wasn't sure I could ever get back." Aaron taps two inked fingers—interestingly enough, the two with the A and V on them—against the Bernadette tattoo on his right arm.

"Wasn't sure," I say, my heart beating like a live thing inside my chest. I feel lightheaded and dizzy, like I might need to reach out and hold onto something to stay standing upright. Unfortunately, the only thing to grab onto right here is Aaron himself. I'll admit: part of me is *afraid* to touch him. I don't know what'll happen between us if I do. "Past tense. But you feel differently now?"

Aaron's mouth curves up into a smile. There's enough good boy hidden underneath that cocky smirk that I feel a bite of nostalgia, but not too much that I don't think he could curb stomp someone for me.

Fuck if Aaron Fadler doesn't make me feel safe. Even after everything. Even *with* everything we're dealing with now.

"You didn't just say it to me," Aaron says, pushing off the tree and stepping forward. He doesn't touch me, but I wish he would. I grit my teeth against the emotion and curl my hands into fists by my sides.

"Say what?" I ask, but I already know. *"You're right. I do love him."*

"You told Vic you loved me." Aaron's smile gets a little wider, but I don't know what he expects will come of this. We can't just go back to the way we were … but then, I don't see why we can't start something new? That rose and sandalwood scent of his wafts over me, and I close my eyes. "I didn't think you'd be able to feel for me ever again. And then to say it to Vic's face?" Aaron chuckles and shakes his head, reaching up to run his fingers through his chestnut hair. "That, I *really* didn't expect." He pauses again, his smile softening into something deeper, more melancholic. "You love Vic though, too, don't you?"

I can't deny that—it would be a lie—but I also can't force my mouth to say the words either.

"Does it matter?" I ask instead, my voice much softer than I want it to be. "Love isn't logical, and it doesn't have limits." I look back up at Aaron to find him watching me like I'm something precious, like dandelion fluff that might blow away in the wind if he breathes wrong. See, Aaron doesn't know the new Bernadette very well. He might've been an expert on the old one, but he has a lot to learn. "What are you proposing?" I ask, and he shrugs.

"Well, to start off, I'd like to take you out for a milkshake." His smile gets a little saucier, ratcheting up into a grin. "And then maybe we can talk about not hating each other?"

"I've hated you in a way I've never hated anyone else," I say, giving a small shake of my head. "I can't explain it, but I think there's a special sort of hate that blooms from love."

"Yeah, it's called love-hate, and I hear the sex is off the charts." Aaron cups the side of my face, running his thumb along my bottom lip. When he leans in close, I get butterflies. Fucking butterflies. Like I'm fifteen all over again. "But we can take it slow."

"Why?" I ask, tilting my head to look at him. He really is gorgeous, always has been, but even more so now that he's filled out and dripping with ink. "The sex is the easy part. It's the feelings I struggle with."

I turn and start down the sidewalk, listening for the easy fall of his footsteps as he hesitates and then follows after me.

"Sex isn't easy, Bernadette. Don't start telling yourself that." Aaron walks a bit faster, overtaking me with his long strides. I catch up to him at the next crosswalk, but neither of us says anything. Instead, he reaches down and takes my hand in his, curving his *HAVOC* stamped fingers around mine.

That gets me right in the heart, an arrow that I can't pull out for risk of bleeding to death.

We walk the last few blocks together like that, like a fairy-tale couple who lives in a tower, safe and solid against the wicked of the world. I notice as we go that Aaron's eyes track side alleys, thick foliage, empty houses with *For Sale* signs in the yards. Occasionally, he nods, and I get chills down my spine.

We're being watched, by Havoc's crew.

"How many people do you have working for you?" I ask, thinking of Halloween and the dozens of skeleton-masked boys —and interestingly enough, *girls*—that appeared from the crowd. Aaron smirks slightly, eyes focused on the old-fashioned soda fountain down the block. It was built in 1915 and used to be a popular Fuller High hangout before Havoc kicked their asses across the railroad tracks. They still serve malts and Shirley Temples and all that old-timey shit in there.

"Even I don't know the answer to that." Aaron pushes the door open, bells tinkling in our wake, and I swear to fuck, every face in that room turns to watch us with wary eyes. Where Havoc goes, trouble follows. "Only Vic and Oscar do," he adds as we head up to the counter and several students clear the red-leather stools to make room for us. "I could ask if I wanted, but I don't."

Aaron orders two chocolate shakes for us and then parks his chin in his hand, elbow resting against the cracked old countertops.

"I can't believe they fire-bombed my van today," he says absently, tapping his fingers against the side of his face. The car is trashed, by the way, a burnt shell of its former self, and yet another flame-washed memory of his mother. We told the cops it seemed like a random act of violence; they didn't believe us for shit. I'm sure the news of today's incident has already made its way back to the Thing.

"Are you going to get another car?" I ask, thinking of the two grand I buried in the backyard. That's enough for a shitty clunker. Maybe I should buy one? I don't have a license, but frankly I need to get on that shit. Having a car and being able to drive it, that's a tool I need in my arsenal.

"Havoc will get me another car," Aaron replies smoothly, sitting up as our milkshakes are slid across the counter to us. He stirs his with a metal straw as I cock a brow in question.

"Aaron, you *are* a part of Havoc. You're the fucking *A* in the equation. How much money do you guys have squirreled away?" It's difficult for me to gauge what the guys have going on finance wise. They all still live in relative dumps, Oscar and Callum don't have rides, and yet, Vic gave me two thousand bucks and told me I have twenty grand to plan our wedding.

Our wedding ...

Shit.

Just thinking about it gives me the chills.

"About fifty thousand," he says, lifting those beautiful eyes of his to mine. They're mosaics of color, like some wicked god dropped to earth for an afternoon to play with gold and green tiles. A lot of care was put into those irises of his. "We'd have more, but Victor likes to reinvest. We pay all our guys, too." He shrugs his big shoulders and gives a caustic laugh. "Once he gets his inheritance, everything will be different."

I exhale and take a sip of my drink, just to give myself a moment.

"Do you have any idea how much is on the line?" I ask, looking down at the ring on my finger. The temptation to run is still there. I think it'll always be there, this sweet far-off promise of a life without worries, without bloodshed and pain. But I've made my bed here, and I plan to sleep in it—even if it's a forever sort of sleep.

"Millions," Aaron says, looking up at me. He leans close, one of his legs going between my own. I swallow hard, but I don't say anything as his knee brushes up against the crotch of my pants. "So much money that it's hard for me to hate the idea of you marrying Vic." Aaron reaches out and slides his warm hand over the top of mine.

"Hard for you to hate it, but you still do?" I ask, and he smiles. This time, it's a real smile, one that's painted in shadows and darkness. He isn't pretending to be the old Aaron, all soft fluffy clouds and sunshine. This time, he's letting me see a little piece of who he's become over the last few years.

"I hate it so much that it keeps me up at night," he tells me, shifting his knee so that it rubs against me in a tantalizing sort of way. There's a dam between us, one that's going to come tumbling down. As soon as it does, I won't be able to resist the flood. It's going to sweep me away and drown me. "You as his wife, Bernie?" he says with another low laugh. His eyes meet mine, and a zing shoots through me, like a bullet pinging around inside my body, making me bleed, causing internal damage. Might be sort of fucked that that's the analogy I go straight to, but I can't help it. Aaron … he's painful to look at sometimes, a reminder of things that could've been. "You were meant to be mine."

I swallow the lump in my throat and turn back to my shake. *Screw you for making me feel fifteen again,* I think as I put my lips around the end of the straw. For some stupid reason, I turn my eyes to his just as I take the damn thing in my mouth.

"If you wanted me to be yours, why do you let Vic push you around? Stand up for me, Aaron." I suck on the straw, and his eyes flash. Aaron reaches out, grabbing me by the elbow and yanking me off of the stool.

"I let him push me around because I feel like I don't deserve you, Bernie. I let you go once; how can I ask you to come back?" He smirks at me, pulling me up against his chest. It's impossible for me to miss the hard bulge pressing into my stomach. Aaron has a huge dick; there's no hiding that. "But maybe you're right? Maybe I'm thinking about this in the wrong way? I'm not the good guy anymore, and I can never be that person again. So, maybe …" He leans down and licks a bit of chocolate from my lower lip. "I just take what I want, regardless of whether I deserve it or not?"

"I'm not sure that I'd say no to that," I whisper, my voice hoarse and low, like I'm in a bedroom, naked and wet, and not standing in a buzzing restaurant surrounded by my peers—most of whom I dislike with a passion.

"What if I were to tell you to get in the fucking bathroom?" Aaron asks, and I swear to god, something breaks inside of me. My numbness, my shields … the final piece shatters, and I'm left feeling like I'm floating. All of a sudden, I don't know who I am anymore. I feel both vindicated and vulnerable, all at the same time.

"Sounds like you're still asking," I manage to choke out.

Aaron wraps an arm around my waist and scoops the other underneath my knees, lifting me up into his arms like I weigh nothing at all. My breath escapes in a rush as I weave my arms around his neck.

"Stay out of the bathroom for a while," he announces, loudly enough that everyone in that room hears him. "And if you think you can quite literally catch me with my pants down, I'm packing a .22 in my boot." Aaron sweeps me toward the bathroom, kicking the swinging door in and setting me down on the counter.

My heart throbs painfully in my chest as he sweeps the stalls, checking to see if there's anyone else in here besides us.

There's not.

And there's no lock on the door, but you'd have to be a total idiot to disobey a direct order from Havoc. You know, like Kali Rose or something. Queen of the morons.

"Do you have a condom?" I ask, and Aaron shakes his head.

"Luckily, we're not far from South Prescott," he teases, grinning at me and running his hand over his beautiful chestnut hair. "No condoms on me—I'm not goddamn Hael or anything —but I do have quarters." He reaches into his back pocket, pulling out his faded leather wallet and dumping several quarters into his palm. Aaron puts them into the dispenser on the wall, twisting the knob until a single condom falls out into the tray. Usually, you only see this sort of shit at, like, truck stops in the middle of nowhere or something, but like Aaron said: we're close to South Prescott, the worst neighborhood in the city of Springfield, Oregon.

For once, I'm a little excited about that.

"If you really are pregnant," Aaron says, pausing in front of me and leaning forward to put his face near mine. He puts a hand on either side of me, pressing our foreheads together, just like we did the other day, just like we did when we were kids … just like we did when we fucked in tenth grade that one time. "Then we'll take care of you. *I'll* take care of you, if that's what you want."

"You'd raise another man's kid?" I ask, certain that I'd visit a Planned Parenthood before I'd become a teen mom, but still …

"Well, this wouldn't be another man's kid," Aaron says with a cocksure smirk. "It'd be a Havoc kid." He kisses me hard on the mouth and I spread my legs to welcome him close. We press our bodies together, and this surge of need takes over me. It clings to my skin, heavy and sticky, as I frantically tear at Aaron's shirt, trying to get it over his head. "Bern," he groans, biting my lower lip and reaching over his shoulder with one hand. Aaron grabs the white tee in his fingers, breaking our kiss just long enough to rip it off and toss it aside.

My fingers play with his belt as our tongues slide together, like two slashes of heat, probing, digging, trying to stir up memories and create new ones, all at the same time.

"Aaron …" His name slips from my lips without my even meaning it to. Tears sting my eyes, and I do my best to swipe them away before he can see. Aaron stops me by grabbing my arm with gentle fingers. With his other hand, he reaches up to swipe away a single teardrop with his thumb. "Cut the sentimental crap," I snap, but … that's because my anger is a defense mechanism.

We all have them, me and the Havoc Boys.

"I can't decide if I'd rather taste your cunt or look into your eyes," he murmurs, putting his forehead to mine. It's a racy statement, but it's said with such affection that I'm not really sure what to do. "I could spend all day worshipping your body, Bern. I want to get to know you all over again, search you until I could map every inch, every tattoo, every scar."

I suck in a sharp breath as he drops his hands to my jeans, popping the button and unzipping the fly.

"I'd like that," I start, feeling that strange rawness in my soul again. Aaron is like an antidote for bullshit. He looks at me like I'm not wearing a leather jacket, like I'm not tattooed, like my tough-as-nails persona isn't a shield against him the way it is for everyone else. He can see past it all, right into the soul of his first love, his first time, his … girl. "Just maybe not in a public restroom, okay?"

Aaron laughs, and the sound is easily the most genuine of all the boys. His girls have given him that gift, allowed him to keep true joy in his heart somewhere. It might be just a pinprick in the black cavern that makes up his chest, but it's there nonetheless.

"Mm, fair point." He curls his fingertips under the waistband of my jeans and kisses me at the same time, savoring the moment, dragging it out until I'm squirming and he's chuckling against my lips. "Okay, okay, I get it. You want my dick."

"Keep talking like that, and there is no reunion of bodies, Aaron Fadler." I'm soaked in sweat already, my heart pounding so loud that I can't hear the chattering of students in the dining

211

room anymore. No, it's just me and Aaron now, just the two of us, like it used to be.

He slides my jeans down my hips, knocking one of my boots off so he can slip my right leg out. He doesn't bother to remove my pants entirely, not here, not with graffiti on the walls and flickering fluorescent lights above us.

Still, even with the less than perfect surroundings, I'm not sure that Aaron's ever looked more beautiful to me. He shoves my jeans out of his way and then steps up close to me again, undoing his own pants. When he takes that beautiful inked cock of his into his hand, my lips part and my eyes flick from his dick to his face.

I almost tell him not to use the condom; I want us skin to skin. But at some point, I need to start taking responsibility for myself, for the possibility of a future beyond the immediacy of my own base needs.

Aaron puts the condom on, slicking it over his cock and then grabbing me by the ass. He holds me easily in his big hands, lifting me up off the counter and then slamming us into the wall next to the bathroom door.

My fingers dig into the back of his hair as he thrusts in, hard and deep, filling me up in one go. For a split-second, neither of us moves, readjusting to each other, letting muscle memory remind us that we were once lovers.

Then Aaron starts to fuck me.

I'm surprised by the wild rapidity of his thrusts, by how desperately he holds me, clings to me. I start to get lightheaded, my breathing shallow, like I can't possibly take in too much air or there won't be room for Aaron. He's inside of me in more ways than one, taking over me, diving deep.

My eyes close and I groan, the sound echoing around the room. Outside the door, I can faintly hear the other Prescott students laughing. Maybe at us, I don't know, but it doesn't matter. Not like they're going to anything to my face.

Aaron is driving into me so hard that I ache in the best possible way. There isn't an inch of me that he doesn't rub against, brush against, touch. He's rubbing against me at the same time he's thrusting, nuzzling my neck, kissing me, making sure I'm really here, that he's really inside of me, that we're really together.

"Oh, Bernie, I missed you," he murmurs, slowing down. Aaron leans back to look into my eyes, slowing the movement of his hips slightly. *In and out, in and out.* There's a tenderness in his eyes, a desperate sort of affection that I want to see him fight for. But later. Later. Right now, I just want him to touch me, press his body to mine, crawl inside my soul.

We stay like that for a while, stuck in an unbroken rhythm that might as well be torture for my overheated body. I'm soaking wet now, probably drenching Aaron's thighs. Doesn't matter though. That's the best part, I think, the mess of it. Sex isn't supposed to be pretty. It's too wild, too base, but it also keeps you grounded.

We are souls having a worldly experience, but we are also *human.*

My body clamps around Aaron, pulsing against him, making him groan as he takes my mouth with his, murdering my inhibitions. My first orgasm is easy and slow, like a lazy star streaking across a night sky. It makes my stomach muscles clench, the pressure in my spine unfurling like a flower.

Aaron, though, he doesn't just let me enjoy it.

No.

Something changes when he sees my face like that, my shields down, my inhibitions stripped raw. His expression shifts, old anger surging into him. Aaron moves away from the wall and drops me to my feet while I'm still shaking and struggling to catch my breath.

He spins me around and then uses a palm on my lower back to shove me over the counter.

He enters me again with a violent thrust and I bite my lower lip, fingernails digging into the countertop as he rams into me, balls slapping, the sound of it taking over the room. I'm drowning in that sound, the noise of our lust.

He made love to me ... now he's hate-fucking me.

And I *love* it.

Arching my back, I press into Aaron, moving my own hips so that we make a pretty little push and pull, our moans mingling together. Mostly, I keep my eyes closed. Because I want to *feel* Aaron, not see him. I watched him for years, dated him, lost him, watched him again. I've done plenty of looking and I'm sick of it.

His fingers wrap my hair and pull my head back but still, I keep my eyes closed. I can feel the fingers of his other hand grabbing my hip, bruising, squeezing. Aaron powers into me, fast and hard and furious, until his muscles clench up and I feel his body tightening behind me.

With a desperate groan of relief, he spills himself while still trapped inside of me. After a few, final thrusts, he releases my hair and I lean my cheek down against the countertop for a moment. My body is still throbbing, but I don't care. It was so worth it.

Before I can stand up though, I feel the air shift around me as he pulls out and then crouches down behind me. The heat of his breath brushes against my pussy just before he makes contact with his lips. His hands slide up my bare thighs and he holds me in place as he dips his tongue into my sweet honey.

Shit.

Aaron is just as good as Hael, but in a different way. Hael is slick, easygoing, confident to the point of arrogance. I could feel all of that in his tongue. Aaron, though, he's more concerned with seeking out my specific pockets of pleasure, two fingers borrowing lube from my pussy to slide across my clit.

He takes his time, too, despite our current situation, working me with his mouth until I'm crying out, slamming one of my palms into the mirror and coming hard against his lips. Also, I probably soaked the shit out of his face.

We sit there for exactly six breaths before Aaron stands up, and I lift my head to stare in the mirror, my eyes locking with Aaron's in the reflection. It's spotty, the glass twisted and warped in spots, but I can still see what's important: Aaron, me, and our feelings for each other.

I never fell out of love with him, that's the truth. I just started hating him on top of it. We just made love … and then he hate-fucked me. It's a dynamic that works. As Aaron steps back and I push up to a standing position, I wet my lips with my tongue.

He groans as he leans back against the wall, fixing his pants while he struggles to catch his breath. I love that, watching his tattooed chest rise and fall with each desperate inhale.

You're so human, Aaron Fadler, I think, and I smile.

"Don't lick your lips like that," he tells me, disposing of the condom and washing his hands. I stay leaning against the counter next to him, watching him. "You'll get me hard all over again, and the poor Prescott kids won't get to piss for hours yet."

"You really think you can go for hours?" I quip back with a grin. I feel weird right now, an emotion I don't understand flickering inside of me. Since I don't recognize it, and I don't want to ruin the moment by trying to delve into it, I just push it aside. "That's some serious bravado, Fadler. I'd like to see you prove it."

He turns his head to look at me, a smug smirk taking over his lips. He might be the nicest of the Havoc Boys, but he's still a boy and therefore, still an asshole.

"Mind if I do that sometime?" he asks, standing up and drying his hands off on his jeans. "Take you to bed and show you exactly how long I can go?"

I just smile back at him. Let him have that smug male sense of satisfaction. The kitty cat inside of me purrs and arches her back. I've taken three of the Havoc Boys to bed. I *knew* that I'd end up sleeping with them when I called out that word. Idiot that I am, I tried to lie to myself and pretend that it was all out of duty and obligation.

In reality, it was obsession.

Do the boys owe me retribution for their wrongs?

216

Sure.

But nothing is as sweet as salvation.

Someone like Kali or the Thing or Pamela, for that matter, will never be worthy of redemption. But the boys will. Are.

I bite my lip.

"Can we get a burger or something before we go home?" I ask, and Aaron laughs, reaching out to grab me by the hips and pull me close. It's strange, I'll admit, how easily we fall back into touching each other. He strokes my hair back, putting his face up against mine. The way Aaron touches me, I can sense it in him: he thinks we're on a timeline, too. He's going to touch me as much as he can because he doesn't know when it might stop, when we might be separated again.

That's how all the kids at Prescott High live, like we have no future at all.

That's something I'd like to change, if I could.

Maybe one day.

"A burger, huh?" he asks, and just his breath against my ear makes my body spasm with need. My fingers dig into the skin of his bare back. We should probably find his shirt ...

"Well, I'm hungry. You tired me out." I *sound* like Bernadette, like the big bitch on campus, but ... on the inside, I'm a kitten in his arms. Whereas Vic turns me into a lion and makes me want to roar, Aaron makes me purr like a baby.

"I suppose I can do that, treat you to a burger and fries. Honestly, our milkshakes are probably melted puddles by now, so I'll guess we'll have to order another round." I nod, but for just a split-second there, I can't speak.

Because I've just felt that flicker of emotion again, like a firefly trapped in my soul.

And, I've just figured out what it is: happiness.

Aaron makes me happy.

How weird is that?

CHAPTER ELEVEN

Two and a half years earlier ...

Aaron Fadler

What the fuck have I done?

I'm kneeling in the grass outside of Prescott High, my head bent over, crushed between my hands. I can't listen to Bernadette scream, not without breaking down and pulling my gun on Victor. How can he be so cruel when he loves her so much? What the hell is wrong with him?

"Aaron, get up," Vic commands, and I turn my head slowly to look at him, looming over me, staring down at me with dark eyes. He's frowning at me, but I don't care. I just gave up my motherfucking soulmate to save my sister and my cousin. The world isn't fair; the world is cruel.

While that's all true, I wasn't supposed to add to Bernadette's cruelty. This wasn't supposed to happen. Giving her up to have a better life was one thing, but sabotaging her? Yes, Kali Rose-Kennedy called Havoc and asked us to destroy Bernie for a year. To be honest, I almost hit her, just clocked that smug bitch in the face.

But that's not how Havoc works.

"This is probably for the best," Oscar had mused, cocking his head to one side in thought. "Bernadette watches us too closely, peers too keenly. We have to put some space between us and her."

"Why's that?" Hael quipped back, frowning hard. "This whole thing is bullshit. Who is Kali Rose? Nobody. We have history with Bernadette."

And he was right.

We do have history with Bernie. Since elementary school, we've tried to look out for her. Shit, we made a pact when we were thirteen to watch from afar but keep romance out of it.

They all wanted her then; they still do, but in a different way. Things have changed a lot since we were thirteen. Bernadette is curvy and beautiful, a young woman with determination and hope in her eyes. For the briefest of moments, she was mine. She was mine. Fucking mine.

"I don't know if I can do this, Vic," I tell him honestly. Seeing Bernie hauled out of Prescott, kicking and screaming? That killed me. I vomited all over the front steps.

Vic crouches down in front of me, still frowning, as unhappy as I am, but most definitely not as undecided as me. He's never undecided about anything, that's what makes him so scary. He's the perfect leader; he oozes charisma. He also scares me a little, but I'll never let him know that. I'd rather die.

"Aaron, when we let you date Bernadette before, we agreed it was because you could give her something that none of us could. Things have changed; you are tainted."

Closing my eyes, I nod. He's right. I know he's right.

"This is going to be hard, the hardest thing we've ever done. But Bernadette is too attached to us, too attached to you. We have to let her go, Aaron. The life of a mobster's wife is short and brutal."

"I know," I growl out, sitting up. Vic claps a hand over my shoulder and rises to his feet.

"You're selfless, Aaron. You always have been." I'm not sure if Vic's trying to compliment me ... or insult me. Either way, he's wrong.

Homecoming night, Hael and I watch from the woods as Bernadette walks home in nothing but a bra and panties. Her eyes are hard, her fists are clenched, but she doesn't cry.

When she gets home, I'm waiting for her. She doesn't know we watched her along the way, that we kept her safe. All she knows is that I'm a monster. Still ... when I approach her, putting my hands on her hips, she looks up into my face and I know.

We can put distance between us, but that connection we have ... it can't be severed. Whether her name is in the acronym or not, Bernadette will and always has been Havoc, one of the family. Mine.

"I hate you," she tells me, her pale skin washed in moonlight as she shivers. "I fucking hate you."

But when I pull her into my arms and kiss her, we both melt.
We fuck in her bed. I go home.
The next day, the torment continues.
Because I don't deserve Bernadette. None of us do.
And yet ... there's not a single one of us that isn't in love with her.
Shame.
It could only work if we could learn to share. But that ... it'll never happen.
Never.

November eighth, Now ...

Bernadette Blackbird

There must be something on my face when I get back that screams *just got my brains fucked out by Aaron Fadler* because Vic takes one look at me and scowls.

"I was starting to wonder if we might have to come after you. Answer your damn phone when you're going to be out for so long."

I just stare at him as he stands up from one of the chairs at the dining table, casting those ebon eyes of his over me and then flicking them up to glare at Aaron when he comes in behind me.

"You're right," Aaron says, somewhat breathless, but

resolute as he returns his leader's stare. "We should've called and let you know we were going to be out longer than expected." Vic taps his nails on the surface of the table and looks away, but not like he's giving in, more like he needs a minute to trap some of that wild violence in his eyes.

"You've worked out your differences?" Vic asks, glancing back at me. He's wearing dark purple cargo shorts and a loose white tank. The holes on the arms are so big, I can see his gorgeous chest and abs underneath. My body throbs in response, and I exhale sharply.

"By that, you mean, *did you two fuck?*" I ask, moving around the couches and coming to stand as close to Victor Channing as I dare. He looks down at me, and it doesn't take a mind reader to tell that he's absolutely furious. Sharing me with Hael is one thing, but Aaron? Aaron is a threat in Vic's eyes. He had to know it would come to this, right? I couldn't just step into Havoc and not come to some sort of understanding with my ex. He took a bullet for me. I won't soon forget that. "The answer, by the way, is that yes, we did."

Vic says nothing, but the shape his mouth makes when he frowns scares me a little bit.

"Why?"

Of all the questions Victor could've asked, that's the one that trips me up the most. Why? *Why?*

"I ... don't know," I say, because I don't. Glancing over at Aaron, I can see that he isn't sure either. Are we back together? If we are, how do things work with Vic? I chew at my lower lip for a moment. "That's what the sex was about, testing our limits." I lick my lips and taste the sweetness of Aaron's mouth.

If Vic is my poison, Aaron is my antidote. One burns so good that you can't help injecting yourself, even if you know it's wrong. The other is violent relief, a desperate soothing balm that feels like old memories and hope.

I'm stuck right in the middle.

"Our girl," Aaron says, voice low. I glance sharply in his direction and see that his head is tilted down, his eyes focused on Vic. He's breathing hard, but he's calm. Almost too calm. "A Havoc Girl. You keep saying she's yours, and I can't blame you. I'd like her to be mine, too, but, uh"—Aaron pauses to grab a beer from the fridge, leaning his back against the door after it closes—"that's not what we agreed on. You're as bound to Havoc's price as she is. Or are you above it, Vic?"

Victor just stares at Aaron, devoid of emotion, as impossible to read as always. The thing is, if you want to consume someone, you have to make room in yourself to hold all of that energy. You have to make space. And what happens to that bit of you that you give away? Sometimes it's eaten by somebody else.

I can feel Victor inside of me—metaphorically speaking, at this moment anyway—and I know him much better than he thinks I do. His dark eyes slide to mine, studying me.

"I can sleep with any Havoc Boy I want," I say, and there's a visible ripple in Victor's demeanor. He stalks toward me, but I'm not afraid. He just doesn't scare me.

His hand lashes out, fingers curling around my wrist.

Aaron steps forward, teeth bared in warning.

"I keep trying to let her go, Vic, because I betrayed her, so I know I don't deserve her. But you know what Bernie and I figured out today? I'm not the hero in the cape anymore. If I want her, I'll have her. You agreed to that, when you slit her palm with that knife."

"What's your point, Fadler?" Vic asks, cocking his head to one side. His entire body radiates with rage, but he doesn't act on it. He told me I needed to master my anger. How can I argue that, seeing as he's most definitely got an ironclad grip on his own? "Your girl, my girl. I'm taking her into the bathroom. If I try to talk to you before I do that, I can't be held responsible for how I behave."

Victor pulls me away from the kitchen and into the half-bath near the front door.

"Are you insane?" I ask him as he steps inside with me, slamming the door behind us. It's dark in here, but for a single nightlight. I notice Vic doesn't exactly rush to turn on the light. Instead, he sits me on the counter, just like Aaron did. Does he know he's mimicking what happened between us earlier? Not likely.

"I can't stand the thought of you hating me," Vic admits, and my brows go up in surprise. He sounds … different, like his voice is fractured in places. Vulnerable and hating it. That's what he is. "You've barely looked at me since the Halloween party. You're not afraid of me, are you, princess?" Victor growls at me, nuzzling against my neck and making me shiver.

I laugh at him.

"Don't be ridiculous," I say, curling my fingers around his strong upper arms and digging my nails into his skin, marking him as my property. God help the next girl who thinks she can look at my man, let alone touch him. Because, even if I'm not ready to admit it aloud to him, that's what Victor Channing is.

Mine.

"Then what? You're upset about the video, I understand that." He kisses my neck, and I shiver. "You want to run, because of what I told you. Because I'm selfish and I want you, have *always* wanted you. Or maybe it's because of what we did to Aaron? Making him give you up …"

"Victor, shut up," I snap, and he leans back, curling his lip at me. The nightlight illuminates the room just enough that I can see his teeth, and the shine of his dark eyes. "Yes, all of those things are bothering me. I felt like you betrayed me and honestly … it was almost a worse feeling than watching Neil hurt my sister. Are you stupid or something? I've been lusting after Havoc for years, watching you guys for even longer. I'm not going anywhere, not even if you'd truly deserve to see me flee."

For a few moments, the room is quiet. Then I hear Aaron's footsteps, moving away outside the bathroom door. He was listening, and I'm glad for it. At least the truth is out there.

"You know it wasn't just me, right?" Vic asks, and I nod, which in reality just rubs my head against his some more. Primal marking, nuzzling, togetherness. I want more. "Nobody wanted to let you go. They're all into you, Bernie. All of them. And that terrifies me." He leans back and exhales. "I haven't been afraid since I was five and here you come, sauntering in and shattering everything. That's what you've done, Bernie, you've ruined me."

"Good," I tell him, reaching down to unbutton my jeans. Victor helps me get them off—along with my panties—so he can grind his own denim-clad pelvis against my bare heat. It feels amazing, little aftershocks from Aaron and his body echoing through me. "I like ruined things. Perfect things make my soul and my teeth ache."

He chuckles at me, desperate and dark, and then lifts his head so that our eyes meet.

"Aaron isn't the only man in this family I'm worried about. If they get the chance, each and every one of them will try to take you from me."

"Even Oscar?" I quip saucily. Sorry, but there's such a thing as stretching reality too far.

"Yes. Even. Oscar." Victor stares right at me as he says it, each word enunciated and thick with jealousy. "You're our dark angel, Bernadette."

I'm flooded with a double sense of disbelief and perverse pleasure at the idea.

Oscar Montauk? No fucking way. Then again, what did he just say to me? Before I left to go with Aaron to the soda fountain ... *"For what it's worth, this particular incident wasn't just Victor's fault. Some boys just don't know how to share their toys."*

"At the same time, that means they'd all die to protect you. We all would. You know that if we could've taken Neil down and kept you safe at the same time, we would've?" I nod, but I'm having trouble responding to Victor's words when his body is singing a siren song that I can't resist. "If you're ever in trouble, Bernie, you just call us. You don't have to say anything, you just let it ring."

I have no idea why he's telling me this, especially right now of all times, but it seems important.

"Of course," I respond, trying to kiss him again, but Vic stops me with a finger on my lips.

"Our safety word is *mare's nest*. Do you know what that means?" He doesn't wait for me to answer; he knows I don't. "It means bullshit. If you need to tell us something is wrong without alerting anyone else, just say that you need to untangle a *mare's nest*." Victor smirks, his face shadowed and scary in the half-light. "It can also mean disorder, *havoc*."

"Telling me all your secrets today?" I ask, choking on a sudden flood of emotion. Between Aaron and that strange flickering feeling, and this push-and-pull with Victor, I'm going to come apart at the seams. I think about Halloween night, about how quick the boys showed up at the house, not long after Aaron and I did.

He must've called them in the SUV, before we came inside. Chills creep down my spine at the thought; it's proof that they think of everything. Speaking of, that stolen SUV was gone when I woke up the next day, like it'd never been. Efficient. I guess the Havoc Boys would have to be, considering they play such reckless games.

I'd still love to know how they managed to get showered up before appearing like shadows in the night. Maybe later though, when my pussy isn't aching for Vic's cock.

"I want to tell you everything, Bernie," he breathes back, sliding his mouth against mine but withholding his kiss on purpose, just to make me squirm.

"Fuck me," I command, and Vic grins, as sharp as a knife.

"Don't have to ask me twice," he snarls, tearing his belt off and tossing it aside. He shoves his pants down his hips like they've personally offended him. When Vic tries to grab me and start off on a wild power-fuck the way he does, I stop him with a hand on his chest.

"Condom," I tell him, looking him dead in the face. The way he snarls, you'd think he was a wild animal. "Now, or no deal."

"You use a condom with Aaron?" he hisses at me, but I just frown.

"Condom," I repeat and Vic growls, reaching past me to shove the glass lid off a small ceramic jar that I just assumed held, like, cotton balls or something. Instead, it's full of condoms.

Wow.

This really was a house run by bachelors, wasn't it?

Not anymore.

Victor puts the condom on his dick in a way that I can tell he'd murder the latex if he could, drown it in the goddamn toilet or something.

"You are such a bitch," he purrs as he wraps an arm around my waist and drags me close, pressing my cunt to his hard lower belly. The way he says *bitch*, though, it's clearly affectionate.

"How's this for a boss bitch move," I begin, adjusting myself and lifting my legs up to put my feet against the side of the doorjamb on one side, and against a shelf on the other. Good thing it's screwed into the drywall because I'm about to abuse the hell out of it. "Don't move, Victor. Seriously. Stay where you are."

"The hell?" he murmurs, because he's such an alpha dick that he can't imagine not doing the thrusting. But I've already been fucked today; it's my turn to fuck someone else. I start to move before Vic can question me further, and that shuts him up real quick. Wrapping one arm around his neck, I use the other to grab his cock, pushing my hips forward and impaling myself on his monster dick.

"Oh, god," I groan, letting my head fall back. Bracing my feet on either side of him, I start to move, pushing off the shelf and the wall to get the movement I need to stir up friction.

Victor quivers as he struggles to stay still, his hands on my hips, encouraging the movement. It feels so good that I lose myself, moving faster, pushing harder. Vic ends up stumbling back against the door as I attack his mouth.

The bathroom is so small that when I put my feet against the wall on either side of him, I can also brace my arms against the wall behind me. I rock my hips forward and back, my body soaked in sweat, trembling with fatigue. But I'm doing it, I'm fucking Victor Channing against a wall.

"Shit, darling, you really are my little Havoc Queen, aren't you?" he murmurs against my mouth, shuddering and moaning as I work his dick into a frenzy, encouraging him to come and loving how vulnerable he looks while he orgasms. *I* am choosing not to finish myself, not right now. I want to hold this over him. I cling to Vic as he shudders, his hips pumping of their own accord a few times before he sags back against the door.

"Well?" I ask, and he laughs at me, a bit breathless and very obviously surprised.

I've just shocked the shit out of him.

"Lemme get you a crown made, baby," he murmurs, his voice thick with sex and satisfaction. "You can have half my kingdom. Fuck, you can have it all. I made it for you, you know, Havoc." And then he kisses me on the mouth, and I forget what I said about not having an orgasm.

I have two before I leave our little cocoon of darkness.

Afterwards, I come out of the bathroom to see Aaron waiting for me. He says nothing, and neither does Vic, but they look at each other with an interesting mix of admiration, respect, and loathing.

"Try to get along, would ya?" I ask, lighting up a cigarette as I move toward the sliding glass door, opening it and leaning against the edge so I can smoke half-in and half-out of the house. "We have enough enemies without making them of each other."

"Huh." Vic just smirks and shakes his head while Aaron scowls at him.

"You guys work so well together," I continue, determined to find some way around their jealousies. Because I'm not eager to give either of them up. "Don't screw it up because you want exclusive access to my pussy."

"Bernadette," Victor growls, but he's already rummaging through the fridge, so he can't be too serious about it. I look at Aaron and he stares back at me.

"Hours," he says, and then he smiles. It's all he needs to say. We both know we have a standing appointment.

"Hey Bernie," Vic says after a moment, looking up and over the fridge door at me. My reverie with Aaron breaks, and I glance back at him. "You know that we never slept with Kali, right? I want to make sure I've clarified that quite clearly."

I just stare at him.

I begged and begged him to answer that question and instead, he screwed me against the wall of his father's house. *Now* he's telling me? But looking into his crow-black eyes, I can see why. What we're doing here, Havoc and me, it's not something they'd ever share with someone like Kali.

"We've never shared any girl," Aaron adds, and I feel my focus on Vic snap. Wow. Blinking, I try to clear my head and focus on them both at the same time. They pull me in opposite directions; I'll have to be strong enough to pull them toward me instead. "Not once."

My body flushes with heat, but I turn quickly back toward the backyard, finishing my cigarette.

I've never heard anything more romantic in my entire life.

My Havoc Boys.

Mine.

CHAPTER
TWELVE

By the following Monday, the entire school knows that Danny Ensbrook is missing.

A cop calls me into Ms. Keating's office, and to make shitty matters even worse, he recognizes me right away as the Thing's stepdaughter.

"You're Neil's delinquent brat, aren't you?" the detective asks, which isn't at all professional. I sit slumped in the chair, my nails digging into the wooden armrests as I glare at the cops with every ounce of loathing and hatred I feel for my stepfather. I don't have to pretend to be nice; nobody at Prescott High likes the police. Already, two students have refused to come in here, another half-dozen have ditched classes for the day, and Jim Dallon threw his drink into the detective's face. Seeing the wet stain on his white button-down makes me want to smile. But then, I wouldn't want him to get the wrong idea.

"Mr. Constantine," Ms. Keating starts, trying to keep things professional. Bless her heart. There's nothing professional about the motley misfits that attend this school. She just keeps trying and trying to save our fucking souls. How long is it going to take her to realize that there's no saving us? "Please try to keep your questions in line with the investigation."

"My apologies, Ms. Keating," Detective Constantine says, his brown hair and brown eyes as interesting as a puddle of mud. He thinks he's attractive, but instead, he's just painfully average with a decent haircut and a nice tie. I hate him instantly.

"You're not allowed to question a minor without the presence of a parent or guardian," I drawl, glad for once that I truly don't know where Danny's body is or what the boys did with him. Less to lie about, less to hide. Not that I'd tell either way. I'd rather jump off a bridge. "I don't see a parent or guardian in this office."

"Well, now, Bernadette," Constantine says, scooting a bit closer to me and trying to smile in that patronizing way that adults often use on teenagers, like we don't have functioning brains in our skulls. "This isn't actually an official investigation just yet. We're just trying to understand why Danny didn't come home after the Halloween party last week."

I yawn and wish I had balls to scratch, just to add a little extra rudeness to my disdain. *Fuck it, I don't need balls.* I scratch my crotch anyway, and smile when Constantine gives me a strange look.

"Sorry, crabs," I explain, which is a total bullshit lie, but I'll admit that it's hilarious to see the detective's face scrunch up in disgust. "Must be all those trains I let the boys run on me."

"I'm sorry, what?" Constantine asks, his innocent face

twisted into an expression of confusion.

"Ms. Blackbird," Ms. Keating warns, but she can't know if I'm lying or not either. Now everyone's uncomfortable.

"By boys, do you mean Havoc?" Constantine asks, his interest in the conversation piquing slightly. I stare at the stubble on his face. There isn't a single hair out of place, like he's carefully shaved the edges and plucked any stray strands. This tells me immediately that he cares a lot about his appearance.

"As a detective, aren't you supposed to, like, shave your face?" I quip, but clearly, he's used to dealing with much bigger fish than me. He just keeps smiling which pisses me off to no end. How dare he sit on the edge of Ms. Keating's desk like that, all casual and young and plucked to perfection. A good guy. Well, putting rapists and murderers in prison and then letting them go to recommit their offenses doesn't make him seem like a good guy to me. My foster brother, Eric Kushner, was accused—but not convicted—of rape *three* times before he tried to come after me.

Keyword here being *tried.*

"Ms. Blackbird," Constantine continues, undeterred by my tactics. "Nobody's in trouble here, no crime has been committed." I smile at that, but the detective pays me no mind. The easiest way for me to get caught here would be to play nice. Nobody at Prescott High ever plays nice with the cops. "But we know how these Halloween parties go, the sorts of pranks kids play on each other."

"Kids?" I echo, raising a brow, but the detective ignores me. I bet he practiced this speech in the mirror this morning, too, right before his wife handed him a coffee while wearing her Betty Crocker inspired apron.

"We just want to find Danny and bring him home safely, that's all." Constantine—who knows what his first name is—ratchets his smile up a notch. "His parents are really worried about him, Bernadette." *Oh, so we're on a first-name basis now?* I resist the urge to scowl, keeping my own smile firmly in place.

"Wait? His parents? You mean the Ensbrooks?" I laugh without meaning to. "Those white trash losers don't give a shit about their son. I'm surprised they even called in to report him missing. They spend ninety-nine percent of their time shooting up, and the rest lying in comatose heaps. They're heroin junkies, Constantine."

He just stares back at me, still smiling, not a single crack showing in his perfect façade. I decide I hate him already. Maybe I'm not being fair. Maybe, because the Thing is such a monster, and I've had such poor experiences with the police in the past, I'm not giving Detective Constantine a fair shake.

Also, I don't give a crap.

"It was actually Ms. Keating here who called in to report him missing. Come on, Bernadette, where is he? Locked in a shed somewhere near the party?"

"I don't know where Danny Ensbrook is," I quip with a roll of my eyes. "He's a waste of life. Why the hell would I keep tabs on someone like him?"

"Maybe because your gang is in a war with his?" Constantine asks, and Ms. Keating steps in to separate us. She needn't have bothered. I'm not intimidated by this ass-fuck.

"Alright, that's enough, detective. You asked your question, and Bernadette answered. If you need anything more, you'll have to call her mother." Ms. Keating crosses her arms over her chest, making it very clear this conversation is over. And she does it all while wearing a hot pink pantsuit. See, her I do like.

At least she's handling this situation and not Principal Vaughn, the asshole who shouldn't rightfully still be around.

Constantine turns to our vice principal and nods once.

"I understand, and you're right." He turns back to me, still smiling. Still fucking *smiling*. "Thank you so much for your cooperation, Bernadette. We'll be in touch."

I shove up from my seat and head into the hallway. Only then do I let my hands shake.

"How did it go?"

A familiar voice stops me where I am, and I turn to find Oscar waiting in the shadows. Even with my instincts on full alert as they always are, I missed him standing there. His glasses catch the light, but that's the only part of him that I can see from here.

I try not to let that icy little shiver trace down my spine, but it happens anyway.

"You are one, creepy psycho, you know that?" I ask, my heart racing as he steps out from between the two banks of lockers, dressed in his usual black suit and white dress shirt, complete with bloodred tie.

"What did the cop want?" he asks casually, but there's something decidedly *not* casual in his expression as he looks me over, like he still doesn't trust me.

I'm not sure that anything has ever pissed me off more.

"He wanted to know where we buried Danny's body," I say with a smile, and Oscar frowns at me. I take a few steps closer to him, reaching up to adjust his tie. He slaps my hand away at the last moment, smiling down at me to soften the blow, to make it seem like he truly doesn't care if I touch him or not. He does. "I told them I'd check in with you guys, grab the murder weapon from Hael's trunk, and then we'd all reconvene at the party house."

Oscar just stares at me, his eyes like cold fog beneath the freakishly clean lenses of his glasses. His ink is intense, crawling out from beneath his shirt and taking over his neck. He's got two demonic hands wrapped around his throat with reaching claws, a fitting bit of décor considering our prior interactions. I try not to think about him shirtless in the bathroom, stitching up the wound on my arm, but I fail miserably.

"Do you think that's funny?" he asks me, and I smirk.

"Actually, I do. You know what's even funnier though?" I reach up for his tie again, and this time, he lets me touch it, lets me run my fingers down the smooth silk. "You. Stop looking for a reason to distrust me; you're not going to find one."

"What if I could get you an out?" Oscar asks, reaching down to pry my fingers off his tie. His are covered in tattoos, as if some cosmic artist dipped them into a can of paint. They're long and wicked, the hands of a devil. I imagine Oscar could cast some black voodoo magic shit if he wanted to, stir up demons and spirits with those hands of his.

"An out from what?" I ask, tucking my hands into the pockets of my old blue jeans to pretend like they're not tingling, like I can't feel every single place he just touched me. *"A princess dress, for a princess."* Oscar's childhood voice rings in my ears, and I can just see him, his skin bereft of ink, his tiny hands wielding round-tipped scissors. "You better not mean an out from Havoc."

His smile turns into an evil smirk, twisting his face into something inhumanly beautiful, but equal parts terrifying.

"What if I told you we'd complete your list, that we'd let you stay with us for the rest of the year, but that you could walk away at graduation? How would you like that? You could even take your cut of Vic's inheritance with you."

My eyes narrow to slits, and I'm so goddamn pissed right now, I feel like I could hit Oscar right here in the hallway and not give a shit what that looks like to the rest of the student body. Maybe if I hit him in the balls hard enough, they'd jam up his throat and stop him from spewing asinine crap.

"What was it that Vic said to Donald?" I ask, musing on that for a minute. I snap my fingers like the memory's just come to me. "Ah, that's right." I step close to Oscar, tugging on his tie. He lets me do it, but he curls his long fingers around my wrist and squeezes, meeting my glare with one of his own. "Do you think I give a *shit* about money? Do you think that's what motivates me?"

"Perhaps not," Oscar purrs, leaning down to put his lips near my ear. "I think it's dick that motivates you."

I laugh at him. How can I do anything else? His response warrants little more.

"You think dick is hard to get?" I scoff, shaking my head and shivering when Oscar's breath feathers against my ear. "I've

239

been fighting *against* dick my whole life. You are aware that all I have to do is walk up to basically any guy I want and ask if he's down to fuck, and he'll say yes. And that's not because I'm exceptionally beautiful or anything; that's just the way the world works."

"Mm." Oscar stands back up, cocking his head slightly to one side before reaching up with his middle finger to push his glasses up his nose. "Let me correct myself: I meant very specific cocks, when I made that statement. For example, Victor Channing's dick."

"What about my dick?" Vic asks, appearing on my right side like a shadow in the night. I shiver, and then add a mental reminder to myself to ask them all how they do it, how they walk around in broad daylight without being seen. That's a skill I could see coming in pretty fucking handy.

"Oscar and I were just having a little chat," I say, keeping my focus on his gray eyes. He's tensed up a bit, now that Vic is standing beside us, like maybe he's a tad nervous I'll tell Havoc's leader what he just said. There's a good chance that Oscar hasn't voiced this idea to our boss. After what Vic told me last week, about how his love was selfish, I don't see him letting me go so easily. "He thinks I'm addicted to your cock."

Vic grunts a laugh, tucking his inked fingers into the pockets of his jeans as he gives his friend a long, studying sort of look.

"What do you care if she is?" he asks, a dangerous edge to his voice.

"I don't," Oscar replies smoothly, turning back to me. I could tattle on his ass right now, tell Vic that he questioned me about my interactions with the cop, as if I would ever tell a pig anything. Victor warned him about questioning me, back when I found the box. He most definitely wouldn't be pleased to hear about this. But then, I'm no snitch. Instead, I just smile at Oscar, letting him know that our little secret can stay between us. "It was simply an observation."

"Well, observe your ass back to class. With cops crawling the campus, we have to be on our best behavior." Vic turns back to me, his stare like glass, sharp enough to cut. "How did it go in there?" he asks me, and I shrug. "I'm guessing you didn't play the good little girl, now did you?"

"I don't trust the police," I say, thinking of the Thing. Sure, some cops are good guys. So are some criminals. They steal to feed their family, or they beat the shit out of a guy that molested their daughter. They still go to prison. But just as the oxymoron *good criminals* serves, so does *bad cops.* There is true evil in Neil Pence. Combine that with unchecked power, a badge, and a firearm, and it spells trouble. "He acted like the Ensbrooks were mourning their long, lost son." I roll my eyes dramatically, a la Regina George in *Mean Girls.* "As if those heroin junkies even know that they have sons, let alone that one is actually missing."

We all pause as the door to Ms. Keating's office opens and she looks at the three of us with a raised brow.

"Mr. Channing, if you would," she says, holding out a hand to indicate he should come into the office. "Mr. Montauk, Ms. Blackbird, I'd like if you attended class today. You're both on track to graduate; that isn't something you'd like to mess up in the homestretch, now is it?"

"Not us," I say, splaying my fingers against my chest. "Of course not. Come along, *Mr. Montauk.*" I scoff that last bit on the end of a laugh as Vic cracks his neck and then sighs dramatically.

"Let's get this over with, shall we?" he says, disappearing into the room as I turn back to Oscar. Pretty sure he's, like, the valedictorian or something. I mean, not that that's a huge accomplishment for Prescott High. There are students here who can't write their own names.

"After everything we've done to you," Oscar says with a small sigh of disappointment, tucking his iPad close to his side. "You fall into bed with Vic then Hael and, of all people, Aaron?"

"Is that what's bothering you?" I quip, fully intending to take my sweet time heading back to biology. I'm not about to become a scientist, so it's a huge waste of time anyway. "That I don't have enough self-worth and dignity for your liking? As Kendall Jenner once said, *you act like I'm not in full control of where I throw this cooch.*"

Oscar snorts at me.

"The only thing that bothers me is the way Vic lets you get away with every little bullshit thing you do," he says, frowning at me. "You're a weak link in our chain. And despite what you feel about me, it's my job to keep Havoc running smoothly. I don't like speedbumps, Bernadette, and that's what you are. You slow the whole operation down."

"Maybe you're just jealous?" I spit back, taking a step away from him and his shiny loafers. He looks so ... out of place here. Even with all that ink. There's just something about Oscar that's next level. I wish I knew a little more about his home life, so I could get some understanding about what makes him tick. "Maybe you care so much about Vic's cock because you wish he'd shove it right up your tight, little ass?"

Oscar just smiles back at me in a placating sort of way. I pretend like it doesn't piss me off, all of that cucumber cool of his, but it does. It *enrages* me.

"Maybe," he says, turning to head back the way he came— which most definitely is not to class. Instead, he pushes open the double doors that lead to the rear courtyard. "I'll see you after school on Wednesday," he calls out as he slips through the doors.

"What's happening on Wednesday?" I call out, but he either doesn't hear me or chooses to ignore me, leaving me alone in the beautiful urban decay that is Prescott High.

CHAPTER
THIRTEEN

"How have your dates with Brittany been?" I ask Hael, glancing over at him as he grips the steering wheel of the Camaro in tight fingers. I've barely seen him since Friday, and it just pisses me all the way off that he's with Brittany when he should rightfully be with ... well, Havoc. I mean, he's the first fucking letter in the acronym, right?

"How do you think? A living hell," he snaps, swiping a hand down his face as I raise my brows. "Sorry, Blackbird. I don't mean to snap, but I just ... I didn't see my senior year being about doctor's visits and cribs and car seats. She wants us to talk to her dad on Friday, too, so there's a good chance I'll be attending my own funeral before the birth of my kid."

"*If* it's your kid," I add, but maybe that's for my own benefit because Hael doesn't seem particularly optimistic. He scowls, and I have to wonder what Brittany told him about the other possible father. He hasn't said anything, but I figure he's just been gearing up for it.

"Listen to you complaining," Callum says with a grin, leaning between the two front seats with his hood down for once, golden hair shining in the sun. Like a poisonous spider with a brightly colored exoskeleton, warning off potential predators. "If you didn't want senior year to include a baby, and all the stuff that goes with it, you could've held back on the sex."

Hael grits his teeth as we wait for Oscar and Aaron. With the minivan out of commission, we're a little short on rides around here.

"It's so easy to say that *now*," Hael growls out, revving the engine and then sighing dramatically. He glances my way, almost apologetically. "Besides, I used condoms *every. fucking. time*. There's no reason this should've happened."

I keep my arms crossed over my chest, my attention focused on his beautiful face. I'm not sure that there's ever been a man quite so pretty, yet handsome at the same time. I've been lusting after him for years, but now that he's within my grasp, he suddenly feels even further away. *Even if it his kid, that doesn't mean you can't—*

Ugh.

I'm as addicted to these assholes as Pamela is to being a cunt. It's impossible for me to stop, to resist, to pull back.

"What are we up to today?" I ask, spotting Aaron and Oscar across the street.

The expression on Hael's face softens slightly, and he adjusts his hands on the wheel, flashing the *HAVOC* tattoo on his knuckles.

"Today's a good day," Hael says, nodding his head briefly. "I shouldn't be harping around Brittany, and all that shit. Today isn't about me."

"Then who's it about?" I ask as Hael opens his door and climbs out to let the others in. He pauses briefly to peep in at me, lifting a reddish-brown brow.

"You, babe. You."

Hael moves out of the way, leaving Aaron and Oscar to squeeze into the backseat with Callum. They're all fucking huge, so the effect is somewhat like a clown car.

"You guys looking ridiculous," I crow, trying to hold back a grin. I wonder briefly why I'm not with Vic, sitting on the back of his Harley. That'd free up another seat and make things way more comfortable. Unfortunately, he's nowhere to be seen, so we're going to have to make do.

My guess: he's still furious about me fucking Aaron.

Speaking of …

I don't look over my shoulder at my ex. Shit, I don't even know if I'd really call him an ex anymore. The sex was … explosive. I'd been expecting good, nostalgic, comfortable. Aaron Fadler could give Vic and a Hael a run for their money.

"Don't get started on that whiny crap," Oscar says, and I spin around to glare at him as Hael revs the Camaro's engine like he's fucking her.

"Goddamn, that's beautiful," he murmurs, giving his crotch a squeeze and winking at me as I glance his way. But then we take off and I turn back to berate Oscar for being a prick.

Oscar's not looking at me though, his attention focused on

Aaron as he closes his eyes and leans his head back against the seat.

Ah.

I'd almost forgotten that he was claustrophobic. It's apparent now that Oscar's quip was meant to shame him. Doesn't make me any less angry, but more so.

"Oscar, do you masturbate by sticking a razor-coated dildo up your ass every morning? Because you sure as shit act like it." I reach back to touch Aaron's hand and he cracks both a smile and a single eyelid, so that he can look at me.

"I even use the blood as lube," Oscar responds smoothly, looking down at a spreadsheet on his iPad. I'm impressed by the quick clapback actually, but I still feel bad for Aaron.

"How long is this drive anyway?" I ask, because I have no clue where we're going. Realistically, for most girls, you'd have to be a brain-dead idiot to get in a car and start driving with four guys to an unknown destination. This, though, this is different. Like I said, nothing about this is normal.

"Fifteen minutes at most," Cal answers, tucking a knee up against his chest and leaning his chin on it. He watches me from sky-colored eyes. "We're taking you to the garage."

"The garage?" I start, before the pieces of this puzzle finally click together. "Like … for cars?"

"As if there were any other kind," Oscar murmurs, and I dig my nails into the back of my seat to keep from punching him. Instead, I focus on the spreadsheet he's playing with and see that it's a list of people.

My list of people.

By first and last name.

My eyes widen as Oscar flicks his gray gaze to me. He doesn't care that I'm looking. Actually, I'm pretty sure he *wants* me to see it.

The first column of that spreadsheet holds names like *Neil Pence* down its vertical length, followed by rows of numbers. At the top of each column, there are acronyms that I don't understand.

"Curious as a kitty cat?" Oscar quips as Hael throws us around curves in the road like he's got something to prove. He rolls his window down to let the air ruffle his red hair, and just laughs. Okay, nope, I was wrong. He isn't proving anything: he's just in love with the road. "Do you want to know what this column is for?"

Even though I know Oscar is baiting me, I bite. Why the hell not?

"What?" I ask as he leans forward and gets in my face, glasses shining with a stray shaft of sunlight.

"These are my calculations for risk. That is, how likely is it that we'd be caught if we murdered the person in question." My eyes widen, flicking back down to the spreadsheet to read the numbers. I barely get a chance to see anything before Oscar is shutting off the screen and tucking it away. He weaves his fingers together around the knee of his crossed leg and stares back at me in challenge, daring me to beg.

I'd rather die.

But at least I saw one thing of interest: Eric Kushner's column for risk ... was only three percent.

Uh-oh.

I'd sure as shit hate to be him right now.

When we arrive at the garage, Victor is waiting, sitting on the hood of some rusty junker without wheels. It looks like it hasn't been in service for, like, decades.

"What the hell is this?" I ask when I climb out, pausing at the end of the grease-soaked driveway and looking around. Off to one side, there's a row of pretty vintage cars, their paint shiny and fresh, their interiors sleek and freshly remodeled.

"Our garage," Vic says with a shrug of his big shoulders. He hops off the hood of the car and parks a cigarette between his lips, talking around it as he cups the end and lights up.

"By *our*, you mean ..."

"Havoc's garage," Oscar says, pausing beside me with his mouth in a thin line. "We collect junkers and flip them for profit."

"You mean *I* collect junkers and flip them for profit," Hael says, moving over to stand beside the rusty piece of shit that's propped up by cinder blocks. He taps the side of the car and flashes one of his shit-eating grins at me. "And this one right here, Blackbird, this is for you, baby."

I lift a brow and then glance over at the baby pink convertible on my left that matches my leather jacket.

"That ..." I start, pointing at the rusted crap-heap. "That's my car? Why can't I have one of those?" I switch my finger over from the junker to the classic beauties on my left. "I'll give you a hint: one of these makes me wet, and the other turns this cooch into the Sahara Desert."

Hael howls with laughter, and Vic grins as Callum hops up onto the hood of the pink convertible.

"Those cars are already marked for sale," Oscar says, glancing down at his goddamn iPad again. Sometimes I want to tear it from his hand and smash him in the face with it. Fairly sure at this point that he's married to the damn thing.

"Besides," Vic says, gesturing with his chin in Hael's direction. "He picked this one out for you, all special and shit. You want to tell her about it, Hael?"

I cross my arms over my chest as Hael walks around the junker, whistling under his breath like he's checking out a particularly beautiful woman.

"Well, my dear Miss Blackbird," he says, grabbing onto the trunk and pretending to fuck the crap out of the car's trunk. I'm not amused. I raise a brow at him, waiting for an explanation.

"I'm sure *you* think having your semen splattered across the trunk of the car makes it more valuable, but to be quite honest, I'm not buying it. Explain, or I'll start to think you don't like me."

"This," Hael begins, flashing a sharp smile. "Is a '57 Cadillac Eldorado."

He pauses for dramatic effect, but since I don't know shit about cars, I just stand there, waiting for the rest of the explanation. Hael sighs and comes back around to stand next to Vic.

"Do you know what one of these things is worth fully restored?" he asks me, crossing his arms over his broad chest. He makes a nice complement to Victor, I must say, like they're two halves of the same deal. Like, maybe, if I were really lucky, I could have them both.

"I have no clue. Enlighten me," I say dryly and Aaron smiles, scrubbing his hand over his chin. He likes seeing me saucy, even if he doesn't care to admit it.

"Girl, come on," Hael says, throwing up his arms in mock frustration. "You impressed me on that first day, when you came sauntering up to us in your leather pants, all sexy and saucy, with that pretty mouth of yours, talking about my baby's grille." He gestures in the direction of the Camaro, and then moves over to stand in front of me, hooking his thumbs into the belt loops on my leather pants.

"Say pretty mouth again and see what happens," I quip, smiling at him. I pretend like I don't enjoy having his hot, tattooed body pressed up against me, but you know, I'm not a complete and total hard-ass.

"I stand corrected: a pretty mouth with an acerbic tongue, and teeth that'd just as easily bite off a dick as suck it. Better?" I cock a brow, and he nods, continuing. "Well, cranky Miss Blackbird, listen to this: a '57 Caddy Eldorado is worth a *hundred and fifty grand* when it's fully restored."

"*When* it's fully restored," I correct, peeking around him at the heap of trash propped up on the driveway. We're in a seedy part of town, not far from Billie's trailer. I wouldn't want to be caught alone out here after dark. Not without a gun, I mean. Or a knife. I could probably handle myself with a knife. "It doesn't even look salvageable to me."

"Yeah, well," Hael says, like the cocky motherfucker he is. He runs his tongue over his lower lip and steps back, walking backward until he gets to the side door of the garage. Hael kicks it open with his boot without even bothering to turn around, and then steps back, holding out a hand to beckon me forward. "You've never had the services of Hael Harbin at your beck and call, now have you?" I step up to the doorway and look aside, finding several other half-eaten rust heaps stacked inside the room. "Between all of these, I've got the parts I need to make this shit happen. I'll even let you pick the paint colors."

I look at him, skepticism riding me hot and hard. I can't figure why the boys would give me a car, when neither Callum nor Oscar ever had one. And now, Aaron doesn't have one either when he needs it most.

"Why don't Cal and Oscar have their own cars?" I ask, truly curious. But even though I don't mean to, my voice is thick with disbelief and suspicion. Nothing good ever comes for free. Fucking *nothing*. I'm under no illusion that I'm a goddess to these boys—these *men*. Victor might be into me, Aaron maybe even loves me still, but I've seen what they can do, how easily I can be thrown away. That, and I'm still pissed about the video. There was a breach of trust there, and it's not something I'm going to get over easily.

"I totaled my last car," Callum says with a shrug of his shoulders, pulling out a packet of salted almonds from his pocket and pouring them into his palm. "Got my license taken away. We pull enough illegal shit without bringing the cops' attention to me on a technicality."

"I have no interest in owning a car," Oscar explains, completely deadpan. "If I wanted to waste my time playing chauffeur, I'd have been born as Hael Harbin." He tucks the iPad under his arm and gives me a look. "Trust me: if it were up to me, I wouldn't give you such a nice car. Hael has enough to do without spending hours every day under a hood."

"Who fixes these up then?" I ask, pointing at the other cars.

"I consult; we have people who do the grunt work," Hael says, moving back over to the shell of a vehicle that's supposed to be mine. He taps the side again, caressing it with tattooed hands like an adoring lover. "But not on this one. I'm going to have everything I need towed to my place, so I can work on it on the regular."

"But *why*?" I repeat, genuinely curious. I can't for the life of me understand why they'd do this for me, not without getting something in return. And trust me: I've been giving them the one thing I thought they truly wanted. Unfortunately, they're going to keep playing the mysterious card on me, and I'm not going to learn shit now am I?

"It doesn't matter why," Vic says, going back to being an asshole. "Don't you know you're not supposed to look a gift horse in the mouth, *Bernadette*?" He drags my full name across his tongue like it's poison.

I ignore the entitled fucker.

"What about Aaron?" I ask, thinking of the girls. I'm not about to accept a car when his got freaking fire-bombed—and likely because of what I did to Kali's face.

"We've already selected one for him," Vic adds, pulling a pair of keys from his pocket and tossing them to Aaron. "Happy early birthday from the rest of us assholes."

"Hint," Callum starts, hopping down off the hood of the car he's standing on and pointing down the row of vehicles. "It's the Bronco."

"It's a '96. Highly desirable. Already a classic. The value on these rises every year," Hael explains, so euphoric sounding that if I didn't know better, I'd think he were rubbing one out over there.

Aaron studies the white SUV with a slight smile.

"What about our other gift?" Aaron asks, looking from me to Vic and back again. "For Bernadette, I mean. Are we really doing that here?"

"Oh, we're doing it now," Vic says, reaching into a bag on the ground beside him and pulling out a box of latex gloves and a tattoo machine before he turns his attention to me, lifting the items up for emphasis. "Get ready, Bernie, because you're about to get your Havoc tat."

"Officially becoming one of us," Callum adds, grinning as he stuffs almonds into his mouth and flashes a monster's smile. It's scary, how pretty he is but how dangerous. I never expected I'd see him kill a boy though, not now, not ever.

Much to my surprise, Victor ends up handing the tattoo machine over to Aaron, of all people. One of my brows goes up.

"Last person to join tattoos the newbie," Vic says with a grin, tossing Aaron a pair of the black gloves. "Hope you've been practicing." My eyes find the letters inked into Victor's knuckles, the lines blown-out and ragged. It adds to his attractiveness though, adding a hint of danger to an already sharp appearance. My attention slides to Oscar and Hael next. I'm not sure who the true second-in-command is, but one look at their knuckles and I can take a guess. Hael's work is fine-pointed and exact while Oscar's is more utilitarian. Oscar then, had to be second. I would recognize Vic's work anywhere.

I look up at Aaron as he fingers the silver machine in his hand, his gold-green eyes contemplative as he studies it with an expression somewhere between resignation and fear. When he looks back over at me, I can tell he's conflicted.

If he does this, it might be too late. I might never escape.

Little does he know: I don't want to.

"Are you sure?" Aaron asks, as if he or I have some choice in the matter. We look at each other, and it's as if the rest of the world falls away. The smell of grease from the open garage, Hael's coconut oil, Callum's cinnamon-sugar almonds. Oscar's intense scrutiny, Vic's unrelenting stare. Aaron takes another step toward me, putting the toes of our shoes together. "I mean, do you want me to do this for you?"

He takes my hand and rubs his thumb over my naked knuckles, igniting every nerve ending in my body.

There's a long pause before Oscar approaches with a small glass bottle filled with black ink.

"Bernadette likes it here, don't you, Bernadette?" he purrs, lifting the glass up between two fingers and shaking it back and forth so that it sloshes around inside the bottle. "Stop dragging your feet, Aaron, and accept it."

Aaron's jaw clenches and he runs his fingers through his auburn hair, taking a step back and turning away, toward the dark maw of the garage.

My eyes narrow, and I exhale, feeling all of their eyes watching me, like they did that day in Billie's trailer, when I stripped my tits bare and changed in front of them. This is worse, though, like my soul is exposed somehow, like I'm emotionally naked in front of them.

"I'm not designed to live any other life," I say, and the words feel too real, like I wasn't quite ready to say them. I move over to the rusted shit-heap that's supposed to be my future car and hop up onto it, shedding my pink leather jacket as I do. "So do it. Make me bleed for Havoc again."

"We need to talk about the video," Vic says finally, and I laugh, shivering as Aaron lays the tattoo machine down on the hood next to me, and starts to slip into the gloves. As he snaps the black latex into place, I get all sorts of dark thoughts, and my mind strays back to his hard body under mine as I rode him into a violent climax. My eyes lift to Aaron's and stay there.

"What is there to talk about?" I quip as Aaron reaches out to take my hand. Even with the latex covering his fingers, I shiver when he touches me, laying my left hand out on my jeans-clad thigh. He weaves our fingers together, and it's impossible to miss the way Vic's staring at us.

"I want to offer up an apology," Victor says, and Aaron goes stone-still, lifting his gaze up to his leader's like he's seriously pissed him off. "I was wrong. No excuses. I fucked-up."

"You're telling her this now?" Aaron snaps back at him as he loads up the ink. It's mesmerizing, to watch his black-clad hands do the work, his tattoos bleeding out from underneath the gloves. "After the fact?" Aaron's tone is incredibly dry, almost enough to turn my damp panties into a damn desert.

Vic just shrugs and slides his hands into the front pockets of his jeans, eyes still on us. Whatever it is that he's got going on between him and Aaron, it's toxic, something we're going to have to deal with sooner rather than later.

"A real man admits his mistakes." Vic's dark gaze moves from Aaron to Oscar, and the two exchange a look of their own. "Isn't that right, Oscar?"

"Mm." That's the only response we get as Hael slips his shirt off, his brightly colored ink catching the sunshine as he gets beneath the hood of one of the car skeletons inside the garage, unscrewing the bumper while Callum waits nearby to lift it off for him.

"Can we be done with this, Bernie?" Vic asks, lifting an eyebrow. He knows he messed up. I'm glad about that at least, but I don't trust him for shit. He can't repair that quite so easily.

"What about the Kevlar?" Aaron asks, wiping my knuckles down with some antiseptic wipes that Oscar brings over to him. He cleans my skin with a careful intensity that has me shivering, even with the hot sun on my bare shoulders. "You gonna apologize about that?"

"What Kevlar situation?" I ask, fully aware that I have yet to accept Vic's apology. He grits his teeth, also fully aware of the situation I'm sure. Although I can't decide if half of his ire is for Aaron, or if it's all just specially cooked up for me.

"At the Halloween party," Aaron says, taking a pink disposable razor from Oscar and running it over my knuckles to get rid of the small blonde hairs there. He switches it out for another antiseptic wipe, giving me one, last scrub down before he takes a seat in a chair brought over by Oscar. "I wanted you to wear Kevlar; Vic thought it would be too obvious."

"Too obvious for what?" I ask, taking in a sharp breath as I prepare myself for the sting of the needle. That's the thing with tattoos; they always hurt. But it's a good sort of hurt, as the ink mixes with the blood, and the pain begins to edge toward a sick, sadistic sort of pleasure. It shouldn't feel good to hurt like this, but it does. It reminds me of what Callum said outside of Principal Vaughn's house, how pain can look pretty to those that have too much of it.

"If we walked in there with you wearing Kevlar over that sexy, little midsection of yours, then the Charter Crew would've known we were on the lookout for their bullshit." Vic turns away, facing off toward the road and the distant rumble of cars. The train tracks are just across the street from us, and we're only about three blocks away from the drive-in. "It was a tactical decision."

"A *risky* tactical decision," Aaron says, turning his attention back to me. "You ready?" I nod, feeling beads of sweat trail down my spine. Once I do this, I'm committed. The only way to scrub Havoc from my body after this would be to get some crazy expensive laser treatments. The thing is, after what I've already been through with them, I doubt I could ever scrub them from my heart and soul. "You put Bernadette's life in danger." Aaron starts the machine with a pleasant buzz, running his tongue across his lower lip and then looking up to meet my eyes. He presses the tip of the needle into my thumb and my breath escapes in a rush. "And you didn't ask her either."

"Right, yeah, we're having a bit of trouble adjusting. But we're getting there, aren't we, Bernie?" I don't look at Vic as he talks, focusing my attention instead on Aaron as he carves the letter *H* into my skin. It hurts like a bitch, I won't lie. It burns through me, and the vibration of the machine makes my hand quiver, like the movement is translating into my bones. It's shaping me, this tattoo, in a way that none of the others have.

I'd thought when I first uttered the word *Havoc* that I was pressing start on this chapter of my life, that I was turning the page to race toward a cliff-hanger of an ending that I may or may not survive. But no. That was the motherfucking prologue. As I look down and see the letters take shape on my fingers, I know that this is it. This is my new beginning.

I glance over at Oscar, finding him watching me and not the tattoo machine. Hael and Callum are still in the process of dismantling the old car, but I can tell they're listening, too. Oscar thought letting me see that recording of Penelope and the Thing would send me running.

Instead, it's only cemented my desire for vengeance.

"Don't make decisions like that without telling me," I say quietly, my voice threaded with steel. I keep watching Aaron's fingers as he moves the needle across my knuckles. "Especially ones that involve my *life*," I snap off the end of my tongue. I'm not sure if I'm pleased that Vic was willing to go so far to achieve his ends … or pissed off. I could've been shot. If Aaron hadn't taken that bullet for me, I would have been. I could've *died*.

And Victor Channing was willing to take that risk.

"She has a point," Hael says, coming over to stand between Vic and the car. "If she's one of us, then she's one of us. If she's not, then …" He shrugs his shoulders and gestures loosely with a grease-covered rag in the direction of my fresh tattoo. "You're going to marry her. Don't you think she has a right to be brought in on everything?"

Callum appears on my other side, tucking his hands into the front pocket of his sleeveless hoodie. He doesn't say anything, but he doesn't have to. His smile says it all. He knew about the Kevlar, about the video, and he didn't tell me shit. Because as nice as he is, as friendly as he pretends to be, he's still the *C* in Havoc, first and foremost.

"Oh, by the way, we're missing a few parts." Cal throws his thumb in the direction of the old car. "I know where we can boost what we need though. There's this investment banker that lives in Oak Park that has a fully restored Eldorado. We'll break in there and grab what we need this weekend."

"I'll go with you," I add as Vic works his jaw, watching as Aaron starts in on the *V* portion of my tattoo. It kills Victor to see Aaron do that, carve his letter into my flesh. He *hates* it. But as per usual, he maintains control of his temper.

"Oh, by *we*," Callum starts, smiling as he leans in close to me. In a surprisingly bold move, he nips the edge of my ear and a small gasp escapes me, one that's impossible to hide. "I actually meant our crew; stealing car parts is most definitely grunt work. We have better things to do."

I nod, licking my lips as Aaron carves admirably straight lines into my flesh. He might *have* a lot of tattoos, but tattoo artist he is not. This could easily be his first time doing this. If I had to choose a boy to do my ink though, it'd be Aaron. While Oscar's lines on Hael's knuckles are a calligrapher's wet dream, they don't have enough … heart.

Aaron's are pretty good, and they smack of emotion. That's what I like best.

"You never answered me," Hael says, his voice dropping

low. Victor turns his head to stare at his best friend, and the mood gets tense there for a moment. "As your future wife, what rights does Bernadette have?"

Vic clenches his jaw and looks away, but Aaron doesn't. His eyes are boring directly into mine.

"All of them," Vic says, sighing deeply. "Everything. I want her to have everything." He glances my way, but I can't turn away from Aaron, not when he's making me bleed in such a delicious sort of way. My bones hurt, my skin hurts, but the injection of ink into my flesh is like an orgasm, taking over me, marking me. It's just with ink instead of cum, I guess. "Aaron was right. Is right. I'm sorry about the Kevlar, too."

There's a long pause as everyone in that garage waits with bated breath to hear what I have to say.

"It takes big balls to admit when you're wrong," I say, nodding, but still looking at Aaron. Lost. Trapped. Mesmerized. "You're all forgiven." A feeling of relief seems to ripple through them. Hael moves off to continue working on the car, Callum lifts the rusted bumper up to move it, and Oscar finds a seat on a plastic chair. "But if you do it again, there won't be a second chance."

"Understood," Vic says, but he doesn't press. This moment isn't about him. It's about me.

Aaron finishes my tattoo and cleans me up, covering the newly inscribed wounds on my knuckles with a plastic wrap made specifically for this purpose. I then grab his hand, dragging him around the side of the garage and to the back of the building. It's shaded, the long grass waving in the wind as I encourage him to lean back against the corrugated metal wall.

"What?" he asks, looking down at me, my hand shaking and bloodied by my side. The wrap will keep it from leaking—which, grossly enough, tattoos are wont to do. "I didn't fuck it up, did I? I'll punish myself forever if I marred your perfect skin."

My lips twitch slightly, but I don't know how to say what I want to say without sounding … lovestruck. *You finally did it. You stood up for me, against Victor.* It was no big thing, but it didn't need to be. Love isn't about sweeping grand gestures, it's about doing little things each day to keep each other happy, little personal sacrifices instead of showy acts.

"I just wanted to say …" I start, stepping forward and putting my hands on his lower belly. Aaron doesn't argue with me about not finishing my sentence, not when I drop down to my knees and free his cock from his pants.

The fingers of my right hand curl around the base as I slip my blue-painted lips over the tip, sucking him deep and taking my time with it.

When he walk back around the building and into the garage, I'm still dabbing at the corners of my mouth with the sleeve of my jacket. There's not much I can do about the smears of blue though.

"Go home to your sister," Vic says when he sees me, scowling like he has any right to judge. I don't hesitate, walking right up to him and leaning up on my tiptoes to give him a messy blue kiss, right on the cheek. He looks dumbstruck over it. *The guy knows how to mate like a lion, but he can't handle a cheek kiss?*

We have serious issues to work on here.

"On it," I agree, happy to climb into Aaron's Bronco with him.

Maybe I suck him off on the way back, maybe I don't.

Either way, there's plenty of room in the SUV for it.

CHAPTER
FOURTEEN

When Kali finally started showing up to class at the beginning of the week, her face was bruised beyond recognition, and her eyes burned with a seething hatred that made my skin itch. At some point, there's going to be a confrontation between us, and it isn't going to end well.

At least now she has something real to hate me for. I *did* just bash in her face in. But before that, what did I ever do to her? We haven't got any sort of relationship where I might be able to ask her *why*. Why did you do those things to me? Why did you steal my essay? Why did you call Havoc?

It never escaped my attention that Kali had eyes for Aaron. I always knew that, but it never bothered me because I knew he was truly and wholly mine. Still is, I think. I mean, he spent years *not* fucking any other girls because of me. I don't care much about words—people lie, after all—but actions, now that's another story.

And Aaron, well, he's told me all he needs to with his celibacy.

By Friday, I'm certain that I'm right about both things: Aaron is still mine … and Kali still wants him.

I'm standing outside the doors to the cafeteria, waiting for the boys, my knuckles throbbing from the fresh ink. I've taken good care of my new tattoo, washing it with Dial soap and rubbing it with Aquaphor, but ouch, the knuckles are a hard place to take the needle.

"How's it healing?" Aaron asks, pausing to stand beside me. I glance his way, and my breath catches in my throat. How can he do that to me, leave me breathless and aching? We were always star-crossed lovers, too sweet to find a happily-ever-after, destined for some bittersweet ending that stings the tongue. Yet here we are, freshly fucked, and gazing at one another like we'd rather be naked and alone somewhere.

"The bruise you left on my hip?" I ask, pressing my hand against my pelvic bone and smirking. "Or the tattoo?"

"Well, since you brought it up," Aaron starts, eyes sparkling with surprise. With the exception of Wednesday at the garage, I've been avoiding him a bit, and he knows it. Unlike Vic however, he's giving me space to breathe. I'm not sure if I love that or hate it. Mostly, I just want him to touch me. "Feel free to discuss either." He tosses back his cherry coke and then leans down to put his lips near mine. "But I'm more interested in hearing about your sexual battle scars." He pauses, licking his lips, smelling like roses and sandalwood, his breath sweet with cherry soda.

"In that case, my ass still hurts, and I have finger-shaped

bruises on my thighs," I whisper back, wondering if I should touch him, curl my arm around his neck, kiss him.

As Aaron's leaning over me, I spot Kali standing down the hall, staring at the two of us from her bruised and swollen face. She's got Billie, Ivy, and a few of their trashy friends standing at her side, but she doesn't approach us. Obviously, there's been no sign of Danny, and the tension in Prescott High is ratcheting up to dangerous levels, but despite their poking and prodding against Havoc, we haven't moved on the Charter Crew.

Yet.

The way Kali is looking at me … I can sense something beyond her usual hatred, a longing, a reaching, a silent pleading. After all, she's known Aaron about as long as I have. I remember her in junior high, twirling her hair around her finger and watching him from across the grassy area in front of the school.

"He's the kind of boy you want to marry," she'd told me in her thirteen-year-old voice, like she knew the secrets of the entire world.

Vic appears before I can decide what to do, and Aaron pulls back slightly. But not out of fear—out of respect. He hates Victor, but he respects the hell out of him. That, and he desperately wants his approval.

"We need to do something about Kali," I say as she turns away abruptly, heading for the front entrance of the school with her girls in tow. Stacey Langford watches them carefully from the vicinity of her locker, eyes narrowed. In general, it's her job to deal with girl drama at Prescott. Kali and Billie are ruining her carefully crafted empire, one that shines, even with Havoc's shadow cast over it.

"We will," Vic says, nodding briskly, eyes tracking Principal Vaughn. He's kept his distance from us. In fact, he hasn't even *looked* our way since he got back. I wonder how long he thinks this careful dance is going to last? Everyone knows that once the requiem is over, the mourners leave the cemetery. "Actually, Callum and I have a special present planned for their crew. We'll drop it off tonight." He lights up a cigarette, passing it my way after a drag. Our eyes meet and something dark travels through me. I'd call it a shooting star, but it's much more wicked than that. Still, it streaks through the endless blackness of my soul before disappearing into the infinite depths of the universe.

Hael catches up to us next, but he isn't smiling.

"I'm going with Brittany today to talk to her dad," he says, raking his fingers through his hair. "Oh, and she wants us to take care of a Fuller High football player that she fucked while we were at the lake house."

Vic raises both brows, glancing over at his friend as I smoke my cigarette. Aaron finally tears his gaze from mine to look at Hael.

"The one she cheated on you with before school started?" Vic clarifies, and seeing someone as built and beautiful as him say something so inane twists up my sense of reality. He's too muscular, too big, too brutal to be a high school student. At least he'll be eighteen soon.

"Nope," Hael grinds out, lighting up a cigarette of his own. The boys disabled the smoke alarm in this hallway on the first day of school. I know, because after I called Havoc, I saw them later that day fucking around with it and, like everyone else at Prescott High, I pretended like I didn't notice. "That was the quarterback, the one Cal nailed in the face with hot coffee. Brittany says he, uh,"—and here Hael stops to give a bitter laugh and a shake of his head—"didn't even come while he was inside of her. *And* she used a condom. The only other possible father for this kid is the fullback, some douche named Rich Pratt."

"You learned this all last night?" Vic asks, and Hael turns away. Clearly, he's been holding onto this information for the last ten days. There's hurt pride in his face that makes me wonder if he ever really cared for Brittany. If she's truly carrying his child, are they going to make a go of it? I could see that happening, based on Hael's white-knight complex.

The thought infuriates me, but I hold it back.

"Let's send some of the boys to deal with Rich," Aaron suggests, and Vic nods. Beating the shit out of some guy Brittany slept with doesn't warrant the actual use of Havoc's leaders. A use for peons, as Cal might say. "Did she say why she thought he might be the dad?"

Hael frowns as Cal sidles up beside us, Oscar close behind him. He looks right at me, but I give him nothing in return. I want him to keep wondering if I might spill the beans to Vic about his proposal. That'd make him feel vindicated, I bet, like I'm truly the loose-lipped snitch that he seemingly wants me to be.

"Brittany slipped out of the cabin and fucked this Rich guy at the lake's clubhouse," Hael says, nostrils flared. "She says he used a condom, too, and that it was only once. My neck is on the chopping block, guys." Hael glances my way, almost apologetically. "I was hoping that with you a part of Havoc, things could be different. I'm sorry, Bernie." I open my mouth to respond when I hear Mitch's laugh from the end of the hallway.

He's standing there with his brother, Logan, as well as Danny's brothers, Timmy and Kyler. They're all watching us carefully, but it's only Mitch who's smirking. Timmy and Kyler have murder in their eyes. Likely, they think they've gotten away with fire-bombing Aaron's van. Guess they don't know Havoc as well as I do. Ever heard the fable of the tortoise and the hare? Havoc is the tortoise. A super fucked-up tortoise with a shell of pain and fury, but there you go.

"Why does she want us to beat him up?" Aaron asks, and I glance back at Hael.

"He won't talk to her. Blocked her on social media. Started spreading rumors that Brittany's been screwing the entire football team. I mean, she's trying her best, but she's only managed to nail two so far." Hael scowls again and rakes his fingers through his red hair. His face has got a full five o' clock shadow going on now, but I don't dislike it. My hands itch to touch him, just to see how he feels against my fingertips.

"What a prick," I say, and all five boys turn to look at me. "What? Brittany cheating on you is fucked, and honestly, I'm praying to the darkest gods I know that she isn't having your baby. But also, this other guy, Rich, he needs to accept that he might have some responsibility in this. He deserves to have his ass kicked."

"Our little feminist in residence," Vic says with a sideways smirk. I give him a look and cross my arms over my chest with the creak of leather.

"You're not a feminist? Because if you aren't, we have a problem." Victor whistles in response to my question and then pauses when he sees Detective Constantine walk by, watching us. He's been at the school every goddamn day this week. I know the boys said they've killed before, but to be honest, the anxiety about the whole thing is starting to get to me. It feels like the guillotine is slowly sliding toward our necks. Between my list, and the Charter Crew, and the cops? How is Havoc going to survive this? I'm starting to wonder if I've put the final nail in their coffin.

"Oh, I'm a feminist for sure," Vic says, but he's not really looking at me anymore, his attention homed in on Mitch. If I were Mitch, and I saw Victor Channing look at me like that, I'd run. Fast. And I wouldn't look back. "A third wave feminist: women are just plain better." He grins and pats me on the head which is extremely patronizing. I can't decide if I should be mad at him or not. "Let's get out of here; we have shit to do."

"Don't we always?" I quip as I fall into step between Cal and Aaron. "A special present for Mitch, huh?" I ask, directing the question at Callum; he grins at me, sucking on the straw that's stabbed into his usual Pepsi can.

"You'll love this one," he tells me with that growling voice of his. The laughter that follows gives me the chills, and I notice both Billie and Kali whipping their heads in our direction to stare. If they aren't afraid of Callum, they should be. "We all agree that what happened with the video wasn't acceptable. Bernadette, you have a right to know us all, as we truly are." My eyes widen slightly, but I'm not displeased by the statement. Well, thank god, *somebody* in this group has brains in their skull.

"Don't look too excited by that," Aaron quips, frowning hard. Callum leans in toward me, a shadowed prince in a hood of darkness.

"You might not like the skeletons in our closet, but I sure do hope you stay," he whispers, kissing me on the cheek.

Doesn't occur to me until about two hours later that he was being literal.

"Oh, my fuck," I gag, covering my mouth with my hands. I'm standing over a hole in the woods, six feet deep, two feet wide. There's a body inside, wrapped up in plastic and taped up to resemble a cocoon.

Doesn't do much to disguise the smell though.

Callum and Aaron, in gloves and rain jackets and hairnets, are at the bottom of the hole, covered in dirt and hefting the corpse of Danny Ensbrook up to Hael and Vic. Oscar stands off to the side, watching carefully and taking notes. I'm not sure what I'm supposed to be doing, so I just stand there and try to process.

Skeletons in the closet indeed.

We've stolen two more cars today—a 2013 Nissan Armada and some 90s Suburban—and covered the interior of the Armada with tarps. Vic and Hael carry Danny's rotting body over to the dirt patch where they're parked and then chuck him unceremoniously onto the ground, like so much garbage on its way to the dump. The smell though … that's what's really getting to me. My head spins, and I try to reconcile those years of fantasizing about Havoc with reality.

They're … awful. In so many ways. So, so, so, so many.

I wet my lips, but the smell gets to me, and I almost vomit again.

"Remind me of the plan," I choke out as I watch Hael and Callum start to fill the hole in with dirt. The oddest thing about this patch of woods is how *many* fresh mounds of dirt there are. My skin ripples with goose bumps. "Nobody is going to find Danny out here." We're two hours from Springfield, and about four hours from the house where the Halloween party took place. "Why are we moving him?"

"Because Mitch pissed me off," Vic explains, using a gloved finger to press the button on the automatic hatch of the SUV. It opens on its own with a cheerful chirp. "We're delivering a message. This isn't just a game of high school chess anymore; it's real. He can either fall back and get in line, or he can play on our terms."

Hael starts to unwrap the body. I tell myself I'm not going to look as he peels the plastic and tape away from the corpse, but I can't stop myself. Danny died because he lifted his gun to my head; Callum killed him to save me. This isn't something I get to stick my head in the sand over.

It's only been a few weeks since Danny died, but holy shit if he doesn't look like a zombie. His eyes are sunken in; there are bugs; he's bloated as shit. I gag and turn away, choking back the bile. I don't want to leave any sign that I was here.

"There are bodies everywhere," I say instead, looking around and wondering what the actual fuck I've gotten myself into. Maybe I shouldn't have been so keen on joining Havoc, after all?

"Not so many as it seems," Callum says with a shrug, pausing to rest his hands on the end of his shovel. He could hit me with it, knock me into this hole and bury me alive. But for whatever stupid reason, I feel certain that he won't. "We have other things buried out here, not just bodies."

"Like money?" I ask, and Vic smiles, moving close to stand beside me. Meanwhile, Hael moves the body to a fresh tarp and ties it up with a bit of rope into a mummy-like shape.

"Money, weapons, drugs, you name it." Victor shrugs and sighs, peeling off his gloves so he can press a warm hand to the side of my face. I just hope he doesn't try to kiss me; I'd probably upchuck yet again. *Shit, maybe I am pregnant?* I think, fear slicing through me like a knife. I can't remember when I had my period last, but that's nothing unusual. My period's been irregular since I started when I was twelve. I'd go to the doctor, but we can't really afford it, and it's not like Pamela has health insurance for us. Fucking laughable.

"Who owns this land?" I ask, and Cal grins at me from across Danny's empty grave.

"Vic's mother's boyfriend," he says, and I lift both brows.

"It's a timber investment property," Victor explains, scowling. "But he'll never sell it. Not the trees, either. Not even if he's destitute."

"Why do you say that?" I ask, and Vic gives me a look.

"Because he killed his best friend and buried him here," he explains, and I have serious trouble keeping my feelings to myself.

"He ... what?" I manage to choke out and Vic frowns.

"My mother cheated on him with his best friend. Tom killed him and buried him out here. I know because I saw the whole thing and followed him. The guy is buried about a quarter mile north of here, close enough that even if Tom were to break the land into parcels and sell it, this area should be safe."

"But far enough away that we shouldn't run into him," Callum adds as Hael mutters curses under his breath and deadlifts the body into the back of the Armada. Impressive. "Tom has enough connections that it'd be hard to nail him with the murder anyway, so we figured we'd rather use it to our advantage."

"The dead guy was a total prick anyway," Vic explains, lighting up a cigarette, like this is business as usual for him. Well, not *like* it's usual. It *is* usual. Jesus. What I've experienced with Havoc thus far, that was like, baby bootcamp or something. His face tells me nothing, cigarette hanging from between his lips as he talks. "His death is serving the world far better than he ever did with his life. Now, when we take out the trash, we have somewhere to put it." Vic turns to me. I should probably be scared of him. Instead, my body ripples beneath his stare, soaking up the attention. *Be very, very careful, Bern,* I tell myself. If I've figured out that I have his balls in a vise, it's only a matter of time before Victor realizes he holds me by the ovaries.

"And Danny ...?" I start, exhaling sharply. Part of me

recognizes that I'm not as tough as I thought I was. This is a lot to take in. And yet … I'm a lot happier than I should be, standing beside a teenager's early grave.

Havoc, spilling its secrets out and into me.

Almost literally, if you consider Aaron, and Hael, and Vic …

"Mitch asked for him back, so we're going to make a special delivery." Vic smirks at me and winks before heading over and grabbing a pair of shovels that are leaning against a tree. He tosses one over to me and I catch it in my gloved hands. "Start digging, your majesty," he says smiling with too much teeth around the cigarette.

Oddly enough, he doesn't sound like he's being mocking. Glancing over in Oscar's direction, I see him frowning and that, that makes me smile.

Aaron looks up at me from across the grave and gives a smile of his own, but his is tinged at the edges with melancholy. It says, *I'm sorry, Bernie, I told you, and I was right.*

"Nantucket," I murmur, swallowing and pushing the end of the shovel into the pile of dirt. "I know, I know."

———————————————

Mitch has been driving a new car the last few weeks, another restored classic that makes Hael whistle like he's just spotted a hot piece of ass out the window of the Armada. It's currently parked outside of Kali's place, this boring ass ranch home that her grandparents probably picked out of a Sears catalog. It used to be an okay house before they died, and her parents inherited it. They've trashed the place.

"Oscar, the cameras?" Vic asks, and Oscar nods. He passes the iPad forward, releasing it into my hands with reluctance.

"Try not to break this one," he oozes, and I have to resist the urge to rabbit punch him. I yank it from his fingers, glancing down to find a graphic video of Mitch and Kali fucking. My brows go up.

"Well?" Vic asks, looking over his shoulder at me from the driver's seat of the second stolen SUV we pinched today. This one's a Suburban though, a bit newer but filled with children's' toys. Makes me feel a little guilty. Hael is driving the Armada with the body in it. That must suck serious ass—even with a mask on his face. Makes me remember the shitty coronavirus pandemic some years back, and I shiver. "Are they otherwise occupied?"

"Oh, they're occupied alright," I say, feeling my mouth twist into a smile. "Kali has small, shriveled looking tits from all her bulimic episodes, and Mitch's dick is short in length and lacking in girth. Plus, his balls are weird as hell." I pass the iPad forward again as Victor grins at me.

"Aren't balls always weird?" Callum asks, leaning an elbow on the edge of the door. I shake my head.

"Not like these balls, Cal. Not like these."

"Focus, please," Oscar purrs as Aaron smiles at me with much less melancholy than he did at the gravesite. "We have a few minutes to get this done, at best."

"You're being optimistic," Cal chuckles, laughter coloring his voice. "Bet Mitch blows his wad before we're done."

"Not taking that bet, the odds suck," Aaron murmurs as Hael reverses the Armada so that it's ass-to-ass with the blue two-seater car. Vic parks beside him and rolls down the driver's side window so they can talk to each other.

"A '69 Corvette Stingray?" Hael says, choking and coughing. I can smell the body from here. No wonder he's got tears in his eyes; the stench is almost unbearable. "Where the fuck is Mitch getting the money for this shit?"

"Slinging coke, that's how. Get out." Vic climbs out of the SUV, and the rest of us follow. I'm given the iPad to monitor as the boys don fresh gloves and unwrap the body. The smell makes me gag, even from all the way over here.

We use the Suburban as a shield for our activities. Luckily, we're on a corner lot across the street from a rundown elementary school. There are no cameras here, no cops, and the next neighbor over is hidden behind an eight-foot tall fence.

Perfect.

Callum picks the lock on the old trunk, then together, the five of them heft the body out. They shove Danny into Mitch's trunk and then slam it shut. I glance back at the Armada and see a few stray maggots. My stomach churns, and I glance down at the iPad.

Mitch's orgasm face is right there, front and center. My lip curls in disgust, and I have to resist the urge to roll my eyes.

"He's done," I say, lifting the iPad up.

"Told ya," Aaron says as Cal flips off the trunk of the car.

"Let's get the hell out of here," Vic says, opening the driver's side door of the Suburban. "Let's stop at our favorite McDonald's and clean that shit out before we return it." Hael nods and exhales, cracking his knuckles before he switches out his gloves yet again, shoving the old ones into a trash bag that he tucks on the passenger seat of the Armada. He puts on a fresh set of gloves as I climb back in Vic's borrowed SUV with the others.

"I feel like we weren't as careful as we could be," I muse, thinking about the few stray maggots.

"Forensics are good, but they can't get you if they don't know where to look. The owner of the Armada is out of town for two weeks on business; he'll never even know his car was missing. How can the police search it for trace evidence if they never knew we were in it?" Vic asks, starting the engine.

"And this one?" I ask, watching as Hael pulls out behind us and we start down the road.

"The owner of this car just had surgery and won't be out of the hospital for days. Her children are with their grandmother; the father is dead." Oscar tells me this in a total deadpan, like it isn't completely creepy that he knows all of that shit.

"How do you figure?" I ask, turning around to look at him. He stares right back at me and smiles. Chills trace over my arms and I shudder.

"Because that's my job, Bernadette, to know things."

What a fucking non-answer if I've ever heard one.

I don't ask how they got the camera in Kali's room. It'd be pretty easy to break in there, if one were so inclined.

"Your favorite McDonald's?" I query, and Callum smiles cheerily, like he didn't just chuck a dead guy's body into a teenager's trunk.

"South Prescott, no cameras, a lot of illegal activity to work under." His smile gets a bit wider. "Plus, they never give out cold fries."

Dark humor. But it works. I give Callum a look that he returns with a private one of his own. We have shit to work through, but it's been—pardon the pun—buried underneath everything else. But I haven't forgotten. I hope he can tell by my expression.

I turn back to the front and lean into my seat.

We just dropped a corpse off to the leader of the Charter Crew.

Talk about a clapback.

CHAPTER
FIFTEEN

We order pizza and smoke weed together, and I start to realize that what I first witnessed when I joined Havoc—that day we chilled and watch South Park together—was like a … calming ritual of sorts, a bonding exercise. Adrenaline was high after the, uh, body heist, and it's calmed down a whole hell of a lot with some community smoking.

"I can't believe you put a dead rat in that guy's Armada," I say with a snort. The smell Danny left in the SUV, it was impossible to miss. Hael cracked the front window, sent one of their Havoc lackeys to find us a rodent and … voila, an easy way to explain the stench of rot.

"This job's all about innovation," Hael says with a grin, glancing down as his phone buzzes. His lips turn down at the corners, and I have to take a guess on whether it's his mother … or Brittany. "Shit, I'm late," he growls, shoving his fingers through his hair. "Time to talk to Britt's dad."

Britt.

The sound of the familiar nickname rolling off Hael's tongue annoys me.

"Keep us updated," Victor warns as Hael grabs the keys to his Camaro. He looks like … well, I was going to say *death warmed over.* But really, I could just say he looks like Danny Ensbrook. "And don't lose your temper."

Hael licks the corner of his lip in an annoyed gesture.

"I won't, boss." He opens the door, and I stand up from the couch, following him out. Aaron and Vic watch me go, Oscar doesn't act like he gives a shit, and it's damn near impossible to figure out what Cal's up to when he hides inside his hood like that.

"You called her Britt," I say as I pause on the path that connects to the driveway, watching as Hael unlocks the driver's side door and turns to look at me. He seems surprised somehow, like he didn't figure I'd care.

"You okay, Blackbird?" he asks, standing up and turning back to me.

I move a little closer, so there's only about a foot of space between us.

"You know, I keep thinking that if this is your baby, that things are over between us," I say, and Hael whistles, letting his body slump back against the Camaro. Seems a little weird, to talk about shit like this after what we did today, but then again, what *wouldn't* seem weird right now? My whole existence is weird.

"I didn't think you thought we even had a thing," he says,

281

giving me a shit-eating little smirk that makes my blood boil. I narrow my eyes on him. Is this the point where I get another lesson in reality? The Havoc Boys have been like fairy-tale boys to me until now. But is Hael really just a cocky prick who likes to screw and run? Am I going to get a dose of his special breed of asshole? "What does Vic think?"

"Not everything is about Victor," I snap back, gritting my teeth. Hael smiles and then nods, closing his eyes for a moment.

"Yeah, I know." He opens those pretty honey-brown eyes of his back up. He had to shower three separate times when he got back, and then cover himself in body spray and cologne. When I lean in toward him, all I can smell is the coconut oil he rubbed into his hands. "But you saw how he acted the other day. I had two choices in there, Bernie: kick his ass or leave. And he's a good leader, even if he is a dick sometimes. I'd follow him into the pits of Hell." I nod, because I've always known it. You could see, looking at Hael and Vic at age eight, that they were destined to share their lives together in one fashion or another. "What does he think about Aaron?" he asks, nodding his chin slightly and then grinning when my eyes widen in surprise.

"You know about that?" I ask, and Hael shrugs.

"I see you two looking at each other differently now. I figured it'd happened." Hael doesn't stop smiling, reaching out a hand and running his knuckles down my bare arm. I shiver, but not because I don't like it. Quite the opposite actually.

"He hates it," I admit, but our conversation didn't exactly go any further than me fucking his possessive attitude into the bathroom wall. That's all we've got, as far as a conversation on the matter. "But I guess I'm still marrying him, so he can't be all that bothered."

"You guess?" Hael laughs, checking his phone for the time again. He sighs, like he's already exhausted. I don't blame him. After what we did today, I think a nap's in order. "You're definitely getting hitched, Bernie." He leans in toward me, smirking slightly. "And on Vic's birthday, no less."

"His birthday?" I ask, frowning. Vic has been insistent that we get married *soon*, but I didn't realize he had an exact day in mind. His birthday … figures. The first possible day we *could* get married, we will. I'm sure his mother, Ophelia, will like that one.

"Yep," Hael says, putting his mouth near my ear. "He turns eighteen just one day after me. how does that get you? That Vic's the younger one between us." Hael bites my ear, hard enough to startle me, but then he grabs my hips in his hands and pulls me close. "Look, if this kid really is mine … I don't know what I'll do. But what I can tell you is this: there's no hope for me and Brittany. There never was."

"Then fuck me before you go over there." The words come out before I can question them. Hael looks surprised, but not as surprised as I am.

"Well, shit, Blackbird, how am I supposed to say no to that?" he asks, grabbing me by the hips and guiding me around to the front of the Camaro.

Hael sets me on the hood of the car, placing a hand on either side of me as he leans in, pressing his lips to the side of my neck. My entire body lights up like it's on fire, and I suck in a sharp breath.

"Where should we go?" I ask, because this is not a good spot to have sex, on Aaron's driveway in the middle of suburbia. Likely, we'd end up getting the cops called on us, and we all know how that'd turn out.

"Go?" Hael echoes, cocking a red brow. "We ain't goin' nowhere, Blackbird. I'm short on time, Vic is probably seething inside the house, and the neighbors around here always look at me like they need to protect their sisters and daughters."

"Well, do they?" I quip back, and he just grins at me. "I'm serious, Hael. Have you been ...?" The words get stuck in my throat because I know I'll sound stupid as shit saying them. *Have you been sleeping with other girls? I mean, I know I've been fucking Vic, and I just screwed Aaron, but hey, I'm jealous as shit at the thought of you with someone else.*

"Um, you mean between the burying of bodies and the gang war on our hands, have I been dating?" Hael pauses, the edge of his lip quirking up in a cocky smirk. "Or ... fucking? Have I been dipping my dick into the sweet waters of a pussy that isn't yours?"

I grab him by the face, my fingers brushing against all of that red stubble as I dig my nails into his skin. His body feels hot between my thighs, scalding really. It's dark out here now, the only light cast from the sconces on either side of the garage. Maybe, if we were really careful, we could screw on the hood of the Camaro?

"Answer me." The words are an order and Hael knows it. He lets out a small whistle of surprise.

"*Cher,*" he murmurs, pronouncing the word like *sha.* I looked it up on my phone after the encounter with his mother.

Apparently, it means like sweetheart in Cajun French or something. "No, I haven't slept with anyone since we defiled my ride." He taps his palm against the hood of the car for emphasis. "Why? You want me all to yourself or something?"

I give him a look.

"Hael Harbin, would I be out here if I didn't?" I ask, gasping as he slides his hand up my leg and into my shorts. His fingers tease the wetness between my thighs, stroking my ember into an inferno with a casual smirk plastered to his face.

"That's not an answer at all," he remarks, reaching down with his other hand to undo his own pants. "I mean, you're screwing Vic and Aaron now, so what use could you possibly have for me?" I grab a fistful of his hair and force his mouth to mine, tasting that finely honed practice of his. It's both simultaneously a turn-on and a serious goddamn thorn in my ass.

I don't like thinking about Hael with other girls.

He pushes his fingers into me, making me groan. The car creaks underneath us as he leans forward and runs his hot tongue up the side of my throat.

"Promise me you won't touch another girl without telling me first," I whisper huskily, but only because I'm too much of a coward to say what I really want. *Promise me you won't touch another girl—ever.* But we're young and this is new, and I just can't bring myself to ask him that.

"Mm-hmm," Hael murmurs, breathing me in as he pumps his fingers in and out of me. "I'll make that promise. You gotta do something for me though first."

"Yeah?" I ask, beyond the point where I could actually find

the strength in myself to resist him. If Hael asked right now, I'd give him everything. *Everything.* He keeps the energy of this group up, keeps us from letting things get stale, perfumes the air with his laughter. We need that. Not just me, but all of us.

"Play a little game with me," he murmurs, kissing across my throat, teasing my clavicle, and then biting my nipple through my shirt. I hiss and grab his head to me. "Whoever comes last wins an oral sex session of their choice, to be redeemed whenever, wherever. How does that sound?"

"Sounds like a game I could easily win," I growl back, using my grip on Hael's hair to bring our faces together. We share breath for a moment before he removes his fingers from my cunt and grabs his dick instead. "Oh, by the way ..." I pat the car with the palm of my left hand. "I'm touching your car. Victor told me to never, ever touch your car."

Hael grins and laughs at me, shoving the shorts aside and then putting his lips right up against mine, so I can feel his words just as much as I can hear them.

"If you were anybody else, I'd break your hand for touching my baby." Hael kisses me, spiking my blood with adrenaline, making me feel sexy and naughty and free. Oh, and young. He most definitely makes me feel young, like we could both truly be seventeen for one, precious moment. "Not you though, Blackbird. Not you."

Hael puts his cock to my opening and thrusts into me. The car groans again, like it's truly part of this interaction, the third person in our little threesome. *Where's the condom, Bernie?!* I remember too late. I try to make myself say something, but then Hael starts to move and my mind is destroyed by the rush of pleasure.

A truck rumbles by on the street and Hael pauses, like just because he's not moving it won't be obvious that his ass is hanging out, that my legs are wrapped around him, that we're joined together in sin.

He waits until the truck turns the corner before he starts to move again, fast and hard and frenzied. In just a short while, he'll be at Brittany's house, sitting on a couch and looking across at her father who just so happens to be a cop, telling him that he got his baby girl pregnant. The thought makes me grit my teeth as I dig my nails into Hael's upper arms, marking him as my own.

"Come over sometime and visit me at my house," Hael murmurs, kissing the edge of my mouth as he cups my ass with soft hands, fingers digging beneath the loose fabric of the shorts. "We can make love *all* over your Eldorado, so long as you don't mind being covered in grease."

A moan escapes my lips at the idea as Hael slides one hand up my side, shoving my borrowed t-shirt up to grab my bare breast. He kneads the heavy flesh with his fingers, thumb stroking over the pert point of my nipple.

"Check this, Bernie," he purrs, licking me again, like he just can't get enough of the taste. Hael seems eager to show off for me, and I have to say, I don't mind one goddamn bit. He drops his hand between us to find my clit, squeezing it between two fingers and making my heart thunder. When he starts to rub it in slow, lazy circles, I feel my body breaking down.

"Tell me I'm tighter than Brittany," I moan, even though I hate to hear her name pass his lips.

"So much tighter," he agrees, thrusting hard and deep. "So much wetter." Another thrust, another flick of my clit. My breasts bounce as the car rocks underneath us, taking the motion of its master's thrusting hips without complaint. "So much prettier, too. I imagined you when I was fucking her, you know that?"

"Oh god, shut up," I groan as he works up the fire between my legs, stoking it with carefully crafted expertise. The orgasm takes over me from the inside, instantly relieving all of my stress, making me forget where I am and why I should be quiet.

A scream of ecstasy escapes my throat, making Hael chuckle as he rides out the tender squeezing of my body around his. He lets me finish before he works on his own climax, holding my panting body and thrusting until he's shuddering in my arms, his body now as soaked with sweat as my own.

We sit there for a second, hearts pounding, just trying to catch our breath.

"I wish you didn't have to go," I say, even though I know that I'm essentially admitting that I want him here, that I'll … like, miss him or something. Gross.

"Same," he says, standing up and fixing his pants. There's not much to do about me; I just have to clean myself up after he leaves. Hael looks down at me, eyes sparkling, face contemplative. I'm sure he's about to say something profound and extraordinary when he proves to me that he's just as much of a cocky slut as I always expected. "By the way, I just won that bet." He taps me on the nose and leans in close, putting his hands on his lower back as he cops a wicked smile. "And I *will* be collecting on that blow job."

I slap him in the chest, but he just catches my wrist and yanks me up and off the hood of the car, planting one, last kiss to my lips before he climbs into the Camaro.

"I'll call you later?" he says, and I nod, crossing my arms under my breasts as Hael pulls out of the driveway and disappears down the street.

"Feel better now?" Vic asks me when I come out of the bathroom after cleaning up. I'm breathless and pink-cheeked, with that freshly-fucked look, I'm sure. He's the only one in the living room now, sitting on the long couch in front of the coffee table, tattooed arms stretched out on either side of him and resting on the tops of the pillows. "Now that you've punished me thoroughly, I mean."

"Punished you?" I ask, taking a step toward him. Fury is rolling off of him in waves, making it quite plain to see that Victor Channing is not about sharing. "You think I screwed Aaron and Hael to *punish* you? You're a narcissistic asshole sometimes, you know that?"

He stands up suddenly, but I don't move, staying right where I am.

"And what about Cal? You want to screw him, too?" Vic challenges, coming around the couch to stand in front of me. I let my head fall back as I laugh. Today should've ranked up there in the worst of my life. I mean, we dug up a dead Prescott High student. And yet, compared to how I felt the day Pen died, this is *nothing*. I feel lighter than I ever have, like I've finally shed the gossamer strands of society, this glittering web of who I should've been, who I could still be, if only I'd run and let my monsters walk.

But oh no, I am *much* more vindictive than that.

"Maybe I do, Victor? So what. Sex is all about expression. You know how I feel about Havoc."

He takes a step toward me. It's dark in here, with just the two lamps on, casting a dull orange glow across the worn hardwood floors and old rugs that decorate them.

"How do you feel, Bernadette?" Vic asks, tilting his head slightly. "Why don't you say it aloud?"

I close my eyes and Vic skims his palms down my bare arms, taking my heated skin and cooling it down, like a pleasant breeze, like the sweet kiss of AC on a summer night. My head clears; my numbness flees.

Sometimes, when you meet someone, you just know they're going to change your fate. For better or worse. I think about saying those words as part of my vows to Vic, and they feel right. They don't feel fake or forced, like a charlatan wedding for a sea of thespians.

"This is where I belong, Vic," I say, opening my eyes back up. He stares down at me from ebon irises, his big body shaking with jealous rage. I should chastise him more for it, but I don't. I can't help myself; I want him like this. Aching for me. Pining. Snarling. Growling. Pissing. He can go all alpha on me if he wants, and I won't stop him. "I've always belonged with the five of you."

His mouth twitches, and he reaches up a big hand, using

inked fingers to tuck pink-tinged hair behind my ear.

"My beautiful nightmare," he confirms, running his thumb over my lower lip. "After we get married, I'm not sharing you. Get your fucking out of the way before then." Vic drops his hand by his side, and I frown. I'm not sure I agree with that statement, but I also feel like I can't possibly say anything, not right now. He'll throw a man-trum and break the magic of the evening.

"Do you want to take these pregnancy tests with me?" I ask, choking on the courage needed to say those words. "I mean, while we wait for Hael to call us and say he's still alive."

Vic's face darkens up, but it's not without kindness.

"Pregnancy tests?" he asks, almost too mildly. My skin erupts in goose bumps. Those syllables spilling from those poison-tinged lips of his, they're loaded. "I didn't know you'd bought any."

"Well," I start, giving him a look. "You keep fucking me without using one. What did you expect to happen?" Victor smiles slightly as I move over to the brown paper bag on the small sofa table that's pressed up against the wall. I take the boxes from it and pop into the downstairs bathroom, reading the instructions as Victor watches me from the doorway.

There's a nightlight in the little downstairs half-bath, shaped like a full moon with little grayed out spots that are supposed to be craters. It's cute, and it casts enough light for me to take a piss and set the stupid white sticks out on the counter.

I fix my pants, wash my hands, and then cross my arms over my chest to wait.

"They only take a few minutes, Bern," Vic says after a

while, watching me with heavy lidded eyes. He'd probably love it if I were pregnant. He doesn't say as much, but it'd be impossible to miss, with the expression on his face.

"You check them," I tell him, but when he reaches out a hand to grab one, I snatch his wrist, fingers curling around him and squeezing tight. *I wonder if Brittany felt like this when she was taking the test, if she wished Hael were there.*

Shit.

I feel like an asshole and yet, the world has only ever treated me like shit. I've tried to do things the right way, I really have. And how have I been rewarded for it? With molestation, suicide, and pain. That's how.

So ... fuck Brittany. And fuck Kali.

I snatch one of the tests off the counter and close my eyes tight. I can feel Victor watching me carefully, waiting with that intense and unending patience of his.

When I open my eyes, I see the words *Not Pregnant* and my breath escapes in a rush.

"I see I've failed to fuck you hard enough," is Vic's response. I lift my eyes up from the test to glare at him. It feels suddenly weird to have him standing here, like the air between us is too thick. I've literally just fucked his best friend on the hood of his Camaro, in the driveway of a tame, suburban neighborhood. How weird is my goddamn life right now?

"You'd love it if I got knocked up," I say, eyes narrowed, but Vic just shrugs.

"Maybe I would? But either way, it's your choice to decide when." He turns away, and I bristle at the arrogance in his words. It's my choice to decide *when?*

"You mean, it's my choice to decide *if* I want to be with you before I even settle the question of *if* I want to have kids at all. Besides, even if I did, what sort of life would this be? The world rewards the rich. We … just moved a body today. You can't do that sort of shit if you have kids."

"Once we get my grandmother's inheritance," he says, pausing to study a framed picture of Kara and Ashley on one of the side tables. It's a newer picture, meaning Aaron must've put it there. Hah. Aaron Fadler and his domestic shit. It's almost … cute. I nearly gag on the thought. "Things will be different."

"Will they?" I ask, some of my skepticism from the last few months fading from me. Do I really think Vic is going to give me an equal share of that inheritance? Kind of … I mean, we'll be legally married, so it'll be mine anyway, whether he likes it or not. The thought warms me immensely. I play with the ring on my finger as I follow him down the hall and toward the master bedroom.

Victor pauses near the hallway, glancing back to look at me with obsidian eyes. He's so impossible to read, and yet … painfully obvious at the same time. I never quite know what he's thinking, but his wants are apparent.

Me.

I'm what Victor Channing wants.

Maybe something he's always wanted, based on our conversation the day after Halloween.

"That much, I promise. We're going to rule this city together, Bernadette. You and me, king and queen." He turns away and keeps going, like he's expecting me to follow him. I just might; I haven't decided yet.

"I'll have no other girl," I tell Vic, and he pauses. His back is broad beneath the dark-colored tee he's wearing, his tattoos bright against his arms. He doesn't look back at me, but I know he's listening, regardless. "In Havoc, I mean. I don't care about all the peons you managed to rope into working for you." Victor laughs, but still, he doesn't turn around. I wonder why? "But not ... like we are now, the six of us."

"For me, at least," Vic starts, lifting up his right hand. I glance up to the top of the staircase and find Aaron looking down at me. I think he's trying to say *us. For us at least ...* "There was never another girl. Enjoy your time as a free woman because I'm counting down the nights until I fuck that wedding dress off of you."

Victor heads into the downstairs bedroom and slams the door behind him.

I glance up at Aaron.

"It's not fair, you know," I tell him, frowning. "That he gets your parents' old room, and you're stuck living in memories of your childhood."

"It's fair," Aaron says, shrugging his big shoulders. "Because he's the boss." His eyes darken several shades and he starts down the steps. It gets suddenly hard to breathe in that room, and my eyes stray to the Bernadette tattoo on his arm yet again.

"Watch a movie with me until Hael calls?" I ask, and Aaron nods.

We end up cuddled together on the sofa, just like in the old days, watching a horror movie that's essentially murder porn. It seems like a weird choice, but all the bodies and the blood, I know they're all fake. Makes it easier to pretend that what I saw earlier today was fake, too.

After several hours and two movies later, Hael finally comes crawling home.

He's got a black eye, red smeared across the lower half of his face, like maybe he got a nosebleed and swiped the blood away with his arm.

"What the fuck, man? You were supposed to call," Aaron snaps, standing up from the couch and knocking stray kernels of popcorn everywhere.

"We have a problem," Hael says, panting heavily, his forehead dotted with sweat.

"What is it?" Vic asks, making me jump as he appears out of freaking nowhere.

"Ivy Hightower is dead," Hael says, surprising the shit out of me. I sit up suddenly, upending the bowl of popcorn to the floor.

"Where is she?" Vic snaps, which is a strange question to ask, if you really think about it. But then, he knows this game a hell of a lot better than I do.

"Outside," Hael says, his mouth turned down in a severe frown. "On the front lawn."

"Well, fuck me," Vic growls, and then he, Aaron, and Hael are moving in unison, like a murder of crows. Perfectly aligned. Perfectly in sync. As it often did when I was in junior high, my heart thunders at the sight, and my mouth waters with the need to belong.

I join them.

And there she is, pale body stretched across the grass like

she's sleeping. Obviously, Ivy hasn't been dead as long as Danny, so she can still fake it. Life, that is. At least from a distance.

"We just saw her in the hallway today," I manage to get out, anxiety flooding my body with adrenaline. It's interesting, isn't it, how perceptions and needs can shift with time? I'm worried about the boys getting caught, more than anything. What if that douchebag detective Constantine were to drive by? What if the Thing were to cruise up in his Dodge Charger?

Shit.

Oscar and Callum join us. One from inside the house, the other from the shadows. The fuck was Cal doing out here? Nobody else seems to care, so I figure he must've been on watch or something. I'll tell you one thing: I would not like to find Callum Park crouching in the darkness, waiting for me.

"Grab the tarps and gloves," Oscar says, yawning. He's dressed in black satin pajama pants, hung criminally low on his hips and showing off all those pretty tattoos of his. Even though it's obvious he's just woken up out of sleep, not a hair is out of place. His glasses are clean. Oh, and he's still a goddamn asshole. "Bernadette, are you deaf? Move your ass and get the tarps and gloves," he snaps, and I scowl at him.

If this were a different time and place …

But a group is only as tough as its weakest link, and let's be honest here: I'm flagging.

I move into the house, glad that the girls are long past the point of waking up for the night, and grab the extra tarps from a plastic bag near the front door. There are dozens of them, and I can't help but wonder if the guys keep them on hand, like paper towels or some shit.

Heading back out into the dewy grass, I pass the tarps to Callum.

"You look rough, my friend," he whispers to Hael as they unwrap one of the tarps with freshly gloved hands. "What happened?"

"What do you think happened? Brittany's dad is the head of the anti-gang force. He's a cop with an extra dose of asshole attached to his title. He beat the snot out of me and then threatened to press rape charges. You like that one?"

"I oughta box your fucking ears for getting us into this shit," Vic snarls, and Hael's entire face flushes with shame. He grits his teeth as he helps Cal roll the body of our dead classmate onto the tarp. Second time we've done that today.

This time, I won't look at Aaron. I hate how right he was about all of this.

"Bernadette, I tried to warn you. We're messed-up. Havoc is fucking messed-up. You just—"

He never finished what he was going to say, and I never got the chance to clarify, but I'm pretty sure it was *you just never saw it.* And I didn't, because they didn't let me. Even when they were metaphorically kicking the shit out of me during sophomore year.

These are my boys.

Mine.

I have to protect them. Even if I hate them a little bit. Even if they're fucked-up and twisted and their spirits are darker than pitch. This is it for me, my endgame.

Yanking on a pair of gloves, I help the guys wrap Ivy up and bind the tarps with rope.

Cal says it's the cheapest goddamn rope you can buy at Wal-Mart. Their guys pick it up on the regular, usually in a large load of groceries, and they always pay cash. It's pretty hard to trace.

When they lift her into the Camaro, I stand back. It only takes Cal and Hael—the clear 'muscle' of the group—to do it. There's no time to steal a car now, not with the shit that's following us around.

"You think this was Mitch?" Aaron asks Vic as Hael slams the trunk closed.

"Doubt it," Vic replies, lighting a cigarette. He moves over to the side of the garage where Aaron's left his lawncare shit. There's a backpack attached to a bottle of Roundup—I'd tell him that shit is cancer-causing, bee-killing garbage, but that would imply I had enough room in my brain to care about issues outside my own life—that he picks up. "He'd be too freaked out by his dead bestie to pull a stunt this elaborate. There's no way he left the house to work on this without at least noticing the god-awful stench of his car. Go check the boys." Vic is spraying the grass with the Roundup, holding his phone with the other hand, and smoking, all at the same time.

It's impressive.

"They're not answering," Oscar confirms, looking down at his iPad. The light catches on the edges of his face and makes him look ghoulish. He glances up at me. "That's not a good sign."

"Definitely not. Especially after how bad they messed up on Halloween," Victor murmurs, seemingly annoyed but not worried. Then again, his shoulders and arms are tight. He's full of shit, isn't he? Just too damn good at playing pretend.

It only takes Cal, Hael, and Aaron a few minutes to report back.

"They're gone," Hael says, nostrils flared. "Every guy in the immediate vicinity, and we had, what, six?"

"Eight," Vic corrects, gritting his teeth. A bead of sweat rolls down the side of his face as Hael pulls his keys from his pocket. Guess I know where he's going after this. "This isn't good. This is bigger than Charter Crew shit. They didn't kill anyone on Halloween. I mean, they might now, since we left that special delivery of ours. But not yet, not this quickly. Even if they did, they'd leave the bodies for us to find."

My blood chills as something occurs to me, and the fine hairs on the back of my neck rankle.

"The Thing," I say, licking my suddenly dry lips. My gaze meets Oscar's, of all people's, but there's no emotion inside his gray irises, like he's either really good at pretending he doesn't have emotions … or else he truly is a sociopath.

"You think he'd go this far, this quick?" Vic asks, looking askance at me. "Because he knows we have one video?"

"Because one monster always recognizes another," I whisper, my eyes on Victor but my focus elsewhere. Hael pauses, one leg inside the car, to watch me. I blink and the fog in my vision clears. "You might be a different breed than he is, but he knows. And now that he's seen me with you, he knows about me, too."

"How so?" Hael asks, and I let out a deep exhale.

"That I'm a monster, too," I tell them, without a shred of

shame in my words. "And he knows exactly what we're going to do to him because, if given the chance, he'd do the same to us."

"Why Ivy?" Aaron asks, but we don't have time to talk about it. We need her body gone like, fucking yesterday.

"Because she was with Vaughn the night we found him," I say, because I know how my stepdad works, the things he does, the way he retaliates.

"What about our boys?" Vic asks, nodding at Hael. The latter climbs in the Camaro with Aaron and Cal, killing my opportunity at having any alone time with Aaron tonight

"I don't know," I say, feeling a cold chill fall over me. And it's not the dew, or the fact that it's nearly four in the morning. It's because I know that once Neil Pence latches on to something, he never lets it go.

It makes me wonder ... if my sister's suicide was really a suicide at all.

CHAPTER

SIXTEEN

The next morning starts out with me waking up in a puddle of blood.

The timing's unfortunate because as I'm sitting up and throwing Aaron's sheets aside, he walks in and sees me staring down at the violent mess of crimson I've made of his bed.

"What the fuck?" he blurts out, tattooed fingers curled around the doorjamb as he leans into the bedroom, like he needs the door to keep himself upright. In an instant, he's moving toward me like I need saving, and I feel myself get seriously irritated.

Yep, it's definitely that time of the goddamn month.

And right after I went to all that trouble to take the pregnancy tests.

"I'm on my period, Aaron," I tell him dryly, watching as he comes to that realization on his own a split-second before the words leave my lips. "I get really heavy ones sometimes; it's not that big of a deal. I mean, for your sheets it is. But not me."

He hesitates about a foot away from the bed, still stuck in that strange limbo we've had between us for years. Are we something or not? Was it just a casual fuck … or not?

"Do you need help?" he asks, eyeing me with a morbid curiosity.

"I mean, you could shove this shit in the laundry?" I suggest, wondering if I'm taking whatever it is we've got going between us too far, too quick. Cute first-time boyfriend shit like shyly helping your girl with her period, we're past that. I'm two years too far beyond getting a bouquet of tampons by a well-meaning high schooler. "This is weird, isn't it? It's freaking weird. Just … get out."

Aaron surprises me by laughing. He buried a girl in the woods last night, has dark circles under his eyes … and he's laughing. Guess he meant what he said about trying to find happiness wherever you can, whenever you can. I can see how and why he changed so quickly. The old Aaron probably vomited at the sight of his first body and fell into shock for days. That old Aaron would never survive this, would most *definitely* not be able to laugh.

"It's no big deal, Bernie. I know what a period is; I'll throw the stuff in the wash."

I narrow my eyes on him, but now that I've asked for help, I decide I don't want it. I'm going to have to run for that stupid toilet, blood running down my legs, dripping across the floor … The last thing I'd ever want is for any of the Havoc Boys—Aaron included—to see me in that state.

I'm Bernadette Blackbird, leather-wearing, face-smashing bitch from hell.

That's the persona I want. This is too real for me. Honestly, it's freaking me the fuck out. I'm pretty sure I have intimacy problems that I need to work through.

"Aaron, screw off," I say, trying to keep my cool as much as possible. Anyone that tells you that women are irrational freaks on their period is probably a misogynistic douche, but that doesn't mean I enjoy having blood all over me and cramps that hurt like a punch to the gut.

"Stop that crap. I'm here to help. Where did you put the tampons and shit you bought?" He crosses his arms over his chest, like he intends on standing there until I tell him.

"Downstairs," I grind out and he nods, disappearing out the door while I scramble to get to the toilet. Unfortunately for me, Oscar is in the bathroom when I get there, and I groan. He's brushing his teeth at the sink and pauses to look my direction with a face painted in abject boredom. When he sees the blood all over my crotch, his expression shifts slightly.

"I can see you need this more than I do," he says calmly, spitting into the sink one last time before he quickly rinses it and puts his toothbrush in a *case*. I try not to judge, but who the hell takes the time to put their toothbrush in a snapping plastic case twice a day? It just isn't worth the effort.

Oscar goes to skirt past me, but as he does, a strange thrill passes over me, and he pauses right beside me, our bodies jammed together in the doorframe.

He's tall, much skinnier than Hael or Aaron or Vic, but with long, lean muscles that move viper-quick in an altercation. I've seen him fight before, when he curb stomped that kid outside the school. I've also used a stun gun on him and watched as he grabbed my arm and electrocuted me, too. I ended up on my back on the ground, twitching, as Oscar stood stoically over me.

He's inhuman.

I move into the room and slam the door behind me. Seeing as the lock is broken, I don't bother with it, climbing into the bathtub with all my clothes on and shivering as I wait for the water to warm up. Blood swirls down my thighs and stains the floor red. I can't stop staring at it for some reason, my mind on Ivy Hightower's perfect dead body.

Just like Pen's.

Too perfect to really be dead, too perfect for any of that morbidity to be real. Because dead people—people like Danny Ensbrook—look ugly when they die. They smell, and they bloat, and they crawl.

Penelope just looked … asleep. Like Ivy.

"You stupid fucker," I growl, closing my eyes under the spray of the water. I strip my clothes off and then stand there with my arms wrapped over my chest, thinking about the Thing. About my sister. About the note on her phone, and the pills on her bed.

But none of that *really* means she killed herself. Neil could've put a gun to her head and forced her to write the note, take the pills. Half of me wonders how I didn't think of this before, and the other half of me is convinced that I must be a moron to come up with a story that's so far-fetched.

I hear the door open and peak around the curtain as thick,

wet fog swirls around the bathroom. Aaron puts the tampons and menstrual cups on the counter, along with a water bottle and some ibuprofen.

"You're our first Havoc Girl," he says, looking down at the items on the counter like he's happy to see them there. This is getting intimate, and I'm not sure that I like it. "And our first period, so take it easy on us, okay?"

"Don't act like sexist pricks, and I'll do my best, okay? And tell Oscar I can still strangle him, bleeding out of the vagina or no."

"I'll make sure to deliver that message," Aaron tells me, watching me for a moment before he steps out of the bathroom and closes the door behind him. My heart flip-flops strangely as I imagine him smiling on the other side of that door, happy to have his girlfriend back, happy to be a part of her life in the most intimate way possible.

Girlfriend ... I still need to unpack that word.

After all, can I really be Vic's fiancée and Aaron's girlfriend and Hael's ... something, all in the same breath?

Once I get out of the shower and put my cup in—it's the disposable kind you can still have sex with, so I'm happy about that—I wrap a towel around myself and head back to Aaron's room to get dressed. I slept alone in there last night, but something about that felt off.

There's no reason for me to sleep alone, not anymore. Aaron might've been in the woods, but Vic was at the house.

I check on the girls and find them immersed in a fierce game of Mario Kart together. I feel a bit like an asshole; I haven't been giving Heather the attention she deserves. *Let's just get through this, and we can be together,* I promise her. But I don't interrupt their game to tell her that. Children are perceptive as hell. If I start acting weird and hugging her, kissing her forehead, murmuring strange shit, she's going to know something is wrong.

She knew on that awful day, when I found Pen. Heather knew before she knew, you know what I mean? I remember her starting to scream, throwing her body against my arms, straining for the stairs.

Penelope was already gone by then, loaded into a bag that looks an awful lot like the tarps we've been using, transported away to Neil's friend at the morgue. Buried. Drowning in dirt. Rotting. My stomach clenches with cramps, and I turn away sharply, closing the door to the girls' bedroom.

Heather and I are staying here enough. Maybe I should get her like, a cot or something? Would that be better than an air mattress?

"Good morning," Callum says in that husky voice of his, standing by the table when I come downstairs. There's a heap of chocolate in the center of it, a literal freaking mound. I narrow my eyes, and he grins back at me. "We heard. Congratulations on not being pregnant with Victor's child."

"Shut your mouth, you smart-ass," Vic says as he leans back on the sofa and crosses his ankles on the coffee table. He's shirtless and wearing only pajama pants. Come to think of it, they're *all* shirtless and wearing only pajama pants. Even Cal, in his usual sleeveless hoodie, has left the damn thing unbuttoned and gaping open to the point that I can't even figure out why he's still wearing it.

They did this shit on purpose, I think, just because it makes me feel like they're being spiteful so I can be spiteful back. In reality, I know we're all just settling into a new normal.

I am a part of Havoc; I am one of the guys.

Except … with a vagina that they all want to fuck.

Okay, maybe not Oscar, but the others.

"Any news about …" I trail off, because there's no point in saying it aloud when we all know what I'm talking about. *Any news about Danny? Or Ivy?* I feel nothing for the former, but there's some shred of feeling deep down inside of me that aches for the latter. Ivy … she was snooty and full of herself, her essays in English last year were as bad as Kali's, and she cheated at every game she ever played, but she wasn't a terrible person. A misguided, gossipy little cunt, but that's about it. She didn't deserve to die for that.

"Nothing," Hael says with a groan, lying on his stomach on the small sofa. I grab a dark chocolate bar from the table and try to forget how stupidly cute it was for them to think of getting me candy. They're not supposed to be cute; they play games with corpses. "There won't be. If the Charter Crew is smart, they'll just put Danny somewhere else."

I come around the end of the couch to look down at his face. Hael is pretty badly swollen still. Worse than that, he mentioned Brittany's dad threatening rape charges. That's not good.

That makes sense, about Danny though. Of course Mitch isn't going to call the cops with a body in the trunk of his car. It *really* wouldn't look good for him. Question is: what are they going to do to us now that we've struck back? And so much worse than firebombing an old minivan.

Havoc escalates things, but never unnecessarily. It's just right, just the correct amount of menace to perfume the air with violence.

"And the other?" I ask, trying to be cryptic. I feel like you can never really know who's listening in.

Callum starts stretching in front of the fireplace, just below the flickering screen of the TV. He glances my way, blond hair hanging into his eyes.

"Likely, we won't see news about her as a missing person for days. In any other regard, she shouldn't make headlines either." Cal curves his body over to touch his toe, and I admire the sinewy perfection of his muscles. Some guys get all bulked up, and turn into these stiff statues, strong but about as limber as the stone they're made out of. Callum is bendy, and vibrant, and I want to know what would happen if we started dancing … and didn't stop.

I sit down on the chair between the two couches, figuring that's the safest place for now. We might be fighting multiple wars on different fronts—real wars, ones with body counts— but there's also an underlying current of male politics, testosterone, and romance. That's the real clincher right there, the most dangerous thread in our tapestry of politics and intrigue.

"What's our plan for today?" I ask as Aaron pads over and hands me a plate with toast and scrambled eggs on it. *The fuck is this twisted reality?* I wonder, staring at my ex and feeling his sweaty chest beneath my fingertips, his hips thrusting between my thighs. My god. How far we've all come.

I guess, when I spent every day last summer debating on

whether or not to call Havoc, that was a smart choice. This isn't the type of decision you make on the fly. No, you either feel it in your soul or you don't.

Because I knew what price they'd give me, all along. I knew. In my heart, I *knew.*

I take a bite of my eggs and do my best to ignore Oscar's intense stare. He's been looking at me more lately, ever since Halloween night. It's annoying the shit out of me.

"What's on the agenda for today?" I ask, focusing on my breakfast and trying to ignore the violent clenching of my asshole uterus. *Dead bodies, you say? Well, have some cramps on top of it, bitch.* My lady parts are out to kill me.

"Couple of things," Vic says, like he's debating the merits of the itinerary he has in his head. We all know he's already decided; this bit is just for fun, to pretend like he might actually be human. "I was thinking we start off by paying your stepfather's partner a visit."

My head perks up at that, and I turn to stare at Vic like he's just suggested he perform his own circumcision.

"You're kidding me? You want to go talk to a cop about another cop? Do you have a death wish? Or perhaps just a dream of incarceration?"

Victor ignores me to glance Oscar's way.

"You really think she can be of use to us?" Vic asks, and Oscar nods.

"Neil Pence's partner, Sara Young, is one of those *save the world types.* She thought she could make a difference by becoming a cop." Oscar chuckles, like that's one of the most ridiculous things he's ever heard. "She wants to save the world.

I figure, either I'm right about her and she'll want to seek justice or, she's as dirty as he is, in which case, she dies, too."

Dies.

There's that word again.

It'd be pretty easy to think the Havoc Boys might just go down my list and start executing people. But killing folks has a tendency to draw attention. They like to inflict damage without leaving permanent marks, just like they did to me. Like they did to Donald. Or Principal Vaughn.

But if anyone were going to die, they had to know it was going to be him.

"You want to tell her about Neil and … what? Wait for her to go vigilante? To report him through official means?" I look up from my eggs and find that Hael's fallen asleep again. Oscar glances his way, but he doesn't seem to mind. Guess even that heartless asswipe figures the other boys need their sleep after a night of unburying, and then re-burying, bodies.

"You're not going to tell her anything just yet. You're just going to talk to her." Oscar leans back into the couch, watching me with empty gray eyes and giving me the chills. He's gearing up to something; I just have no idea what, exactly, that is. "Confide in her, make her your friend. You can handle that, can't you, Bernie?" Oscar asks, but then, he doesn't get to hear my answer because Victor's phone rings. He glances at the screen, still casually slumped into the old sofa.

"Mitch," he purrs, and I wish I could truly describe the way Vic smiles then. There are demons there, twisting up the edges of his lips. It isn't a natural or normal smile and yet, my blood pressure spikes as soon as I see that malicious expression spread across his handsome face. It's pure … I don't want to say evil, because Victor is far from evil. Real evil, I've seen that, in the Thing's face, in Eric's bleeding scowl, in Kali's pink painted sneers. But it's something dark and wicked, something that glitters like the edge of a bloodstained blade. By the time he answers with a curt "*Yeah*", I'm soaking wet.

"You sociopathic nightmare!" Mitch screams, now on speakerphone. Hael startles awake, his hand snaking underneath the cushion, likely to grab a weapon of some sort. He cracks one brown eye to watch Vic set the phone down on the coffee table. Victor leans forward, putting his elbows on his knees and clasping his hands together in front of him. "We've been *fucking* with you until now. You've just opened the floodgates, motherfucker."

"What on earth are you talking about?" Victor asks, completely deadpan. His entire stance though, that speaks to violence. I take a bite of my eggs to hide the involuntary shiver that passes through me.

"You think I wouldn't notice the goddamn *corpse* you put in my trunk? Are you nuts? You're lucky I've got Kyler and Timmy on a short leash or you'd already be dead, motherfucker."

"Try a different word. You've used *motherfucker* twice," Vic says, and I hear the crash of something on the other end of the line. Mitch is clearly in a mood. Maybe he should've thought about what could happen when he decided to challenge Havoc? "And slow down. A corpse? What corpse? Should I notify the police?"

"You are going to *bleed* for this. I'm going to hold your girl down and fuck her until she begs me to end her life. You hear me, Victor?" Mitch is panting and cursing; I hear voices in the background but they're too faint to make out.

Vic's eyes narrow, and his face darkens into something truly terrifying. I hear Mitch's words, but they pass over me like a light breeze. How many times have men threatened to rape me? More than I can count. I'm not afraid of Mitch Charter.

"If you speak about my girl like that again, I will drown your mother in her bathtub. Do you understand me?" Vic's as calm as could be, his eyes on the phone, his shoulders tense. I have no doubt in my mind that he's telling the truth.

"And if you think we're done avenging Kali's face, you're seriously deluded. Tell Bernadette her stepdad says—"

Victor hangs up on Mitch and then promptly blocks him.

Wow. Dismissive. I love it.

"My stepdad says … what?" I ask, feeling my stomach hollow out. If Mitch is somehow working with the Thing, that won't go well for us.

"Irrelevant," Vic says, waving his hand at me. "We have to deal with the Charter Crew, and we have to deal with your stepdad. It's all one in the same to me." He stands up from the couch, and I find my eyes drawn down the muscular length of his body. He's built like a dark god, and I'm here to worship on my knees. *Shit, fuck, goddamn it …*

I frown.

"Everyone get up and get dressed," Oscar says, making Hael groan. Aaron is perched on the edge of the couch, finishing his breakfast. He takes my empty plate from me before heading into the kitchen. "We have a lot to get done this weekend."

"Like moving more bodies?" I quip as Cal finishes his stretches and stands up, arching his arms above his head with a yawn.

"Better," Oscar says, glancing over at me with a smile that's as sharp as a garrote, wrapping around my neck and sucking the air from my lungs. "We're going to look at a wedding venue."

CHAPTER
SEVENTEEN

Sara Young is a pretty young blond who lives in a pretty yellow house on a pretty little street.

I stand at the end of her driveway, staring at the bright, red color of her front door. I'm not a fan of this plan, not at all. I don't trust the cops. But … I do trust Havoc. Even though I shouldn't. Even though their secrets are buried as deep as the bodies in the woods.

The video.

Vic's confession about my price.

The truth about the incident with Kali.

Yet, here I am, walking up to Sara's front door in a crisp linen summer dress that I watched Callum pinch from Nordstrom. He even had a tool tucked away in his backpack that he used to remove the security tag. Impressive.

I feel like a fraud in it.

Taking a deep breath, I lift the tattooed knuckles of my left hand up and knock softly.

It takes Sara a minute to show up. She answers the door with her hair wrapped in a towel … but her hand on her gun.

As soon as she sees me, she relaxes … and then spots the tattoos on my hand and tenses up again.

"Can I help you?" she asks, and I do my best to smile. The expression feels forced, like it's stretching my lips in an unnatural way. I don't even know what it means to smile anymore.

"Maybe. I'm Bernadette Blackbird, Neil's stepdaughter." I watch the information wash over her. The fingers on her gun relax and she pulls the towel from her hair. I wonder if Neil is supposed to be picking her up soon in the cruiser; she's already dressed in her uniform.

"Bernadette," she says, like the name is familiar enough. Sara's face is so little, her features petite and delicate. I have a hard time believing she commands authority in cold-hard criminal types. "Yes, it's nice to finally meet you." Her eyes flick to my knuckles again, and I realize then that Oscar wasn't exaggerating when he called her a *save the world* type. She's one of those black-and-white, good-versus-evil hero types.

And those types … they are dangerous as fuck. Their morality is the most important thing to them. They only *think* they know what justice means. Sara Young here probably thinks pedophiles like Neil deserve life in prison … with three hot meals a day, unlimited access to HBO, and feather pillows in their cells. Because, like, that's humane.

I frown, even though I know I'm supposed to be playing a part here. The thing is, Sara is even worse than I thought. She's seen my tattoo; she already knows I'm a gangbanger. I may as well be wearing an orange jumpsuit in her mind.

"Sara Young," she says, trying her best to smile. I mean, I'm still a teenage girl, so her conflicted inner sense of justice is struggling to make my presence make sense. "As glad as I am to have finally met you, may I ask what you're doing at my house?"

"The ..." *Don't say the Thing, not outright.* "My stepdad's driven us past your house and pointed it out once or twice." I shrug my shoulders. It's a lie, a pretty terrible one, if I'm being honest with myself, but it doesn't matter. That part of this interaction is irrelevant, as Vic might say. "I know it's weird for me to just show up on your doorstep, but I don't have your number or anything and I thought ..."

I try to remember what the old Bernadette used to believe. Oh, that's right. People in positions of authority are there to help. Report bad things. Be honest. Ask for assistance when you need it. I mean, it's laughable to me now, but I used to believe those things with my whole heart.

"I thought you might be able to help me," I say, making sure I maintain eye contact with her. She has soft brown eyes, like those of a baby deer. *Jesus Christ, what am I doing here?* At best, I'm going to get Sara Young killed. At worst, she might end up hunting the Havoc Boys down as a part of some justice warrior plot.

Sara frowns, but only a little. Unlike me, it seems as if she's used to smiling. She's young—I'd peg her in her late twenties —but she has little marks on her face from smiling too much. Looking at her is like shoving an entire stick of cotton candy down a parched throat. I'm choking on sugar and sweetness; it's basically poison to me.

I crack my knuckles in the awkward silence and her eyes find my *HAVOC* tattoo again.

Something shifts in her expression, a flood of hormones that I liken to … empathy?

Oh.

Oooooh.

She thinks I'm here because I want to leave the gang, I bet. I think about Ms. Keating and the soft sympathy in her face when she told me I had *options,* that she used to be in a gang herself once upon a time.

"Do you want to come in, Bernadette?" she asks me. "Neil should be here soon. The three of us could sit down before our shift—"

I cut her off by raising both hands and taking a step back. This time, I don't have to fake the revulsion in my face at the mention of my stepfather.

"No, I … I don't want him to know I was here," I start, and Sara pauses a moment before nodding briefly. She's probably making up some story in her mind, where I'm too afraid to talk to my 'father' or some shit. In reality, he's the monster I hate most.

Sara combs her blond hair over her shoulder with her fingers as she waits for me to continue.

"How can I help, Bernadette?" she asks after a moment, when I just stand there in that stupid white dress, wondering if my cup's going to overflow and I'm going to bleed all over it. I glance to the right, down the row of fifties bungalows with their

American flags waving in the wind. There are no trees left in this neighborhood. Over the years, the homeowners have cut them down, one by one. I don't think it was intentional, but the look of it is … austere, at best.

I turn back to Sara.

"Do you think it'd be okay if I came and talked to you sometime?" I ask, tilting my head to one side, hoping I look young and desperate enough for her to take pity on me. "I know we don't know each other, but … I don't have anyone I can trust." I blink my green eyes and keep my face as neutral as I can.

"Are you in danger, Bernadette?" Sara asks me, stepping out onto the small front stoop of her home and looking up and down the street, like she can sense the Havoc Boys waiting around the corner for me.

"Yes," I tell her, because that's the truth. I am in danger. From her partner. From the Charter Crew. From my own strange, black, fractured little heart. "Would it be okay if I came over here sometime? I mean, if you can't talk to a cop, who can you talk to?" I almost gag on the words, but I feel like I just pulled that off. Sara's face softens and she nods, smiling at me in what I can only assume is a sincere way.

"Why don't I give you my phone number? Text me, and we'll set up a time to chat. Whatever it is that's going on, Bernadette, it isn't too late. It's never too late. We can always fix what's broken." I almost laugh at that, but the sound would be so caustic, it'd burn Sara's pretty face off. Is she kidding me? When glass shatters, it cannot be fixed. You can collect the pieces, but your hands will bleed after. There is no putting those little shards back together. They will forever remain dangerous fragments of a thing that used to be.

"Thank you," I tell her instead, handing over my phone so she can input her number. I wonder if I'm being too awkward or weird, but maybe that's what helps my case? Gives my lies a sense of believability. "I'll be in touch. I really appreciate this."

"If you ever need anything—beyond just a chat over coffee —call me. Don't leave yourself in a dangerous situation because you're scared to ask for help." Sara looks down at me on the second step of her porch, her savior complex shining so bright that I want to look away. Instead, I stare at her until there are white splotches in my vision.

"I appreciate it," I say after a moment, turning and heading back down the pathway. The grass has been cut back on either side, but there are no other plants of which to speak, adding to the strange fifties catalog-style Americana bullshit with the freakishly green lawns and shiny cars in the driveways.

It's a relief to climb onto the back of Vic's Harley and wrap my arms around him.

"Don't ever stop me from riding with you," I murmur against the sun-warmed leather of his jacket. I might be showing my cards a bit, but I can't help myself. Victor isn't *allowed* to cut me off from his influence. Not anymore.

"Even when Hael finishes your car?" he asks, a bit of a laugh hiding in the smooth fluidity of his voice.

"Even then," I confirm. "Don't cut us off from each other to punish me, Victor."

He stays still for a moment before kicking the engine to life.

"Never," he agrees, the wicked purr in his voice telling me

that it's just clicked for him. He's figured it out, and I am *fucked.*

We take off down the road and into an entirely different sort of business transaction.

———————————————

"What the hell is this place?" I ask as Vic parks his bike in the dirt outside of what looks like, quite literally, a haunted house. "*This* is your idea of a wedding venue?" Victor climbs off the bike, lighting up a cigarette as the Bronco and the Camaro pull up alongside us. I'm getting mad déjà vu from when we visited Billie's trailer to find a dress for the brunch thing at the country club.

"You don't like it?" Victor asks, studying the admittedly beautiful foliage. This place is the opposite of Sara's neighborhood. The house is falling apart—not all shiny and perfect like hers—but the land is *alive.* There are mature trees with lineages far deeper and more beautiful than my own. And the ancient rhododendron near the porch? It's such a far cry from South Prescott with its tract housing and shitty duplexes, all that cement and chain-link and urban decay.

"Whose place is this anyway?" I ask as the other boys climb out to join us. I'm surprised they're all here, seeing as Vic is possessive as hell over this whole wedding idea. "*Enjoy your time as a free woman because I'm counting down the nights until I fuck that wedding dress off of you.*" I'm still not entirely sure what Victor expects after the wedding, but … glancing

Aaron's direction, I know that I'm not ready to give him up, not with all the time lost between us.

He doesn't look like he wants to give me up either. His gaze is angry, and his fingers are squeezing into fists and then relaxing, a sign of the tension riding hard and heavy inside of him.

"My grandmother's house," Victor says, throwing a smile over his shoulder at me. Well, I'm not sure that I'd really call whatever that expression is, a smile. More like a fucking anti-smile. Yep, that's what it is: an anti-smile.

"Such a shame," Oscar sighs, leaving his iPad on the front seat of the Camaro as he looks up at the house. He rode with Hael while Callum tagged along with Aaron. "A Gothic Revival with an original kitchen and original bathrooms. It might've been worth a fortune, were your mother any less of a sadistic cunt."

Victor pounds up the front steps as I eye them warily, wondering if they're even going to hold his weight.

"If you don't like this, Bernie, just speak up and we'll find somewhere else," Aaron says, smiling at me in that way of his, like his mouth is made of sunshine. It's a different sort than it used to be. Freshman year, I might've said his smile was as open and bright as a summer afternoon at the lake. Now, he's like the dusky, filtered light that percolates through tree limbs and decorates the shadowed forest floor with stars.

"First though …" Cal starts, slipping up beside me. His blue eyes meet mine, and I find an invitation there, one that I didn't quite expect. I know he's been waiting for me to decide, but I'm pretty sure I already have. Actually, no, that's a copout. I've always known what I've wanted, and it wasn't just the V in Havoc; it was every letter in their wicked, little alphabet.

But how I go about making that happen, I don't know.

Victor is possessive. Aaron wants to skin him alive. Hael is ... wrapped up in Brittany's bullshit.

I exhale.

"First though?" I echo, and he grins, pushing his hood back, so I can see his face. His pink lips echo whatever dark thoughts are drifting through that head of his.

"Come see what we've brought you," he says happily, his voice a velvety purr that has texture to it, like it's more than sound. When Callum Park talks, I sometimes think I can feel it, kissing across my flesh and crawling inside of me.

I glance over at Hael, but he just smiles. He's here, but he's also ... not. Yes, we had that talk—and that fuck—on the hood of his car, but where are we really? Waiting for a fetus' DNA test and stuck in limbo.

"This should be good," Hael crows, throwing his head back anyway and howling with laughter. He shoves his sunglasses up and into his hair, ruffling that red faux hawk of his as he opens the front door of the crumbling manor and then pauses, like he's reconsidering. "Right," he purrs, crinkling his eyes up as he smirks, "you don't like the chivalrous shit."

"Come the fuck off it," Aaron snaps at him, elbowing Hael out of the way when he laughs and lets go of the door, leaving it to swing in our faces. Aaron stops it with his palm and lets Callum lead the way into the darkness, following after Vic and Oscar. Hael takes up the rear.

We head straight for the stairs and up. All the while, I'm

wondering if we're going to fall through to our deaths.

The place is hauntingly beautiful on the inside, but very clearly beyond saving. This isn't a place you move into with hopes, dreams, a shoestring budget, and YouTube videos on how to DIY shit. No, no, this place is a shell, with holes in the ceiling and floors, sunlight trickling down and highlighting drifting brown leaves. Technically, it's still autumn, but winter is right around the corner.

It's cold in the creepy, old place, even in my leather jacket. I'm thinking about that, about my leather jacket, as the boys guide me down the hall and … into a room where an older gentleman is bound to a chair.

Oh.

Crap.

"Who is this?" I ask as the boys fan out around their prisoner, like demonic gods attending a dark ritual. But I already know who it is. I just want to hear them say it.

"This," Vic tells me, putting his hands on the man's shoulders and giving him a little shake. "Is Todd Kushner." Victor gives me another anti-smile and then stands up straight, letting his hands fall to his sides. "He's got earbuds in," he explains, gesturing at the blindfolded man with the too-perfect skin. That was one of the things that always weirded me out about Todd, how smooth and babylike his skin was. Maybe that's what he was really doing, drinking the youth of his victims.

However it happens, his youth doesn't suit him at all.

"Earbuds blasting music, Vic should say. *I Prevail,* most specifically," Callum corrects, mentioning one of my favorite bands. Whenever I hear the song *"Gasoline"*, I think of the Havoc Boys. It suits them, the mood of that one.

"What is he doing here?" I ask as I circle around Todd, noting that he, too, has pissed his pants in fear. Isn't that ironic, how some monsters get so scared when their time finally comes to play victim? I have a feeling that the Havoc Boys wouldn't cower like this, pee themselves and whimper like kicked dogs.

Not a chance in hell.

"That's up to you," Vic tells me, watching as I complete my circle and pause next to Oscar. It's not like I've forgotten what his boss told me. *"If they get the chance, each and every one of them will try to take you from me ... Even. Oscar."* Hmm.

He moves away from me, which in reality, gives me all the information I need.

I look at Oscar, and his glasses flash as he pushes them up his nose, flipping me off at the same time. If he didn't care about me at all, he wouldn't move away like that. It's an emotional response that makes me wonder what I could do, if I pushed him hard enough.

My mind flashes to that moment in the hallway where I persisted on touching his tie, until he finally let me.

"We could tell Eric we've kidnapped his father," Callum suggests, shrugging his shoulders as he slips his hands into the pockets of his black cargo shorts. "But we're of the opinion that he doesn't care whether his dad lives or dies. So, a better choice would be to use Todd to convince Eric to come here."

I can only imagine the tortures they have in store for the Kushners.

I don't have to explain what happened to me there; they

know. I told them all, when I was thirteen. I told them everything.

"We thought you could help with the phone call, act like you're a girl that Todd's rounded up for Eric," Aaron adds, and I cringe slightly. I wonder if I'm suffering from my PTSD shit again. I've never been diagnosed, but again, kooks and quacks aren't really in the budget of someone whose little sister doesn't have shoes without holes in them.

I should probably dig up some of that money and buy her some. That was old Bernadette who buried that money, a Bernadette who was a lot more afraid than she realized. Things are different now.

"So, we use my voice to lure the pervert to a haunted mansion on the edge of Oak Park?" I ask, shaking my head. "If he chooses to resist his perversions, he escapes free and clear. If he doesn't, he suffers, something like that?"

"Well, I wouldn't go that far," Hael says, snickering at me. "If he resists, we'll just get him later. That's pretty much it."

I pause in front of Todd, and then reach out to remove his earbuds. I tuck them in my pocket and then slip the soggy wet gag down his chin, curling my lip and then wiping my hands on the front of the hideous white frock I'm wearing. It looks like something from Abercrombie and Fitch. I don't quite feel like me without my regular clothes.

"Listen to me," Todd starts, stuttering slightly as he moves his head around, like he can actually see anything through the black blindfold he's wearing. "You need to repent. It isn't too late. Jesus can always heal a sinner."

Callum grabs Todd by the hair, yanking his head and

pressing the edge of his knife—the same one I stabbed Kali with—against the front of his throat. Cal doesn't even seem unhappy doing it. Actually, he smiles.

"Wait, wait, wait," Todd pleads, but it's clear from his tone of voice that he hasn't fully grasped the sincerity of his peril. "If you bow to God, you *will* find salvation. If you bow to the devil, you will burn."

A strange laugh escapes Victor as he comes around to stand beside me.

"I wouldn't bow to Satan anymore than I'd bow to God," Vic says, slipping a fresh cigarette between his lips. I stare at him, and he lets his dark gaze slide to mine. We're caught up in each other all of a sudden, and my head spins. *He sounded way too hot when he said that,* I think, tearing my gaze away to look at Todd. "Try a little harder than that, pervert. You think God wants a child-fucker in his kingdom anymore than he wants assholes like us?"

Victor approaches the chair where Todd's sitting, Callum's knife still pressed to his throat, and he leans down in front of him. Lucky for Todd, he can't see the way Vic looks at him, like he's so much trash that needs taking out.

"Listen to me, Todd. We don't want to hurt you." *Lie.* The feeling of it coats my skin like ash, and I shiver. I won't survive it if Vic lies to me ever again, by omission or otherwise. I'll have to tell him that. "But, what we do want is money." I almost laugh at that, biting my lip to keep the sound back. Callum grins at me, adjusting the knife just enough that a small drop of blood slides down the front of Todd's pale throat.

"Money?" he asks, sounding hopeful. "I have money. In

cash, too." Callum pulls the knife back and then hits Todd upside the head with the handle, making his head flop forward with a groan.

"Shut your fucking face," he whispers, and the sound makes me go cold inside. *Holy crap.*

Vic just stays right where he is, waiting patiently. Aaron and I exchange a look, and I can see in his expression that he wants to spirit me away from here, take me somewhere—anywhere—else. He doesn't want me to see this and, since this is my request, I can walk away at any time.

I make zero moves to do so.

Todd filmed me in a bikini; he bought me for his son.

That, and I don't know what he did to Penelope when I wasn't around.

"Coraleigh Vincent," Victor continues, standing up straight. Hael takes a seat on an ancient chair, its frame skeletal. All that's left in the seat are rusted metal springs. "We know she brings you girls. That's what we're interested in. We don't want a onetime payout; our game is longevity."

Victor Channing is such a talented actor that I almost believe what he's saying. I'd be shocked if Todd didn't. After all, when has a vigilante gang ever come after a pedophile purely for the sake of justice?

No, it's much more believable—and much more likely— that we'd be in it for money, as willing to trade girls into sex slavery as Coraleigh. If a woman who works for the department of human services can be that twisted, that cruel, then why not us?

"Yeah, yeah, I know Leigh," Todd says, shaking so badly

that he rattles a bit on the chair. "I can get you in touch with her for sure." Victor and Hael exchange a look, and the former nods. Hael stands up from the chair and grabs a black latex glove from a box on the table, snapping it onto his left hand and then doing the same for his right. He picks up a cell phone from a rickety side table and holds it up to show that the screen is locked.

"What's your pin code for your phone, Todd?" Vic asks as Oscar watches the scenario unfold with disinterest. Aaron is the only one who looks actively uncomfortable, but when his eyes glance Todd's direction, they shimmer with the sort of darkness that nightmares are made out of. He hates Todd as much as the other Havoc Boys, he just doesn't revel in the chase like they do. Maybe that's the difference between monsters who are made … and monsters who are born? Vic is a born beast, for sure.

Todd hands out his code and Hael opens his phone up, searching the contacts for Coraleigh's name. She comes right up, and Vic smiles.

"Perfect. Now, here's what we're going to do."

I accept the phone as Victor explains his plan to Todd, scrolling past Coraleigh's number to find Eric's. If I analyze my feelings too deeply, I'll chicken out here. Calling Eric, letting Todd tease him with the idea of me, and then using my voice to warm him up to the idea of coming here. It grosses me out.

It also excites me.

Who knew vengeance could be such a turn-on?

CHAPTER
EIGHTEEN

The trees in the front yard of the property are magnificent, old and untouched by the greediness of human hands. Most of them are evergreens, so they're still pretty, even though it's verging on the edge of winter. Here and there, a barren oak tree sits, a reminder that this property was once a part of the Springfield elite; they always marked their land with oaks as a status symbol.

Victor and me, we're both old money turned dirt poor.

"Do you like this place?" Callum asks, pausing nearby, hunched over in his hoodie with his hands in his front pocket. His hood is down, which is surprising. It's one of his shields, and he uses it well. "I mean, do you really want to get married here?" He pauses as I glance his way, studying his exposed calves and knees and all the silver scars crisscrossed over his skin. "I know Victor does, because it's his grandma's place and even if he's too stubborn to admit it, he loved her more than anything."

There's a strong pause there, but I don't bother to fill in the blanks aloud. I know what Cal is thinking: *except for you.* Except for Havoc, maybe.

"I like it here," I admit, looking around the front yard at the collapsing gazebo, the patchy grass, the porch that has definitely seen better days. "It used to be something, but now it's nothing. It's a good reminder that life can turn in an instant." I reach into the pocket of my leather jacket and extract a joint. Cal steps forward before I can ask and removes a lighter from his own pocket, lighting me up before I can even ask.

My eyes lift to his, and he smiles.

"Todd being here, that doesn't bother you?" he asks, but I shake my head. Each drop of blood that Todd sheds belongs to me. It's penance, and it sinks into this hallowed ground like a blessing. The earth is thirsty, and I am hungry.

I'm owed the sweet taste of vengeance.

"Every name on my list becomes a sacrifice," I say, taking two drags on the joint before passing it to Callum. Our fingers touch, sparking joy in my hands that travels straight to my heart. "It's like an offering to the dark goddess that rests inside my heart."

Callum throws his head back with a laugh, one that's husky and broken and oh-so beautiful.

"You make pretty metaphors, Bernie," he says, flashing teeth at me. The tattoos on his bare arms draw my attention, highlighting the thick, rounded curves of his biceps. In junior high, when Cal was thin and lean and angelic looking, I never would've believed he'd bulk up the way he did, or that he'd be covered in so much ink. Pain changes a person though, doesn't it? "Don't ever stop. Life was so much more boring without you."

I smile as Cal hands the joint back. For a moment there, everything is easy and casual, just two teenagers hanging out on an abandoned lot.

Then Callum's entire demeanor shifts, and he steps around me, like he's protecting me from something. The sound of a car on the empty country road echoes to me just a few seconds later.

Eric is here.

I mean, we *did* send him an invitation.

The thing is, when I took Todd's phone from Vic's hand and put my lips near the speaker, I almost thought Eric would recognize my voice.

He didn't.

"Your daddy says that if I'm a good girl, you'll give me some money. I could really use some money to help with the rent."

Gag.

The other thing I was worried about was that I might sound too old for his perverted tastes.

Guess not.

Cal and I stay where we are, hidden by the tree as Eric parks near the front porch, climbing out to look up at the house with a wary expression. I watch him from where I am, a lioness on the hunt.

He looks exactly as I remember him: like some sort of Ken doll with bleached-out skin and white-blond hair. When I was eleven, and we first met, I thought he was handsome. He skeeves me the fuck out now, even from all the way over here.

"He's going to bolt," I whisper to Cal, my eyes taking in Eric's stiff form, his hand still resting on the door handle of his Mercedes.

"I think you're right," he agrees, his big body curled over mine, watching, protecting. I feel so goddamn safe with Callum Park at my back. Invincible. We exchange a look and he nods, slipping away and crouching low as he runs across the field on my left.

"Eric," I call out as sweetly as I can, stepping out from behind the tree and pitching my voice high and clear. He turns around to look at me, face flashing with triumph ... and then fear.

No ... not fear, *terror.*

He's terrified. Because he recognizes me as soon as he sees me. That much, I'm sure of.

When he spins around, desperately grabbing at the handle of his car, Callum is just there, crouching on the roof like a spider.

"Hello Eric," he says, and then he grabs the back of Eric's head and smashes his face into the side of the Mercedes, leaving him to crumple onto the ground in a heap.

I walk slowly over to my perpetrator as the other Havoc Boys come out the front door, slow and casual and fully confident in me and Cal to handle the situation.

"Let's get him inside, shall we?" Oscar asks, slipping out of his jacket and rolling up the sleeves of his white button-down.

His gray eyes meet mine, and I can tell that we're about to take a step forward together. Not sure what that step will entail, but it's coming.

And quick.

I asked the Havoc Boys to show me all their secrets.

Guess that's why that old adage exists: be careful what you wish for.

Eric is on the floor bleeding, his eyes wide as he stares across the narrow space between him and his father. Between the two of them, he's the most clearly fucked-up, his skin bloody and raw, his fingers broken, his shins smashed with a baseball bat.

I haven't moved from my spot near the door, letting the boys do the work. This is, after all, my request. My reward. Eric molested my sister, tried to molest me. He rapes little girls. I feel nothing for him, nothing at all.

"How many girls have you raped and killed, hmm?" Oscar asks, bending low and digging the barrel of his revolver into the front of Eric's skull. "I'm sure you don't know an exact number, but guess what?" Eric whimpers, closing his eyes as blood runs down the side of his face and into them. I hope it stings like hell. "I do. I'm very good with numbers, Mr. Kushner. I fucking *love* numbers." Oscar grinds the weapon in until Eric lets out a scream, moving his arm back just enough to shut the man up. "Numbers don't lie, but people do. In totality, Mr. Kushner, I've estimated that you've murdered thirteen underage girls."

Oscar rises to his feet suddenly, moving the gun away from Eric and over to his father. Eric lets out a whimper of relief, but Todd begins to weep silently.

"I don't think he's killed anyone," Oscar continues, gray eyes darkening to a near-black pitch behind his blood-spattered glasses. He gestures in Todd's direction as the other boys look on in silence, letting the man I'd sort of written off as Havoc's, uh, IT guy, elevate this shit to another level. "But he knows what you do, and he lets you do it."

"He's my son!" Todd screams, thrashing in his bindings. "I'd do anything for him." He probably thinks he sounds strong as he struggles, eyes focused on his only child. He doesn't. He sounds weak, and my stomach churns.

I'm still in the process of contemplating the whole scenario when Oscar lowers the weapon, so that it's pointing directly at Todd's head ... and fires off a single round. The sound of it makes me jump, like a car backfiring in an enclosed parking garage. My ears are ringing so badly that it takes me a good two minutes to realize that Eric is screaming.

Havoc has just shot and killed Todd Kushner.

On the inside, my spirit writhes a bit. I don't know how to process any of this.

After Don and Scott, I didn't think ... But then, I remember Oscar's risk assessment. *Three percent. Good odds for a killing.*

Aaron sidles closer to me, putting his arm around my waist and dragging me close. His scent is so strong that when I bury myself against his chest for a moment, all I breathe in is rose and sandalwood. The sharp copper scent of blood disappears for the briefest of instances, but then I look up and see the body and time starts up all over again.

"Anything else you'd like to say Eric before I shoot him in the face?" Oscar asks mildly, unmoved by the situation. At least, on the outside. On the inside, a little boy with broken glasses and round-tipped scissors is screaming.

I stare at him for a moment before I push away from Aaron and move over to stand beside Eric. Crouching down, I reach out and swipe hair away from his bloodied forehead.

"Please," he sobs, shaking, his hands bound behind his back, his ankles lashed together. "I don't like to hurt people. I just have needs that can't be met any other way." I smile, but there's no mirth in the expression. My fingers find the scar above Eric's eye, where I hit him with the metal truck.

"You changed my life for the worst, Eric. Foster care was my escape, away from my mother, from my rapist stepfather. You stole that chance from me, from us." Closing my eyes, I imagine a different world, one where Pen and Heather and I found a loving home, somewhere safe, and we all made it to adulthood without the marks of monsters on our skin.

I open my eyes.

I'm surrounded by my monsters now, but at least I hold the leash of some very pretty ones.

Shit, but did you really think they were just going to execute the Kushners? I didn't. This is next level. There must really be some sweetness left in me somewhere because it still hurts, in a weird way. If murder only sparked joy in me, I'd be worried. But also, I feel no regret.

"Please, please, Bernadette. Please. I'm sorry. I won't do it anymore. I'll stop. I'll stop." Eric is sobbing now, snot running out of his nose and over his lips. His spittle is foamy; he's definitely hurting. Also ... he must sense that he's not walking out of here, right? Like I said, monsters always know to look for other monsters.

"Did you see what I did to your house?" I ask him and he nods, almost eagerly, like he thinks that admitting to this will please me. "Did it scare you?" He nods again, and I smile, standing up and moving back to stand next to Aaron again.

Oscar doesn't ask me any questions, just steps forward and points his revolver at Eric again.

"No, please!" Eric screams, his voice shattering the still air.

Even though I'm expecting it, even though I want it, I still jump when Oscar pulls the trigger.

Two years earlier ...

Oscar Montauk

It's not as if I enjoy doing violent things. No, it's that violent things are necessary. You can't create order without a little chaos. You can't stir Havoc without a little pain.

Bernadette is sitting at a café across the street, a black coffee in front of her, blond hair hanging around her face. She doesn't want to go to school today.

Because of us.

I put my elbow on the table and rest my chin in my hand, watching her. She probably thinks that only happens now, her being under the eyes of Havoc. But that's not the case at all. The five of us were as fucked-up as children as we are now. We've always watched Bernadette Blackbird.

At first, we thought of her as a lost, little bird, someone that needed protecting because they were too weak and too soft to defend themselves. Life proved to us that we couldn't save her, no matter how hard we tried. We couldn't save her from her abusive mother, or her pedophile stepfather.

All of that because we didn't have the power.

We do now. And the reason we have that power is because of the violence.

"Anything new to report?" Hael asks, flopping into the chair across from me. When he looks at Bernadette, I can see it in his eyes. He's in love with her, but in a different way than I am. The love I have for her hurts. *It stings. I grit my teeth against the sensation while Hael isn't looking, but by the time he turns back to me, the emotion is gone. I keep it locked away in a silver chest inside my heart, and I always make sure to toss away the key.*

I smile.

"Nothing. She hasn't touched her coffee or checked her phone."

Hael nods and sighs. He doesn't like this plan, but there isn't much more we can do. We watch Bernadette, but Bernadette will not stop watching us. There's no goddamn place for her here. Like I said, Havoc is violence. Violence is not fun. I just want Bernadette to leave.

She doesn't seem to be going anywhere, unfortunately. And I really hate doing this under the guise of helping Kali Rose-Kennedy. She's an opportunist and a silver-tongued liar with an inferiority complex; I'd never hurt Bernadette just to please her, regardless of her calling Havoc.

Above all, Havoc means two things: loyalty and family.

It doesn't feel like we're being very loyal to Bernadette right now.

"Shit, I hate this," *Hael says, chewing at his lip for a moment. He shakes his head again, but he does nothing to change her fate. None of us do. Hael knows he has a mother who lives inside her own head, a murderer for a father, and very poor prospects for the future if he doesn't help Havoc build something better. We could all very easily get stuck living our parents' lives on repeat—and we could doom Bernadette along with us.*

"If it weren't difficult, it wouldn't be the right thing to do," *I say, shoving up from my seat and heading down the sidewalk toward Prescott High. If Bernadette doesn't show up today, we'll have to go and find her tomorrow, drag her from her cozy bed, make her fear the only people in the world she shouldn't have to be afraid of.*

I curse under my breath, exhaling sharply and then reaching down to fix the cufflinks on my jacket.

I tell myself not to look back at her, but I do anyway. Our eyes meet and something inside of me shifts and breaks; lava appears in those cracks, scalding and dangerous. Bernadette lifts her coffee to her lips and drinks, watching me like I said she would be, like always.

For two years, I regret that moment because that's the moment I could've put a stop to it.

And I don't mean by being nicer to Bernadette; I mean by becoming her worst nightmare.

Then she could have left, then she could have avoided all of this.

She could've missed me, shooting her would-be rapists in the head. It still had to be done—after all, they'd touched her in ways that only I or one of the other Havoc Boys should touch her—but I wouldn't have ever told her about it. She wouldn't have had to see.

Our eyes meet over the blood-stained floor, and I have to wonder why, after they all treated her so badly, she lets them touch her, kiss her, fuck her. Victor, especially. He's the worst of all, the one who nailed her coffin shut by bringing her into Havoc. She should spit in his face, not suck his dick.

I lower the weapon.

"Bernie," Aaron whispers, holding her in the way I wish I could. I watch him tuck her close, and my fingers twitch on the revolver. I would never hurt Aaron, but hell if I don't want him to back off of her a bit. "Do you want to go home now?"

"I'll go home," she says, almost absentmindedly. She's clearly still struggling with all of this, despite her bravado. Vic nods, like this is the acceptable answer, and sends Callum back to Aaron's house with them.

My eyes drift back down to the pair of bodies. The world is a safer place today, even if the cost was high. I put the gun back in the holster under my jacket.

"Since you fucked-up with the video of Neil and Pen, you can clean this mess," Victor tells me, and I just lift my gaze to stare at him. He stares right back, like I need a reminder that I messed that up, too.

"Yes, boss," I tell him, grabbing the edge of one of the tarps and helping Hael roll up the bodies. Victor knows I won't argue with his orders ... not much anyway. Any well-functioning organization needs a leader, and we both know that's not my thing.

Despite outward appearances, Victor has a much, much longer fuse than I do.

"Bernadette," he calls out, just before she disappears out of view down the stairs. "Don't go home anymore, okay? You and Heather stay with Aaron now." She pauses for a long moment, and even from here, it's impossible to miss how much she wants that to be true.

She takes out a wrinkled envelope from the pocket of her leather jacket, unfolds it against the side of the newel post at the top of the stairs, and then uses a tube of red lipstick to make a slash across it.

I don't have to see the paper up close to know that it's her list.

You're welcome, Bernadette, *I think, hiding my smile as I bend down and start the laborious task of scrubbing up blood.*

CHAPTER
NINETEEN

November seventeenth, Now ...

Bernadette Blackbird

I sit up, shrouded in darkness, my face covered by something. For a minute there, I start to panic, but then I remember that Cal gave me his hoodie in the Bronco on the way home.

"Pretend it's me, holding you so tight you can't breathe," he'd whispered, and even though that statement should've come across as creepy, it didn't. Not at all. Sitting up now, I push the hood of the sweatshirt back from my face and exhale sharply.

I wish I could say that I was surprised by what happened last night, but I'm not.

The Havoc Boys have hard limits, but their lines are drawn far further down the road of depravity than most would dare dance. They don't rape; they don't hurt kids. But they *do* shoot pedophiles in the face and not lose any sleep over it.

Aaron is breathing softly beside me, shirtless and beautiful in the starlight trickling in through the sliding glass door opposite the bed. It's cracked just slightly, and I can hear birdsong. Must be early morning rather than late night.

I yawn and stretch my arms above my head, my eyes drifting over to Aaron again. He has both of his girls' names tattooed on his back. My lips twitch into a small smile, and I reach out with two fingers to brush across the ink. He stirs and groans but doesn't wake up.

To be honest, I barely remember climbing into bed with him. He drove me home; Callum asked to stop at Wayback Burgers on the way. That's all I remember.

A rush of hot liquid between my thighs makes me curse, and I shove the covers aside. As I stand up, I squeeze my legs together against the rush of blood, cursing myself for not dumping my menstrual cup last night.

On my mad sprint to the bathroom, I leave red splatters on the floor, like a morbid little nod to Hansel and Gretel's breadcrumbs. Only … if I were in the tale, I'd probably be the witch, so maybe that's not an apt metaphor?

With a groan, I sit down on the toilet and try my best to remedy the situation.

When Oscar opens the door, I'm sitting there with my fingers and legs covered in blood.

It's a weird situation, I'll be the first to admit. Oscar Montauk … watching me deal with period stuff? Not even remotely okay.

"Get the *fuck* out," I snap at him, hating this damn bathroom lock and all the bullshit it brings me. First day I get off work—meaning, a day in which corpses and guns are not regular parts of my schedule—I'm going to the hardware store to get a new knob. Might even get a chain-lock while I'm at it.

Oscar stands there far longer than propriety's sake would indicate. His eyes are unreadable behind his glasses, his shirtless body lean and painted like a canvas. Looking at him, it's impossible to forget the sight of him with a gun in his hand, red spattered across the lenses of his glasses.

"And I thought the situation at the old house was a bloodbath," he remarks, smirking with that annoying devil-may-care attitude of his before he finally leaves. I'm cursing him out as I clean up as best I can with toilet paper, and then head out into the hall with fury riding like a cloak around me.

I find Oscar in the kitchen, listening to *CEMETERY* by AViVA on his phone. The volume is cranked fairly low, but the haunting sounds of the music still stain the air like fog on a cold night.

He's making himself a cup of tea which both weirdly suits him and also seems like the antipathy of who he was tonight when he was brandishing that weapon. Oscar Montauk is a reptile in beautiful, tattooed skin.

"Don't think I don't see the way you look at me," I tell him, watching as he stirs milk into his tea with a small spoon. I rarely—if ever—see him eat or drink. This is truly a rare occurrence.

He lifts his eyes to me, and I find that they're the color of a graveyard, when the moon is high, and the trees are barren of leaves. A shiver takes over me that I can't fight off.

"And how, exactly, is that?" he queries mildly, setting the small spoon aside and lifting the mug to his lips with hands drenched in blood and secrets and ink. I watch those hands and wonder what it'd be like if they were on my throat instead of mine on his …

Eww.

The fuck?

No.

I banish the thought and move around the kitchen peninsula to face off against him.

Why I'm choosing to do this now, I have no idea.

Oscar stares at me, quietly sipping his tea as he waits for me to elaborate.

Lying to other people is insane; lying to yourself is suicidal. That's what I read in that damn book, right? *Devils' Day Party.* Ask me later why I bother to read bully romances. My *life* is a goddamn bully romance.

I'm confronting Oscar now because I can't stand the fact that he acts like I don't exist sometimes, like he appears disappointed at others, because he won't let me touch him.

"Like you both hate me and love me, all at the same time," I say, my words breathy.

"Those things aren't mutually exclusive, you know," is what he says in response to my statement. Not *of course I don't love you, silly little bird.* The song ends and then starts all over again; it must be on repeat.

That's an interesting fact to note about Oscar. Some people are playlist people, some are radio people with their custom

Spotify stations, and others … are repeaters. I often listen to the same song on repeat for hours on end. Used to drive Penelope nuts.

And it's something that Oscar and I have in common.

"So you're in love with me?" I ask dryly, mouth hanging open as I lick the edge of my lip, Cal's sweater bagging and hanging around my arms. He might not be a hulking monster like Vic or Hael, but wearing his sweater reminds me of how much bigger his muscles are. I need to start working out, like, yesterday.

"You're bleeding," Oscar replies, choosing instead to glance down at my pale thighs instead of answering my question. A slither of hot red liquid runs down and stains the tiled floor. Crap. In my frenzy to fight Oscar, I forgot to put my cup back in.

I glance back up at his face.

He likes the sight of it, the blood.

"And you're deranged," I quip back, but he just shrugs his shoulders. The way his hands are holding the white mug, they mimic the demon hands tattooed on his neck. The sight is eerie —especially with this creepy ass song playing on repeat. "Why are you always so goddamn mad at me? I get it: you didn't want me in Havoc. Too late. Blood in, blood out, right?"

"So much blood," Oscar says, looking back up at my face. "Is this a normal flow for you?"

I laugh then, because I know he's just trying to needle me, get underneath my skin like a worm and *crawl*. I hate to admit that it's working.

"I've had an irregular period since I was twelve. Find

another target to attack, you dick."

Oscar sets his mug on the counter and then starts toward me. I forget sometimes how tall he is, since he's always trying to keep his distance. He puts his right hand on the counter and leans over me.

"I wasn't attacking; I was admiring," tells me, and my body ripples with an emotion that feels like fear and lust, all twisted into one unspeakable thing. I can smell Oscar now, that spicy-sweet scent of cinnamon wafting over me.

"Admiring my period? Man, you're creepier now than you were at the house." I lean back, so that I can meet his eyes. My gaze traces the sardonic smile on his lips, one that radiates bemusement and superiority both. It occurs to me that I'm standing in a dark kitchen, having a casual conversation with a man that killed two people just hours prior. Also, I'm bleeding everywhere. Really, I should just haul my ass to a bathroom.

"Am I though? Creepy?" he asks, reaching up with his left hand and dragging his knuckles through the air next to my face. I notice that he doesn't touch me, even as close as we are. Oscar is aware of every breath. "You look at me the same way, you know, with that dichotomous intensity."

I exhale, and then draw in a huge inhale. My chest inflates, my sweatshirt-covered breasts brushing up against Oscar's bare skin. But just barely. Just *barely.* He registers it though, and shudders.

"Why are you always so pissed at me? Seriously, I want an answer, and I want it right *now.*" Oscar turns his head, watching the darkness behind me. A ripple passes through me, one that speaks of creeping predators and shadows. It's Vic, I know it is.

He watches us for a moment before heading upstairs to the bathroom.

"Jesus, Bernadette, there's blood everywhere," he calls down, but I ignore him. I was going to clean it up, but eh, it's his problem now. If he wants to be my husband, he can deal.

"Why am I pissed at you?" Oscar asks with a sharp laugh. I notice he doesn't put any space between us. My eyes find his pierced nipples, drifting lower and wishing I could see his pierced cock, too. "Because of that." He points toward the staircase and frowns, nice and violent. "Victor doesn't treat you well. None of them do. Why do you reward them with your affection? It disturbs me, Bernadette."

I refocus on his face, carved of shadows and sin, and blink in surprise.

Seeing Havoc murder number six on my list and cart his corpse off to the woods certainly didn't. This though, it's a shocker.

"You're mad because I hang out with the people I'm supposed to be family with?" I clarify and Oscar grits his teeth. He waits as Vic comes down the stairs, as quiet as a cat. He watches us both again for several seconds before finally disappearing into his room. I hear him murmur something under his breath, but it isn't worth the time or effort to figure out what it was.

"I'm mad because you kiss and fuck and fawn over them, after everything they've done to you." Oscar pauses and rattles his long fingers against the countertop, like the inked legs of a venomous spider. He looks back at me. "After everything *I've* done to you."

He pauses then, and the room gets real quiet as the song ends once again. It starts up soon after, but I can feel that pregnant pause like a punch to the gut.

"Are you upset because I fuck them …" I start, taking a gamble and lifting my palms to Oscar's bare chest. Joining Havoc has made me brave. It's only been a few months, but I'm surprised at how much I've changed. What will I look like after a year? A decade? "Or upset because I don't fuck you?" I press my fingers to Oscar's skin, and he hisses at me.

His hands snap up to grab my wrists, but he doesn't push me away. Instead, he traps my palms against his skin. He's burning up beneath my touch, and I'm finding it really hard to breathe.

"You wouldn't want me to fuck you, Bernadette. I'm not sure I could behave myself."

I snort at that, breaking a bit of that strange magic in the air. Oscar releases me, stepping back to put some space between us. His face tells me nothing, but his body is tense, his cock hard beneath his pj pants.

"You? The master of control?" I quip, watching him as he moves over to grab his mug again. "I highly doubt you'd have much trouble behaving. Is it just that you hate me more than you love me? Is that it?"

"Hate you …" he murmurs, sipping his tea and giving a low, cultured laugh. He's extravagantly uncivilized, now isn't he?

"You've said it before," I challenge, giving Oscar a dark look. "You hate me. I get it. But why? Because I'm over your shit."

He smiles at me, but the expression is sharp, cutting.

Without his shirt on, he's a colorful mess of tattoos. His ink owns every inch of his lean, muscular form, a story made of blood and needles. Unsurprising, considering his soul is clearly crafted of darkness and pain.

"You're bold, Bernadette," Oscar says, stepping close to me once again and wrapping me up in his dark scent. He smells of danger and uncertainty, of wild, moonlit nights, and orgasms made of hot embers and poisonous kisses. I close my eyes as he cups the side of my face in long, elegant fingers, the fingers of a master pianist or a Renaissance painter. They're warm, too, from the tea.

When I open my eyes, I find Oscar far too close to me again. We could kiss, if we were so inclined. But how could we be? When he hates me so goddamn much. He sets the tea down, adding his right hand to the other side of my face, touching me. Willingly.

"You, in Havoc," he starts, letting a low chuckle curl past his lips like smoke from a slow-burning fire. "I've never wanted anything less."

I reach up to slap his fingers away, but he catches my wrist with his other hand, holding me prisoner. Captivating me with gray eyes the color of a tumultuous sea, slow-moving but capable of unfathomable destruction.

"Should I be surprised by that?" I quip, my tongue as caustic and acidic as his own. We can have a verbal sprawl, me and Oscar. But I hope he knows I'll kick his ass in repartee the same way I did with my hands around his throat.

"Maybe," he bites back, smiling in just such a way that I feel my knees go weak. "Because I don't think you understand my motivations, Bernadette Blackbird. You're incandescent; I'm just trying to keep your flame from being snuffed out."

"That doesn't make any sense," I snarl, quickly losing my patience with him. His hands tighten against the sides of my face and I reach up, placing my own hands atop his.

"You glow from the inside out," Oscar whispers, and then he does something I never expected: he drops his mouth to mine.

I've been hit before, many times. In many fights. By many people, much, much bigger than I am.

None of those incidents knocked me back in quite the same way as Oscar Montauk's kiss.

His kiss is one of shadows and spiders, of darkness and strands of old moonlight woven into webs. When I kiss him, I can taste both his violence and his desperate need for love. There's a void inside of him, one that's even bigger than the one inside of me.

Nobody has ever taken care of him.

Nobody has ever loved him—except for Havoc.

Except for ... me.

"Since elementary school," I murmur against his ice-cold slash of mouth. Oscar doesn't let me finish, kissing me harder, pushing me back. I stumble a bit, but he keeps me upright, guiding me where he wants me to go.

The backs of my calves hit the side of the couch, and then I'm going down.

With Oscar on top of me.

Shit, shit, shit, Bernie, you're on your period; you're bleeding. I tell myself all of that, but it doesn't matter. This is happening. It has to happen. It *needs* to happen, and it's happening now.

Oscar cups the back of my head in his sinful fingers, his tongue taking over my mouth, his long, lean body between my thighs. I'm so surprised and excited by the fact that he's actually letting me touch him that my hands begin to wander all over his body, finding his strong shoulders, sliding down his arms.

When I find the little metal swords pierced through his nipples, I give them a tug with both hands.

The sound that escapes that man's throat undoes me completely. I moan in response, thrusting my hips up against his pelvis, feeling his right hand slide up my waist toward my breast. As soon as he grabs ahold of it, he growls.

"Thought you liked bigger boobs than mine," I snap back at him, flushed from head to toe and shaking all over. Oscar pauses briefly, lifting his gray eyes to mine. I lift my hands up and grab his glasses, pulling them aside so that I can look into his eyes without interruption. I need to see them without a protective cover, bare and endless and deadly.

This man killed two people today. The thought should be sobering; it's not.

"Bernadette, you have huge fucking tits. You must be kidding me? You were intended to read between the lines." He bites my lower lip as his words settle over me. He said he liked bigger breasts; there aren't many girls with bigger breasts around that don't have implants.

Oscar is an asshole.

"I hate you," I grind out between clenched teeth, but it's

impossible to maintain that caustic vitriol in my voice, not with him caressing my breasts the way he is, like he's savoring the weight of them. My thumbs trace over his nipples, teasing the metal pieces and flicking them back and forth until Oscar responds the way I want him to by thrusting against me. "The blood ..." I murmur, but he shushes me with another kiss, one that bites, one that cuts.

I'm wearing a loose pair of basketball shorts that I stole from Aaron. Oscar soon finds his way to them, pushing them over my hips. His fingers delve between my legs, finding that hot, wet heat.

Normally, I'm not one to get shy during sex, but I can't seem to keep the flush off my face as Oscar slides two, long fingers into my cunt. His eyes meet mine, and my throat gets tight with emotion. I'm bleeding all over him and my body feels even more raw than usual, the ache between my thighs nearly painful.

With his other hand, Oscar shoves my shirt up so that he can see my bare breasts.

The way he exhales makes my body clamp down around his fingers in excitement.

"The devil take me," he mutters, dropping his face down toward my chest. At the last second, he flicks gray eyes up to my face. I can tell he's trying hard to maintain his usual coldness and biting wit, but it doesn't work. His face is a mosaic of need and tenderness. Oscar's sharp tongue flicks out, wrapping my nipple and sucking it into his mouth. Those lips of his are just as acerbic and deadly sucking on my breast as they are flinging witty repartee.

His thumb slips across my clit, nice and slippery, causing my hips to buck against his hand.

"Bernadette," he growls out, moving his bloodied hand from my cunt to my hip. We're making a huge mess here, but I don't care. My heart is too full, my eyes stinging with strange tears. I have no idea why I feel like I'm about to cry, but it doesn't matter. If I hold them back, Oscar shouldn't be able to see them in the dark.

He adjusts himself, pushing his pants down his hips until his cock springs free. It's impossible to see the ink in the low light, but the piercings on his dick glint in a stray shaft of moonlight. Not that he gives me long to examine them anyway.

Oscar lowers himself over me, rubbing his body against mine. For someone that hates to be touched, he sure does seem desperate to connect our bare flesh. It's as if he's a starving man who's just finally found his way to a picnic.

He's going to eat *everything.*

My fingers weave together behind his neck as he fits himself to my opening and then pushes inside. There's a moment there where he freezes up, his body shuddering as we adjust to each other. The smell of blood is in the air, but it doesn't bother me as much as it should. As weird as it sounds, it actually seems to suit us, having our first time with the scent of copper surrounding us.

Oscar moves his hips with long, slow, undulating strokes, the metal in his cock teasing me in strange places, making me squirm. Hael is pierced, too, but Oscar must have some unique metal because the sensations he's giving me are new.

He kisses me again, but I find that I suddenly don't

recognize him at all.

He's ... kissing me softly, almost reverently. His body moves the same way, at complete odds with his personality.

Jesus fuck, Oscar Montauk is making love to me.

My entire body flushes hot as I press my cheek to his, closing my eyes and enjoying the way his lean form feels on top of mine. His hips push me into the couch cushions, staining us both with the red of my womanhood. It feels extra good, actually, to do it like this. Whenever I get my period, I always feel like my cunt is more swollen, more desperate than usual. The blood even gives us extra lube, adding to the slip and slide, the beautiful friction.

We spend, quite literally, over an hour on that couch, locked together, moving together, joined into one person. I come more than once, but it's hard to say how many times, lost in a fever of pleasure and connection.

We have something here, me and Oscar. I didn't expect that, not at all.

Things change as soon as he comes, shoving his cock deep and hitting the end of me, making me cry out as he fills me with hot seed. His muscles tighten, fingers digging into the sofa on either side of my head. But there's no release after that, no collapse, no panting.

Instead, he just sort of ... freezes.

Crap.

He's panicking, isn't he?

"Oscar," I start, trying to head off whatever unhealthy emotional response he's having. He pushes up on his forearms to look down at me like he's never seen me before, like he isn't even sure how he got here.

"What." Just that one word, but really, there's not even a question mark at the end of it.

I'm so stunned by the shift in attitude that I just stay where I am, heart thundering, my emotions twisted into a violent tangle.

Without a word, Oscar sits up and pulls out of me, looking down at the red on his pelvis, his lower belly, his upper thighs, and scowling fiercely.

He stands up, yanking his pants over his dick, and takes off.

"Where the fuck do you think you're going?" I shout after him, struggling to get up. My body feels heavy, used, but in the best possible way. Whatever that just was, I want more. "You can't leave me to clean this up by myself!"

Oscar acts like he can't hear me, pounding up the steps and slamming the bathroom door behind him. My cheeks burn as I get up and pad to the downstairs bathroom, wiping myself down, and then leaning my palms on the countertop to look at my reflection in the mirror.

"God, that was weird," I murmur to myself, but I can't deny that it was incredible, too.

The question here is: what the hell is Oscar so freaked out about?

I decide I don't care. But I am pissed. Royally fucking pissed.

He's going to owe me for this, big time.

CHAPTER
TWENTY

Only a total dick fucks a girl on her period and then doesn't help clean up. I spend another hour scrubbing the couch cushions before Vic finally comes out of his room to stare at me.

"Jesus," he murmurs, lighting up a cigarette before heading outside the sliding glass door to smoke.

"Thanks for the help," I snap out through gritted teeth. That gets his attention, and he comes back in to look at me, leaning his big body against the inside of the sliding glass door.

"If you think I'm cleaning up a mess you made while fucking another guy, then you've seriously missed the boat on my personality. Who do you think I am, Bernadette?" I ignore Vic, but I know he's right. Doesn't rankle any less. "By the way, isn't it like Thanksgiving next week or some shit?"

I pause in my scrubbing and then glance back at him in surprise.

Oh. Crap. It is, isn't it? Well, in like a week and a half or something.

We've been so busy this month that I spaced it completely.

Victor doesn't want me to go home anymore. I agree with that, but it also means that the danger level is amping up. My mother isn't going to take this lying down. The Thing most *definitely* won't. He loves to pick at me from across a dinner table—even more so on holidays. He laps my pain and anger up like a lizard sticking its long tongue to a fly.

"It's on the twenty-eighth," I say, but I don't really care. It's an okay holiday, and I get the modern meaning of it, but there's also just a wee bit of genocide in there, too. Heather, though, she might get upset if we don't do anything at all. I put my forehead on my arm, the fingers of my right hand still curled around the sponge.

I cannot believe I had sex with Oscar Montauk this morning.

At this point, I've screwed every Havoc Boy but for Callum. *I'm sure we'll get there soon,* I think, and then sigh. Not because I don't want to see what Cal might be like in bed, but because I hate holidays and all their stupid rituals.

"The girls will want to do something," I say as Vic comes over to sit in the armchair on my left. I lay my cheek against my arm and turn my face to look at him. He stares at me with equal parts possessiveness and tender adoration. I'm not sure he's even aware of the latter bit. "But I'm not sure I have the energy."

Victor nods, sweeping his palm over his purple-dark hair. He doesn't like me sleeping in Aaron's bed, but I keep doing it anyway because I have a feeling that after the wedding, I'll rarely be out of Vic's wicked fingers.

"Hael can make tacos with that ground turkey meat shit you like. How does that sound?" Vic lights up a joint, the smoke drifting toward the open sliding door. "Gobble motherfucking gobble."

I smile, but I don't have the energy to laugh.

"Tacos and Havoc Boys. This might be my most exciting Thanksgiving yet." I sit up and plop the sponge into the bucket of pinkish water. Victor and I don't talk about me screwing the other guys, not really. It's implied that I stay within Havoc. I'm dead certain that if I fucked a guy outside of this circle, he would kill him, and I would most certainly suffer.

Not saying our relationship is healthy or hashtag-goals or anything like that, but it is what it is.

And I revel in it.

"The day after, can we get a Christmas tree?" I ask, and Victor gives me a weird look as I push to my feet.

"You're one of those people, huh? A sentimental asshole with a need for dead pine trees and lights."

I glare at him as I climb to my feet, swiping a hand across my forehead. When I reach out for the joint, he passes it my way and then yanks me into his lap. Victor's lips brush my ear, and my entire body flashes white-hot before relaxing into a desperate sort of cool, like a dip in a pool after getting a sunburn.

"Why do you have to mess with me like this?" he continues, and it takes me a second to realize he's not talking about the Christmas tree. No, he's talking about Oscar. "You know how I feel when I see you with another man, don't you?"

"Grateful for a night off?" I joke, and his hold tightens on me. I pretend not to notice, smoking the joint with two, tattooed fingers. The *A* and the *V* from my *Havoc* tattoo stare back at me.

"Murderous," he tells me, and then he takes the joint back and pushes me off of his lap just as Callum comes down the stairs.

"Off to the studio?" I ask, lifting the bucket. Cal shakes his head, coming over to take the bucket from me. I almost don't let him. After all, he doesn't know what the pinkish water in it means, but then I decide to just enjoy not having to dump the heavy thing in the sink.

"Not today," he tells me, rinsing the bucket with the detachable sprayer on the sink. He looks ridiculously comfortable cleaning up blood. Not his first time at the rodeo, am I right? "I was going to climb onto the roof and watch the sun rise."

I stare at him as goose bumps prickle across my arms. I'm wearing his hoodie again, drowning in fabric and the fresh smell of talc and laundry soap. Callum turns around and leans his ass against the sink. His hood is down, but he's wearing a sweatshirt similar to mine, tucking his hands into the front pocket.

"My grandmother and I used to do that, every Sunday morning." He shrugs, like it's no big deal. It is. It's huge. I focus on his blue eyes and try not to get lost in the vibrancy of them, but it's impossible, like falling into the ocean during a storm and praying that you don't drown. "When she could still get around well-enough to do it, that is." He ponders on that for a moment. "I might go home in a bit to check on her."

Obviously, I knew each of the boys had a family and a backstory and all that crap, but I guess I'm just as much a narcissist as the next asshole because I never really let myself think about that. To me, they were always just … mine. My boys. My property. I would piss on them if I could.

All of these revelations, though, they're rocking me.

Vic has a socialite for a mother and a drunk for a father; Hael's dad is a murderer and his mom is broken; Callum only has a grandmother to his name. Of course, I know all about Aaron, but when it comes to Oscar? He's an enigma. I wouldn't know if he lived with snakes in a wild tangle in the woods.

"Do you mind if I join you on the roof?" I ask, feeling my heart stutter a bit. The animal side of me says, *Bernie, you fucked four of your boys; get that last one.* But I need some time to process what happened with Oscar, what's happening with me.

My sexuality is opening like a dark lotus inside of me, and I need to at least say *hi* to her before I test her limits again.

Callum smiles at me, tilting his head just slightly to the side. The diffused gray of early morning light colors his hair, but all it does is turn it silver. It can't diminish the shine of it.

"Of course you can," he tells me, his voice as rough and beautiful as always, a tumble of dead and dark things that makes the wicked part of me happy in ways I can't explain. His scars are silver, too, shiny in the strange light, marks of his past stamped into his skin much like his tattoos. As usual, the ballerina on his arm crouches over her legs and weeps, eternally broken. Until Callum is dead and rotting, she will always cry.

Cal pushes up off of the sink and leads the way upstairs, taking me into the room with the bunk beds. Oscar and Hael are still sleeping. The latter looks cute with his red hair all mussed up, one arm thrown across his forehead. The former … I climb on his bed and kick him as hard as I can, slamming the heel of my foot down on his chest.

The piece of shit catches me before I can make contact, opening his eyes and throwing me into a vivid memory of last night. His inked body above me. Blood hot between my thighs. Gray eyes watching, always watching.

I jerk my foot away from him and stumble off the edge of the bed and into Cal. He catches me easily, his fingers making me ache in all the places they touch. He sets me upright, and I flip Oscar off. It's not my most distinguished moment, but I can't help it. I'm annoyed. I've never had sex on my period before, especially not without a cup in. It was an intimate moment; it smacked of vulnerability.

And I just had to take that plunge with Oscar Montauk of all people.

"Is there a problem, Bernadette?" he asks, turning toward the wall. I notice he gets the queen-sized bed while Callum and Hael share the bunks. It'd be easy to see whose bed was whose, even without their presence. Oscar has silken gray sheets, and a matching comforter. He has one pillow, and a cup of water on the nightstand beside his glasses. Hael, on the other hand, sleeps in a tangle of mismatched children's sheets with cartoon patterns on them. He also has a single pillow, but it's not all perfect like Oscar's. Instead, it's folded up and ratty at the edges. Callum's bunk is the top one, decorated with a blue threadbare blanket, a sleeveless hoodie draped over the safety railing.

"A problem?" I ask, peering at him like the nutcase he is. "We just had *sex*, you half-wit fucker. You're not going to write me out of my own story." Oscar pretends not to hear me, but the muscles in his back tense up. That's enough for me, knowing I've rankled him in some way.

I refocus on Callum, taking his hand as he helps me out the window and onto the gentle pitch of the roof. We're still holding hands as he walks me around to face the east side of the house and the rising orange ball of the sun.

We sit down, side by side, our arms pressed close together.

For a while, neither of us says a damn thing.

"You know," he starts, removing a pack of cigarettes from the pocket of his hoodie and lighting one up before offering it to me; I take it. "When I told you, at the dance studio, that we do whatever is best for Havoc …" Callum trails off, slipping another cigarette between his fairy-tale lips and lighting up. It's odd, to see such a beautiful boy with smoke billowing from his mouth. That mouth, it should be kissing your forehead, telling you everything is okay, saying *I love you.* That's how Callum was built from birth, to be someone special. He still is, but his energy now is dark and muddled; the only thing he's certain of —besides the rising sun—is that pain is a constant.

"What about that?" I ask, edging closer to him. By all rights, I should move further away. But each day … no, no, each minute, each *second* that I spend with the Havoc Boys, the more I'm drawn into the deep, dark well from which they call came.

We're forged from the same primal soul, me and these boys.

I take a drag on my cigarette, lifting a brow as Cal pulls a Pepsi out of his hoodie pocket. He cracks the top and takes a sip. This, too, he offers me, and I accept, just so I can press my lips to the same spot he did. An indirect kiss. My mouth tingles as I hand the can back.

"You know that I meant you, too, right?" he asks, still staring into the sun. It's getting a bit bright for me, so I glance away, but Callum manages to hold its fiery stare for much longer. "Because you're a part of Havoc. It might not have been official until recently, but it was always true."

I say nothing, staring down at the shorts I stole from Aaron's dresser. I'm addicted to wearing his clothes apparently. Even when I know I have my own things in a duffel bag on the floor, I want something of his. Paired with Cal's hoodie, I feel safer than I ever have in my entire goddamn life.

Yes, Havoc kills people, but they kill people for *me*. To protect me. To protect my sister.

"Somehow," I start, smoking my cigarette with no small amount of pleasure. Sure, it might kill me one day, but the slow murder of nicotine is delicious. Sorry, but it's true. Just … don't start. That's what I always tell Heather. *Don't start. Don't get mixed up in something that could kill you. Don't fall in love with five boys on an elementary school playground.* "I knew that was what you meant."

Callum chuckles, and I'm just so done with trying to find metaphors to describe his perfectly imperfect voice that I lean over and kiss him. It's a sloppy, weird kiss, and it makes me feel my age, but it also makes my mouth sparkle and glitter.

Jesus.

Flushing, I turn back to the sunrise. Doesn't mean I miss Cal's saucy smile out of the corner of my eye. He reaches up to rub a hand over the scars on his neck.

"You should know, we thought about killing your stepdad years ago, even before we found the video." Callum says that as easily as one might mention how they like their eggs for breakfast. I stare at him, but he just smokes his cigarette and sips his Pepsi, taking his time before he answers me. "Hael tried to do it for real once, but back then, we had nothing. We were nothing." Cal snickers, eyes crinkling up with a genuine sense of emotion. "We became something for you, Bernadette. Havoc is a blade; wield it."

"Hael tried to … kill Neil?" I clarify, blinking at him. Cal nods, his blond hair turning gold in the light of the rising sun. Even though mornings make me sad—because they always remind me of Pen and the way she used to say *rise and shine* when she'd wake me up—I can at least take a moment to say this is shaping up to be one of my bests. I'm here, and not with Pamela and the Thing. I'm here with Callum freaking Park.

"Not my story to tell," Cal explains, glancing my way. His eyes are as blue as the sky behind his head. My breath catches, and I find myself looking away. *I can't believe I screwed Oscar before Callum. What a dick move.* In any hand, in any game, Callum beats Oscar. "You should ask him though; bet he'd love to tell it." I think about that, about Hael Harbin facing off against Neil Pence for me. My lips twitch against the beginnings of a smile. "We might've let Hael do it—helped him do it, actually—but the world was stacked against us." Cal keeps watching me, like he's trying to gauge my reaction. "We didn't want Neil's murder pinned on you. That, and someone would have to go to jail. That would mean never seeing you again. We were all too selfish to let you go." Cal stops smoking, ashes his cigarette on the brown roof tiles, and then flicks the butt into the netherworld. "I won't make that same mistake again, Bernie." He looks out toward the other suburban houses that surround Aaron's, their backyards all butt-fucked up against each other. Not that I can complain. Still better than the sandbox-sized dump they call a backyard that Pamela has back in South Prescott.

"Please don't talk like that," I say as he laughs at me, giving my scrunched up face a curious onceover with that beautiful blue gaze of his. Birds twitter in the trees around us, singing songs that are more cheerful than any living creature has a right to be. "If I were reading a book, I'd peg you as the sacrificial type, the first one to die."

"Foreshadowing?" Cal jokes, but it's not funny to me. I don't want any heroic bullshit moves ruining what we're building here. *And what, exactly, are we building here, Bernie?* I ask myself, but I'm not ready to answer that question, so I don't bother.

"We haven't slept together yet, so … it'd make narrative sense for you to be killed off." My voice cracks a bit on the words because the thought of losing a Havoc Boy when I've only just gotten them … that kills me.

"Yet," Cal purrs in his husky voice, expelling the sunlight from my aura and replacing it with star-studded darkness. I shimmy even closer to him. "There's no rush, Bernadette. Just enjoy yourself. I don't date, and I haven't slept with anyone since school started." He keeps smiling, but his eyes are far away and full of wicked whimsy.

"Victor acts like there's a rush," I say, wondering if Oscar or Hael is listening in on our conversation. They can if they want; I don't give a shit. The shower was on when I came up the stairs, so I figure Aaron is naked, and wet, and his soapy hands are trailing down his inked body …

"There isn't," Cal tells me, voice firm and maybe just a little bit scary. "Vic is good at what he does. He created Havoc; he owns it. He's fair, and he's smart, and his fuse is long, but he's also an asshole. Don't listen to him. Sooner or later, he'll understand."

"Understand what?" I ask, but really, I don't need Callum to answer me. We both know what he means. *Havoc Girl.* Not Vic's girl, not even if I heat up on the inside every single friggin' time he says it.

"Do we need a turkey for Thanksgiving?" Callum asks after a long pause. He lights up another cigarette and holds it between two fingers, his nails painted blue like always. "My grandma probably has one in her deep freezer. I could bring it over here after I check on her."

I wet my lips.

I'm *dying* to ask about Cal's grandma, about his homelife, what his bedroom looks like … but we've already had a tender moment up here, and my heart still feels a bit raw. That's a subject for another time.

"Won't she need it?" I ask, but Callum shakes his head,

flipping his hood up to cover his hair. Defense mechanism. I'm getting good at recognizing the boys' little tics. Or … I always knew what those tics were, because I've stalked them like a creeper for half of my life.

"She always makes me buy one for her, but she can't cook it, and I'm no good with that shit." He keeps smiling, even though there's melancholy laced in those words. "It makes her happy though, when I bring one home. Maybe I should've made more of an effort to learn to cook?"

"You mean, in your spare time, after all the free dance lessons for impoverished little girls, the murdering, the burying of bodies …"

"Bernadette, show some tact," Oscar says from somewhere behind me, probably leaning out the window of the upstairs bedroom. But if he can leave me to clean blood off the couch by myself, he can deal with my quips.

"Is your mom going to be okay with you staying here indefinitely?" Callum asks after a minute or two. We both know we need to get started with our day, but neither of us has moved. It's hard to want to leave that spot, with our arms pressed close, hips abutting one another. The sunshine is nice, too. We don't get much of that these days.

"Probably not," I admit, pulling my phone out of the hoodie pocket. It's off, the screen black, all of its horrible secrets hidden away. The last thing I feel like doing is turning it on. After he finishes his cigarette, Callum takes it from me and powers it on. He doesn't ask me my pin code; he just seems to know it (which is not at all surprising).

"Mm," he says after a minute, passing the phone back to

me. There's a text message pulled up, just waiting for me to read.

You're an idiot, Bernadette. But I'll do it. Let me know when to meet you at the courthouse.

That's it, the only text I have from Pamela.

There's nothing from the Thing either.

I smell a rat.

Well, that, and a snake.

"Victor," I growl, shoving up to my feet and heading for the window. Callum follows close behind, as dexterous as a cat. I'm certain that if I started to fall, he'd catch me.

Hopping into the room, I manage to land just as Hael is pushing his pajama pants down his hips. His cock is hard, and my fingers twitch as I pass him by.

"Morning cutie," he purrs as I roll my eyes and slip into the hall.

Callum even follows me down the stairs, falling back as I open the downstairs bathroom door to find Vic pissing. He glances casually in my direction, cigarette hanging from his mouth.

"What?" he asks, ebon eyes—and yeah, Mr. Darkwood, ebon is a fucking word because it's in the Merriam-Webster dictionary, you twat—watching me as I lift up my phone, screen facing toward him.

"Courthouse? Why is Pamela asking me about the courthouse?"

"Oh." Vic finishes peeing, shakes his dick off, and then tucks it away. He moves over to the sink to wash his hands, taking his sweet time responding to me. "I paid your mother ten-thousand dollars and a Burberry bag for your hand in marriage."

I just stare at him. And then I chuck my phone at his head. Unfortunately, he manages to catch it like a boss and looks cool doing it, cigarette clutched in his opposite hand.

"When?" I ask, and Victor shrugs.

"This morning. I was worried Pamela might not like you staying here permanently." He steps forward and hands the phone back to me. When he leans in and puts his mouth against my ear, my eyes close of their own accord and my fingers fist in the front of his t-shirt. "I'd have told you sooner, but Oscar's dick was shoved up that sweet cunt of yours." I punch Vic in his man-tit, but it doesn't do any good. His muscles are like rocks.

"Why the courthouse?" I ask as I move aside to let him out of the bathroom. "Don't we have to have a proper ritualistic Western marriage to get your inheritance?" He glances back at me, grinning big and showing teeth.

"Sure, yeah, but we need a marriage license at least three days before the wedding." Vic turns away from me to watch as Aaron comes down the stairs, his hair wet from the shower. He was in there a *long* time, so I can only guess he was doing something other than chastely washing his body. Our eyes meet and an awful sense of dread washes over me. I have to tell him that I had sex with Oscar. Like, *now.*

"We are not getting married in three days," I snap with a roll of my eyes. Aaron continues down the stairs and heads into the living room, grabbing his boots before he goes to sit down on the long couch. His face very clearly says *the fuck happened to my furniture?* I pretend not to notice, at least for the moment.

"No," Vic agrees, nodding his head as he pauses in the archway that leads to the kitchen. "We're not. We're getting married in six. Right on my motherfucking birthday."

CHAPTER
TWENTY-ONE

One year earlier ...

Callum Park

There is nothing more beautiful than Bernadette Blackbird, bathed in moonlight and sleeping peacefully beneath my overly protective gaze. When I first started coming out here and climbing to the roof to watch her, I felt like she could sense me somehow. I'd place my fingers to the glass and let my breath make little clouds in the cool air.

Her unease would quiet, and she'd finally find a chance to rest.

Now that I've been doing it for a year, I'm sure of it.

She only truly sleeps when I'm around.

I sit down and cross my legs in front of me, resting my elbows on my knees and parking my chin in my hands to wait, to watch, to keep her safe. I don't trust that her stepfather will *stay away because of the video, so I make certain of it as often as I can.*

Instead of letting myself be shackled to a broken dream, I've found a new one in the face of a girl who thinks she's jaded to a fine point. In reality, there's an innocence in her that's rare and precious.

Even in the face of hate, of pain, of ruin, Bernadette has never stopped watching us.

Never stopped loving us.

And we, we love her.

Me, most of all.

She just doesn't know it.

I touch my blue-painted fingernails to her window, wishing I could open it and crawl inside, curl my body around hers and hold her tight.

But I don't; I can't.

I sit there, and I make sure her door remains locked, her eyes closed, her mind safe from the destruction of her stepfather. With my chance at escaping South Prescott dashed to ashes, I've found a new mission.

Bernadette will be happy, whatever it takes. It doesn't matter what sacrifices I have to make—even my life is not too much. And if it truly took the death of my dream for me to understand this, then it will have all been worth it.

I chuckle and light up a cigarette, turning my head to look at the moon.

Silver light bathes my face as I close my eyes, dreaming of a day where I don't have to sit in the cold outside her window, when I can actually touch her, when she'll talk to me.

Of all the things, that's what I like best of all, hearing her sweet words.

When the sun begins to peek its head above the horizon, I leave, climbing back down and landing in a crouch in the side yard of the duplex. I don't like to leave my grandmother home alone, but if it's between her and Bernadette, I know the hard choice I'd have to make.

Still, my grandma is the only family I have left, and I'll take care of her for as long as I can. I have a bad feeling that the darkness coming for her is something that I can't fight with guns and fists.

I walk through the dawn without fear because I know that I am the thing in the darkness to be afraid of. There's comfort in that, being the monster under the bed instead of the person inside of it.

Later that day, when Bernadette sees me in the hallway, she gives me a wide berth and I pause, turning to look at her over my shoulder. She thinks that I barely know who she is. In reality, I've turned into a fucking stalker, my eyes following her even when she thinks no one is watching.

My lips tilt in a sad smile as I turn away, remembering a time when I held little hands out to a crying girl and pulled her into the magical language of dance. Words are hard for me, but the body ... the body can say it all without a sound.

Flipping my hood up blocks out the voices of doubt, the fears, the regret. It keeps me calm, hides me in a world of my own making, one where I am the captain of my own fate.

"You've been going over there again?" Vic asks, and I nod, turning to look at him as he leans up against the lockers near

the front entrance to Prescott High. I say nothing as he looks after her, turning to me only after she's gone. "Anything I should know about?"

"Nothing at all," I say, but there is, really. Because with each passing day, Bernadette is drowning. The harder she fights, the deeper that struggle works its way into her bones. It's only a matter of time before the shell around her innocence is so sharp that it cuts.

One day, she'll join us. Even if we wish she wouldn't. We can try, but eventually, you have to accept the inevitable.

"Good," Vic says, but in his voice, I can hear it.

He wants her, and he isn't letting her go.

Fine by me, because I don't want to let her go either.

Not ever.

November eighteenth, Now ...

Bernadette Blackbird

At school on Monday, the boys manage to surprise the shit out of me.

"We're going to deal with Vaughn today," is the only thing I'm told when Aaron and I roll up to the school to find Oscar waiting for us.

We walk into Prescott High as normal, passing through the metal detectors, skirting the German Shepherds ... I almost—

check it: *almost*—miss Hael slipping a wad of cash to the campus cop. I don't ask any questions, making sure I keep up as we sweep down the hallway as a group.

Vaughn sees us coming, but doesn't change his course down the hallway, like he thinks this stalemate we've been at for the past few weeks is permanent. He thinks the Thing's status protects him.

He's wrong.

As we pass by, Callum slips away from our group and throws an arm around Vaughn's neck, effortlessly dragging him into a chokehold. His eyes are wide as he struggles, silently pleading for Nurse Whitney to help him as she steps out of the nurse's office … and turns away.

We surge into her office together, and Aaron locks the door behind us.

"What are you doing to me?" Vaughn asks, coughing and sputtering as Callum releases him and cracks his knuckles in a menacing sort of way. If the move's intended to instill fear, it works. I can sense Vaughn's terror the way a wolf might sniff out a rabbit by the pheromones of its pathetic cowering.

"Oh, Vaughn, come on," Vic says, hopping up onto the sterile little table in the center of the room. He plants his elbows on his knees and puts his face in his palms. "Did you *really* think you could come to Aaron's house on Halloween and walk away unscathed? We take our privacy very seriously."

Aaron picks up a pair of bolt cutters that are lying on the stainless-steel countertop. They seem so out of place in a school nurse's office. I'm certain they weren't left there by accident.

Scott notices the bolt cutters right away, and all the color drains from his face.

"You can't touch me," he whispers, but he doesn't look away as Aaron opens and closes the bolt cutters, as if he's testing out the force. "Neil—"

Victor bursts out laughing. I'll admit, even I jump a bit from the sound. Hael glances my way and winks, trying to lighten the mood. Bit difficult here considering the air is quite literally perfumed with violence. It smells like testosterone and long-awaited revenge.

"Oh, Scott, come on," Vic says, shaking his head slightly. "You were punished for a reason. To be quite frank, we went easy on you. But you just *had* to come crawling back. Even a snake knows that when its burrow is kicked in, that it should slither away. You know what that makes you, Vaughn?" He continues as Callum and Hael step forward, shoving Vaughn into a plastic chair, each of them with a hand on the principal's shoulders. As usual, Oscar stands to the side in his suit and tie, observing but keeping his hands relatively clean.

"Please," Vaughn whispers, looking around the room and finally settling on me. "Please don't do this." He leans forward, teeth gritted, eyes wide. His glasses slip down his nose. He must think because I'm a girl, that I'll be softer on him somehow, the most likely person in this room to grant him mercy.

Silly him.

"It makes you a rodent, Scott," I finish, filling in the blanks in Vic's metaphor. "I told you my stepfather was raping my sister, and you felt me up. You invited me to do pornography for you, at the age of fifteen. Don't look at me like a savior.

Vaughn, part of the reason you're here is because you did me wrong." I nod my chin at Aaron, and he steps forward, bolt cutters in hand.

"No, please!" Vaughn screams, his voice echoing around the small room. That's when I hear the speakers in the hall begin to play music, disguising our wicked intent from the world. It'll take Ms. Keating a while to figure out how to stop it, I'm sure.

Part of me is worried about that detective guy—Constantine or whatever the fuck his name was—but I know how thorough the boys are, so I figure he must not be on campus today.

"Quiet," Vic snaps, going dark as he lowers his head, his dark brown eyes turning black, like a demon's. "You're going to take your punishment and your lover is going to patch you up. Afterwards, you're going to consider doing what we say. A trained dog is fed treats, Vaughn. A rabid one is put down. Do you understand what I'm saying?"

"No, no, no, please," Vaughn is sobbing as Aaron pushes the metal rolling table toward him. Callum takes the principal's hand and puts it flat against the surface, splaying his fingers out. That's when it clicks, for both me *and* Vaughn. He begins to keen like a cornered animal as I watch sweet, little Aaron Fadler slip one of the man's digits between the end of the bolt cutters.

"Bite down on this," Oscar offers up, passing over a leather whip that he removes from his bookbag. "You left it at the cabin; we thought you might want it." Hael slips the item in Scott's mouth as tears roll down his cheeks, staining his blue-striped button-down. "Now, bite down and taste the sweet metallic bite of vengeance."

Aaron glances at me one last time, his green-gold gaze connecting with mine, and then squeezes the bolt cutters closed, severing the tip of Vaughn's middle finger. His scream is muffled by the handle of the leather whip as blood floods the surface of the metal table. Not two seconds later, his eyes are rolling into his head and he's passed out.

"Pathetic," Oscar murmurs as he steps forward and cracks some smelling salts beneath the principal's nose, reviving him. Scott's eyes flick wildly around the room as Aaron moves onto his next finger, positioning the bolt cutters just below the first knuckle of his pointer finger. Reminds me of this one time when I broke the tip of my finger in the panels of our garage door. I was trying to close it manually from the outside, but my finger slipped in and was crushed. The pain was nearly unbearable, especially for a fourteen-year-old, but I survived.

So will Vaughn.

Lucky him.

"Wait," I say, before Aaron can squeeze the ends of the cutters together. All five boys glance my way, and I see something like triumph flash in Oscar's gray eyes. *Asshole.* He thinks I'm here to free Vaughn? What an idiot.

The way Aaron looks at me though, like I'm both more and less than he ever thought I would be, I can tell he knows what I want. Without a word, he hands the cutters to me, and I step up to the table.

It's my list, after all.

When I asked Havoc to help me with it, I thought it was because I was too weak to take control of my own vengeance. Now, I know that's not the case at all.

I'm here because I want to be.

Vaughn looks up at me the way I once looked up at him, with a sincere pleading in his gaze, a cry for help.

I put the bolt cutters against his finger, and squeeze until bone breaks and blood sprays.

Some of it gets on my face, but I don't care.

Oscar is right: the sweet metallic bite of vengeance was the perfect way to describe it.

After we're finished with Vaughn, we clean up in Nurse Whitney's sink and scrub the room until it shines. Callum pockets the bolt cutters in his dance bag as Nurse Yes-Scott tends to the principal's injuries as best she can.

We only removed five fingers; he still has full use of his left hand.

Consider that a kindness.

"Okay, Scott," Vic says, after he's all bandaged up and sipping orange juice from a straw. There's a glazed look in Vaughn's eyes that makes me wonder if he's still all there. He passed out after each cut and had to be woken up. And after each cut, he seemed less and less coherent. "You're going to take the rest of the day off. If you need to go to the hospital, you'll tell them you had an accident with a circular saw. When I call your phone next, you'll answer it, won't you?"

Vaughn nods, and Vic smiles, patting him on the cheek in a patronizing sort of way.

"Off we go," he says, letting Hael crack the door and check the hall. Once he decides it's safe, we slip out together. "Get to class, you delinquents."

Victor glances back at me, narrowing his eyes slightly, like he's deciding if he should walk me to class or not. But he must see the way I'm gravitating toward Aaron, and decides to turn and stalk off, like he's in a pissy mood. Let him be, that's his problem.

"You don't hate me, do you?" I ask Aaron, wondering if I've just shattered any leftover illusions he might've had about my being a good girl underneath all the leather and tattoos. Cal heads for the front doors and we follow him, in no hurry to actually get to class. The security guard looks up at us, nods his chin at Cal, and buzzes him out the front door. We follow, but Callum disappears down the sidewalk like a shadow.

I'm guessing he's off to bury those bolt cutters.

"Are you kidding me?" Aaron asks, smiling to soften the blow as he lights up a cigarette on the front steps of Prescott High. The steps where he stood and watched as I was dragged and thrown into the back of a van, on my way to a week of darkness and granola bars. The start of my new, hellish life. "I love you, Bernadette. You know that, right? I would die for you."

I smile, because even though I'm pretty sure I have Vaughn's blood still stuck under my black-painted fingernails, I do know that Aaron loves me. I really do.

"You took a bullet for me, Fadler," I say, because like I said, actions over words. He's given me both, and I'm loving it.

We share a cigarette together before something strange

happens. Aaron ... hugs me. He just grabs me and squeezes me against him until I give in and fist my fingers in his shirt. He holds me there for a while, so long that the next bell rings before we pull apart.

"Remember to stay human," he warns me, and then he reaches down to grab my hand, pulling me down the hall to my classroom.

After school, I step outside to find the Thing's police cruiser waiting across the street from Prescott High.

My mouth goes dry and my palms fill with sweat. For a moment there, I'm eleven years old all over again, peering around the corner of the kitchen as Neil palms my older sister's budding breasts and then laughs.

"What on earth is he doing here?" Oscar asks, and I blink, coming to like I've just woken from a coma. I glance his way to find him frowning, his iPad tucked under his arm, purple silk tie smooth and wrinkle free.

"You think Vaughn called him?" Callum asks, cocking his head to one side, hood up to hide his scars. The way he looks at that police cruiser, I can only imagine the violent slideshow that must be playing in his head. The weirdest part about it all, is that he smiles while he's imagining it.

"There are no outgoing calls from Vaughn's phone," Oscar says, checking his iPad. He must've installed spyware on Scott's phone while I was severing his fingertips. What a dreadful team we make. "So, likely not."

"Kali?" I wonder, because I'll admit, it seems a bit overdue for her to come at me with some level of retaliation for what I did to her face. The fire-bombing was a nice touch, but not personal enough for her liking. While some people play in tropes and clichés, she likes to steal personal experiences and twist them into dark, ugly things. Like … how she ruined my homecoming for example. Or how she asked the boys to convince horse-faced Kaydence Mane to kick my ass for no reason at all.

It's been a month, and we still don't know why she was with Neil on Halloween.

His motivations I understood perfectly: *I'm watching you, Bernadette, and I'm coming for you.*

But Kali's? And what's up with her dating Mitch, but hanging out with some guy at Oak Park Prep? Shit, she has as many possible fathers for this future baby as I might've had for mine, had I been pregnant, too.

Speaking of …

Hael comes out the front doors of Prescott High, his mouth turned down in a sharp frown. He's still pretty, with that red hair of his, those honeyed eyes, his ass encased in tight denim. He's got a goddamn bubble butt, too, and he knows it, the way he swaggers around town.

"Aw, come the fuck on," he groans, gesturing at Neil's car with a tattooed hand. "I've got to deal with Brittany tomorrow, and now this? When do we get a trip to Hawaii, huh Vic? We work hard here in South Prescott." Victor steps out beside his best friend, his emotions locked away behind a stoic face, as always.

"There's no rest for the wicked, Hael," I tell him, quoting Oscar. The dickhead in question glances my way, but I return his stoic look with one of my own.

Aaron is the last to appear, pausing with his arm brushed up against mine. It's meant to seem like coincidence, but I can feel the sharp intention in the move. So can Vic. He looks at his friend for a long moment before turning back to the idling cop car.

"What the fuck is that about?" Vic asks, cigarette hanging limply from his lips. "Is he stupid or something?"

A shiver crawls down my spine as I shake my head.

"No. He's watching us," I explain as the car starts to roll slowly down the road, turning the corner and disappearing from sight. "He's waiting."

"Let him," Hael says, cracking his knuckles and glancing over at Vic. "Because we have something planned for him." He flashes teeth at me. "And soon, something soon."

"I sure as shit hope so," I murmur. "Because if he's here, then he's looking to start something soon, too."

And I don't like that. I don't like it at all.

CHAPTER
TWENTY-TWO

Hael is under the hood of the Eldorado when I walk into his garage on Tuesday, pausing near the open door to lean my shoulder up against the jamb. He doesn't notice me at first, music trickling from his phone, the sound of metal on metal ringing pleasantly around the small space as he tinkers around with the Caddy.

Fortunately, his mom isn't home or else I wouldn't have stopped by without asking. She seems to be a pretty sore subject for him, and I don't want to stir the pot—especially since today is the day we get the results of Brittany's DNA test. My teeth clench as I think of her weepy face and all the bullshit that spews from her lips. Maybe dousing her in her own pumpkin spiced latte wasn't the best idea, but I don't give a crap.

Hael is mine now. Period. Baby or no baby.

I've made up my mind for good.

I lick my lips and shift nervously as Hael slides out from under the hood, shirtless and covered in grease. My heart stutters when I see him sit up, raking dirty fingers through his red hair. When he spots me, he smiles in the most infuriating way possible. *Cocksure asshole,* I think as he stands up, the muscles in his abs and chest rippling with the movement.

The baby can't be his; it just can't be.

"Hey, Blackbird," he says, his voice this melodic purr that's so at odds with his filthy appearance. I pretend like I don't give a fuck that he's shirtless and covered in grease, that I don't want those dirty hands leaving dark handprints on my jeans. It's a lie. "Didn't expect to see you here today. What's up?"

"Well," I reply, studying the metal shit heap that's supposed to be my future car. "We figured you might want company when you get the news." I shrug my shoulders, like it's no big thing. In reality, my stomach is in knots.

"Ah," he murmurs, grabbing a rag and coming over to stand beside me. The smell of coconut oil is unmistakable, and my nostrils flare as I take it in. Mix that with a bit of motor oil and some fresh sweat, and I'm sold. A single drop slides down his stomach, falling into the valley between his abs. *Jesus. This boy was born to make me wet.* That, or maybe I'm just a thirsty bitch. Who knows? "Right. That. I was about to head inside and get dressed." Hael glances over my shoulder toward the street, where Aaron is waiting with the Bronco, Vic with the Harley.

I flick my eyes up to Hael's face, realizing that I haven't heard a single word he's just said.

"Miss Blackbird," he murmurs, stepping close and putting his palm on the wall beside my head. "Were you just checking me out?" He's smiling, but there's something more to his expression, something darker and far less pleasant.

It's because of the Brittany thing; of course it is.

Not a soul on this earth could smile knowing what's at stake, not sincerely.

"I might've been," I say, putting my fingers on his bare lower belly and savoring the hot sweaty slickness of his muscles. "But that's only because I'm so damn confident that it isn't going to be your kid."

Hael shoots me a grin, but the expression doesn't quite reach his eyes.

"That confident, huh? You want to make another bet? If the baby's mine, you owe me another blow job at a time and place of my choosing. If it isn't, I'll owe you some, uh ..." He makes a 'V' shape with his fingers and flicks his tongue between them to indicate cunnilingus and then laughs.

"Sounds a bit like a win-win for you," I quip, even though my stomach hurts, and I'm afraid. I'm so afraid. I don't want Hael to be connected to Brittany through a child. If he is, then I can never truly just have him to myself. He'll be a dad; he'll have responsibilities.

And that's the allure of Hael Harbin, isn't it? How free and wild and wicked he is?

"The oral sex part is," he agrees, but the playfulness is already draining out of him as he checks the time on his phone and sighs. "Not so much the rest of it. Wait here for me?" I nod as Hael slips into the house to change. When he comes back, he's still wearing the dirty grease-stained jeans, but he's got on a fresh red tee.

And damn if he doesn't melt the panties right off me.

"Let's go, Blackbird," he says, breezing past and tossing his keys in the air as he walks. "You can ride with me."

Hael leads our caravan of vehicles to a coffee shop—not the one where we got in a fight with the Fuller football team—and parks crookedly across two spaces. After he turns the engine off, he just sits there with his hands on the wheel, staring down at it like he's trying to get up the courage to go inside.

Brittany is already in there, waiting at a table near the window. As soon as she turns and sees me in the Camaro with Hael, her face flushes with angry heat and she slams her coffee mug down, splashing liquid everywhere.

"Hey," I whisper, reaching out to lay my fingers atop Hael's. He lifts his face finally to look my direction, all of his false bravado and cocky bullshit stripped bare. To be fair, I like all of that cocky bullshit, but this … this is intense. I want to see more of Hael without his mask and his flair and his sex appeal hiding what he's truly feeling. "We can do this. No matter what happens, we'll figure it out."

"Looking at her now, can you tell?" he asks me, and I glance back to find Brittany staring at me like she's got murder on the mind. "Like, does she look upset or …?"

"She looks furious, to be quite honest," I reply, and he grins. "Good."

Finally, he takes his hands off the wheel and we get out together, meeting the other boys just inside the front doors of the coffee shop.

"Why are they all here?" Brittany demands, looking past Hael to glare at the other boys—but mostly me. "This is a private matter between us, Hael."

"Eh," he says, giving a loose shrug of his shoulders. "You

sort of called Havoc in order to get me to play along, so it's really more of an *all of us* issue." He pauses for a moment and then cocks his head to one side. "So, you gonna tell me or not? I'm guessing since you haven't thrown yourself at me with tears of joy running down your face, that it's not my kid?"

Brittany pauses for a moment, swallowing hard, eyes flicking to Oscar as he fires up his iPad like one might discharge a weapon.

"If you lie to me, I will know," he says, without even looking up from the screen. I have no doubt that the boys will find a way to verify the results of the test from a means other than Brittany herself.

"Hael, please ..." she whines, and his attention snaps over to her in a way I've rarely seen before. The predator in him is coming out, and he is *pissed.*

"You made a deal, Brittany. We've done everything you asked on our end. I've taken you to the movies, to the mall, out to dinner. Our boys beat Rich up; I got beat up by your shitty dad. Tell me the fucking results *now.*"

She stares at him, eyes watering in a way that makes me realize that she really and truly loved him. Still does. The baby isn't even important to her. That's not what this was about, not ever.

It was about Hael and how much she craved him.

My stomach flips, and I exhale sharply.

"This isn't fair," Brittany says, burying her face in her hands and letting out a deep sob that draws the eyes of everyone else inside the building. "It's just not fair. You were mine. You were fucking mine." Her shoulders shake as I exchange a look with

Aaron.

"We should go, maybe," he says, because we already know the answer to our query, even if Brittany refuses to say it outright.

The baby … is not Hael's.

But also, this moment is personal and sad and weird, and I just want to get the fuck out of there.

"I'll stay for a bit," he says, tucking his fingers into the front pockets of his dirty jeans. Brittany sniffles and lifts her head up to look at him, but when she reaches out to touch him, he moves back. "Hands to yourself and we can talk. Otherwise, I'm out of here and you will never see me again."

It hits me then that Hael—despite the things he does in Havoc's name—is actually sort of … *nice*.

Oscar seems to realize this, too, and scowls like he's a disappointment.

"What a fucking relief," Victor murmurs, exchanging a look with Callum. "Not our baby, not our problem. Let's roll. Hael, meet us back at the house in twenty? We have wedding shit to plan today. You can be my best man as long as long as Callum is Bernie's maid of honor."

"Just so long as I don't have to wear a dress," Cal quips, giving a dark anti-smile. "They don't suit my frame very well."

"This isn't a joke!" Brittany screams, but she just sounds reedy and desperate.

We ignore her, turning right back around to head outside. Just … not before I put my hands on Hael's massive bicep and rise onto my tiptoes to kiss the corner of his mouth.

"You owe me oral sex now, too," I whisper, just loud

enough for Brittany to overhear. Hael grins at me as I drop back to my feet and follow the other boys outside.

As soon as I'm situated safely inside the Bronco, I just throw my head back and laugh, and I don't stop until we get back to Aaron's place.

Two years earlier ...

Hael Harbin

I cannot, for the life of me, understand how Batman sleeps at night. He holds the power to kill the bad guys, but yet ... he lets them go. Every. Fucking. Time.

That's my problem, right? Like, I go home, and I lay my head down on that goddamn pillow, and I can't stop thinking about Bernadette Blackbird.

Sure, my friends and I have been into her since she showed up at our inner-city elementary school, quiet and reserved and too pretty for South Prescott. The other children didn't like her because when she first started going to school with us, her clothes were too nice, her hair plaited, like a little doll.

The thing is, while they saw all of that and thought of wealth and snobby Oak Park assholes, we watched Bernadette morph from a doll into a statue. Day after day, the same clothes. Her hair got wilder and more knotted, her shoes worn.

For years, we watched her dip lower and lower into poverty and pain, and we felt powerless.

The only thing we could agree on was that none of us could ever have her. Because as much as we loved Bernadette, we always loved each other, too. She could destroy us from the inside out and we knew that, even at a young age.

Thinking back on it, I'm like, what the fuck, bro? Destroy us from the inside out? Huh? How? By being the perfect Havoc Girl? By fitting in and getting along with five fucked-up misfits that barely belong in society?

No way.

The only reason Bernadette couldn't be one of us at first, was because we were all selfish.

Well, not today, Satan.

My hand squeezes around the handle of the knife. We have guns, Havoc does. I mean, we didn't used to, but things are changing. We've morphed from a kiddie gang ruling a high school into something else, something sinister and wicked and black.

"You can do this, Hael," I tell myself, waiting for the front door of a particular motel room to open, for Neil Pence to step out. Once he gets down the steps, I can move out of the shadows, wrap my arm around his neck, and drag him into the trees at the edge of the park.

I can kill him.

Quietly. Painfully. Cover my hands in blood for Bernadette.

My entire life I've watched my father beat on my mother, use her as a punching bag for his drunken nights and his jobless days. There's nothing I hate more than a man who chooses to treat a girl in his family with disrespect.

Nothing.

Besides, I've turned into something strange, a whore who can't stop fucking, who doesn't know what to do with his feelings, or how to help anyone. This is the least I can do, really. Dad is still in prison and, god-willing, he'll stay there. Mom is safe, at least for now. I mean, if the parole board doesn't jam their heads up their own asses and decide to let him free.

I lick my lips, adjusting my grip on the knife. Neil Pence is out here, fucking a prostitute who looks about the same age as Bernie. Blonde hair, big tits, curvy. I should kill him just for that.

Mostly, I'm killing him because I'd do anything to make sure that Bernie makes it to adulthood without falling into the hands of a predator.

That's all I want. I've got simple needs, you know. I'm easy to please.

Something in the darkness draws my attention, and I shove to my feet, spinning around and swinging the knife in an arc at my would-be attacker. Fortunately for me, the person coming at me is just as good as I am and manages to miss having his throat split open from ear to ear.

I would never forgive myself if I killed Aaron Fadler.

"Dude, what are you doing here?" he asks me, sounding tired. We've stopped chasing Bernadette around, sure, but it's impossible to miss her when she steps foot on campus every morning.

Her sister is dead; she looks broken.

I drop the knife to my side as Aaron studies me, waiting for an explanation of some sort.

"You know what I'm doing here," I retort, glancing over my shoulder to make sure that Neil hasn't left the motel yet. All seems quiet on the Western front. I look back at Aaron, and in his eyes, I see a reflection of my wants and needs.

"We followed you," Aaron adds, stepping back to lean against a tree. He looks like a strong wind might blow him over. I slip the knife—the very same one my dad used to cut me once upon a time—back in its leather holder and then tuck the whole thing in my pocket, so I can cross my arms. "They're all here, around the corner." He pauses and looks away. "Waiting for me to bring you back."

"Is this an order from Vic?" I ask, not even sure why I'm bothering. I know the answer to that.

"You know it is." Aaron looks up, meeting my eyes just as I hear the door swing open and look back to see Neil swagger down the upstairs walk toward the stairs. Fuck. I look back at my friend. "Bernadette is a part of us, but so you are. Havoc has to look out for every member, not just Bernie. You going to prison for life for stabbing a cop doesn't do anyone any good. Pamela will still have Bernadette, she'll still be trapped by Heather, by Heather's grandfather and uncle …"

I touch the knife at my side, knowing that my time for jumping Neil is running short. It's now or never, but looking at Aaron, I don't feel quite as sure as I did. Giving up Bernie for life, I don't want to do that, but I will. Because I'll never be selfish when it comes to her again.

"Besides, who's to say killing him now won't find its way back to her? Everyone knows she hates him. He's sent her to *juvie for attacking him before. We can't take the risk, Hael."*

I frown, and my hands squeeze into fists at my sides. But I already know that he's right, just like I knew about Vic. I might act like an idiot sometimes, but I'm not as stupid as I look.

"Every night he's in that house, there's a risk that he might touch her, that he might put his hands on her. Aaron, I couldn't live with myself if that happened."

"It won't," he tells me, reaching out a hand, palm up. It takes me a minute to realize that he's asking for the knife. With gritted teeth, I give it to him because I'm not sure what I might do with it if I don't.

Well, okay, I do know. I'd destroy Neil and I'd probably howl with laughter while I did it.

I reach up to scratch at the back of my head.

"Well, you gonna explain or what?" I snap, listening to the sound of a car door being shut. After a few seconds, the engine starts up and Neil disappears into the night. I didn't do it. I wanted to, but I didn't. Am I still that same selfish asshole I've always been? The thought infuriates me.

"Look, he knows we have the video now. He knows we'll come for him if he touches her. Right now, we have to work on building Havoc, so we can help her later." Aaron plays with the knife for a minute. "Someday, she's going to come to us, and she's going to call Havoc. We have to give her a weapon she can actually use, something that'll help her escape."

He stops talking. I get it. We all want that for Bernadette, a normal life. A life that is, specifically, not the one we live. Well, except for Vic. I love the guy, he's my best friend, but he can be ... intense.

"I love her, too, you know," I say, and Aaron nods. He's lucky. He's the only one of us who got to pretend, at least for a little while, that she could be his. "So we use the video to keep Bernie safe?" I scoff and rub my hand over my face. "I don't like this. We shouldn't be using a video like that as a weapon."

"We can, if it means keeping both Havoc and Bernie safe."

Aaron meets my eyes again. We're similar in a lot of ways, me and him. We both want to be the good guy yet we both do evil things. We're both inextricably lost somewhere in the middle.

"Okay," I say, exhaling and putting my hands on my hips. "Okay. But someday, he has to die. You know that, right?"

This time, Aaron actually smiles. It's a sad smile, but it's a smile, nonetheless.

"I know," he replies, and together we walk down the block and climb into the welcoming arms of my Camaro. She isn't done yet, but she's getting there, and when she is, I'm going to paint her a violent cherry-red.

And one day, I'm going to take Bernadette for a spin.

Mark my words.

November nineteenth, Now ...

Bernadette Blackbird

"She didn't take it well," Hael says, sitting at a stool in front of the kitchen peninsula, his chin in his hand, a frown on his face. "She threw her coffee in my face and tried to knee me in the balls. I'm a little worried, to be honest with you."

He watches as Oscar goes down a checklist of things that need to be done before the wedding. It isn't a huge affair—after all, besides the Havoc Boys, we've only invited six guests. With Victor's choice of venue, it wasn't difficult to put together a ceremony in the twenty-thousand-dollar budget.

Actually, I've only spent about half of it—most of it on the dress.

"Worried about Brittany?" Aaron asks, making a scoff of disbelief in his throat. "You really think she'd break the deal she made with us?"

"I have no idea," Hael says, narrowing his eyes slightly. He's clearly thinking about Brittany's father, the chief of the Springfield police and the leader of a newly developed anti-gang squad in the area. The fact that he ever got involved with her shows me that even if Havoc seems to have its shit together, we're all still in high school.

There's a lot to learn.

"Hey kiddo," I say when Heather comes tromping down the stairs to search in the fridge for some juice. She gives me a look that very clearly says, *I'm busy, so what the fuck do you want?* I raise an eyebrow and she whines at me.

"I'm in the middle of a game, Bernie," she complains as Victor slips past her and into the kitchen, wrapping his arms around me from behind. My eyes narrow, but Heather gives a dramatic groan.

"Why are you *always* kissing on each other?" she demands,

slamming the fridge door and turning to glare at us.

"Whoa," Hael whistles with a laugh. Victor's big body shakes behind me as he chuckles.

"Because we're in love," he murmurs, resting his chin on my shoulder. I can see Aaron rolling his eyes at the comment.

"Well, I don't want you to be in love," Heather declares, lifting her chin and crossing her arms over her *Spiderman* t-shirt. "I ship you and Aaron."

"You ship us?" Aaron echoes, and it's like he can't control his face anymore. His lips twist up into a shit-eating smirk. "Seriously?"

"Seriously," Heather says as Vic stands up straight and frowns at her. Kara and Ashley come down the stairs just a moment later, and my sister wastes no time in asking them their opinion. "You guys agree, right?" she says, cocking her hip out like she's sixteen instead of eight-going-on-nine. Holy fuck, I'm going to have trouble with her as a teenager I bet. "You ship Aaron and Bernie?"

Kara looks nervously at Vic as he stands behind me, looming over everything like he always does.

"I don't want to be rude ..." she starts, proving that she has most definitely been raised by Aaron and not by me. Look at Heather: you can tell it's in our blood to be bitchy. "But I think Aaron and Bernadette are meant to be together." She glances down at Ashley who, shockingly enough, actually decides that today is the day she's no longer afraid of me.

I must truly be a part of the family now.

"I ship Bernie and Callum," she says, and he snorts from behind me, perched on the edge of the counter as he taps his heels against the lower cabinets.

"So two votes for me, one for Callum, and zero for any of you assholes," Aaron clarifies, pointing at Oscar, Hael, and Vic. "I'll take it."

"From the mouths of babes," I murmur, grabbing the black veil I laid out on the counter and tucking the comb-part of it in my hair. It hangs over my face like I'm attending a funeral. Gross. I take it off and chuck it across the peninsula, deciding that I'd rather have my face bare anyway. I want to actually *see* Vic when I marry him, not hide behind a mosquito net while I walk down the aisle.

"Yeah, well, from the mouth of the boss, you're marring me regardless of who they 'ship'," Vic growls, snatching an apple and flipping the girls backs off as they run up the stairs. They don't see him do it, but it's honestly funny as shit. "You ready for tomorrow?"

I nod.

Because the wedding is not the hard part, the courthouse bit is.

After school, we're meeting Pamela so she can sign the papers of our marriage license.

I'd rather give myself an enema with battery acid.

"Not really," I reply, because out of all the people on my list, Pamela is the one who holds the most weight.

Neil, arguably, is my most hated … but Pam? She was supposed to be my mom. There's no bigger betrayal than that.

"Too bad," Vic says, grinning around a bite of apple. "Because it's happening, whether that bitch mother of yours likes it or not." He pauses to look down at the piece of fruit in his hand, like it's Snow White's poisoned apple or something. "I hope for her sake that she cooperates. She wouldn't want to see the extent of my temper if she doesn't."

CHAPTER
TWENTY-THREE

I'm quite literally shaking as I stand on the courthouse steps in the sexy white dress that Havoc picked out for me inside of Billie Charter's trailer. When I put it on after school and looked in the mirror, I didn't recognize myself.

To clarify: I didn't recognize myself in a good way.

I do not look seventeen. The dress clings to my curves and the back dips low, showing off a pale arch of spine and what little there is left of me that isn't inked. The ends of my hair are dyed a fresh pink, and the blond waves are hanging loose around my shoulders.

To be fair, I haven't looked my age for a long time. Pain and loss and violence, those things worm their way into your eyes; they change a person. So if someone were to look at me, they could see in the emerald green of my irises that I'm an old soul.

Today, it's my makeup, and my body, and my tattoos that tell a different story.

"The combat boots were a hideous choice, really," Oscar

says, checking the time on his iPad and frowning hard. Pamela is late and he doesn't like it. Sorry to tell him, but she hasn't shown up on time to an appointment in her damn life. We might be waiting awhile.

"Shut your face, Oscar Montauk," I grind out, shivering, my teeth chattering against the frigid frost of late fall. "Have you ever stood on cement in heels? It *hurts*. I wasn't about to wander around the courthouse in them."

Oscar just purses his lips and pretends like he doesn't care what I have to say. My argument to that would be … why did you bareback fuck me on my period? I mean, come on, man. He can't fool me anymore. He literally confessed to being in love with me. Did he think I was just going to forget that happened?

"I suppose this wouldn't be a good time to offer you up the birth control pills that we stole?" he asks in just such a way that I *know* he's needling me on purpose. "You'll most definitely need them for the honeymoon though."

"As soon as this is over," I say, gesturing at him with the bouquet of white roses in my hand, "I'm going to beat the snot out of you, do you understand that?"

"So you don't want the pills then?" Oscar asks, lifting his head up to look at me. Something he said the night we went after Donald pops into my head at random, and I feel my cheeks flush with heat. *"I'm a master of knots."* Is he really, though? I'd be curious to find out.

"I'll take them," I snarl and Vic laughs.

"Or not," he says, shrugging his shoulders. I ignore him, which is actually a pretty difficult thing to do, seeing as he's wearing the tux he bought for the wedding. Since today is more casual though, he didn't bother with the pink tie I picked out.

Pink, of course, for Penelope.

The only reason we're dressed up at all is because getting the license is the important part. After this, all that has to happen is we sign and date and mail that shit in on Saturday. The rest of this operation is just for show.

Plus, I knew it would piss Pamela off. She'll recognize this dress as designer, recognize the value of the ring on my hand, recognize that I've moved past her and her shit.

"There she is," Hael says, pointing across the street at a curvy blond in a short, red dress.

Hah.

That's Pamela for you, trying to outshine me, even on a day like this.

She notices the Havoc Boys before she even finishes crossing the street. No surprise there. You'd have to be blind, deaf, and dumb to miss these assholes. Not only are they handsome, but they're covered in tattoos, and they look at the whole world like they're on the verge of taking control of it.

"Bernadette," Pamela says as she pauses near the courthouse steps. The wind tousles her hair around her pretty face. Her green eyes scan me from head to toe, evaluating, sizing me up, judging me. I can tell the moment she decides I'm prettier because she scowls. Everything is a competition to this woman. "Do you have the money?"

Callum tosses the Burberry bag full of cash at my mother's face, smiling as she scrambles like a rat to catch it and checks inside to verify its contents.

CHAOS AT PRESCOTT HIGH

"Don't worry, Mother, my dowry is all there." I clench my teeth together as she pretends to count the bills inside. There are far too many, and she's far too dumb to count to a high enough number to actually verify that there's ten grand worth of bills there.

She looks up at me again, like she's never seen me before, like she has no idea who I am.

I don't suppose that she ever has though, so it's not surprising.

"Let's get this over with. I have a luncheon to attend." Pamela waltzes up the steps like she's important, sauntering past the Havoc Boys and failing to notice the way all five of them turn their heads, stalking her like prey.

Name number seven on my list.

I only know that I don't want her dead. I can't explain why, but I feel strongly about it. I should probably tell the guys before they get an idea in their heads that I can't scrub lean.

"You heard the woman," Victor says, nodding with his chin in the direction of the front entrance. We head inside together, and thank fuck we find out that the marriage office is down the righthand hallway and not the left. To go down that one, toward the courtrooms, you have to pass through a metal detector.

The boys consistently fail those at Prescott High five days a week, but they just pay off the security guards, so it doesn't matter. Might be a bit harder to do that here.

Once we get to the office, Victor and I use one of the ancient computers in the room to fill out our information. When we get to the final screen that asks how we'd like our names written out, he clicks the option that reads *Bernadette*

Channing before I get a chance to stop him.

"You goddamn prick," I snap, and the woman behind the counter looks up at us with wide eyes. Her look very clearly says, *How can you get married if you talk to each other like that?* She doesn't understand the sort of passion we have though.

It's … explosive, but in the best possible way.

To pay Victor back, I click *Victor Blackbird* on the second screen and hit submit.

"You cheeky cunt," he snaps right back at me, and then we end up sitting in silence with Pamela until our number is called.

She does what she has to do, flashing her ID and signing the papers with sharp, angry movements. When she's finished, she doesn't say goodbye. Shit, she doesn't even *ask* about Heather. Instead, she just clutches her Burberry bag in tight fingers, her red nails digging into the handle the way they used to dig into my arm.

Pamela leaves the way we came in, and she doesn't look back, not once.

"She isn't invited to the actual wedding," Vic tells me, putting his big hands on my shoulders and giving them a squeeze. "She knows that, right?"

"You could only get her to come if you paid her," I tell him, closing my eyes as he kneads the tightness from my muscles.

There's only one thing that's worrying me.

Pamela usually likes to make a scene. Even with all the money Victor paid her—which came right out of our wedding budget—she should've been more … well, more of a bitch.

It makes me wonder if she isn't up to something. Or at the

very least, if she knows that her husband is.

"Do you know what you eventually want to see?" Vic asks me mildly. I open my eyes, watching the other four boys smoke in the breezeway outside as people walk by and gawk at their brazenness. My boys in black. I smile.

"You mean, as far as Pamela's punishment?" I shake my head. "Not yet. All I know is that I don't want her dead."

Victor grabs my face in his hand, turning me to look at him.

"You're too kind for this world, Bernie," he says, leaning down to steal my soul out through my lips. I don't believe a damn word of that, but I appreciate the effort. "Now, tell me how the hell I'm supposed to wait three days to marry your ass?" He growls at me, and I shiver.

Several women passing by the open door of the office turn to gawk, rubber-necking the fuck out of my future husband.

I narrow my eyes on them

"You know, the only advice Pamela ever gave me that was worth any salt was this: find your man and lock his ass down." I turn to smirk at Victor. "I always thought it was bullshit, but hey, here we are."

"Ah, right, lock my ass down," Vic purrs, kissing me again. "Mine, and four other guys', right? Should be a romantic honeymoon."

He laughs as he moves past me and into the hallway, but I can tell the idea pisses him off royally.

I'm sure the honeymoon week/Thanksgiving break will be fascinating, a study into the emerald green depths of human jealousies.

My mouth twitches.

I'm looking forward to it already.

CHAPTER

Friday, November twenty-second, is Hael's eighteenth birthday, and yet another long drag at the coal mine known as Prescott High.

"Things are going to get lit tonight," he crows during our break between second and third period, leaning back on the front steps and basking in the sun like a snake. He's grinning so big that the sunlight catches on his white teeth, reflecting back at me. Victor has paid Stacey Langford to throw a party for his best friend in the old Prescott High building, so it's pretty much guaranteed to be good.

Then tomorrow ... marriage. To Vic. My heart lodges in my throat, but I banish the feeling of dread. That cold lump in my stomach isn't about Victor; it's about the Charter Crew and the Thing. Last time we had a party, Danny died.

Then Ivy died.

And now here we are, in a war that's fought in shadows and surprise. I chew my lower lip.

"Don't stress, Blackbird," Hael says as he sits up and the other boys start to trickle out of the front doors to take their seats around us. Cal sits close to me and offers up a fresh cigarette and a cold chocolate milk with a straw. My favorite. "We're *expecting* trouble." Hael leans in close to me, nuzzling my face with his. "Girl, that's what makes it fun."

"Don't pray for trouble, Hael," Oscar chastises, watching as the Thing's police cruiser crawls down the street yet again. It's a scare tactic that isn't working, so he can fuck all the way off with that shit. "We have enough of it as it is."

"Let's just get through this weekend alive, and I'll be happy," Vic murmurs, lighting up a cigarette and watching my stepfather's car with narrowed eyes. "By the way, Bern, we have a wedding present to give you tonight." He pauses, flicking me a cocksure smirk that has me smoldering. "If you're a good girl, you don't get it at all. Now, if you're a bad girl …"

"You can have it at three a.m.," Cal finishes as Aaron takes a seat on Hael's other side. "The witching hour." He smiles at me and sips his Pepsi. "Bad things always happen at the witching hour."

Goose bumps rise up on my arms, but I don't say anything. I'm not displeased by the idea of a gift.

"You'll like this one," Aaron promises me, his attention shifting back to the Thing's car. Now all the boys are watching. "Actually, I think you'll love it."

"Nah," Hael says, shaking his head, his smile darkening for a moment into something truly wicked. "I *guarantee* she will;

she's just as bloodthirsty as the rest of us."

Nobody there disagrees with him—not even me.

On any normal day, my third period class puts me to sleep. I mean, it's biology. I know all the important stuff—like how an alpha male and alpha female clash in the wild, how violence begets power, how it's survival of the fittest out there. The rest of it ... I have no use for.

A bit of commotion sounds from the hall, like the pounding of heavy boots. It's not an entirely unusual sound. There are always cops at Prescott High, sometimes SWAT. Okay, well, that was only one time, but most of us just yawned our way through their visit.

Today though ... feels off.

I know as soon as the call comes into my phone from Hael, ringing once and then going dark, that something bad is happening.

My entire body goes cold.

"Havoc just got dragged out of class by the VGTF!" someone chortles, and the class explodes into action, ignoring our teacher's tired, dreary pleas to sit down. If you work at Prescott High, you're either a do-gooder like Keating or else you're just bored and drained of life (i.e. every other staff member except maybe Mr. Darkwood whom I still hate).

I shove up from my chair and the crowd parts to let me through.

The VGTF.

The Violent Gang Task Force.

Oh. Fuck.

I'm already panting as I stumble into the hall, my eyes widening as the world around me slows down, like the hungry ticking of time is being filtered through sand.

There are my boys, all five of them, handcuffed and being marched down the hall in a single file line. They're each being escorted by two cops, decked out in full SWAT gear, with face shields and rifles and everything.

My mouth goes dry as Victor glances my way, his expression bored, dark eyes admitting nothing.

I move up to him, ignoring the shuffling of the cops, the lifting of guns.

"Finish class. Act like nothing's wrong. Hit Aaron's house after school and one of our guys will meet you there to get the girls," he whispers before he's cuffed in the back of the head and I'm dragged backward by Ms. Keating. One glance at her face, and I can see that she's worried. That's when I know for certain that she's the best, most genuine human being I have ever met.

While Sara Young and her type aren't bad people, they're twisted in their own way from following a rigid set of moral rules. Ms. Keating is just kind, through and through. She doesn't like seeing her students manhandled like criminals.

I mean, they are, but that's not the point.

I'm starting to hyperventilate as I watch each letter in Havoc walk by.

"*Last time you'll fuck with my daughter, you punk,*" a bald man without a helmet says, his fingers clamped so tightly on Hael's bicep that I can see angry red marks where his skin is indented.

It doesn't take a genius to put the pieces together.

Brittany's dad. The anti-gang squad. Her rage at Hael when the DNA results came back.

Either her father acted on his own in response to his daughter's grief ... or she betrayed Havoc. Broke her price. Wrote her own epitaph.

Hael looks at me in apology as he's ushered past, Aaron close behind him. He says nothing to me, but his look says it all. He knew this might happen one day. He pushed me away from Havoc because, unlike Vic, his love is not selfish. It's endless and infinite and pure.

Shit.

Oscar comes next, frowning hard, his glasses askew, one of the lenses cracked. If I were the police on either side of him, I'd be afraid. Even handcuffed, even being assorted out of a high school surrounded by rifles, he's dangerous.

"Hey, Bernie, you're beautiful in the worst possible way," Cal chortles as he walks past, laughing and laughing and laughing, his blond hair shimmering under the fluorescent lights.

They hit the front doors of the school as I stand there in a panic, my mind blank, my mouth hanging open.

But ... but Havoc is untouchable ... right?

"Looks like even Satan makes mistake," Mitch calls out, and then one of the nameless Charter Crew assholes sets off a party popper, exploding confetti across our classmates. They start to whoop and chant, a near deafening sound in the crowded hallway.

Kali giggles and cuddles up against Mitch's side, flicking a poisonous glance my direction as she throws up a fist in the air and cheers.

It'd be impossible right now to look around this school and miss the dark, quiet expressions on some of the students' faces. These are the Prescott kids with skeleton masks in their lockers. I feel a solidarity with them. *Blood in, blood out.*

"Alright, everyone," Ms. Keating says, giving my arm a comforting squeeze. "That's enough of that. Back to class." Laughter and groaning echo around the school as people file reluctantly back into their classrooms, whispering behind cupped hands, their eyes darting straight to me.

The disgraced Queen of Havoc.

A queen who isn't entirely sure what to do just yet.

"Aw, look, the bitch is about to cry," Billie purrs, and I swear, I nearly fracture my jaw when I grit my teeth against a surge of violence. As much as I'd love to recreate what I did to Kali by smashing her face into a locker, there are too many witnesses around and clearly, this is not a good moment to be stirring up trouble.

"Don't pray for trouble, Hael," Oscar said. Damn but he was dead-on.

"Do you need a minute to calm down, Bernadette?" Ms. Keating asks, standing close by, her face pinched with concern. I look back at her, dressed in her yellow suit jacket, BLM t-shirt, and black pencil skirt, still colorful, still alive.

"Nah, I'm good," I say. The words sound normal enough,

but to my ears, they ring with a hollowness that reminds me of dry bones and roadkill. I turn and head back into the classroom, taking my seat and pretending like I don't notice everyone staring at me.

We never went over this scenario, and I never asked, because I didn't think it could happen. I didn't think. I did. Not. Think.

During lunch, I check my phone, but there's nothing from the boys. Likely, they used their one phone call to lawyer up. Bet they already have one on retainer. Chewing my lower lip, I lean back on the bench in the cafeteria, ignoring the gossip and acting like I don't have a care in the world. *Yeah, we knew this was going to happen. No big thing. Got it handled.*

Victor told me to finish class. I see the wisdom in that. I need to stay here, surrounded by the Havoc crew, under the eyes of the administrators. When I leave, I'm going to have to be very careful that the Thing or the Charter Crew don't come after me.

By the time sixth period rolls around, I'm soaked in sweat and jittery as I check my phone, waiting for the bell to ring so I can get the hell out of there. First, I'm going to find someone with a somber face and ask to see their mask. Then I'm going to inform them that they're my escort back to Aaron's.

Hopefully they have a car. If not, I'll walk back to my mom's place, dig up the cash from the backyard and get a taxi.

Get the girls.

Find out how to summon Jennifer Lowell to babysit.

And then, I'll start making phone calls. I need to figure out where the boys are being held, if they have lawyers yet, what

412

the charges are against them exactly.

It's going to be a long night.

Also, I'm probably not getting married tomorrow, now am I? Disappointment slithers through me, but I push it aside. Keeping the boys safe and out of prison is my only priority right now.

With only thirty minutes left in class, I decide I'm going to bail. I've played along all damn day, and I'm over it. Just as I stand up, the door opens, and a student assistant hands me a pass to summon me to Ms. Keating's office.

I strongly debate taking off anyway, but then I remember her face. She was truly upset by the situation; she might even be privy to information that I'd struggle to get anywhere else.

Tucking the note into the pocket of my leather jacket, I head down the hall, around the corner and past the dark zone where I beat Kali, and then I slip into the vice principal's office.

Ms. Keating smiles at me, but it's a tight smile. I don't think anything of it, seeing as five of her students were dragged away in handcuffs today.

Stepping forward, I grab the back of one of the chairs in front of her desk, intending to slip into it. I'm distracted by the door opening behind me, and my eyes flick back to see my stepfather, dressed in his uniform and smiling like a reptile.

No.

"Hello Bernadette," he says, blocking me from the door with his body, hand resting casually on his belt, just a few inches from his gun. Ms. Keating doesn't look at him with any sort of fondness either, like maybe she can sense how evil he is beneath his average Joe exterior.

"What is he doing here?" I ask her, recognizing that I have at least one ally in this room. My eyes find the locked windows behind Ms. Keating's desk, and I curse myself for ruining her trust enough that it's actually handicapping me now. Talk about karma.

"Bernie, sweetie," Neil says, making my skin crawl as his eyes undress me right there in the VP's office. He doesn't care who's watching because he knows he can get away with it regardless. I hate him. I hate him. I fucking *hate* him. "You're not exempt from this little raid today. Actually, the only reason you weren't dragged out and embarrassed in front of your peers is because I stepped in. I do have to take you to the station though." He pulls a pair of metal cuffs off of his belt, and my mind goes white with panic.

If he gets me in those cuffs, in his car, I am dead.

I am raped and killed.

I am buried with Pen.

Heather is ruined.

A shudder ripples through me, and I turn back to Keating with every ounce of panic I feel in my blood showing on my face. She notices right away and rises to her feet.

"Please don't let him take me," I tell her, slipping my phone from my pocket. I use the speed dial for Aaron's phone and let it ring. Even if he can't answer me now, if he sees this later, he'll know.

"If you're ever in trouble, Bernie, you just call us. You don't have to say anything, you just let it ring."

The Thing steps forward, lightning quick, his reflexes honed in dark alleys and seedy bars. I'm ready for him, spinning to intercept his blow, but he isn't going for my face like usual. Instead, he smacks my hand and sends my phone flying. It hits the ground with an awful crack as I dart into the corner between Ms. Keating's bookshelf and the row of windows behind her desk.

Not a great place to make a stand; I'm essentially trapped here, but I have nowhere else to go.

"Mr. Pence," Ms. Keating says, her voice alarmed, a true fear working its way into her gaze. She knows what she sees here: a black woman and a teenage girl, trapped in a small office with a white male cop. Who is she supposed to call if things go wrong? And yet, I watch her stand up for me anyway. "I'm going to have to ask you to leave and return with either a warrant, or a partner, or preferably both."

Neil tucks his thumbs into his belt for a moment, nodding his head like he might actually listen to her. But then his elbow flies out and he cracks Ms. Keating in the face. She groans and stumbles back, but even as I move to help her, I know I can't do shit.

The Thing levels his weapon on Ms. Keating, holding the barrel even with her head as blood streams down her face and she sags back against the windows. At least she's still conscious. I know firsthand how bad an elbow to the face can hurt. Neil's, in particular. My eyes dart his way.

"Put the cuffs on," Neil commands, tossing them onto the floor at my feet. He smiles at me in that way of his, like a gator on the hunt. He's scented blood, and he sure as shit isn't going to stop until he tastes meat. "Or I'll kill this—" I close my eyes against his words, against the rush of emotion. Neil calls Ms.

Keating the worst things you can call a person—a cunt, a whore, the n-word—and then he pistol-whips her in the goddamn face. "Now, Bernadette," he snaps, and my eyes fly open just as Ms. Keating slides to the floor, still moaning, still trying to stand up.

I know my stepfather; this isn't false bravado.

He feels untouchable.

He feels like he can kill us both and get away with it.

There's a second there where I weigh my chances of escaping, where I wonder if I could really sacrifice someone like Ms. Keating to save my own ass. I've tried in the past to be a good person, but all I got in return was pain. I had to change to meet the challenge of the world, become something different.

But I will not let myself sink to my stepfather's level.

Ms. Keating has shown me kindness when nobody else would, given me chance after chance after chance to prove myself.

If she dies here because of me, then I'll find myself sinking through the muck to Neil's level. That, that would be my true rock bottom.

I clasp the cuff on my right wrist, heart pounding. By putting these cuffs on, I put myself at the mercy of Neil. I put myself in the trust of the Havoc Boys.

"That's a good girl," Neil purrs as I hook the other side, now bound before him. But not helpless. Never that. He lowers the gun, but at the last second, turns and starts beating Ms. Keating in the face with it. When I charge him, he swings out and whips me across the cheek, making me bleed and see stars. "Let's go."

Neil leaves Ms. Keating choking on her own blood and then

gestures me toward the door with his gun. If I don't leave willingly, it's likely that he'll shoot me in the leg, rape me over the desk, and then kill me.

It'd be easy to blame it on someone else: one of Havoc's crew, Mitch's people, self-defense.

But I know the step-thing like I know the back of my hand.

He feeds on pain and suffering. He *wants* me to know that he's won. And he wants to play with me first.

Neil opens the door and gestures me into the hall, marching me past the lockers and toward the front door. Since it's a Friday, and this is South motherfucking Prescott, there are no students hanging around. They've all bailed for Hael's birthday party, knowing that he won't be able to attend, but loving the idea of gossip.

This is literally my worst nightmare.

Or rather, I thought it was until I come around the corner and find Kali waiting for me.

"Baby!" she squeals, running forward and throwing her arms around Neil's neck. She nuzzles the side of his face and then turns to look at me, like she's studying a wolf caught in a farmer's trap. I give her nothing. I won't cry or scream or even curse her out, because that'd give them both pleasure, and I'd rather die than see either of them smile. "How the mighty have fallen," Kali quips with a roll of her eyes. She tosses her green and black hair over one shoulder and then comes to stand in front of me. "You only think you're better than me because you're weak," she says, and this time, I have to laugh.

I mean, come on.

"Weak?" I query, cocking my head to one side as Principal

Vaughn slinks from his office like the rat he is, bloodied fingers bandaged, his hand in a sling to keep the severed stumps from jostling. He's sweating profusely, and honestly looks on the verge of passing out. "Kali, honey, if you thought you were in trouble before, you've just dug your own grave."

She sneers at me and then reaches out to backhand me across the face. I'm proud to say that I take the blow without stumbling, lifting my head up to look at her with blood running into my mouth.

"Where are you taking her?" Vaughn simpers as he moves over to stand beside Neil. My stepfather is studying me curiously, eyes glinting with possibilities. This is his greatest dream come true, a chance to break that wild mare in that he's always wanted. Crush my spirits, take what's left of me, rape me into an early grave the way he did to Penelope.

"Oh, don't you worry about that," he says, scowling as he looks the principal up and down, like even Neil finds him pathetic and weak. "I'm just gonna take her to pay a visit to her sister." Neil moves over to give Kali a kiss as Vaughn watches me with fear in his eyes. The thing is, when he glances at Neil, I get the idea that *he* isn't the one that he's afraid of.

"Call an ambulance for Ms. Keating," I whisper, just before Neil shoves me from behind and Kali's laughter fills the hallway. Scott doesn't respond to me, stepping back and watching as I leave Prescott High with my worst nightmare holding me hostage.

Kali watches as Neil puts me into the back of his squad car, wrapping her arms around his neck and kissing him in a way that makes my stomach churn. Well, I don't know if the baby she's carrying is his, but it very well might be. I wonder if Mitch knows, and then file the information away to use against him later.

I could scream, but then, I'm a girl in cuffs and Neil is a cop. Who would care? Who would try to help me?

Nobody.

Until the Havoc boys come, I have to save myself.

Glancing out the window at the brick walls of Prescott High, I wonder where the rest of the Havoc Crew is.

Or … I do until I see a skeleton mask lying on the sidewalk beside a spatter of blood.

Charter Crew.

My jaw clenches as I turn back around to watch Neil climb into the driver's seat.

"You ready, Bernadette?" he asks me.

I might not be, but I can tell from his voice that he's been waiting for this moment for years.

I'm sure he plans on savoring every wicked, awful moment.

CHAPTER
TWENTY-FIVE

The Thing drives me almost an hour outside of town to the cemetery where Penelope is buried. I could bike that route with my eyes closed I've been there so many times. Resting my head against the window, I listen to *"Tiptoe Through the Tulips with Me"* by Tiny Tim, a 1968 nightmare of a song that makes my bones hurt.

It's featured in plenty of horror movies because it's scary as shit, like a maudlin clown with a knife. It's always been Neil's favorite song. It sets the tone for the afternoon as he winds up a quiet blacktop road toward the parking lot of *Our Lady of Mercy* cemetery. My father was Catholic, so we have a family burial plot here.

The nicest thing Pamela ever did for Pen was to bury her here beside our dad.

Probably because it was pre-paid so therefore, in her eyes, free.

Neil parks the car, humming the words to the song under his breath as he loads his pistol with a fresh magazine, bobbing his head in time with the music.

This primal sense of survival takes over me as I exhale, sitting in the back of his cop car, fully aware that he could kill me at any moment.

That's not what he's here for though, not yet. If I died now then he'd never get to stick it to me, show me he was boss, punish me for all my years of resistance. Nah, it wouldn't be near as fun. I'm sure he intends on raping me, too.

I swallow back my fear, letting that icy lump crash into my stomach as I let my alpha female side take over.

Fight, Bernie, always.

The boys will come for me. I just need to buy them time. That's my job right now.

Neil climbs out of the car and then opens my door, gesturing with his gun to indicate that I get out. For a moment, he just studies me, but then his lips curve up into an insidious smile.

"We're going to play a game together, Bernadette," he tells me as I lick dried blood from my lip, staring back at him as I wait for the rules of this nightmare. Memories flicker in my mind, but I push them back. Not going there, not right now. The Thing makes a show of checking his gun to ensure that the safety is off. "You remember when we used to play hide 'n' seek when you were a kid?"

I do.

And I wish I didn't.

"Come out, come out, wherever you are …"

Neil used to force Pen and me to play with him, chasing us

through the dark as we scrabbled like rats to avoid him. If he found us, it usually wasn't good. He was always drunk back then, and he'd knock us around a bit, just for fun.

"I'm going to give you a fifteen second head start," Neil tells me, tapping the butt of his gun against his palm. "But if I find you ..." he trails off and then aims his weapon at the angel statue above Penelope's grave. My eyes widen and my breath quickens, but I can't do anything but watch as he pulls the trigger and blows off her head. Bits of marble that look like skull fragments explode across the grass as I take off running, weaving between tombstones and around mausoleums.

I need to find somewhere to hide, I think, eyes darting around the cemetery as the sun dips low in the sky and the birds call out their final songs from the trees around us. The Thing is laughing, the sound echoing across the freshly-mowed grass as he counts down from fifteen.

"*Twelve,*" he continues, his voice a maniac growl. He's planned this all perfectly, lying in wait on his belly and watching with eyes above the swampy water for us to venture too close to the watering hole. See, Neil isn't about showy moves like dumping a kids' corpse in a trunk. He just crawls around on curved claws until an opportunity arises.

Just like it has today.

And this, this is why he's always been so goddamn dangerous.

"Eleven."

I keep running, being careful not to trip. I need every second I can get to put space between me and him. But the issue with this graveyard is that it's carved from the woods and surrounded by a cast-iron fence that'd be very difficult to climb in handcuffs.

I have to find a way to get the jump on Neil, I realize as his countdown ends, and I swing behind a statue of the archangel Michael. He's the defender of justice, right? Seems a fitting place to stand as I struggle to control my breathing, to stay quiet, to channel the cat-like silence of the Havoc Boys.

If you don't get him, Bernie, he'll get you. Be proactive, not reactive.

"Ready or not, here I come!" Neil calls out as I close my eyes to block out the graveyard, focusing on his footsteps and the clinking of the keys at his belt. "Bernadette …" he oozes, working his way toward the woods.

I imagine he'll keep a close eye on the exit and the fence, assuming that I'll try to make a run for it. Instead, I'm going to do the opposite and head into the thick of the graveyard, using the tombstones to hide.

"You know how good your sister's pussy felt?" he asks, causing my eyes to fly open with angry tears. I grit my teeth to keep from crying out. Hearing him say that … it's like torture, pure torture. He knows it, too, and like a hunter with a dog, he's trying to flush me out. "The last night that I fucked her was the last night she was alive. Did you know that, Bernie? Did you?"

A gunshot explodes into the quiet, sending a flock of songbirds into the sky, their voices high with fear. I use the moment to peek around the corner of the mausoleum, spotting Neil just forty feet from me. He's just knocked the head off of another statue, leaving destruction and disrespect in his wake.

I exhale and then duck low, struggling to crawl with my

arms bound by the cuffs. I don't make it nearly as far as I want, rolling over and sitting up with my back against another tombstone.

"Does it bother you that she killed herself?" he asks, moving slowly across the grass, gun held ready, clasped in both of his hairy hands. I close my eyes. "Left you here to suffer the way she did? What sort of big sister does something like that?"

Count to three and then keep going. You can do this. You've got this.

I open my eyes again and roll onto my belly, crawling closer to Neil. He's just in front of and to the right of me, and I know I only have a few precious seconds to find a new hiding spot before he turns and sees me.

There's a large tomb on my left that I head for, putting my back up against it just before I hear Neil pause. He's listening for any sound, any clue.

"When I find you," he tells me, his voice thick with lust. I can hear him smacking his lips in anticipation. "I'm going to shoot you in the leg, and then play with you until you stop screaming. If you're a real good girl then I'll take you to the hospital and you can tell them how your boyfriend's gang jumped and killed your vice principal and then turned their sights on you. This doesn't have to end in your death, Bernie. It could be fun for both of us."

Fuck you, I think, feeling my eyes sting with angry tears. *The next chance I get, I'm going to kill you, consequences be damned.* Neil Pence's expiration date has come and gone.

I hear him start to walk away and get ready to move again.

"Boo," Neil growls, appearing from the opposite side of the

mausoleum. Luckily, I have quick fucking reactionary commands. Turning, I lean back and then kick up as hard as I can with both feet, nailing Neil in the balls. He fires the gun into the air as he howls with pain and I struggle to my feet.

I barely make it three steps before he's on me, grabbing me by the hair and shoving my head as hard as he can into the side of an obelisk. Stars fill my vision as my knees buckle and Neil follows me down to the grassy ground.

He's struggling to control me with one hand and fire the gun with the other, so I take advantage of him being off-balance to turn over. Better to be on my back than my belly. I bend my knees, keeping my legs together so that when I use them to push at him, I have more power.

My boots hit the arm holding the gun, sending the pistol flying.

"Fucking cunt," Neil snarls, grabbing my legs with one arm and swinging at my face with the other. He manages to crack me across the cheek, but I shove him off of me, scooting back to put space between us. He chooses to go for his gun as I get to my feet and start running.

Another gunshot explodes the grave on my right as I sprint with everything I have and disappear around the side of another mausoleum. As soon as I'm out of sight, I start looking for somewhere else to hide.

I have seconds, at best.

There's a huge hole not far from me. It's very clearly a grave awaiting a body.

The idea of crawling into it makes me sick, but I have nowhere else to go. I'm trapped between the mausoleum and the fence. The thing is, once I get down there, I won't be able to get out. I discard the idea and decide to run for it.

"I *see* you," Neil calls out, firing his gun at me again. I trip and fall then, struggling to catch myself with the cuffs on. I go down hard, certain that this is it, that I'm done for. But when I roll over and sit up, I see Neil replacing the magazine on his gun. That gives me just enough time to crawl behind another grave.

It's not much help though because he saw me.

He knows where I am.

I'm panting like crazy as I sit up, glancing around the tombstone to see him coming straight for me.

This is it.

My last chance.

I wait for Neil to get close. I don't expect him to shoot the gravestone I'm hiding behind, and I cry out as bits of cement hit me like projectiles. Oddly enough, the move works out for the best. I use the rush of adrenaline, the cloud of dust, and the echo of the gunshot to shove up to my feet and slip around the other side of the tombstone.

For the briefest of seconds, I'm behind Neil.

I throw my handcuffed arms around his neck as he curses at me, slamming his back against another statue and crushing me against it. The move knocks the breath right out of me.

He gags as I hang from him like a noose, using my bodyweight to put stress on his airway. Neil collapses to the grass and rolls to his back, sandwiching me between his body and the ground. He throws his elbow back over and over again, battering my ribs. After a moment, he stops, and then I realize that he's fumbling with something at his belt.

The next thing I know, he's shoving a key into the handcuffs and the right side comes undone.

Neil turns on me as I move to back up, the cuffs hanging from my left hand, the one with the *HAVOC* tattoo. He tackles me into the grass, getting me underneath him, putting gravity on his side. His forearm goes into my throat, cutting my air off.

"You like that, Bernadette?" he growls out, voice husky from being choked. Spittle flicks my cheeks as I writhe, desperate for air, my nails gouging his forearms bloody, even through the sleeve of his uniform. "Does that turn you on?" Neil leans down and kisses me, his stubble scraping my face as I kick and flail.

One of my knees manages to slip between his legs, and I nail him in the balls for a second time. As soon as I get some space to move, I launch myself forward, wrapping my hands around his neck like I did with Oscar.

He even falls backward, letting me get the upper hand.

I squeeze harder, putting every ounce of my weight into trying to choke him. There's no malice in me right now however, no joy at seeing him suffer. This is purely about survival. For me to escape this place alive, I have to kill the step-thing.

"And here we thought you'd be needing some help," Hael says from beside me. I glance up just in time to see his boot come down on Neil's face. Blood sprays as my stepfather screams, and I'm lifted up under the armpits by gentle hands.

Callum tucks me under his chin, wrapping his arms around me.

The relief I feel in that moment nearly sends me to my knees.

"Ah, Neil," Vic says, appearing on my stepfather's other side. "You got started without us."

Aaron and Hael haul Neil to his feet and slam his back against the side of a crumbling stone crypt while Oscar steps forward with his revolver in hand. He keeps it trained on Neil as my stepfather's shit-brown eyes flick between the boys like he can't possibly understand how they got here.

Frankly, I don't know how they did, just that I knew they would.

"How the fuck did you get out of the station?" the Thing snarls as I cuddle into Callum. I don't want Neil to see how scared I really was, how vulnerable I felt, like a child all over again. Cal just squeezes me close, enveloping me in his scent and his hoodie and his eternal calm, like a dark sea under a full moon. "You shouldn't be here."

"Yeah, well," Vic says, shrugging. "We are, and just in time to see our girl strangle the life out of you." He laughs again and moves forward, getting up close and personal with Neil as Hael and Aaron hold him back. "To be honest with you, officer, you'd have been lucky if Bernie had strangled you. We have something much darker in mind." Victor works his jaw for a moment, like he's thinking, and then hauls back to punch Neil in the face.

Just one hit is all it takes to knock my stepfather's head back against the stone and plunge him into unconsciousness.

The boys let him crumple to the ground like a discarded toy.

"Find the key to those cuffs," Vic orders, but Aaron's

already on it, bending down to retrieve the small, silver key from the grass. He quickly unlocks the remaining cuff from my wrist, and then places both sides on Neil's wrists instead.

"Hey," Hael says, stepping close and peering in at me, still trapped in the safe circle of Callum's arms. "You okay, Blackbird?"

I glare at him.

"Of course I'm okay," I snap back, pretending like I don't notice how badly I'm shaking. The boys extend me the same courtesy, which I appreciate. "I had him. Didn't you see?"

"You're the only woman I know who could go from being handcuffed in the back of a squad car to choking the life out of an armed police officer in less time than it takes most people to decide what movie to watch on a Friday night." Oscar tucks his gun away again, confident that Neil is out for the time being. I'm not sure if Oscar's statement is meant to be a compliment, but I take it as one anyway.

"You made the right choice, calling us," Aaron says, trying his best to smile at me. But he's shaking, too, and it occurs to me that they were probably as afraid as I was. Maybe more so. I know I'd rather be the one in danger than see any of them hurt. Likely, they feel the same way about me.

"How did you know where to find me?" I ask, finally taking a step back from Callum. As soon as I do, I wish I were pressed up against him again.

"Weirdly enough," Hael starts, doing his best to keep smiling, to keep the mood light. "Vaughn called to tell us that Neil was, uh, 'taking you to see your sister'." He scoffs and rolls his eyes. "Looks like our dog has properly come to heel, at least."

"Thankfully," Vic agrees, looking down at me with crow-black eyes. I can see the strain in them from holding back; he wants to touch me like Cal is, hold me close, check me for wounds and fuck me into a restful sleep. Instead, he takes on his role as leader. "Are you sure you're okay? If you want to have a breakdown later, I'll hold you all damn night. Right now, though, if you can function, we need you. We've got urgent business."

I feel a sense of relief in that, in knowing that I have to push my feelings aside for the sake of Havoc. I'm good with that sort of thing, with violence and intrigue. Not so much with my own emotions.

"I'm okay," I say, and I mean it. I'm hurting all over, and deep down, there's a little girl crying inside my heart. But that can wait. I can unpack later. "What do we need to do?"

"We need to start a riot, that's what," Cal says, and I flick my attention to him, brows raised.

"A riot?" I echo as he nods with his chin in the direction of a black SUV that I've never seen before. My guess: they boosted it for a quick ride out here.

"Let's load Neil up and we'll explain on the way," Callum tells me as Hael and Aaron each grab one of the Thing's legs, dragging him across the grass with zero regard as to where his head falls. If he smacks his skull against a tombstone here, a metal memorial plaque there, eh. Not our problem.

The boys chuck him into the back of the SUV, leaving him with Aaron and his .22 since we don't have any ropes or gags on us. Gotta improvise where you can, right?

"I've scrambled the camera feed," Oscar tells Hael as I sit in the SUV with Callum, feeling useless as the guys deal with picking up the pieces of this mess. "I can't say what it recorded before now, but it's the best I can do in the moment."

"Good enough," Hael says, climbing in the driver's seat of Neil's squad car and slamming the door. He takes off down the winding cemetery road as the other boys join me in the SUV and we follow after.

I have no memory of that drive into town, only of laying my head on Cal's lap and feeling his fingers stir my hair.

When I wake up, I find us parked outside the old Prescott High building, music blasting from inside. Neil's car is in front of us, and there are about a dozen girls waiting beside it. Pretty sure Stacey Langford is one of them.

"Hey there, sleepyhead," Vic says with a tired smile, watching as I yawn and stumble from the SUV with Callum beside me, like my own personal guardsman. Hael, Aaron, and Oscar are already on the sidewalk waiting for me. "I was just about to give Stacey the go-ahead."

"Go-ahead for what?" I ask, glancing over at her and her strange posse of girls, all of them dressed in pink sweatshirts and matching ski masks. Stacey yanks hers on and smiles as I cling to Callum, cranky and tired but alive. Alive and *safe*.

"We paid Stacey to start a riot, didn't we, Stacey?" Oscar asks, and she shrugs.

"We would've done it for free, as a favor," she clarifies, showing me teeth through the hole of her ski mask. "You ready?"

Vic nods, just once. He doesn't need anything more than

that. That's what makes him a leader, all of that insane charisma and confidence. "Light it up."

"Girls," Stacey says, and then they all move forward, putting their palms up against the side of Neil's police cruiser and rocking it forward and back, until it tips over with a groaning creak of metal. Windows shatter, covering the pavement with shards of glass. One of Stacey's girls steps up and douses the damn thing in gasoline.

"Bernie?" Cal asks, holding out a matchbox as chaos erupts around us. People pour from the building in pink ski masks and skeleton masks both, wielding baseball bats and hammers, shovels and torches.

Without hesitation, they start flipping cars along the edge of the street.

Holy fuck.

I lift my head and see that Callum is still waiting for me to take the matches. I lick the blood from my lips as I grab them, staring down at the overturned police car as the night lights up like the Fourth of July.

"Do it," Victor purrs, watching me carefully. "Finish it."

Goddamn these boys. They've managed to find the perfect cover-up.

"You've got this," Aaron reassures me as I strike the match.

Neil's cruiser will be gone. He'll be missing. And yet, his disappearance will be steeped in havoc, chaos, and mayhem. What we're going to do with him after tonight … that's another matter entirely.

I chuck the match at the car and watch as it goes up in a swath of brilliant, vibrant flame.

"Let's go home," Cal suggests as I stand there in the crackling heat, the sound of sirens piercing the distance. "We still have a wedding to attend tomorrow." With a nod, I let him escort me back to the SUV and we take off, dragging Neil's comatose body along for the ride.

CHAPTER
TWENTY-SIX

I don't stay awake long enough to remember getting home, only that I open my eyes and find myself in Aaron's bed. He isn't there, but when I head downstairs, I find him in the kitchen drinking coffee with the rest of the Havoc Boys.

Their conversation stops when I come into the room, bleary-eyed and exhausted from yesterday. I can hardly believe that we have to deal with Neil *and* have a wedding today. It doesn't seem possible. Besides, the guys might've walked from the station, but that doesn't mean they're free and clear.

No, this shit is just beginning.

"Coffee?" Hael asks, lifting up his mug and saluting me with it. "A little caffeine to get you through the horror of a wedding night with Victor."

"Heh," Vic snorts, looking askance at his best friend. "You're just salty because your birthday got fucked. Well, instead of cake, I'm going to eat Bernadette all night long. Be jealous, dickhead." Hael just grins and laughs as I slide onto a stool at the peninsula next to Oscar.

"What are we going to do with Neil?" I ask, thinking of him, bloodied and still in the back of our stolen ride. I'm guessing the guys took turns watching over him last night. And with the stress the riot put on the Springfield police, it's likely nobody will notice he's missing until later today.

"That's the wedding present I was talking about," Vic says, smirking at me over his coffee. "Your stepfather, wrapped up nice and tight. The perfect gift for a Havoc bride."

"You were arrested by the VGTF yesterday and you're, what, plotting murder today?"

Victor shrugs his muscular shoulders, like it's no big thing.

"No rest for the wicked," Oscar reiterates as Aaron makes me a cup of coffee and slides it across the counter. It's spiked with chocolate milk and whiskey, my favorite. I hide my smile behind a sip. "Finish up and I'll help you into your gown," he purrs, and I close my eyes against a shiver.

This is happening, actually freaking *happening.*

I set my mug down on the counter and exhale.

Yesterday felt like it lasted a century. I was afraid in ways I've never been afraid before. I was worried.

But I never doubted Havoc.

Never.

I won't doubt them today.

"You sure I should wear my wedding gown to deal with Neil?" I ask, raising a brow in question.

"Oh, we're sure," Cal says, grinning at me. "Just trust us."

And I do.
Always.

_____

The hole that I decided against hiding in yesterday has now become the focus of our morning.

Neil Pence is lying in a beautiful black coffin at the bottom of it, the lid flipped open, the bloodred satin interior shiny and pretty and wicked. His eyes are neutral, his mouth stuffed with a gag, hands and ankles bound. He just looks at us like he isn't afraid, like he doesn't believe any of this is actually going to happen.

"Give him some time," Callum says softly, his face painted silver in the early morning light. Fog drifts lazily around our ankles as I stand there in the black Lazaro wedding gown that I picked out with Oscar. My hair is still slightly damp from my shower, hanging loose around my shoulders. "They always break, eventually." He smiles as he crouches down, staring at Neil with an intensity that reminds me of a blue-eyed wolf stalking prey. "Don't they, Neil?"

Hael uses a long stick to stab Neil in the face, scratching him up a bit as he pushes the gag from the Thing's mouth. He coughs for a moment and then laughs at us, like he's still the one in charge.

"You don't have the balls to kill a cop," he jeers, a metal tank tucked between his legs. I'm not sure what it's for. It, or the plastic bag tucked under his arm. He barely fits into the coffin with all of that, but I'm sure it's not built for comfort.

I figure this is a scenario similar to the one with Donald, where the boys pretended to hang him from a tree. We aren't actually burying Neil, but we want him to think we are.

"Bernie," Vic says, glancing over at me. "I wanted this to be your wedding present. The best part of it all is that Neil *actually* drove himself up here to preview the attraction. Now, this gift was supposed to be from the five of us, but I feel like he deserves at least a bit of credit." He turns back to my stepfather and smiles. "Seems fair, right?"

Oscar removes the revolver from inside his suit jacket and pulls the hammer back, leveling it on Neil.

"You going to shoot me, boy?" Neil taunts, still unfazed by the situation. "You'll spend the rest of your life getting fucked up in the ass in prison. You ready for a life like that?"

"Listen up," Aaron begins, ignoring Neil's rambling. "We're not without compassion. If we were, we'd be as bad as you." He sighs and shakes his head, pulling out a knife and sliding down into the hole with Hael's help. Aaron cuts the bindings on Neil's hands then drops the knife beside him as my stepfather shakes them out with a twisted smile on his ugly mouth.

When Aaron turns to grab Hael's hands for a boost up, Neil goes for the knife and tries to stab him.

Instead, he ends up with a gunshot to the thigh, his screams echoing around the empty graveyard. Up here, only the dead can hear his cries.

Hael pulls Aaron up and out of the hole, and we all take a step closer, so that we're circling the space. The boys are all dressed in their tuxes for the wedding today. Most of their shirts are undone, ties loose or missing, but they still look fly in their pressed slacks and shiny loafers with metal skulls on the tops. Barker Blacks, I think the shoes are called.

I'm standing at the foot of the grave in my dress and combat boots with Victor opposite me in a pink tie. Aaron and Hael are on my right, Callum and Oscar on my left. At a nod from Vic, they all remove skeleton masks from their pockets and slip them on.

Even me.

I put the rubber mask over my face, my mouth a flat line, my face bereft of emotion.

"I'm going to kill you!" Neil wails, clutching his leg. "And I'm going to bury you, Bernadette, you fucking whore."

"I think," I say, crouching down at the side of the hole. "That you're the one who's getting buried today, Neil." I wait for a moment as he struggles to stand up, clutching the knife like he thinks we'll actually let him climb out and fight us. "This is for Penelope. You understand that, right? That you're being punished?"

"You just wait, you little cunt," he snarls, bleeding everywhere, struggling. It's sort of pathetic, actually, how much he seems to want to live. For someone that does the things he does, he needs to accept that this is fate. This is how it ends. *I wish.*

But I mean … this isn't a realistic way to finish things is it? Especially since Neil's a cop?

"You have two choices," Aaron continues finally as I stand up. It's clear that Neil is not listening. "You've been provided with an oxygen tank that holds about six hours of air. You also have water and snacks. Then again, you have a knife."

"What Aaron's trying to say," Hael adds with a sharp laugh. "Is that you can choose to use the items we've given you to survive a bit longer and prolong your own pain, or you can end it. That is our only kindness."

"Close him up," Vic orders, as efficient as always. He lights up a cigarette as Hael uses the stick—which I think is an old pool cue—to hit Neil in the face. With the injury to his leg, it's pretty easy to knock him over. Hael then uses the stick to hook a bit of rope on the lid of the coffin, pulling it closed.

Just before the lid shuts completely, I see Neil look up at me, his mouth opening to spew vitriol. I don't hear any of it. The lid closes and there's a breath or two of silence before he starts to scream.

"Ah, there it is," Cal says cheerfully, "he just broke."

I wonder how long the boys plan on leaving Neil in there until they let him out, lead him into the woods, and execute him.

"Death is too sweet a release for some," Callum adds, nodding as he grabs a pair of shovels and then offers one up to me.

I just stare at him.

"Wait …" I start as the boys—including Vic and Oscar—step forward and start to shovel dirt. "Is this … are we really doing this?"

"Do you like it?" Vic asks, looking up at me with sincerity in his dark gaze. "Your wedding present?"

It's then that I know they're serious.

We are burying Neil Pence alive for the crime of rape. For

the suicide—or murder—of Penelope Blackbird. We are burying him alive for making me feel scared and unwelcome in my own home. We are burying him because he is a monster.

I fall to my knees in the dress, collapsing next to the hole and putting my forehead on my arm as I start to hyperventilate. After a moment, Aaron comes over to crouch beside me, rubbing my back in soothing circles and whispering sweet nothings in my ear. If I listen really hard, I can hear Neil screaming as dirt piles on top of his shiny black coffin.

"I'd say, based on the size of Neil and the size of the coffin, that he has about twelve hours of air if he chooses to use the tank," Oscar explains, continuing to shovel. I wonder for a brief second if they might just be doing this for dramatic effect, and that we might dig Neil up later.

But … no.

No, that's not what's happening.

This is it.

The final chapter of my book that includes Neil Pence.

And I do nothing to stop it.

It takes a while for the boys to finish filling in the hole, patting it nice and flat when they're done, helping blend it into the landscape. Callum gathers leaves and twigs, scattering them over the surface, until it's hard to tell that there was ever a disturbance here at all.

I crawl forward, laying my body across the grave and putting my ear to the dirt. The echoes of Neil's screams travel up to me, as faint as my sister's cries in the night after he visited her bedroom. My fingers dig into the dirt and I squeeze my eyes shut against the tears.

I lay there until the screaming stops, and then for another hour beyond that.

The boys are patient, parking their beautiful inked bodies on nearby tombstones, smoking cigarettes or joints, passing around a bottle of whiskey.

Aaron stays beside me the whole time, his hand on my back for comfort.

After a while, Neil starts to scream again, and I realize that he is not going to use the knife. Because he's desperate to keep living, to keep hurting people, and he won't give the world even a small favor by killing himself.

I sit up and the boys still around me.

"Today, I become queen of Havoc," I say, my eyes on the dirt beneath my knees. On Neil's grave. A place that nobody will ever visit, that they'll walk over and ignore, just the way it should be. I lift my eyes to find Hael's. Then Aaron's. Vic's. Oscar's. Callum's. "And I won't share my crown with anyone."

Nobody challenges me as Aaron helps me to my feet, leading me away from Neil and toward the parking lot.

I'd stay longer, but then, we have a wedding to attend.

Sorry, Neil.

CHAPTER
TWENTY-SEVEN

The nice thing about burying a monster alive is that you don't get any blood on your clothes.

I'm standing in front of a full-length mirror in the disheveled downstairs parlor of the old house. There isn't much left to indicate the antique splendor that used to fill the space. No, instead it's just so much urban rot.

"You sure you're okay?" Aaron asks, leaning up against the old peeling wallpaper and lighting a cigarette. He's beyond handsome in his tux, but then, aren't they all? My Havoc Boys. I might be getting married to Victor today, but I can never really be just his, can I? We're a family, me and my former tormentors.

"I'm okay."

My lips twitch, and I lean in toward the old mirror, reaching up a single black-painted fingernail to scrape at a bit of stray pink lipstick near the corner of my mouth. It seems a strange color when paired with the black dress and its raven-feather neckpiece, especially being married here, in the woods of an abandoned mansion.

But I chose that color for a reason. I dye the ends of my hair for a reason.

Pink was Pen's favorite color and since she can't physically be here with me today, I want her here in spirit. Oscar already offered to hold a séance for me, to see if we could talk to her, but I don't buy into voodoo magic and bullshit.

You buried a man alive this morning, I remind myself, trying to stay humble, to stay grounded, to remember to be human. Reaching over to grab my phone, I see that it's been about six hours since we buried him. That means he's got about six hours left. Six hours to change my mind.

Only … I have no intention of doing anything of the sort.

"Hey, Bernie," Pen says, leaning down to kiss my forehead. I've always resented her being taller than me. I frown and wrinkle my nose when she kisses me. I do that because I believe, like all little sisters do, that she'll be here forever to take care of me. Right now though, I'm an asshole sophomore and she's the kind-hearted senior who panders too much, worries too much, cares too much. "You know I love you more than the moon loves the stars, don't you?"

And I did. And I still do.

My hands clench in the shimmery black fabric of the gown.

It was supposed to be a fake dress for a fake wedding for a fake marriage. The thing is, I love Victor too much. He loves me too much. Havoc is too important to me. I could never give it up.

"I know, Pen, and I love you, too. More than the sun loves the clouds. Wish me and Vic—me and Havoc—luck. I have a feeling the honeymoon is going to wreck me in the worst way possible."

There's a soft knock at the door, but really, it's just a courtesy knock. There are too many holes in the walls to pretend like Callum can't see me and Aaron in my makeshift dressing room.

"We're ready," he says, smiling at me in that way of his, like pain is pretty and the world is a fragile monster with hungry jaws. I like it, though, his smile, because it also says that he doesn't care about any of those things. If Callum Park loves something or someone, he will, quite literally, murder the world. "Are you?"

There are so many shades of meaning to that question, but I nod anyway, standing up and turning around so he can see me with my hair and makeup done. We hired one of Stacey's girls to do it. She wasn't bad, but she's no Ivy Hightower.

I wet my lips.

Nope.

No more thinking about business today. Business was yesterday. Business was watching Ms. Keating (who's now in the hospital, thanks to Vaughn) get pistol-whipped. Business was being chased by the Thing through the cemetery. Business was putting him in an early grave.

"I'm ready," I say aloud, offering my arm to Aaron. I haven't looked outside yet to see who's actually come for the wedding, but it doesn't matter because the Havoc Boys will be here. That's enough of an audience for me. Although ... part of me would have loved to see Pamela's face when Aaron walks me down the aisle.

Aaron hooks his arm through mine, leaning over to give me a kiss on the forehead. His signature scent surrounds me, calming my nerves and blocking out the wet stink of rotten floorboards and crumbling plaster ceilings.

I've chosen to walk down the aisle to the tune of *Numb Without You* by The Maine, but the orchestral version, not the one with lyrics. For some reason, when I first heard it, I thought of me and Vic. If couples truly have their own songs, then this one is most definitely ours.

Callum slips back outside, waiting by the doors until Aaron and I give the knock to indicate that we're ready. I can just barely see the altar through the grimy windows that flank the double front doors. An arch of pink roses soars above Victor's purple-dark hair, Oscar centered beneath them, our sadistic little wedding officiant.

"Fuck, I'm scared," I murmur, and Aaron laughs softly. I glance briefly in his direction.

"I'd be worried if you weren't," he tells me, putting his hand over mine. His touch comforts me, and I close my eyes for a moment, just to catch my breath. "But as much as I hate Vic sometimes, I trust him with my life." Aaron pauses a moment, and I open my eyes to look at him. He's staring at the floor and not at me, but his expression isn't unpleasant. Actually, he looks a little surprised. "I trust him with the love of my life, too, apparently." He scoffs a harsh laugh and then glances back at me.

All I can do at that point is smile.

My stomach is a mess of black butterflies, reminding me that I am, in fact, still human.

I'm a seventeen-year-old girl who's about to get *married*.

Of all the things that I am, that I've become, that one is definitely the strangest.

Without another word, I reach up and rap my knuckles against the wood.

Deep breath, Bernie, deep breath.

Callum opens the doors for me and Aaron and then steps aside, pressing play on his phone and sending spirals of beautiful music out of the speakers placed on either side of the porch. It takes a second for me to adjust to the sight of a wedding, a *real* wedding, before I can force myself to start walking.

Victor is waiting, his best man by his side. Hael Harbin grins at me and winks, giving me a little salute with his inked fingers. In his gaze, I can read so many things that have been left unsaid. *It's not my baby; I feel free; I want to move on with you, Bernie.* He said as much before, when we had sex on the hood of his Camaro.

I glance at the white folding chairs on either side of the walkway. There are only a half-dozen in total, and I smile when I spot Kara and Ashley in the front row. Kara grins over her shoulder at her brother and gives us a thumbs-up, but Ashley just buries her head in the puffy sleeve of her cousin's dress.

Heather stands in front of me, holding a basket of pink rose petals. She smiles at me, but I know that when she told me that she shipped me and Aaron, and not me and Victor, she was serious. I don't know how to explain to her that I don't intend on keeping just one for myself.

The breeze picks up around us, making the trees shiver and shaking off whatever leaves they have left. Heather takes that as her cue to turn around and start walking, dropping rose petals in her wake.

I follow after, nice and slow, my combat boots comfortable beneath the voluminous magic of my dress. With my left arm, I hold onto Aaron. My right, I tuck into the pocket on the dress, fingering the old, wrinkled envelope that contains my list.

Victor's mother, Ophelia, is here, glaring at us. So is her sleazy car salesman-like boyfriend, Todd. I'm surprised to see that Vic's dad is in attendance, too, and I just suddenly miss my own so much it hurts.

If he hadn't died, things would've been different. Penelope would probably still be alive. But then, would I have met the Havoc Boys? Can I quantify my love for my sister and my love for the guys enough to compare them?

No, fuck that.

You can't change the past, but you sure as hell can dictate your own future.

I start walking, my dress trailing in the patchy grass, Aaron by my side. I wonder if, like Callum mentioned, I smell like leather and peaches to him the way he smells like rose and sandalwood to me.

Ophelia wrinkles her nose at me as I walk past, her obsidian eyes so much like her son's that it's scary. She made Victor Channing. She's just like him. We should be, if not afraid of her, then at least wary. Because she's coming, I just know she is.

I do my best to ignore her, climbing the steps of the small dais under the trees. Aaron gives me one, last kiss on the cheek and moves to the side with Cal beside him, like they're my bridesmaids or some shit.

"Welcome, friends," Oscar says, the word *friends* dripping from his lips like a poisonous joke. We all know that this wedding is as much an attack on Vic's mom as it is a union.

I turn to look at Victor, his face filled with tenderness and dark, possessive domineering, all at the same time. My breath catches.

We didn't need a wedding to become one; we always have been.

He reaches out his hands to take mine, our *HAVOC* painted fingers curling together on either side.

"Marriage is a dark and desperate sort of union," Oscar begins, the words of the ceremony penned by his own elegant fingers and promptly memorized. I notice that, for once, he doesn't have his iPad by his side. "It's one person begetting the soul, the love, and the sins of the other. It's about forging a bond in legality that tries its very best to adhere to the age-old adage: blood in, blood out."

Vic grins at me, and I grin back. Meanwhile, Hael snickers with laughter and the tree branches above us fill with a murder of crows.

How ominous.

"My only question to you today is," Oscar continues, reaching up to adjust his glasses as he looks between us. "Are you willing to bleed for each other?" Callum steps forward to hand the wedding bands to us. They're artfully tied to a black rose, using silken ribbons that remind me of Cal's ballerina tattoo. "Victor, please repeat after me. I, Victor Channing, am an asshole who in no way deserves Bernadette Blackbird, but who, through some strange fault of the universe, will be marrying her today. I will bleed for her; I will die for her. I agree to marry her."

Victor laughs, even as his mother's cursing drifts over the fading sounds of the music.

"This isn't some sort of sick joke! Who does he think he is, Tom? Huh? Who?"

But there is no law that says that your dick of a friend can't make up whatever vows he wants.

Speaking of …

Vic takes the wedding band and then leans in toward me, putting his lips up against my ear.

"I have vows for you, but I'm not about to read them in front of my mother. But tonight, I want to tell you everything. And then I'm going to tear that wedding dress off and fuck you until you're mine." I scoff at Vic's words, but how can I respond to that now, up here in front of my sister?

Instead, I wait for Vic to lean back and repeat Oscar's words back to me as he slips the simple wedding band on my finger, joining it to his grandmother's ring. Oscar repeats the vows and asks me to recite them, and I do.

I do.

When Vic cups the back of my head and kisses me, destroying me with that hot slice of sin he calls a tongue, I am lost.

Forever trapped in Havoc.

We walk down the aisle together and head straight for his Harley.

The infinite black of my wedding gown ripples as we drive away. I'm not sure where we're going at first, because my head is lost in both the clouds, and the soft earth in which we buried Neil Pence.

I'm not surprised, however, to find myself back at the cemetery.

Vic parks the bike, and I know what we're here for.

Closure.

That's what this is about: saying goodbye to Pen, saying goodbye to one of the monsters in my closet, and saying hello to whatever my next chapter is supposed to be.

Victor can't keep his hands off of me as we stumble through the cold, quiet of the cemetery, our panting breaths the only sound here, the only proof that life still goes on, even when the dead lie quiet and sleeping.

We collapse on the grass at the edge of the woods, halfway between where we buried Neil, and where he—whether through action or design—buried Penelope.

My arms wrap Vic's neck, desperate to keep his mouth on mine. I'd never imagined that marrying someone—especially at the age of seventeen—would be so fucking erotic. But standing up there with Victor Channing, his purple-dark hair slicked back, suit pressed and perfectly tailored, was foreplay of the best kind.

It's left us both shaking and sweating, frenzied for another taste of our drug of choice: each other.

"You've made all my dark, little dreams come true, Bernadette," he growls against my mouth, his hands planted into the green grass on either side of my head. Victor undulates his hips forward, rubbing our pelvises together and making me groan.

We buried the Thing alive.

The thought slithers into my brain, but it doesn't disturb me as much as it should.

I am tainted. I am broken. I belong to Havoc.

Vic shoves the skirts of my Lazaro gown aside, reaching down and fumbling with his belt. He curses under his breath, dark eyes heavy lidded and liquid with sin and want. He frees his heavy shaft into his tattooed hand, giving it a few pumps as I look up at him from my back. Right this second, he can have me anyway he wants me.

Before the wedding, I made my wants and wishes clear.

I'll be Queen of Havoc.

We'll finish my list.

We'll crush the Charter Crew.

And with the way Ophelia was looking at me and Vic during the wedding, it's obvious we'll need to do something about her, too.

Victor leans over me, licking the side of my face before stealing my soul through my lips. His kiss is the most exquisite sort of torture, like licking the brownie batter spoon before you wash it. There's just enough chocolate to tease, but the real dessert is in the oven; you're just waiting for it to heat up.

"Make me yours, Vic," I moan, giving into my sweet obsession for him. Usually, I'm too prideful to let him see how I really feel.

But not today, not during our first fuck as husband and wife of Havoc.

"Princess, you already *are* mine," Victor murmurs, pushing my pale thighs apart. The sunlight makes my skin glow gold as he drives into me with his bare cock. We're all about risk, me and Vic. Doesn't mean it's smart or right, only that it's fact.

We ache for each other.

Our mouths clash again as Vic curls his big body over me, seeking a kiss but unwilling to stop the manic thrusting of his hips. His musky smell mixes with the earthy odor of freshly turned earth. There are no living witnesses to our consummation, but plenty of quiet spirits, watching two demons rut in a tombstone-ridden field.

Havoc's boss sits up and looks into my eyes with two, dark pools of obsidian, his expression fierce and possessive, unforgiving and domineering in a way that almost scares me. Almost. To be with someone like Victor, you have to be able to match him, blow for blow.

I cup Vic's head in my hand and, with very little pressure, manage to bring his mouth to mine again. That's how easy he is for me to control; I only wish I had a leash to show the world the truth about how easy he is to command.

He fucks me even harder, the sound of our bodies joining echoing around the silent space. My own hips rise up, eager to meet his, stirring up a delicious sort of friction that I can feel in my teeth, my bones, my cunt.

My body throbs around Vic's, squeezing him, rewarding him.

The emotions of the day twist around inside of me as Victor pleasures me with his cock, and then it all comes pouring out in one, last surge of emotion. Finishing my purge. I end it much hotter than I began, with an orgasm that rips through me like an electric storm, frying my brain, burning me from the inside out.

It's violent and messy, when Vic gathers me close and comes inside of me, holding me to him, marking me. The scratches I've left down his back don't hurt either; they very clearly say *Do Not Fucking Touch.*

Victor is panting above me, doing his best to regain control of both himself and his breathing. His head is bent, dark hair wet with sweat.

"I love you, Victor Channing," I tell him, and he freezes. I swear, he even stops breathing. After a moment, Vic exhales and his tense muscles relax.

"I love you more, Bernadette, and I always will." I frown at him, but he just lifts his head and lets his mouth twist into a villainous smirk. "Don't argue, just enjoy."

"You're a fucking prick," I growl as he rolls off of me with a laugh. I sit up, still dressed in my black gown, the fabric thoroughly fucked into the dirt and probably irreparably damaged and stained with cum.

Whatever.

It's symbolic, right? The wedding dress, I mean. There's a reason I got married in black.

Victor turns onto his back and lights a cigarette, passing it to me as I sit there with my attention on the gravestones all around us. Somewhere beneath us, there's a dead—or soon-to-be dead—cop. A dead stepfather. A dead rapist.

I'll never know if Neil Pence actually killed my sister or not. Either way, it doesn't matter. Because he ruined her, with his lust and his greed and his narcissism. He ruined the person I loved most, and I will always love the sweet taste of vengeance in my mouth.

Confucius says, *dig two graves before embarking on a journey of revenge.*

Well, bitch, I've already dug more than that. What next?

"Let's get out of here," I say, finishing the cigarette in my hand and stabbing it out into the grass beside me. Victor turns toward me, his own smoke still clutched between his lips, and smiles.

It's not a very nice smile.

It never is.

"Whatever you say, my love," he growls, shoving up to his feet and looking down at me. Vic, his shirt undone, his tattoos glowing in the sunlight, stares down at me with smoke curling from his lips and grins.

I take his outstretched hand and he hauls me to my feet.

Vic then pulls a small pocketknife from his jacket, cuts his palm, and offers the blade out to me. I take it, slicing my own palm and curling my fingers through his, our wedding bands brushing together. We look at each other, past our clasped hands, and he smiles.

"Blood in," Victor tells me with a nod of his chin. "Blood out."

Together, we walk hand-in-hand through the gravestones toward Vic's waiting bike.

———————————————————————

1.   *the stepdad.*

I take the tube of red lipstick from my purse and pop the cap off. Victor waits beside his Harley, the back decorated with a *Just Married* sign, cans and flowers tied to the saddlebags and dragging. I wonder which one of the boys found the time to do that? It had to be one of the Havoc Boys; Victor would never let anyone else near his ride.

The eyes of my new husband are dark as he watches me kneel down on the pavement in my wedding dress, silence rolling through the cemetery as the sounds of our moans fade into a distant memory. My hands are dirty, staining the old envelope as I smooth it out in front of me.

I don't bother reapplying my lipstick. Instead, I use the pretty pink color of it to cross out the first name on my list, obliterating Neil Pence from my life, my mind, and the endless abyss of my pain.

Fat, juicy tears fall from my eyes and splatter against my wedding ring, the ink of my *HAVOC* tattoo, and the crinkled piece of paper that holds all my worst memories in simple words and titles.

"I'm sorry Penelope," I whisper, wishing she were here with me, missing her with every breath. *You'd have hated Vic, huh?*

I bet you'd be just like Heather; you'd ship me and Aaron, I'm sure. He always got along well with you, didn't he?

"Bernie," Vic says, gently commanding me. Just the way I like. Just the way I hate. I can't decide if I should be his queen, if he should be my king ... or if we should rule together. We have a long way to go.

I tuck the list—and the lipstick—into the pockets of my black gown and stand up.

Victor waits for me by his bike, reaching out to put his big, warm hands on my hips so he can pull me close and kiss me in a stray shaft of sunshine. His mouth tastes like iniquitous love and romantic sin, all twisted into one dark, wicked tongue.

His fingers fist in my hair, bringing me closer so he can consume me with that impossible venom of his, its taste as sweet as the peace I feel inside of me. I had to fill that dark void to quiet the voices crying out my seemingly endless and infinite pain.

I should feel sorry for Neil, but I don't.

Not in the least.

"Let's go, wife," Vic says, flashing me those white teeth of his as he grins big. "I haven't fucked you near enough to satisfy my inner demons." A shiver takes over me, but I'm not displeased by Victor's words. He's right: we haven't had near enough of each other.

"Can we play some music?" I ask, and he nods. His Harley's hooked up with a sound system that fills the cemetery when he turns it on, letting me choose the song that will forever define this moment for us.

I decide on *"A Little Wicked"* by Valerie Broussard.

Victor hands me a new leather jacket in hot pink that he gets from one of the saddlebags, the word *Havoc* scrawled across the back. It's like, the dark version of the *Pink Ladies* jacket from *Grease*. I slip into it and then climb onto the Harley behind him, wrapping my hands around my husband's strong waist.

"You ready for this, Mrs. Channing?" he asks me with a dark chuckle. He knows I'm not changing my name, but whatever.

I have no idea where we're going, but it doesn't matter because Vic is driving. He loosens his tie, lights a cigarette, and kicks the engine to life beneath us.

"I'm ready," I tell him as the song oozes from the speakers, perfuming the air with sound. Victor takes off down the curving road toward the street and, as we pull onto it, the Camaro and the Bronco slide into formation behind us.

And off we go.

Havoc on a fucking honeymoon.

All bets are on and I'm throwing my money at the possibility of mayhem.

No, no, the *certainty* of it.

TO BE CONTINUED...

THE HAVOC BOYS #3
FLIP FOR A PREVIEW OF "MAYHEM AT PRESCOTT HIGH"

CHAPTER
ONE

Vic's hands are hot as he grabs my pelvis in inked fingers, thrusting into me with deep, long strokes, sweat beading on the glorious lines of his chest and trailing down to the spot where are our bodies are inextricably joined together.

"Oh, fuck, Bernie," he groans, throwing his head back, a glorious dark king trapped between my thighs. I own him, just as he owns me. It's a give and take sort of situation, neither of us really willing to accept that we're equals just yet.

COMING JULY 2020

FILTHY RICH BOYS

RICH BOYS OF BURBERRY PREP, YEAR ONE

FILTHY
RICH
BOYS

ALL BETS ARE ON ...

USA TODAY BESTSELLING AUTHOR
C.M. STUNICH

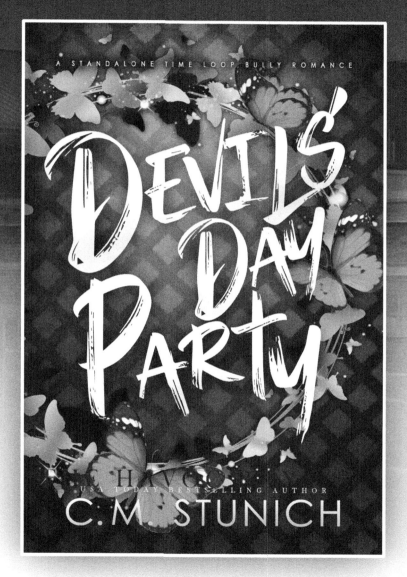

A STANDALONE TIME LOOP BULLY ROMANCE

DEVILS DAY PARTY

HAVOC

USA TODAY BESTSELLING AUTHOR

C.M. STUNICH

A STANDALONE TIME LOOP REVERSE HAREM

I WAS BORN RUINED

I Was Born

RUINED

DEATH BY DAYBREAK MC

FIRST IN
A NEW SERIES

INTERNATIONAL BESTSELLING AUTHOR
C.M. STUNICH

DEATH BY DAYBREAK MOTORCYCLE CLUB #1

STALKING

LINKS

JOIN THE C.M. STUNICH NEWSLETTER – Get three free books just for signing up
http://eepurl.com/DEsEf

TWEET ME ON TWITTER, BABE – Come sing the social media song with me
https://twitter.com/CMStunich

SNAPCHAT WITH ME – Get exclusive behind the scenes looks at covers, blurbs, book
signings and more http://www.snapchat.com/add/cmstunich

LISTEN TO MY BOOK PLAYLISTS – Share your fave music with me and I'll give you my
playlists (I'm super active on here!) https://open.spotify.com/user/12101321503

FRIEND ME ON FACEBOOK – Okay, I'm actually at the 5,000 friend limit, but if you click
the "follow" button on my profile page, you'll see way more of my killer posts
https://facebook.com/cmstunich

LIKE ME ON FACEBOOK – Pretty please? I'll love you forever if you do! ;)
https://facebook.com/cmstunichauthor & https://facebook.com/violetblazeauthor

CHECK OUT THE NEW SITE – (under construction) but it looks kick-a$$ so far, right? You
can order signed books here! http://www.cmstunich.com

READ VIOLET BLAZE – Read the books from my hot as hellfire pen name, Violet Blaze
http://www.violetblazebooks.com

SUBSCRIBE TO MY RSS FEED – Press that little orange button in the corner and copy that
RSS feed so you can get all the latest updates http://www.cmstunich.com/blog

AMAZON, BABY – If you click the follow button here, you'll get an email each time I put out
a new book. Pretty sweet, huh? http://amazon.com/author/cmstunich
http://amazon.com/author/violetblaze

PINTEREST – Lots of hot half-naked men. Oh, and half-naked men. Plus, tattooed guys
holding babies (who are half-naked) http://pinterest.com/cmstunich

INSTAGRAM – Cute cat pictures. And half-naked guys. Yep, that again.
http://instagram.com/cmstunich

About the Author

C.M. Stunich is a self-admitted bibliophile with a love for exotic teas and a whole host of characters who live full time inside the strange, swirling vortex of her thoughts. Some folks might call this crazy, but Caitlin Morgan doesn't mind – especially considering she has to write biographies in the third person. Oh, and half the host of characters in her head are searing hot bad boys with dirty mouths and skillful hands (among other things). If being crazy means hanging out with them everyday, C.M. has decided to have herself committed.

She hates tapioca pudding, loves to binge on cheesy horror movies, and is a slave to many cats. When she's not vacuuming fur off of her couch, C.M. can be found with her nose buried in a book or her eyes glued to a computer screen. She's the author of over thirty novels – romance, new adult, fantasy, and young adult included. Please, come and join her inside her crazy. There's a heck of a lot to do there.

Oh, and Caitlin loves to chat (incessantly), so feel free to e-mail her, send her a Facebook message, or put up smoke signals. She's already looking forward to it.

Printed in Great Britain
by Amazon

45799049R00280